THE VIRGIN AND THE VISCOUNT

Also by Charis Michaels

The Earl Next Door

THE VIRGIN AND THE VISCOUNT

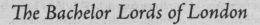

The Bachelor Lords of London

CHARIS MICHAELS

AVONIMPULSE

An Imprint of HarperCollinsPublishers

Excerpt from *One Lucky Hero* copyright © 2016 by Codi Gary.
Excerpt from *Stirring Attraction* copyright © 2016 by Sara Jane Stone.
Excerpt from *Signs of Attraction* copyright © 2016 by Laura Brown.
Excerpt from *Smolder* copyright © 2016 by Karen Erickson.

EPub Edition JULY 2016 ISBN: 9780062412935

Print Edition ISBN: 9780062412959

Avon, Avon Impulse, and the Avon Impulse logo are trademarks of HarperCollins Publishers.

AM 10 9 8 7 6 5 4 3

For Barbara Denise Taylor, MD, MS
A real-life heroine who seeks to heal those from
whom everyone else turns away

PROLOGUE

On April 12, 1809, Franklin "Frankie" Courtland, sixth Viscount Rainsleigh, tripped on a root in the bottom of a riverbed and drowned. He was drunk at the time, picnicking with friends on the banks of the River Wylye. According to an account later given to the magistrate, his lordship simply fell over, bumped into a fallen log, and sank.

It was there he remained—"enjoying the cool," or so his friends believed—until he became too heavy, too slippery, and, alas, too dead to revive. But they did dislodge him, and after that, they claimed he floated to the surface, bobbed several times, and then gently glided downstream. He was later found just before sunset, face down and bloated (in life, as also in death), beached on a pebble shoal near Codford.

At the time the elder Courtland was sinking to the bottom of the river, his son and heir, Bryson, was hunched over a desk in the offices of his fledgling shipping company, waiting for the very moment his father would die. It had been an exceedingly long, progressively humiliating wait. Years long—nay, *decades*.

Luckily for Bryson, for his ships and his future, he was capable of doing more things at once than waiting, and while his father drank and debauched his way through all respectability and life, Bryson worked.

It was unthinkable for a young heir and nobleman to "work," but Bryson was given little choice, considering the impoverished state of the Rainsleigh viscountcy. He was scarcely eleven years of age when he made his first foray into labor, and not so many years after, into private enterprise. His life in work had not ceased since. On the rare occasion that he didn't work, he studied.

With his meager earnings (he began by punting boats on the very river in which his father later drowned), he made meager investments. These investments reaped small gains—first in shares in the punting station; later in property along the water; later still in other industry up and down the river.

Bryson lived modestly, worked ceaselessly, and spared only enough to pay his way through Cambridge, bring up his brother, and see him educated him as well. Every guinea earned was reinvested. He repeated the process again and again, a little less meagerly each time 'round.

By the time the viscount's self-destructive lifestyle wrought his river- and drink-soaked end, Bryson had managed to accrue a small fortune, launch a company that built and sailed ships, and construct an elaborate plan for what he would do when his father finally cocked up his toes and died.

When at last that day came, Bryson had but one complaint: it took fifty-two hours for the constable to find him. He was a viscount for two days before anyone, including himself, even knew it.

But two days was a trifle compared to a lifetime of waiting. And on the day he learned of his inheritance—nay, the very hour—he launched his long-awaited plan.

By three o'clock on the fourth day, he'd razed the rotting, reeking east wing of the family estate in Wiltshire to the ground.

Within the week, he'd extracted his mother from the west wing and shipped her and a contingent of discreet caregivers to a villa in Spain.

Within the month, he'd sold every stick of furniture, every remaining fork and dish, every sweat-soaked toga and opium-tinged gown. He burned the drapes, burned the rugs, burned the tapestries. He delivered the half-starved horses and the fighting dogs to an agricultural college and pensioned off the remaining staff.

By the six-week mark, he'd unloaded the London townhome—sold at auction to the highest bidder—and with it, the broken-down carriage, his father's dusty arsenal, what was left of the wine stores, and all the lurid art.

It was a whirlwind evacuation—a gutting, really—and no one among polite society had ever witnessed a son or heir take such absolute control and haul away so much family or property quite so fast.

But no one among polite society was acquainted with Bryson Anders Courtland, the new Viscount Rainsleigh.

And no one understood that it was not so much an ending as it was an entirely fresh start. Once the tearing down ceased, the rebuilding could begin. New viscountcy, new money, new respect, new life.

It was an enterprise into which Bryson threw himself like no other. Unlike all others, however, he could do only so much, one man, alone. For this, he would require another. A partner. Someone with whom he could work together toward a common goal. A collaborator who emulated his precise, immaculate manner. A matriarch, discreet and pure. A paragon of correctness. A viscountess. A proper, perfect wife.

CHAPTER ONE

No. 22 Henrietta Place
Mayfair, London
May 1811

"Will that be all, my lord?" Cecil Dunhip peered over the edge of his thick portfolio and raised his brows.

Bryson Courtland, Viscount Rainsleigh, pushed back against the soft leather of his chair and breathed a heavy, agitated sigh. "Teatime, already, Dunhip? It's only half past one."

The secretary's swollen cheeks shot crimson, and he shook his head, his three chins keeping frantic time. "Begging your pardon, my lord. Of course, by that I did not mean to imply that *I* required—"

"Easy, Dunhip." Rainsleigh tossed his pen to the blotter. "You'll have your tea. But I do have one thing more." He took up his agenda and glared at the hastily scrawled last line.

Wife, read the note.

Solve.

Marry by year's end.

The viscount looked away. "I'll need to go about the business of getting a wife."

Dunhip blinked and inclined his head. He raised his pen high above the parchment, ever ready. "The business of getting a…"

Rainsleigh folded the agenda into the shape of a bird and sailed it into the fire. "This townhouse is complete. I'm in London now year-round. It was always the next thing." He paused. "I'm not a randy bachelor, and I won't be seen as such. The natural next step is to find a mate, carry on as husband and wife, fill the nursery, et cetera, et cetera. Besides this charity prize, I have no reason to put it off. I need to acquire a proper viscountess and start a family."

Dunhip stared across the desk, his mouth slightly ajar. Rainsleigh raised one eyebrow. He hadn't wasted time or energy on female distraction these last diligent years, but he was hardly a monk. Surely the man would not make him say it again.

"Very good, my lord," agreed Dunhip, idling only a fraction more. His face was impassive as he began to scribble. What notes the man took down, the viscount couldn't guess. Rainsleigh's own strategy for wife procurement was vague and theoretical at best, and Dunhip was a confirmed bachelor who lived with his mother. What could he possibly add?

Still, they had to begin somewhere. To his credit, Dunhip shed all hint of challenge and began to pepper the viscount with questions.

Would his lordship prefer a lady from here in London, or should the whole of Britain be considered? What ages appealed to his lordship? With regard to the look of the girl, should the candidates appear olive-skinned and raven-haired, or pale and fair? Should their figures be reedy or robust? And what of the demeanor of the candidates? Bookish or social? Serious or gay?

Straightforward, sensible questions, these. Rainsleigh knew Dunhip would approach the whole thing methodically. He was just about to venture thoughtful answers when his library door swung open and crashed against the wall.

"I always announce myself," called a voice from beyond the door. "There's a good man. Trust me, *his lordship* prefers it."

Dunhip slapped his portfolio shut and spun toward the sound. Rainsleigh closed his eyes. *Finally*, he thought, drawing a grateful breath. *Thank God.*

"*Ah*, there you are!" said the voice, now attached to a man. Tall, lanky, untucked. Clothes wrinkled, boots caked in mud. A three-day growth of beard.

"*Beau*." Rainsleigh leaned back in his chair, crossing his arms over his chest.

His brother whipped off his hat and spun it into a chair. "Before God. Before man. Before—oh, what the hell, Dunhip, we'll include you with the men."

Beau Courtland strode into the room, looking around the spacious library with a low whistle. "Wasn't sure I had the correct street; then I saw *the castle*. Three-times larger than every other house in the vicinity—and I knew."

"My lord! Apologies!" Rainsleigh's butler, Sewell, scrambled through the door behind his brother. "This fellow would not permit me to announce him. I did not realize you were—"

"Expecting him? How could I"—Rainsleigh sighed—"when I believed him to be *in* India? Don't bother, Sewell. This *fellow* is my brother, Beauregard Court—"

"Damn it, Bryson, for God's sake, *mind the name*," Beau interrupted. "Do me this one, small favor." He turned to the gawking butler and held out his hand. "Beau Courtland. How do you do?" Sewell stared in uncomfortable confusion.

Bryson watched him. "Do you have baggage?"

"I'm not taking a room, if that's what you mean."

"You look like a sailor and smell like a still. I hope you'll stay long enough for a wash and shave and procure a clean set of clothes." He nodded to the secretary. "That will be all for this morning, Dunhip."

"Dunhip, old man," said Beau, slapping both hands on the man's shoulders, shoving him back into his chair, "still taking down every golden utterance my brother says? Who knew your chubby fingers could write so fast? Kindly *remind my brother* that I look like a sailor because I *am* a sailor."

Bryson narrowed his eyes. "You have no title whatsoever—none of which I am aware." His brother did not bother to correct him, and Rainsleigh tried again. "What are you doing here?"

"India became too warm for my taste." Beau circled an empty chair and then sprawled into it.

"Too occupied to send word?"

"I could ask the same thing of you."

Rainsleigh sighed. "What word? I'm not a shiftless resident of the world at large. I am here, as I always am, as you clearly *knew*, considering you're slouched in my library."

"No, you're not always in London," countered his brother. "You're usually in Wiltshire…in that ancient pile of freezing rock, counting sheep and money with Dunhip, here. I disembarked three days ago, if you must know, but I only learned you were in town today. Read it in the bloody papers."

Bryson eyed him, weighing his options. He couldn't have asked for a more opportune inroad to a conversation that was long overdue. But experience had taught him to tread lightly. His brother had been known to bolt if he said too much—if he expected too much.

"I've moved to London to be closer to the shipyard," Bryson told him. "We'll launch a new ship next year. But perhaps that's what you read. It's a venture in which I hope you will take no small amount of interest."

"Hmmm," said his brother, who managed to look bored and restless at the same time. He closed his eyes.

"And"—Rainsleigh paused—"I'm in London to find a wife."

Beau opened one eye. "I beg your pardon?"

"Yes, you heard. I intend to *pay you* to use whatever you may have gleaned in the Royal Navy to captain my new ship."

"Not the bloody boat," said Beau, sitting up in his chair. "The bit about a wife. Surely you're joking? How the devil will a *wife* fit into your ambition to make more money, build more boats, and prove to the world that you're not Father?"

Bryson sighed. "I see your impression of my life equals the pointlessness and lack of regard with which I view yours."

"One thing I don't do is judge. If you want to make money and prove to the world that you're a bloody saint, that is your prerogative. It's my prerogative to heckle you from the aisle. But a *wife*? Truly? When have you ever spared time for a female?"

"Clever. As always. I suppose you won't mind if I marry and turn out a handful of heirs? You'd likely never inherit if I have a son."

"The chief reason," Beau said with a sigh, reclining again, "that I will be the first to congratulate the lucky miss, whoever she may be. Godspeed, Bryse. Honestly. Marry immediately and conceive a copious number of sons. The farther I am from the title, the better. God knows you'll be popular on the marriage mart. All your lovely money. The shiny new polish you've put on the title." He made a low whistling noise.

"Yes, well, that remains to be seen," Bryson said. "However, I won't be subjecting myself to the so-called 'marriage mart.' Dunhip?" He turned to his secretary. "You might as well take this down, as you're still here."

"No marriage mart?" Beau said, marveling. "This is a shock. I thought you were incapable of straying from convention. You know this is how the *authentic* aristocrats do it."

Bryson pushed back from his desk. "I loathe that statement, and you know it. Our title is one of the oldest in England. We *are* authentic. Which is why I'll go about finding a wife any way I please."

"Oh my God," Beau said, "you're afraid they won't let you in. After all this time and all your money, you think they'll withhold their precious, blue-blooded daughters from your tainted fingers. You're not Father, Bryson. If you want a debutante, you should have one."

"It's not the rejection, although I've never seen you endeavor to be received anywhere but the corner public house." He stood. "The shipping venture is my first priority, and I haven't the time to flit about from drawing room to theatre box, passing brief moments with adolescents about whom I ultimately know very little. Proficiency at idle chatter is no proof of character. When you consider the whole business practically, as I have—as I *will*—you'll see it is not a debutante that I want." He walked to the alcove window that overlooked the garden.

Beau drawled, "No debutante, then. Do as you like. Why I would expect anything less? You'll forgive me if I cannot get the scene out of my head: You, standing in the corner of a ballroom at five o'clock in the afternoon, sipping tepid punch and discussing needlework, while a crowd of eager seventeen-year-olds and the mercenaries they call chaperones bat their eyelashes at you. You cannot possibly think of spoiling that for me."

"Yes, but I'm not looking for a seventeen-year-old, eyelash-batting wife. A respected family will be important, of course. It is imperative for my future children that my wife be quality."

"Dunhip, I'd underline that twice, mate," Beau said. "*Quality*."

Bryson ignored him. "But the other hallmarks of, er, gently bred maidenhood hold no interest for me. I don't care about form or figure, or even beauty, for that matter. I don't care about wit or clever banter. Obviously, I've no need for a dowry. All I want is someone who is morally upright to a fault. Who is pure. Who can be a proper hostess, bear me healthy sons, and remain faithful to me and to our family." He looked back at his brother.

"You're looking for the opposite of Mother."

"Yes," he said grimly, uncomfortable with Beau's baldfaced honesty. "I am looking for the opposite of Mother."

Beau nodded. He rolled from his chair. Through the window, a finch lit on the stone fountain in the garden, and they watched it in silence.

When Bryson went on, his voice was low. "I know you would prefer that I speak less frankly. To be always in jest, like you. But it can never be said enough: no aspect of our years at Rossmore Court need ever be repeated, Beau. Not a single miserable moment, save that we rely upon each other."

Beau turned to him. "I hope by that you don't mean that I, too, will be expected to marry a plain, penniless, pious wife who holds no attraction for me."

Bryson laughed. His brother was shiftless and randy, and he drank far too much, but he was amusing. He slapped him on the back and caught his shoulder, hanging on. "No, brother," he said. "Leave that to me. Leave that to me."

Wiltshire, England
Fifteen years prior...

"*Leave it to you, should I?*"

Frankie Courtland, Viscount Rainsleigh, held his son painfully by the left arm and dragged him down the hall. On Bryson's right, his cousin Kenneth pinched his shoulder with a thumb and forefinger and kneed him in the kidney. Bryson was nineteen, tall, and strong from punting boats on the river. As victims went, he wasn't an easy boy to drag from a house or stuff into a carriage. So they came for him in the dead of night and set upon him when he was fast asleep.

"Let me go," he ground out, scrambling to find his feet. "I will not go."

Laughter, wheezing, profanity. They hauled him down the main stairwell of Rossmore Court and through the great hall. The front door stood open, and they chucked him onto the stoop.

His father stalked him. "You will go." His voice had gone breezy and light, but Bryson knew what to expect, and he braced himself. The backhand was swift, opening his lip and speckling his vision with tiny flecks of white light. Bryson reeled, and they pounced again.

"As will your cousin Kenneth, your uncle, and myself," Lord Rainsleigh went on. "Tonight, my pious boy, you'll become a man."

The starless night was disorienting, and they easily overtook him, fighting, one against three. A carriage stood ready in the drive, and they shoved him in and climbed in behind.

Bryson scrambled to the far bench. "You plan to forcibly carry me inside? Haul me around like last week's wash? Against my will? While people watch?"

"Be agreeable for once in your life. It'll be over before you know it, and then you'll be fighting to get back in the wench's arms instead of conspiring to stay out."

"Ah," Bryson scoffed, "this is for my own good, is it?"

"See for yourself."

"As if you ever had the smallest interest in anyone's good but your own, particularly mine. You can go to hell."

"Oh, I intend to," said his father. "But first I will go to this brothel, as will your cousin and your uncle. As will you. We're all going. So you can cease your sanctimonious babble and prissy crying about my miserable turn as your father. It spoils everyone's fun, *not to mention that it makes me drowsy."* He leaned his head back on the seat. *"How tiresome your pious sneering has grown...all summer long...carrying on like lord of the manor...as if you're better than the rest of us."*

"This is because I am better than you," Bryson said. *"But that's what bothers you, isn't it? This has nothing to do with how I conduct my life. I'm keeping the lot of you out of debtor's prison; meanwhile, the world knows you're a degenerate wastrel of man, an addict, and you don't deserve to be viscount."*

Lord Rainsleigh chuckled. *"Call me names if it cheers you, Bryson. But let us not forget that I am not the nineteen-year-old virgin in the carriage."*

"What could you possibly care about that?" Bryson worked to make his voice sound light.

"Why, it taints the otherwise virile reputation of the Rainsleigh crest, of course." His father laughed. *"You don't want to make a name for yourself as a sodomite, do you?"*

"Eloquently put, as always," Bryson ground out, speaking over their laughter. *"I have school at the end of the week. St. James is the opposite direction."*

"Oh, we're not going to London!" This from his cousin Kenneth, on an eager laugh. Bryson's father silenced him with a swift elbow to the rib.

Bryson looked out the window. *"If we're not going to St. James, then where are you taking me?"*

"Kenneth cannot contain his excitement"—the viscount glared at the fat relation—*"because he has located an establishment in Southwark where we all may indulge in delights that suit our particular needs. Scouted it out himself last night. Do not fret,*

Bryson; there will be an experienced wench there, well suited to your nervous, novice bumblings."

Bryson let the curtain drop. "Southwark? The river slum? You're joking."

His father raised his eyebrows cryptically, flashing a cruel grin.

Bryson pressed. "If you must go whoring, why not go to Town? To somewhere civilized and comfortable? With clean sheets and a decent meal, for God's sake?"

"St. James has grown…tiresome," his father said, turning to look out the window.

Of course, Bryson thought, coming to understand. "Your reputation precedes you. They've shut you out. That's it, isn't it?" He laughed. "Excellent work, my lord. Excellent. You're a peer of the realm who can't even fornicate in bloody St. James. Good God, Father, is there no person or establishment that you will not offend?"

"You're only making it worse for yourself, boy." His father yawned.

"No, my lord," Bryson said. "You make it worse with every breath you draw."

CHAPTER TWO

Denby House
Grosvenor Square
May 1811

The breakfast room of Denby House in Grosvenor Square was canvassed with maps. Greater London. Mayfair. Chelsea. Seven Dials. The River Thames. They covered the dining table, smothered the centerpiece, and draped the chairs. A magnified rendering of Hyde Park lay unfurled on the floor.

In the corner of the table, leaning over the largest sheet, Lady Elisabeth Hamilton-Baythes studied the hive of crooked streets that crisscrossed the south bank just beyond London Bridge.

In and out. Over, then south. Down the alley… Using a tiny white spoon from the sugar dish, she traced routes. The fastest escape. The least likely to flood in case of rain. A second route to lose pursuers. Side streets in which to hide. A switchback. There was potential, but also the risk of becoming disoriented in the narrow, winding mews.

"Oh, darling! *Must you?*"

Elisabeth looked up. Aunt Lillian stood in the doorway, balancing a wobbly green pear on a plate.

"Hello," Elisabeth said, blowing a wisp of hair from her face. "It's awful, I know. I had hoped you'd taken breakfast in your rooms so as not to be subjected." She tossed the spoon into the Thames.

Aunt Lillian affected a patient expression and drifted to the sideboard with the pear.

"The raiding team will do deep reconnaissance tonight," Elisabeth said. "These couldn't wait for the office. Ah, yes. Look. Here's a spot for you..."—she pointed to the map at the end of the table—"in, er, *on* Hampstead."

Lillian settled near the window. "The mess can be tolerated, but these maps force me to acknowledge the gravely dangerous nature of the work you do. I prefer to imagine you seated at a sunny desk, you know. Writing letters or tallying up contributions. On occasion, perhaps you impart the stray encouragement to a young girl. Instruct her on serving tea. Or arranging flowers in a vase. But this? Elisabeth? You promised."

"Hmmm." Elisabeth nodded, turning back to the maps. "Yes, but we only arrange flowers on *Tuesdays*, Aunt, and today is *Friday*."

The countess sighed and took up the pear.

"But you needn't worry," said Elisabeth. "I've kept my promise. I only assist with the planning. I'm never in the street. Stoker would soon edge me out, you know, if I did not acquire this working knowledge on my own. I don't know the river as he does, but I can learn." She straightened and looked around. "Quite a lot of mess for your breakfast, I'm afraid.

The most convenient place would have been the kitchens, but Cook wouldn't allow it. She was already in the throes of culinary hysteria. Said you're hosting a dinner?"

Lillian drew her eyebrows. "Yes, but you knew this. In honor of the new viscount, just moved to town. He's a parliamentary connection of Lord Beecham. Lady Beecham and I will host together. Feign ignorance all you like, but I want you there, Elisabeth. No excuses, please." She sliced the fruit and took a dainty bite. "'Tis but a meal and conversation. The only guests will be the viscount, Lord and Lady Beecham, and a few old friends. Some ladies not much younger than yourself—"

"*Oh, no.*" Elisabeth pointed at her aunt with a rolled map. "*Young ladies?* Young ladies only mean one thing: this viscount is a bachelor. Admit it. And you're tossing me in on the vain hope that he won't notice that I'm too old and too preoccupied with my work to be anyone's wife." She crossed her arms over her chest. "We've been over this, Aunt Lillian. It's a poor strategy. And it makes everyone uncomfortable. Especially me."

"Stop. You are young and beautiful and will outshine every girl there, despite your age. Be preoccupied if you like…although I'd term it more like 'enthusiasm.' Discuss your foundation with the guests, but wear a new dress when you do it. Allow Bea to style your hair. It won't matter what shocking thing you say if you look your very best when you say it."

Elisabeth shook her head and reached for another map. "Has it occurred to you, Aunt, that if I dressed as fashionably as you liked, I might supersede the beauty preeminence that so rightfully belongs to you in this house?"

"But this is what we *want*, of course. You are young and beautiful. You aren't forced to eat raw fruit—better intended for the horses than the people—in order to remain slender and attractive." She took another bite. "When I was a girl, I traveled to Paris to be outfitted in styles that were seasons away from the drawing rooms of London. Before I was parceled off to marry decrepit Lord Banning, Mama's front door saw a continuous stream of gentleman callers."

"Which was one of the reasons you were parceled off, or so I hear," Elisabeth said absently, returning to her map. "I suppose this is what you want for me. A line of men wrapping around the house? So many men that you're forced to marry me off simply to be rid of the bother?"

"Ah, but you must know that I want what *you* want, darling. My point is merely that you are only young once—"

"Ah, but perhaps I'll be beautiful forever, like you, Aunt."

"That is entirely beside the point. Do not distract me with compliments. No doubt you *will* be beautiful forever. But regardless, you will never be as beautiful as when you are young." She took up the fruit again but then put it down. "And why shouldn't you let me dress you? Why won't you indulge your old aunt in being more of a true mother to you?"

"Oh, Aunt Lillian…" Elisabeth sighed. She crossed to the back of her aunt's chair and draped her arms around her shoulders. "You have been an ideal mother to me, as you well know. You restored my life when I wanted to roll up into a little ball and float away. You made me a happy girl where a miserable girl could have been. This is far more valuable to me than fine clothes or hats or shoes or bags. *You* are the great unsettling beauty, Aunt, and you know it. The infamous Countess of Banning. I am the niece who has other plans."

Elisabeth dipped to give her aunt a kiss on the cheek, and the door from the kitchens swung open. Quincy strode into the breakfast room bearing a silver tray of fragrant scones. "These," boomed the gardener, "have just come from the oven, my lady. Made with our very own gooseberries from the garden."

Elisabeth chuckled at her aunt's exasperated sigh. Lillian turned away, but Quincy was not deterred. Elisabeth helped him clear away maps so he could edge out Lillian's pear with the heaping tray. The countess squinted at it with open animosity.

"Pruning today, Quincy?" asked Elisabeth.

"Aye. Only the west garden remains."

Of all the ornately decorated rooms in Denby House, Benjamin Quincy was most out of place in the frilly, pale-pink breakfast room. His well-worn leathers and salt-and-pepper beard were like an unfinished oak beam against the countess's chintz. When the house was empty of outsiders, Quincy moved freely through every room, pink or otherwise, with a verbose, earthy jocularity that was distinctly, endearingly Suffolk woodsman. Despite Lillian's exaggerated irritation, Elisabeth knew her aunt would have him no other way. The countess had been in love with her gardener since the summer her husband, the old earl, had died and left her a young widow, some twenty years ago.

"When I've finished," Quincy went on, "every bed will be cut back for the summer. How do you like that?" He winked, collected three scones, and strode out the door with a loud whistle.

"He would fatten me up to the size of an ox," vowed Lillian, making a show of pushing the tray away.

"Oh, surely one cannot hurt." Elisabeth took up a scone and nibbled.

"I shall eat the whole tray if you will come to dinner tonight. Did I mention that it was for charity? Knowing this, I should think you would *want* to attend."

"Hmmm," Elisabeth mused. She began rolling the maps and sliding them into a basket. "You said it was for Lord Beecham's parliamentary something-or-other."

"Yes, yes, the viscount. Beecham arranged the meal because they are acquainted. But Lady Beecham and I intend to approach him about our committee for the hospital expansion. You've coerced me to join a cause, Elisabeth. The least you could do is support my effort to raise funds. They say he's very rich…"

"Is that what they say?" She rolled another map.

"And now he's just announced his plan to donate a sizable sum to three worthy charities in town. 'Tis a competition, in a way. The three winning charities will each receive a donation. And why shouldn't one of them go to the hospital? We are determined to reach him before those vultures from the Widows and Orphans League."

"Never let it be said that the widows and orphans have an advantage. But this is a bit provoking, isn't it? Forcing charities to compete? Why doesn't this person simply select one charity and quietly donate the whole sum?"

"Publicity, I suppose. He's been working for an age to rehabilitate the reputation of his title and family name. Wants to be viewed as the right sort. Generous. Noble." She took another nibble of pear. "But perhaps you should toss your hat into the ring, Elisabeth. For your foundation? Win the charity prize for your girls. There now, you see? Another reason to attend."

"If his goal is to generate publicity, the last cause this viscount will wish to support is mine. We never get the flashy donations. More of the same, really." Elisabeth ran a charity that rescued girls from the streets of London and set them up in a better life. She looked at her aunt. "But you've invited the man to dinner in order to win his favor? Is this how the decision is to be made? He'll give the prize to whoever makes the biggest fuss?"

"Oh, no. There'll be an application process, and interview, a tour of the facilities. We'll do all of this, naturally. But Lady Beecham felt we might sweeten the pot with a lovely dinner. Considering he's new to town. It's why we've invited the young ladies—yourself included." She shot her niece a pointed look. "Rumor is, he's come to London looking for a wife. We simply want to appear helpful and accommodating. It's the least we could do."

"The very least." Elisabeth rolled another map. "Quite an effort for a charity gift. How much is the prize?"

Lillian dabbed her lips with a napkin. "Oh, 'tis a thousand pounds, each prize."

Elisabeth's head shot up. "You jest! A thousand pounds? No one gives away that amount of money unless he's dead.

Why, a charity could realize the goals of its wildest dreams with a donation of that size."

Aunt Lillian nodded, "'Tis no jest. But I can't believe you haven't heard of this, darling. It was a headline in today's *Times*. According to the article, the viscount has money to spare. He's spent two years and God-knows-how-much restoring a mansion near Cavendish Square. In Henrietta Place, just down from old Lady Frinfrock. You remember Lady Frinfrock, from St. George's? She'll be here tonight as well, which is very rare. She's not been seen out for an age. It would appear everyone wants a glimpse of the viscount."

"Forgive me if I haven't kept up on who spent what to live where, but *a thousand pounds*. Truly?"

"Oh, yes. And to three different groups. Three thousand pounds in all." Lillian paused. "If it's a splash he wants, he'll get one with that sum." She chuckled to herself. "Aren't you curious about the prize or the philanthropist, Elisabeth? Even a little?"

"The prize? Possibly. The philanthropist? Not really." She stooped to retrieve the maps from the floor.

"Even so," said her aunt, "I should like you to make the effort. Wear a pretty dress. Wear a flower in your hair."

Elisabeth tucked the maps beneath her arm and sailed to the door. "And ever the burden grows," she said.

"What burden?" her aunt called after her. "'Tis but a meal—three hours at most." Her voice raised to a shout. "You'll do this one small favor to help me, won't you, darling?"

"I don't see how this is helping," Elisabeth replied, already moving on.

The Bronze Root Tavern
Southwark Docks on the River Thames
Fifteen years prior…

"**I** don't see how this is helping," Elisabeth whispered to Marie, scuttling down a cramped brothel hallway in the dark. "Please, Marie! This is not helping me."

"Hush," hissed Marie, whipping them around a corner and falling back against the wall, "and come on!"

"How is it helping me to run deeper into the building?" Elisabeth peered around the corner at the main stair, which grew farther away with every turn. "We're going the wrong direction!"

"Lesser of two evils," Marie whispered. "I'm rescuing you from the old man—the father. There'll be no getting around the son."

"But I don't want either of them!"

Marie laughed. "You only think that because you don't know what a rotter the father can be. Coming here especially for you, he is. Partial to soft-skinned innocents. Virgins, the sick bastard. For the son, they've asked for an experienced professional. Like me. If it really is his first time, he'll be harmless—even for you. Far better than the father, believe me. The son won't last ten seconds." She laughed.

"But Marie." Elisabeth fought for control. "We talked about an escape. Actual freedom. All the way outside. Not another room with another man!"

"Ha." Marie chuckled, drawing a shaky hand to her brow. "What we want doesn't matter now, does it? Means to an end, this is. Stop arguing, and do as I say. You will go to the boy—the son. Best I can do. Why don't you tell him what's happened?" she went on. "Tell him your parents have been shot, and you've been left here to rot. Let him hear that plummy accent of yours." She shrugged. "Maybe he'll be the one to get you all the way out."

"But you can get me out," Elisabeth insisted. "We can both go. Together. Out the front door. Or the back door. Out any door."

Marie only laughed.

"You're smarter than these men, Marie," Elisabeth said. "The man in charge? He may be strong, but you are clever, and I am fast."

Marie shook her head. "Forget about the doors. Forget about me. You've got one job tonight, and that's to please the young lord. Whatever he wants, you do it. Do it with a smile on your pretty face. And when it's all said and done, ask him for a little boost, patient and pretty, like. I'll keep the father busy all night long. He'll never know the difference."

"There must be another way," Elisabeth whispered, her voice cracking.

Marie shook her head. "Been here five years, since I was younger than you, and I've not seen it." She studied Elisabeth with sad, shrewd eyes and yanked the remnants of Elisabeth's ill-fitting shift back over her wounded shoulder. "We've had some bit of luck with those men last night, sniffing around, getting a nice long look at you. Their little taste gave us fair warning, didn't it? And when do we ever get that?"

Elisabeth nearly retched at the memory of the men who had arrived the previous night. She'd been dragged her from her bed and presented to them like a meal. At the urging of the eager proprietor, they had ogled her, pinched her—touched her. The feel of their hands on her body had made her actually pray for death.

"It cannot be so far to London," Elisabeth had whispered to the wall. "My parents and I were only to Windsor Road when our carriage was attacked. The highwaymen rode only a few hours to reach this place." Elisabeth could recite the circumstances of the last forty-eight hours, but she could not dwell on it. She'd set aside the sickening grief of her parents' murders and her abduction, and her unspeakable first night in this place. She would not think of her future without her mother and father. She would not think of the searing burn on her shoulder. Instead, survival had become her entire world. It was survival or choking on her own fear and pain.

She implored Marie again. "If it's even a day's walk to town, I can make it on foot, truly I can."

"Put it out of your mind," Marie scolded. "This won't be so bad. A lot easier than walking back to London in the wet, I'll tell you that."

"Marie," Elisabeth's voice broke. "I cannot be given to any of them."

Marie went on as if she hadn't heard. "The young men are quite shy, really. Timid-like. Easy to manage. How old are you? Sixteen? Seventeen?"

"Fifteen," Elisabeth said. "Only just."

"Oh. Well." She thought this over. "Nothing we can do about that, is it? The old lord wanted a young one, didn't he? But the boy will expect experience, remember. He will expect me."

"This is not helping me," Elisabeth repeated. She would say it again and again and again.

"It will be what you make it. Tell him who you are; tell him what happened to you and your parents. Show him the mark that

Snill burned into your shoulder. It'll heal, by the way. Leave a scar, but it will not pain you forever."

"*I don't want to talk to him! I don't want to see him at all. Marie, please. I cannot do this.*" *Elisabeth pulled the course, torn garment over the fiery wound on her shoulder.*

"*You can do it, and you will do it,*" *Marie said, taking her by the hand.*

Voices, loud and slurred, intruded on the hushed tones of their conversation, and Marie held up a hand to quiet her. It was a group. Four men, maybe five. In the taproom below. One of them angry, others laughing. A piece of furniture splintered. Elisabeth squeezed her eyes shut.

"*They've come,*" *whispered Marie.* "*'Tis time. We'll stash you in my room, and I will go to where Snill left you to wait for the father. Exactly as I've said, little miss,*" *she continued, pulling Elisabeth along.* "*You must do everything exactly as I've said.*"

CHAPTER THREE

Denby House
Grosvenor Square
May 1811

It rained the night of the Countess's dinner, a foggy, fitting damp. Rainsleigh welcomed it—what else could he expect for his first foray into the inner sanctum of London's social elite? He'd toiled years for an invitation such as this, but he refused to sail into the evening thinking it would be easy. Old habits died hard. A lifetime of exclusion had prepared him. At the very least, it should rain.

Ah, but it was just a meal, and on a day when Parliament sat. This guaranteed that the dinner would not run long. Few people of distinction would attend. The best wine, he knew, would not be served. Considering the stack of work waiting for him at home and the rare appearance of his brother, Rainsleigh didn't really even want to attend. What he'd *really* wanted had been the invitation. Simply to make the bloody list. The real triumph was access. Now that he had it, it meant inane chitchat with lofty strangers. He immediately wished attendance had been optional. Or not tonight.

But he had said that he would come. And he was mildly curious. And really, these sorts of engagements were necessary, he knew, if his ultimate goal was to be regarded as equal. A reclusive viscount would be known as a degenerate one, if no one ever saw him.

Rain meant carriage traffic, lurching and slow, and after ten minutes of waiting, Rainsleigh bade the coachman park behind the last vehicle so he could walk. Soames had outfitted him with hat and umbrella, overcoat and boots. He had not come so far that he could not get wet.

"*My lord…*" enthused the hostess, Lady Banning, five minutes later, smiling inside the warm confines of her sprawling entry hall. She reached out, two delicate gloved hands clasping his, and ushered him in. "What a pleasure it is to meet you at last. We're so pleased that you've been able to join us on such short notice, especially when you must be terribly preoccupied with settling in."

Rainsleigh bowed over her hands. "The pleasure is all mine, Lady Banning. It was a delight to receive your invitation. We're practically neighbors now. You are between my new house and the park."

"That park!" the countess complained, smiling still. "My niece spends half her time there, regardless of the weather. But you've met my niece, Lord Rainsleigh? Lady Elisabeth?"

Rainsleigh bristled. It was common knowledge that he'd been introduced to practically no one, especially young women. He put on a neutral face. "I don't believe I've had the pleasure."

"I don't see her at the moment," Lady Banning said, "but we'll find her, and you must be introduced. She knows every corner of Hyde Park, especially the damp, boggy bits, judging from the condition of her boots. I'm sure she will be happy to educate you about where the trail has washed out or where the best shade can be found."

"That would be most useful."

He bowed again, making way for the dripping older couple behind him. The countess easily soothed them, all sympathy and smiles. Charming woman, he conceded. She'd shown him no veiled slight or indignity. Attractive, too, despite being twenty years his senior.

A footman led him down the wide hall to an adjacent salon. It was a small gathering. Mostly elderly couples and young women. There was a glaring lack of gentlemen and no one easily identifiable as his equal in rank or wealth. Possibly a statement about his inclusion, possibly harmless.

Two more young women strolled into view, which made five girls, all told. He rubbed his jaw. A footman passed with a tray of drinks, and he took a glass, counting in his head. Five young women, the widowed countess, and a clutch of elderly people, old enough to have met Christ. He took a drink. This dinner made no sense.

But now here was Lord Beecham, making for him at a slow waddle from a chair beside the fire.

"Rainsleigh!" the baron called, his politician's smile wide on his ruddy face. "So good of you to come. Lady Banning and my wife have been determined to welcome you to town before the others."

"Others?" Rainsleigh took another drink.

"But of course! Point of pride, really. Wanted to be first and to make an impression. You've seen the lovely debutantes? Convened the lot—oh, there must be four or five of them—in hopes of lighting the tinder of a brilliant match."

Rainsleigh choked on his drink. "The young women are for me?"

"Oh, but do not think to keep secrets in this town, old boy. London hostesses can smell a marriage-minded gentleman as far as Middlesex. They'll know it's time to get shackled before you do."

"How accommodating. I hadn't—"

"But before you become distracted by the young ladies, I must bend your ear about my shipping levy…"

And he was off, lobbying on behalf of the maritime legislation he'd been touting to the shipping magnates for weeks. Rainsleigh nodded, only half listening, and allowed his eyes to wander. He surveyed the room.

Four or five young ladies for me? This had not occurred to him. He took another sip. But he had no idea what to do with four or five young ladies. Mincing through marriage prospects was to be Dunhip's job. Rainsleigh intended to sweep in at the eleventh hour and consider the finalists, perhaps the top four. Or even two.

He narrowed his eyes, studying the girls. *My God*, but they were young. Barely out of the schoolroom. He was thirty-four years of age, head of his family, shipbuilder, landholder, viscount. Certainly maturity in his future bride was a priority. With maturity would come reserve, calm, discretion, self-control…

One of the girls looked up and caught him in a stare. She was tall. Frocked in yellow. Brown hair, strong nose.

Rainsleigh considered her. She appeared elegant enough. He gave a curt nod. The girl smiled coquettishly and lowered her eyes without breaking the stare. She blinked. While he watched, she discreetly extended the tip of her tiny pink tongue and licked her upper lip. At him. *For* him.

Rainsleigh turned away.

No. Absolutely not. No boldness. First and foremost. Especially no provocative, flirtatious boldness. He'd spent his boyhood with a mother who batted eyelashes and licked lips before she even arose from bed. More often than not, a footman walked away in a better mood. It was a disgrace, one of many. He would not repeat the phenomenon with his own wife.

He drained the last of his glass and nodded along to Lord Beecham's drone, raising his eyebrows in faux interest. He was just about to gesture for another drink when movement caught his attention. A flutter. A flash of blue. Out of sheer boredom, he turned to follow it, craning his head.

It was yet another young woman. In the opposite direction, separate from the party. She was alone, clipping down a staircase at the end of the great hall and holding a piece of unfolded parchment. As she descended, she read. *Must be a relative or member of staff,* he thought. Clearly, she wasn't part of the countess's party. She paid no mind to the raised voices or clinking crystal at the end of the hall, and she was dressed in a simple blue muslin day dress. Rainsleigh almost turned away. Almost, but not quite.

Casually, he looked again.

Perhaps it was that she did not descend the stairs so much as float over them. Purposefully but not stridently. Gracefully but with no flounce. She ignored the handrail and did not glance at the rapidly descending marble beneath her feet. The parchment in her hand obscured her face, but he could make out a serene profile, a small ear.

He looked harder. She appeared…Rainsleigh found himself unable to put words precisely how she appeared.

"Rainsleigh? *Rainsleigh?*"

Lord Beecham called to him from five feet away.

The viscount looked up. The baron stood on the threshold of the salon, sputtering and confused.

"Forgive me," Rainsleigh said, stepping back to him. "Lord Beecham, do you know that girl, there? On the stairs?" The question was out before he realized. He pointed. "The young lady?"

"Eh?" Beecham craned around.

"No, not in the salon. There, in the hall. She's just come down the stairs. It's difficult to see for the parchment in her hand, but I believe she has—" He blinked. "Yes. Her hair is an odd sort of pale ginger."

Beecham squinted down the hall. The young woman had stopped at a sideboard and was rustling in a drawer. She closed it, took up the paper again, and moved on, still not looking up. Now she walked in their direction but stopped at a closed door, halfway down. She reached for the doorknob and pulled it open, speaking to someone on the other side. She gestured. She nodded. She waved the paper in the air. She moved inside the door a step but not all the way.

Rainsleigh could not see her face. He swore and stepped to the side, angling for a better view.

"Oh, *there*," said Beecham, drawing his brows together. "'Tis only Lady Elisabeth, the countess's niece. My wife did not expect her to attend the party, and it appears she was right. Look how she's dressed at this hour. But she does live here in Denby House. Been a ward of the countess for these many years."

"*Lady Elisabeth,*" mumbled Rainsleigh, studying the tall, thin half profile visible behind the standing door. He looked at the baron. "Why is she not expected to attend?"

"Bit of an odd duck, I'm afraid. She's lived with the countess since her parents were killed in a carriage raid, years ago. Tragic business, really, but she seems well enough. Although she is never really seen out socially, or so they say. Lady Banning never compelled her to make a proper debut, and she did not, as far as I know. Egad, Rainsleigh, with all the other girls here, you'd do well to stay away from that one. On the shelf, really."

Rainsleigh studied the parts of her he could see beyond the standing open door. The slender point of her shoulders. Her elegant back. The gentle slope of her bottom beneath the soft blue skirt.

A footman walked past her, ferrying drinks on a tray. He offered her a glass, and she used the paper to gently wave him off. The servant proceeded toward Rainsleigh, but she must have called him back because he returned to her. She pivoted, telling him something.

And that's when he saw her face.

For the second time that night, he could not look away.

Her eyes were light. Blue? Perhaps green. He was too far away to tell.

Her hair, he saw, was not strictly ginger but gold and blonde and pale red, all spun together.

Rainsleigh took an inadvertent step toward her. The footman with the drinks passed him now, and he took a glass, not taking his eyes away.

Without warning, she looked up, and their gazes locked. Her eyes grew huge. She sucked in a startled breath.

For a long, taut moment, they stared.

Beecham, reliably, broke the trance. "Egad, Rainsleigh, but you look as if you've seen a ghost. Are you acquainted with Lady Elisabeth?"

Rainsleigh shook his head: one slow, firm shake. He was not.

His mouth had gone strangely dry. His voice was a low rasp. "I've never met her before in my life."

Fifteen years prior…
The Bronze Root Tavern

*B*ryson awakened in the world's smallest, most uncomfortable bed. He blinked at the ceiling, smoky and water-stained, and lifted his head to look at his feet.

Boots, he thought. *Thank God. At least they'd left him in his clothes and boots.*

His head throbbed. They'd drugged him—his father and his uncle and his cousin Kenneth. Or they'd knocked him out with a blow to the head. Or both. His vision blurred, sharpened, and then blurred again. When it came to the pranks of his father and cousin Kenneth, his priority had always been consciousness. Remain conscious. At all costs. Clearly, he'd failed again.

He swore and shoved up in the damp, unfamiliar bed, willing his eyes to focus. When the room stopped listing, he saw it was small and cold and spare. The adjacent door was closed tight, naturally. If previous abductions were any indication, it would also be locked.

He looked to the opposite wall, and—

Bloody hell. The room was small, cold, spare, and occupied.

Bryson rolled out of bed, blinking against his throbbing headache, and gaped at the silent figure huddled against the far wall.

A girl.

She stood beside a window, clutching a fireplace poker diagonally across her chest. Her hair hung unbound down her back. Her dress, or rather her shift, was marked with an ominous stain that seeped through the fabric at one shoulder. *Blood.*

He looked at her face. Her eyes were wide with terror.

"Hello," he said carefully. He held out his hand in a reassuring gesture. "You're all right."

He took a step, and she gasped. She pressed herself more tightly against the wall.

"Door," he told her, taking two steps. "I'm merely going to the door. Is it locked, do you know?"

She didn't move, but he was careful not to turn his back on her and the poker. He reached for the knob.

"Locked," he said, gripping the knob more tightly, rattling it left and right. It refused to give, and he added his other hand, his shoulder, his foot, kicking the base with his boot. He forgot about the girl and raged at the unmoving door, shouting profanity and threats.

No one came.

He spun back to the room. "The window," he said, pointing beside the girl.

"It's locked," she said, her first words. He stopped. *My God, but she was young.* This had been obvious from across the room, *but her voice sounded like that of a frightened child. Was she fif-teen? Sixteen? He couldn't guess.*

"Careful," *he said, starting again for the window. The girl leapt back and skittered down the wall, wedging herself between a heavy wardrobe and the corner.*

He held out a hand to calm her. "Be assured, miss, the sooner I can discover a route to the street, the sooner I will be out of your way." *He peered out the window and swore. They were at least three stories up.*

"But you don't mean to…" *Her question trailed off.*

"I don't mean to stay the night," *he assured her, feeling around the window facing and clattering the lock.* "I don't mean to stay five minutes, if I can help it."

She thought about this and then asked, "Can you take me with you?"

His hands stilled. "With me? Take you with me…to Cambridge?"

She shook her head. "Take me with you out of this room. Take me out of this building. Out of Southwark. To London?" *She raised up a little, having said this. She watched him.*

Her eyes, he thought, were a curious color. Aquamarine. So unexpected. He'd prepared himself to be matched with the fattest, most tired, most garish woman in the history of the occupation. Instead, he found himself staring into the aquamarine eyes of a girl who wanted exactly the same thing that he did.

"We'll go together, then." *The words left his mouth before he'd realized he'd said them.* "Why not? Since we're a team now, could I trouble you for the loan of your poker?" *He smiled.*

She looked at the iron rod in her hands.

"Window's painted shut," *he explained.* "Many times over. We'll be here all night if we bother with the lock. If no one came when I raged against the door, I'm doubtful they'll come at the sound of breaking glass. Especially if you scream."

"Scream?" she repeated.

"To cover the racket. If you stand by the door and affect something shrill and perhaps a bit desperate, that should do it. You'll, er, know what's a common enough sound for a…er…" He turned back to the window. "For this time of night."

He saw her think about this. He thought of her shoulder, the fear in her eyes, the torn shift. Likely she'd done enough screaming for a lifetime.

"Or we can give it a go without the scream." He stretched out his hand and nodded toward the poker. "I'll let you decide."

"I can scream," she said. She knelt and placed the iron poker on the floor and slid it in his direction.

"Right," he said, scooping it up. "Wait—let's block the door with this wardrobe, shall we? When they do come, it will slow them down."

She stood back as he muscled the heavy, uneven piece of furniture in front of the door.

When the wardrobe had been safely lodged against the door, he tapped the sharp end of the pointer three times against the glass, testing it. It would shatter easily with one thrust.

He nodded to her. "Go on, then," he said.

The girl stood stock-still for three or four beats, and then she took a deep breath, braced herself on the wardrobe, and screamed.

*F*ive minutes later, they hit the wet ground of the alley outside the window with a one, two, smack.

"Bloody hell," Bryson grumbled, launching from the ground and swatting at his knees. "Not only are my boots scuffed but my trousers torn as well."

The girl bounced up and scrambled against the wall.

"You all right?" He glanced at the tear in his trousers. "These breeches were new, and I needed them to last for at least a bloody year. Typical. My father does these things intentionally."

He straightened and looked up and down the alley. "And now where are we? With torn breeches and only two days to get half-way across the country?" He looked at her. "Which way to the river? Do you know?"

She reached for the wall beside her and said nothing.

"The river?" he prompted. "The River Thames? Wide? Dirty? Lots of boats?"

She considered this.

"Separates this sodden slum from the outskirts of London?" he added. "Look, I know you can speak, so please. If you can impart anything about where we are, now is the time to share it. Surely it's clear that I'm not going to harm you. I only landed on your, er, head when the drainpipe snapped. I lost my hold those last three yards. Sorry." He grimaced. "You broke my fall. For which I'm grateful." He flashed her a smile.

She looked away.

"Right." He sighed. "Let's try a new tack. What's happened to your shoulder?"

She shuffled down the wall two more steps. "Stay back," she whispered.

He nodded. "Right. Very well. I'm back. What's happened? A cut? Oh, God is it a...," He forgot his promise to stay back and closed in on her. She cowered, flattening against the wall.

"*Easy,*" he said. "*I only want a look.*"

"*Please,*" she whispered brokenly, "*do not touch…*"

"Bloody hell, it is," he said, marveling. "You've been branded. Is that it? A cattle brand burned into your shoulder?"

She turned her face away and leaned her forehead against the wall.

He peered over her, fighting the urge to pull away the blood-soaked shoulder of her shift. The wound was festering, angry, red and black.

"How far down your back does it stretch?" he whispered. He moved to take better advantage of the moonlight.

Her face crumpled against the wall. She let out a broken sob.

Bryson swore. "Look, we've got to get out of here."

He left her to cross the alley and look around a corner. They would have miles to walk in the cloud-filled darkness before they reached reliable civilization.

"You mentioned London. Is this where you would you like to go? I've a schoolmate there who might be persuaded to give me a ride back to Cambridgeshire."

Her head popped up from the wall. "London—yes, please. I'll need only the direction to Mayfair. To Grosvenor Square."

He craned around. "Mayfair? What business do you have in Mayfair?"

She shook her head.

"Right," he said. He wouldn't pry. "Mayfair. That is as good a place as any for me to start. We can hardly stay here." He looked left and right. "The last thing I remember was my father's carriage rolling over Blackfriars Bridge. If we are near Blackfriars, we can walk to Mayfair by morning. Assuming we can find the direction of the bloody Thames."

"The river is to the left," she said. She took a step from the wall.

"Ah, that was going to be my guess. Great minds think alike."

"It was the smell."

"Great noses, then."

"If you please," she said, louder now, "I cannot be found out. I cannot be taken back. I'll die before I go back."

"Then we really do think alike. Can you manage if we begin at a run?"

"Yes."

"I meant with your wounded shoulder."

"My legs are well."

"Right." At the mention of her legs, his eyes roamed, unbidden, down her body and up again. He cleared his throat and looked away. "Let's put a little distance behind us, several blocks or so. Then it should be safe to stay parallel to the water but not in the full view of the bank."

He shoved off in that direction at a trot, and she darted behind him. He'd planned to lope for a quarter hour and then allow her walk, but she kept an enviable pace, and he felt safe enough to slow down to a walk after just two blocks. They breathed in unison, deep, hard breaths. Bryson stole a look. He wondered again about her age.

Her face, furrowed now with fear and fatigue, was quite pretty—beautiful even. It was not often he saw a female with unbound hair. Not even a braid or a pin to keep it back from her face. Red-gold waves fell down her back like a cape. He fought the irrational urge to reach out and tuck it behind her ear.

He cleared his throat. "Do you have a name?" he asked.

She shook her head, a barely perceptible shake. She returned her focus to the road.

"Not the talkative sort, are you?" He nodded. "I understand. What a devil of a night this has been. Unfortunately, I am accustomed to these sorts of misadventures. I can frequently be found crawling out of windows or leaping from speeding carriages. It becomes old hat, I'm afraid."

She looked at him, and he gestured toward a street to their left.

"My father," he provided.

When she said nothing, he felt compelled to explain. "He has a bad habit of subjecting me to his diversions by force, which, unfortunately, seem to become more unpleasant, not to mention more illegal, by the year. The truth is, it amuses him to humiliate me."

They turned down a long, curved thoroughfare with no torchlight, and he glanced at her again. One thing was certain, she'd never jeopardize their escape by making any sort of fuss. Even her footfalls were quiet on the gravel street. The hem of her shift barely rustled as she took two steps to his one.

"I'm called Bryson," he said after a moment. "Bryson Courtland. One day, God willing, I shall be Viscount Rainsleigh. My father is the viscount now, unfortunately."

Bloody hell but that was chatty. He told himself that he'd heard this about prostitutes. That you could say things to them that you wouldn't ordinarily risk with someone you would see again.

"Likely you've never heard of him," he continued darkly. "This is because my father makes no effort toward the title. Nor does he mind the property. His reputation precedes him, but only with enraged creditors, gamblers, addicts." He looked at her and then asked, inspired, "Or perhaps you do know him?"

"I am not in acquaintance of your father, sir."

Sir.

No one called him that, although, rightfully, they should. But there were very few servants left at Rossmore Court—servants had to be paid—and he kept to himself at school.

They heard a carriage in the distance, thank God. He needed a reason to stop talking. It was probably nothing, but he held up a hand to stay her. They ducked around a corner and collapsed against the side of a building. Making no sound, he spidered his fingers across the brick until he found her hand, and he covered it with his own. The conveyance rolled past without incident, and he said, "Harmless," and waved her back to the walk.

"Will your father be cross that you left him behind?" she whispered.

"I don't really care," he said with a sigh. "My main concern is getting back to school. My holiday, such that it was, is over, and I must be to Cambridge by Monday. After tonight, I'd say that going home would be imprudent. But I will need my belongings. If I don't send for them, my father will sell them. Eventually I will go back, because I look after my brother, God save him."

A cat skittered in front of them and disappeared under a rise of steps. He watched her follow it with her eyes. "And what will you do? What business do you have in Mayfair?"

"I have an aunt there—in Grosvenor Square," she said.

"I wish I had an aunt in Grosvenor Square." He looked right and left and crossed the street, motioning for her to follow. "Will there be a doctor for your shoulder? In the care of your aunt?"

"Yes."

"And, perhaps…Honest employ?"

They rounded a corner before she could reply, and there it was. Blackfriars Bridge. It lay across the inky water of the Thames like an outstretched arm.

"Is this it?" she asked.

"It is." He squinted through the mist rising from the river at the bridge. "Hmmm. More traffic than I had hoped this time of night, but we needn't worry. My father would never find it worth his trouble to come after me now." He scanned the bridge. "These are farmers mostly, headed to market...setting up stalls for the morning crush. We'll keep our heads down. Make quick work of it. We can easily be on the other side in a quarter hour."

She nodded but held back, waiting for him to lead.

"Right," he said, and he shoved off the ledge toward the bridge. She hurried after him and then surprised him by grabbing his hand. Her grip was warm and firm and...familiar, as if he'd been holding her hand all of his life. He was unaccustomed to being touched by anyone and certainly not by a girl, but it was surprisingly easy to clasp back, to gently lead her. He grew surer of their safety and direction with every step.

She let out a shaky sigh when they descended the steps on the opposite bank, and he said, "It won't be far now," but he didn't let go of her hand. The sun was beginning to warm the horizon, and birds called from deep inside the leafy canopy of the street. They walked toward Westminster. He held her hand.

When they neared Green Park, he said, "It will be daylight soon. People will see us...servants making preparations for the day. Grosvenor Square is just a handful of blocks away. I wouldn't want you to appear suspicious to the other staff who work with your aunt." He cleared his throat. "That is, the focus should be on your wound and reunion and not who the devil I may be."

She dropped his hand, just like that. He looked down at it his empty palm, fighting the urge to take a step closer.

"I should like to walk alone from here," she said, staring across the park.

"I didn't mean to dismiss you," he said. Now he took the closer step. "I have every intention of seeing you the rest of the way. I'm simply trying to…" he trailed off, frustrated. He had no idea what he was trying to do.

"I know the way," she said. "You have been more than kind. You needn't trouble yourself. As you said, you must find your way back to school."

"Yes," he agreed, a reflex.

She backed away from him. "Thank you so much. Godspeed to you."

And then she turned her back and jogged a diagonal path across the park.

"May I—" he called after her, but then he stopped.

He ran a few steps to be heard and started again. "I will inquire after your health on my next holiday. I should like to know that you've been looked after."

"Please do not follow me," she called over her shoulder.

"Of course," he mumbled to himself, watching as she grew smaller and smaller in the distance. When a milk cart passed between her silhouette and his view, he lost sight of her altogether.

She was gone.

Chapter Four

Elisabeth darted into the servant's stairwell and whipped the door shut on her aunt's party.

Bryson Courtland.

Bryson Courtland stood not ten yards from her, on the other side of the door.

In her aunt's entry hall.

Sipping wine from a goblet. Staring at her.

Oh, God. After all this time. She closed her eyes and put a hand over her mouth, willing her breathing to settle.

But how had he—

And then she realized. Bryson Courtland was Viscount Rainsleigh now. *He* was the viscount her aunt had invited to her party. He was the bachelor lord with all the money, the benefactor, the charity prize, the new house in town. It was *for him* Lillian had cajoled Elisabeth to attend tonight.

She stared at the closed door, her heart pounding.

Bryson Courtland. Here. Staring at her.

Recognizing her.

Fifteen years reconvened in the blink of an eye. The last time he'd seen her, she had been all of fifteen years old, terrified, out of her mind with grief.

Meanwhile, he was…

Well, he looked very much the same as he did now. Less wiry as a full-grown man. Broader chest. Thicker.

He was still—

"What's happened to *you?*" Four steps down the stairwell, Elisabeth's errand boy and lead raider, Stoker, chewed on a green bean from the kitchen.

The letter! "Stop there, Stoker," she managed, staring at the parchment still clutched in her hand. "A word, if you please. You may not go until we've spoken."

He took another bite. "You look like you've swallowed a beetle."

She scanned the letter, seeing nothing. She scanned it again to the same result. In her head, she saw only the viscount's gaze, locked on her face, or Aunt Lillian's innocent expression this morning, casually inviting her to live out one of her most mortifying dreams while society friends slurped soup around the table.

"I won't go to Yorkshire," Stoker said, jerking her back to the letter.

"You *will* go," she shot back. "You've barely considered it." She could have had this conversation in her sleep, thank God.

"You can't force me, Lady E, and I won't do it. Even if I have to stop raiding for you."

"I don't intend to *force you*, Stoker. I intend to convince you. And that begins with reading the letter. What luck that you turned up." She extended the letter to him. "The formal acceptance arrived only today. I was counting the minutes until I could show you. Here, take it. Read it yourself. See what they've said about you."

He didn't move.

Elisabeth sighed and continued. "It's a lovely school, Stoker. It will change your life. You won't be restricted to rescuing girls from brothels for me and living in Rotten Row. You'll never have to set foot in a brothel ever again. You may take a job in a bank. Or as a teacher. You may work in an office or a laboratory. Who can say what you might achieve? The tutors have given you a fine basis of knowledge, but you are cleverer still, and there is so much more to know. Literature. Art. Mathematics. Languages. For this, you'll need a proper school, and this one *wants you*. They want you, Stoker." She waved the letter again.

Stoker leaned against the wall of the stairwell. "And what would I do, working in a bank? Sounds like a bloody bore. I'd rather work for you, Lady E." He pulled a half-smoked cheroot from his pocket.

"Do not smoke in here, Stoker. You know I cannot bear it." She scanned the letter again. "Don't you see? This means that you will have choices. Your notion of a fulfilling occupation may change after you've been to school. Why, after graduation you may work in the foundation *offices*, not in the streets."

"The office? While who runs the raids?"

"You...you may train Lewis to do the raiding." This would never happen, but she said it again. "Before you go, Lewis can learn." Stoker had been working as a stable boy for Elisabeth when she'd welcomed her first-ever prostitute to the foundation. It had been Stoker who volunteered to breach the brothel's high security and steal the girl out. He and a ragtag team of street boys had been raiding brothels for girls on Elisabeth's behalf ever since.

"Lewis?" Stoker scoffed, naming his hapless second in command. "Lewis gave us the slip tonight. Again. It's why I've come. We're down to five lads. But don't worry. It's sorted. Less is better, actually, in the rain."

"If Lewis cannot replace you, I'll find someone else. I refuse to keep you from a hopeful future so you can muck around in the gutter for me. This has always been my fight, Stoker. I am grateful for your help, but this is why I am sending you away. I owe it to you."

"I muck around in the gutter to keep you out of it, m'lady."

Elisabeth sighed. "You are loyal to a fault, Stoker. I would not have bothered with your education if you had not been so loyal or so bright." She raised her eyebrows, waiting. The boy spun his hat on his finger.

Elisabeth tried again, "Look, Lady Banning and I have gone great pains to have the school consider you. You are sorely mistaken if you think I will simply let it go. You must come to terms with it. This is your future. You *will* go."

"I won't."

"You *will* go, even if I have to drag you to Yorkshire myself!"

"Think of the girls we save, Lady E. Think of them."

She wanted to stomp her foot in frustration. "I will take on more help. Paid muscle is readily available in the London streets, but only a few, choice young men—and literally no one with your history—have the opportunity to attend to a real university."

"Paid muscle?" The boy looked as if he would cry.

She shook her head vigorously. "Stop. No one can fully replace your instincts or courage, but you may assist when school is not in session. In the interim, I will hire off-duty policemen. Or soldiers on leave."

"Less money for the girls."

"So be it. We can only do so much. Or I will raise more money. You have gifts, Stoker, and you cannot—"

A knock sounded on the door behind her, and Elisabeth jumped, dropping the letter. She lunged for it in the same moment as Stoker. They both came up with a corner, ripping it in two. Elisabeth exclaimed in frustration, half sigh, half shout.

Another knock, more insistent this time. Elisabeth whirled around, irritated. "Who could—"

The door opened, just a crack.

"I beg your pardon, but are you quite all right?"

Oh, God. Elisabeth shut her eyes.

"I thought I heard...conflict."

She opened one eye, but he was still there.

Bryson Courtland, Viscount Rainsleigh. Inexplicably, mortifyingly. Standing in the hall outside the now-open door.

She opened her mouth; closed it.

The viscount prompted. "Miss? I heard shouting. Is the boy causing a bother?" He leaned to one side, studying Stoker on the stairwell. Stoker dropped his gaze and slouched down to steps, the embodiment of supplication.

Miss?

Elisabeth's mind raced. *Miss?* Was it possible that he *did not remember?*

She shook her head. "There is no trouble," she said to the half sheet of parchment in her hand.

He waited.

Elisabeth stifled a shout of frustration and then elaborated. "This boy is in my employ, and we have disagreed about an errand. Our voices were raised but not in anger. There is no bother. I apologize for disrupting your evening."

"'Tis no disruption," said the viscount carefully. "I am inconveniently attuned to raised voices." A pause. "I apologize for the intrusion."

"'Tis no intrusion," she said quickly. She glanced at Stoker in time to see him quietly retreating down the stairs. *Traitor.*

She was forced to look at the viscount. "You are kind to inquire."

He nodded but remained in the doorway.

She ventured, "If you'll excuse me."

He didn't move.

She tried again, "Good night to you, sir."

Nothing.

Right, she thought. *Fine. I will go.*

He blocked the door to the hall, so she had no choice but to follow Stoker down the stairs. She turned, collected her skirts, and began to descend.

"Forgive my boldness, miss," he called after her, "but are you…"

She paused, her foot hovering above the fifth step. Her heart hammered. She squeezed the handrail.

He finished, "Are you the countess's niece? Lady…*Elisabeth?*"

Her lungs tightened and the knots in her stomach cinched into a tight pit. For a horrifying second, she thought he would call her out, right there and then. She averted her face and nodded to the wall.

"Forgive me again, but…won't you attend the dinner?"

She forgot herself and looked up.

His stare did not waver, and before she could stop herself, she scanned him, head to boot. His height and breadth filled the doorway. He'd worn buckskins and shirt sleeves that night, so long ago, but tonight his evening attire was solid black wool, leather boots, a creamy white cravat. The fit was precision, despite his considerable size. His face had grown to accommodate his strong features—wide jaw, aristocratic nose, ice-blue eyes, now creased at the edges by tiny lines. Surely he would have been freshly shaven before the party, but now his jaw was smudged with the shadow of a beard.

He cocked his head, just a little, aware of her scrutiny.

She cleared her throat. "I'm afraid the party is out of the question." She gave a dismissive smile and turned to go.

"Why is that?"

She stopped. "I beg your pardon?"

"I wonder why the party would be out of the question."

His persistence was rude, even by her standards, and she almost laughed. She was about to venture an outright lie—a headache, another engagement, an allergy to the fish—when Aunt Lillian swept through the doorway behind him.

"Aha, so you've found her," trilled the countess. She shot her niece a heavy look. "But what an unfortunate corner of the house. Elisabeth, darling, what are you doing in the foot-man's stairwell? Please, come out at once, so I may introduce you."

Elisabeth gritted her teeth. "Actually, I was just—"

Lillian continued, "After that, you may run upstairs. I will hold dinner while you dress."

Oh, no you will not. Elisabeth looked at her aunt, then the viscount, then back to her aunt.

The viscount coughed. "I beg your pardon, my lady. I made the acquaintance of your niece—outside the bounds of the party, I'm afraid, with no formal introduction. But I heard shouting in this stairwell. I was alarmed and feared the worst. I did not mean to—"

"Shouting?" Lillian chuckled, feigning shock. "Oh, hor-rors, what you must think. Yes, well, we reside in a very spir-ited household, I'm afraid. Thank you for your chivalry, but do not allow the odd ruckus to alarm you. Elisabeth," she continued, her voice tight, "please. Come into the hall so you may be properly introduced." She looked over her shoulder. "Lady Beecham would not speak to me if she knew the guest of honor had been lured away by a ruckus in the stairwell."

Elisabeth shook her head slightly and stepped down one step. She could feel the color burning in her cheeks. If he had not recognized her, it was only a matter of time. If he *had* recognized her, he was feigning ignorance for the purpose of...She had no idea why he would lie about it, but she could guess a myriad of humiliating revelations, each worse than the last.

She would not give him the opportunity. The life she'd built since her parents were shot had been carefully, painstakingly rebuilt. It included her aunt and Quincy, her charity, and the girls she saved. It did not include him.

"*Something has come up*," she told her aunt firmly. "With Stoker. I was just managing it. He and I had not yet finished speaking; in fact, I believe that I mentioned to you that I am *otherwise engaged* tonight, Aunt. For the party. I would prefer—"

"Ah, but the *viscount* would prefer the pleasure of your company, and he is my honored guest. If you come to dinner, you may tell him all about dear Stoker and the shouting match that so alarmed—"

"It was hardly a shouting match. We were merely—"

The viscount interjected, "Truly, my lady, if she does not wish to attend…" His voice was cutting and flat.

The countess interrupted, "Nonsense. Of course she wishes to attend. Come, darling, up, up." She extended her gloved hand and gave an urgent *flick, flick* with her pointer finger and thumb.

Rainsleigh tried again, his voice now a sharp grind. "If the lady does not wish to make my—"

Elisabeth shook her head and said, "It's nothing to do with you, my lord. 'Tis merely—"

"'Tis *everything* to do with you, my lord," cut in Aunt Lillian. "She wishes to approach you about your charity prize, but she does not wish to compete with my cause." To Elisabeth, she said, "I will not tell you again; the viscount has seen quite enough."

In the end, Elisabeth was given no choice. She nodded. She took up her skirt and raised her chin to hold her head high. It felt momentarily better—at least she no longer spoke to the wall—but she refused to go so far as to look Rainsleigh in the eye. Not that it mattered. If he recognized her, he gave no indication.

She glanced at him quickly—one swift look and then away. His expression had gone stony, almost grim. He nodded curtly, watching her ascend.

"It would seem that I shall attend the dinner after all," she said primly, looking straight ahead.

"Indeed." He blocked half the door. The polite thing would be to step back, but he did not budge. She was forced to maneuver around him.

"Aunt?" she called over her shoulder, sailing briskly to the stairs. "A word? It will only take a moment. While I change?"

"But of course, darling," came the answer, as she knew it would.

Elisabeth clipped up the marble steps to her chambers, ready to do battle.

CHAPTER FIVE

"You are cross." It was a statement, not a question, said on a sigh. Aunt Lillian opened Elisabeth's wardrobe and began yanking gowns from the rod and tossing them on the bed.

"Yes," said Elisabeth, watching colorful silks arc through the air. "I am cross. 'Cross' states very mildly how I feel, I'd say. Lilly, how could you? Without even consulting me? This man? *This* man? You have no idea what you've done."

"Oh, I think I have some notion, and"—the countess pulled a turquoise gown from the wardrobe—"I would do it again." She held the gown high, considered it, and then added it to the pile.

"Of this I have no doubt." Elisabeth began to pace. "Of all the machinations, the manipulations, of all the chance meetings that were not so chance—this is, by far, the worst. And to think. If I had consented to attend the dinner from the start, I would have been taken completely by surprise."

Lillian tsked. "Quincy predicted you would react this way."

"Well, Quincy was right. Where is he? He'll be the only one on my side, as usual."

"Whatever do you mean?" asked the countess, watching her pace. "He insists upon watching over me during these affairs; you know this. He's with the footmen, serving drinks."

Elisabeth considered this—considered the entire conversation they could have about it. The abject strangeness of her aunt's secret love affair with the gardener was a rare but explosive topic. If ever she wished to change the subject, dear Quincy was a sure bet. But not tonight. Her aunt's audacity could not be let go. Elisabeth had her own secrets to detonate.

While she paced, Lillian circled the bed, considering the dresses. "Would it have been so bad to be taken by surprise by the viscount? Rainsleigh has pursued you himself. Of all the young women the baroness has invited tonight, it was *you* he sought out. I watched the whole thing from my place by the door. To be honest, I've never seen anything like it."

"How gratifying for you—to witness your ambush play out before your very eyes."

"Ambush—please, Elisabeth. It's not like you to resort to dramatics."

"Perhaps, but it is exactly like *you*, and now I'm meant to reckon with it? *This* goes beyond the bounds of reason. How could you invite him here and not tell me?"

"Oh," she mused, fingering the hem of each dress, "you know the answer to that. If I had told you he was coming, you would have refused. You refused anyway. You always refuse. Honestly, I hardly see what could be so harrowing after *fifteen years*."

"That's because you have no idea about that which you speak. The passing time makes no difference. It only matters that I am *not ready*."

"But what if you're never ready? This is my fear." Lillian held up the ivory silk, and Elisabeth made a face. The countess nodded and moved on to the next.

"How can I make you understand?" asked Elisabeth. "The...ordeal we suffered together does not translate into the direct need to meet again. Ever. Despite your years of asking, suggesting, wheedling—and now delivering the man to our dining table. And he doesn't even recognize me—thank God. My one saving grace."

Lillian opened her mouth to counter this, but Elisabeth forged on. "Surely you know that most reasonable people would say my history with this man calls for the opposite of a reunion, surprise or otherwise. It has been prudent and self-preserving to stay away from him."

"True, perhaps, but lucky for you, I am not most reasonable people. Certainly I am not prudent." She pulled the lavender gown from the bed and held it high. "The lavender, I think, don't you? Come, let us try it."

Reluctantly, Elisabeth crossed to her aunt and turned, allowing her to unfasten her perfectly pleasant, exceedingly comfortable blue muslin.

"I would never have pressed," continued Lillian, "if I had not seen your reaction to him."

"What reaction?" Elisabeth craned around. "He cornered me! In the stairwell! Whilst I harangued Stoker. I hardly looked at the man at all."

"Not *tonight*, Elisabeth. Before." She jostled Elisabeth this way and that, working the gown from her shoulders.

"When before? Before what? I've not seen the man in fifteen years, and you've never met him in your life. It's his first time to dinner; you've said so yourself. You're making no sense."

"Am I not?"

Elisabeth let out a noise of frustration and dropped her face into her hands. Her stomach churned with frustration and anger, and the sickening, nervous stew of it almost outweighed the anxiety of seeing him again. Almost.

The countess filled the silence. "I've said nothing about it, mind you. I do try to honor your privacy, darling. But that doesn't mean I have not seen it, all these years. The blushes and the bright-eyed interest. If anyone even utters his name, in any stray piece of inane gossip…"

"This is ridiculous," Elisabeth said reflexively.

"Ridiculous, is it? What of the newspaper clippings? For years you have followed him in the papers." Elisabeth stepped out of the blue dress and hugged her shoulders against the coolness of the room. Her aunt had seen the brand on her shoulder many times, but Elisabeth hated the scar to be exposed, even in private.

"I can read about the man and wish him well without making his acquaintance," Elisabeth said lamely.

"Or you could meet him again on your own terms. As the beautiful young woman you have become."

Elisabeth shook her head. "You misconstrue my interest."

"Do I? I do not misconstrue your gratefulness to him for his rescue." Her aunt leaned over the bed and picked up the lavender dress, giving it a gentle shake. "How much have we heard about this young man? You would speak of little else over the years. We know virtually nothing about what happened the night your parents were attacked. We have respected your privacy. But forgive me if I have clung to the few details you are able to share. The rescue. *This man*. And now, he's waiting to have dinner with you."

Elisabeth was shaking her head. "But I—I cannot bear to meet him," she said softly. "*I am not ready*. I think it is my fate never to be ready."

"Fate?' But what is fate?" Lillian lowered the lavender dress, and Elisabeth hesitated only a moment before stepping into it. "Resistance is all you've ever known, so of course it seems like the only path. What have I always said? *There. Is. More.*"

"*More* may be a risk I am not willing to take," she whispered. "I have the inheritance. I have my work at the foundation. With or without a…man in my life, these mean freedom. Not everyone has the opportunity to fall in love, like you."

"Well, certainly no one who refuses to try."

Elisabeth scoffed, "I'll consent to *try* to fall in love when you consent to tell the world that you *are* in love."

She knew it was wrong the moment she said it. Behind her, Lilly went still and then her diligent hands fell away from the back of the gown. Silence settled in the room. It was not unfair to invoke her aunt's relationship with Quincy, the coward's way out. Hastily, she added, "When you are ready."

The countess was quiet a long moment, and then she said, "Now 'tis *you*, my dear, who speak of things that you do not know." She turned away.

Elisabeth was unaccustomed to motherly rebuke. Her aunt chided her and teased her, but rarely, if ever, did she scold.

"That was exceedingly rude of me," Elisabeth said softly. "I'm sorry, Lilly. I…I know you have your reasons. Aunt Lillian?"

She would not respond.

Elisabeth tried again. "We all have secrets."

The countess turned to her. "Yes, but only you bear yours alone. Come." She returned to Elisabeth and took up the loose sides of her dress and pulled the bodice together. "And *this* is why I am forcing you to dine with the viscount."

"So I will no longer have secrets?"

"So you will no longer be alone!" She attached the tightest hook with a yank, causing Elisabeth to gasp at the constriction of the gown.

"You are too ambitious," said Elisabeth. "A surprise meeting? How could this possibly work?"

Lillian sighed impatiently, smoothing the closed bodice over Elisabeth's spine. "We will not know until we try."

"Even better, we could never kno—"

"Ah, ah, ah," interrupted the countess coming around to smile at Elisabeth's appearance in the lavender gown. "Too late for that, darling. It's finally too late for that."

CHAPTER SIX

If the distinction of *viscount* did not allow Rainsleigh to leave a party early, the notoriety of being Frankie Courtland's son certainly did. His parents routinely left parties early, arrived late, refused to leave, or didn't attend at all. Boorish rudeness was a Courtland family tradition.

It was also precisely the sort of bad behavior that Rainsleigh worked so hard to expunge, but he'd be damned if he would remain in the presence of an unknown niece who, clearly, could not bear the sight of him.

He hadn't even known the countess was in possession of a niece. And now this young woman would reject him? According to Beecham, she was an on-the-shelf spinster who rarely left the house.

Rainsleigh scanned the salon, looking for the baron and his wife. He'd make some excuse. He had no idea what. *I lost my head and behaved like an idiot in front of a pretty girl* would obviously never do, but he'd think of something.

What lunacy had taken possession of his brain? He had conditioned himself over the years to ignore the distraction of females in general and beautiful women in particular. He was an active, virile male, well in his prime, but temptation could be (and had been) locked down for the sake of productiveness. And his reputation. And to prove a bloody point.

He would never be a slave to his own impulses as his father had been.

And now, look at him. After one exchange, it was no wonder that Lady Elisabeth had sprinted up the stairs. He'd all but chased her into the bloody kitchens.

If nothing else, it made him realize that the new wife he sought should not unleash any sort of unchecked base desire. Another reason that Dunhip was better served to sift through the early candidates. The very last thing Rainsleigh wanted, even less than a young girl or a bold girl, was a distractingly beautiful girl. Especially one who considered herself too superior to sit beside him for the length of one meal. He made a mental note for Dunhip's file: *Should pose no particular temptation.*

Temptation, he thought bitterly, *that's putting it very mildly.*

He located Beecham and his wife near the fire but paused just short of making an excuse. Of course he couldn't leave now. To go before they'd eaten would be considered strange at best, rude at worst.

He should use the event to demonstrate that his manners were sufficient. That he could keep away from closed doors and servant passages. That he was in no way preoccupied with the hostess's obviously disinterested niece.

"Ah, there he is," called a female voice behind him.

Not preoccupied, he reminded himself, waiting a beat before he turned 'round.

Lady Banning stood smiling behind him. Behind her, stood the niece, Lady Elisabeth. Her expression read…concern. Concern about what, he could only guess. She would not look at him. She stared resignedly at the bobbing feather in her aunt's coiffure with a pained look on her face. Gone was the blue day dress; the wispy, tumbling curls; the bare hands. Now she wore an evening gown of pale purple, delicately trimmed in a darker shade of merlot. Her hair had been slickly gathered into a full poof of curls on the top of her head. Silk gloves of the same pale purple sheathed her arms from elbow to fingertip. Distractions set in immediately, and he found himself staring at those fingertips, her dainty elbow, her curls. Only the faintest sense of self-preservation caused him to return his gaze to the countess.

"My lady," he said. He inclined his head graciously.

The countess went on, "Please accept my apologies for the delay, my lord. You must be ravenous. But I have rung for dinner, and the soup is divine."

She looked to her niece—one quick glance and then a second, longer look. "Come along, Elisabeth," she enthused. "You've made the acquaintance of the viscount, so he may escort you. Lead the way, won't you?"

Rainsleigh was given no choice but to offer Elisabeth his arm. For a long, painful moment, he thought she would reject it, her aunt be damned. But then she stepped wordlessly forward and slid her gloved hand over his sleeve. Her fingers closed firmly, and he felt her warmth through the wool of his jacket. She was so close. His body surged with awareness, like a magnet drawn to its opposite pole.

As they walked, he had some vague sense of the other guests falling in procession behind them—the plod of canes and heavy footsteps from the old couples, the rustle of gowns and giggling from the young ladies. He had intended to take in every detail of his first London party. Now his sole focus was every detail of the woman beside him. Her profile—soft skin and a serene expression. Her red-gold hair. The faint scent of her hair wafted against him, clean, fresh. *Like a bloody meadow,* he thought. She smelled like daylight.

"It's just here." She gestured to the right.

He allowed her to lead him. What else could he do while his mind swam with her nearness? In no way was he detached or measured or rational. He was totally preoccupied, and the weakness made him angry. To stem the tide, he leaned to her ear.

"Loser's lot?" he asked softly.

"I beg your pardon?"

"Oh, come now. Let us drop the pretense."

She missed a step. On reflex, he tucked his arm, drawing her close. He felt the warm contour of her body up and down his side. He swallowed hard.

"Pretense?" she asked.

"The quarrel with your aunt just now. You lost, clearly. And now here you are, forced to eat dinner with me."

She stopped. "Is that what…"

Her pause made him look. She stared back, her eyes large. They were blue *and* green, he could now see. Turquoise. A mermaid's eyes. A flicker of a memory—some long-forgotten moment in time—danced on the edges of his consciousness.

He ignored it, determined to expose her rejection of him. "Yes?" he asked.

"Is that why you... *That* is what you think? That my aunt has forced me, and I don't wish to attend?" She stole a look over her shoulder at the other guests. They were nearly to them, filing past with sidelong glances. Rainsleigh looked up long enough to see the young women do more than glance. They stared openly, and Elisabeth slid her hand from his arm and stepped away. It felt immediately wrong, and he fought the urge to grab it back.

"We needn't pretend," he said, an excuse to return to her.

To this she had no response. Her mermaid's stare did not waver. "No. Let us not pretend."

She chuckled then, a sad, disbelieving sort of laugh, and slid her gloved hand over his arm. The other guests had trickled through, and she tugged him to catch up, around a corner and through an arched door. "Here we are," she said.

She let him go and drifted to the table, nosing round, chair to chair. Other guests had begun to settle up and down the table, but they watched him. He felt every curious glance. The young women watched him openly. He waited to feel gratified or flattered, but his sole focus was Lady Elisabeth.

"Heavens, the outlay," she whispered, walking back to him. The table was set with a glinting landscape of china and silver. Crystal goblets reflected the light of fifty candles. "I have no idea where I'm meant to sit."

"You'll sit beside his lordship, Elisabeth," said Lady Banning, sailing into the room behind them. She gestured to two seats near the head of the table.

Elisabeth nodded and followed. Rainsleigh followed, too, watching how she maneuvered the crowded room with a silent, graceful pride that seemed to ignore the audience of onlookers. When she reached the designated seat, a footman leapt from the wall to pull out the chair. She smiled gently and murmured to him, sinking in.

In the corner of the room, a fierce, whispered exchange arose between the countess and Lady Beecham. Lady Elisabeth leaned to Rainsleigh and said, "My aunt is pulling rank. A rare sight, indeed."

"Except in the stairwell," he said.

"Pardon?"

"The countess forced *you* to attend this meal on my arm."

"You are mistaken, my lord, about what happened between my aunt and me." She studied him.

He raised one eyebrow.

She looked down at the glistening place setting. "Lillian has probably shuffled the place cards."

"To accommodate our seats," he guessed.

"To accommodate herself—but yes, she is pulling rank to trap you between me and her. You should feel gratified; Lady Beecham would swarm you on all sides with the young ladies." She inclined her head toward the girls casting disappointed glances in their direction from the far end of the table. "My aunt would have you less…encumbered."

"Instead, she encumbers you?"

"I am not encumbered by you, my lord," Lady Elisabeth said.

He stared at her, searching for some slight or deeper meaning. He tried to predict what she might say next, but he realized that he had no idea. Everything out of her mouth had been a surprise. He wasn't accustomed to surprises; if asked, he would say that he wasn't fond of them. And yet he found himself eager to hear what she might say next. Too eager.

But now the countess was settling at the head of the table and signaling the footmen to serve the soup.

"Lord Rainsleigh?" she called to him. "There are several people who would delight in making your acquaintance, and I hope you'll indulge us. My, er, *errand* upstairs precluded proper introductions, but you must meet a few friends and neighbors."

Rainsleigh glanced at Lady Elisabeth. "It would be a pleasure."

A procession of names and nods followed, including the young ladies now relegated to the far end of the table and the elderly couples scattered between. The final guest—a marchioness, who, according to rank, was seated directly across from Rainsleigh—was presented last.

"Perhaps you already know Frances, Marchioness of Frinfrock?" the countess asked, gesturing to the diminutive old woman. "You are neighbors, I believe, in Henrietta Place."

Rainsleigh nodded. "How do you do, Lady Frinfrock?"

The wizened old woman could barely see above her soup, but she gazed at him with suspicious, narrowed eyes. "The *castle* you've constructed in my street is a vulgarity, Rainsleigh," the marchioness said.

Rainsleigh swallowed a laugh. "I'm sorry to hear it, my lady."

In the same moment the countess said, "Come now, Lady Frinfrock. I'll admit I've nearly starved you, but let us strive to be pleasant."

"'Tis no unpleasantness," he assured the countess. To the scowling woman across the table, he said, "Pray, your ladyship, which house in the street is yours?"

"You'd know my property if you made an effort to learn the character and population of the street before you devoted an eon erecting your Tower of Babel."

"Yes, well, I've only just moved in, but you make a fair point. It's been builders and craftsmen you've seen in and out. I should have called on neighbors by now."

"Had you deigned to make the acquaintance of anyone in Henrietta Place, you would also know that your 'craftsmen' have hauled every manner of timber, stone, and Lord-knows-what material into the street, rendering the road nearly impassable. Pocked with trenches and pits from your delivery wagons. Strewn with spilt gravel. All the while, they raise your monstrosity higher and higher, blotting out the very sun."

Again, Bryson swallowed a laugh. In fact, he had met with neighbors—he'd bought the house from a neighbor and friend—and he had been mindful of inconvenience and damage to the area. But this woman was enjoying herself far too much to be challenged. And it wouldn't do to be ungracious to a lady.

"But perhaps you did not notice, your ladyship," he said, "the repairs I commissioned to restore the road? The new road was meant to give residents—"

"*Perhaps* we preferred the road as it was," the marchioness interrupted, pointing with her spoon. "Another thing you would have known if you had bothered to introduce yourself to anyone of consequence in Henrietta Place."

"Yes," he allowed, taking a sip of wine. He gave Lady Banning a wink and tried again, "Although were you aware that I, in fact, bought the house *from* a neighbor? The Earl of Falcondale? He and his lady-wife live next door; that is, when they are not traveling abroad—"

"I said anyone of *consequence*, and Falcondale hardly qualifies. His wife is lovely, but I take frequent issue with the earl. He offered nothing to the house but abject neglect. You are no better, burdening us with an extended construction; widening and raising and embellishing. Domed turrets, ogling gargoyles, and that ghastly tangle of iron trim. It's difficult to say who has done more harm, you or the earl."

"Oh, I'll happily concede this distinction to Falcondale," Rainsleigh said. "He may revel in it." A footman cleared his soup, and he leaned back in his chair, smiling at the engrossed faces up and down the table. "But you make it very clear that I must make some sort of amends, my lady. I've no wish to embark on my new life surrounded by enemies in my own street. May I call on you in the coming days and provide a tour through the house? Perhaps you could tolerate the work if you were to see the inside."

The marchioness harrumphed. "Doubtless I have the strength to traverse such a vast expanse or climb such a great many stairs."

"I find that very hard to believe," he said, eliciting chuckles from around the table. "Come now, you must be curious."

The tiny woman set down her spoon and raised her eyebrows. "How perceptive. *Curious*, am I?"

A footman removed her soup and replaced it with a dish of vegetables. She muttered something disagreeable to him and then turned back to Rainsleigh. "Now that you've made mention, there is one thing about which I am *exceedingly* curious…"

Something about the way the sentence trailed off, about the look of determination in her keen, gray eyes, signaled the end of their discussion about his "castle" and heralded weightier topics. Her tone, certainly, could not have been more clear. He felt the stares of everyone at the table but kept his face impassive.

"My curiosity has nearly eaten me alive over the topic of your *parents*, Lord Rainsleigh," the old woman began. "Your sire is dead, of course, but tell me—what of your mother? The viscountess. Lady Rainsleigh?"

For a moment, Rainsleigh said nothing, allowing the footman to place a plate of vegetables before him. When the man was gone, he said, "My mother resides in Spain."

"Spain?" repeated the marchioness. "She will not relocate to Henrietta Place?"

"No."

"And you have a brother, have you not?"

"I do. Mr. Beauregard Courtland. A retired naval officer and current merchant marine. He is in residence now, actually. You may have seen him in the street. He *will*, I can assure you, be a guest in my home when he is not at sea."

He had expected this, of course. Some manner of interrogation. Not necessarily here, during the meal, with a captive audience, and certainly not in front of the disdainful niece, but he had given some thought to what he might say. Direct answers. Levelness. No shame. He'd answered for his parents often enough. It was the wrong play to grow defensive. It only showed weakness and guilt, and he felt neither.

Lady Banning obviously discerned his waning patience and strove to intercept. "I know *I* would relish a tour of Lord Rainsleigh's house, if the offer extends to more distant neighbors," she enthused. "The papers describe quite a marvel of modernity and high art. Won't you tell us of your architect, my lord? I read you had him brought over from France?"

He forced a smile. "Germany." He turned back to the small woman now examining a hank of potato on her raised fork. "But I wish to satisfy Lady Frinfrock's curiosity," he said. "Please, my lady. What other questions have you for me? Not more offenses piled on my house, I hope."

"The less I know about your German-built atrocity, the better." She took a small, skeptical bite.

He took up his glass. She stared back, chewing. Rainsleigh went on, "But surely you do not intend to tick off every relation I have, asking if they each have a bed. Come now, don't be shy. What do you *really* want to know?"

"Very well. What I *really want to know*," she said, inclining her knife at him in little taps, waving it like a composer's baton, "is what manner of person *you* may be, Lord Rainsleigh. The reputations of your parents precedes you, as I'm sure you are aware. But what of you, my lord? So far, all I know is that you commissioned a towering mansion for a family of *one*, and that you spent a fortune to do so." She paused, took another bite, and chewed.

Rainsleigh crossed his arms over his chest as the marchioness went on. "Your late father could scarcely keep a roof over his head by the end. He commissioned nothing, built nothing; certainly he funded nothing." Another bite. "The obvious question from a concerned neighbor is, what of you, my lord?"

A fourth bite. "Do the differences between you and your disreputable sire begin and end with houses and money? Or do you go your own way in all things? I will not tolerate a reprobate in Henrietta Place, I don't care how much money he has, and furthermore—"

Beside him, the countess's niece, Lady Elisabeth suddenly, inexplicably, surged to her feet and planted her hands on the table.

"I beg your pardon, Lady…Lady…Forgive me. Aunt Lillian?" She turned to her aunt. "Pray, remind me of the name of your esteemed guest."

A table full of heads swiveled to the countess. Lady Banning appeared as shocked and speechless everyone else, Rainsleigh included. Only the diminutive old woman casually stabbed a third potato, showing no alarm.

Lady Frinfrock took a bite of potato and eyed Elisabeth levelly. "The Marchioness of Frinfrock," she answered. "And who, pray tell, are you?"

"I am no one of consequence," said Lady Elisabeth, "but I am a guest at this table, along with other friends and well-meaning people, and I should like to speak for all of us when I ask you, with respect, to cease your interrogation of the viscount. 'Tis uncomfortable and unnecessary and rude."

Rainsleigh's jaw would have dropped into his plate if his manners were not bolted so tightly in place. He stared at the woman beside him.

Lady Elisabeth went on. "You need only read the papers to learn of Lord Rainsleigh's years of quiet work to build his shipping company and his subsequent devotion to philanthropy. Of his serious and thoughtful influence on political debate. The care with which he has rebuilt his family's home in Wiltshire, including new prosperity for the land and tenants, advances in agriculture, and the restoration of historic relics. If these very public acts do not convince you of his character, then an extemporaneous defense of his parentage—a circumstance of which he is wholly innocent—will do even less." She sat back down. "Now, I implore you. Please. Leave the man alone. For God's sake. Let someone else or some other topic draw breath at this table."

All around the dining room, white faces stared in stunned silence.

Rainsleigh glanced at the marchioness, still eating potatoes.

He looked at Lady Elisabeth beside him. She stared into her full plate. Her chest fell and rose. Color stained her cheeks. One lone red-gold curl had worked its way free from her coiffeur and fell against her face.

Beside him, Rainsleigh heard Lady Banning make a small, desperate sound. She cleared her throat. "Lady Frinfrock, perhaps you remember my niece and ward, Lady Elisabeth Hamilton-Baythes? Her late father, Lord Cay, was my brother."

"So she is," the marchioness said, her voice unchanged. "Then let us hear from you, my lady." She turned her gaze to Elisabeth. "What business is it of yours? And don't *you* know quite a bit about a man who, by all accounts, has just moved to town?"

CHAPTER SEVEN

Elisabeth's lone consolation was that Aunt Lilly had *asked* for this.

Nay, Aunt Lilly had *forced* this.

The party. Her insufferable friends. Pretense. Gossip-mongering.

But most of all, proximity. To *him*.

The result was, of course, she'd embarrassed herself by calling out a marchioness. She'd embarrassed the viscount by leaping to his defense. She'd embarrassed her aunt for—oh, well, Lillian received nothing more than she deserved. But now Elisabeth must see it through.

"I was…unacquainted with the viscount before tonight," she told the marchioness, "but I…I intend to apply for his charity donation on behalf of a cause that I support. Naturally, I learned as much about the man and his history as possible. In order to have every advantage. For my charity." Taking up her fork, Elisabeth stabbed a carrot and ate.

The marchioness waved away a hovering footman. "A charity, you say? And what is this cause you support?"

Elisabeth weighed her options. This question would be next; it was *always* next. It was one thing to defend the viscount but quite another to defend her own life's work. Not with any delicacy. Not in a way that did not betray the girls she fought to save or put off small-minded people. And here the stakes were very high indeed. She glanced around the table. The busybody marchioness. A roomful of esteemed strangers. Young, sheltered debutantes. And—*oh, God*—Rainsleigh himself.

If she intended to apply for his charitable gift, she would need to term the whole thing very vaguely. Too much detail had scared away legions of well-meaning benefactors. Not to mention, the specifics might trigger a memory she would rather not share. With the viscount. Not now. Not ever.

She looked up, smiled brightly, and said, "The charity is called 'The Well,' and it is a foundation for lost girls and young women of London."

"Lost, you say?" asked the marchioness.

"Hmmm," Elisabeth confirmed. "Lost. Without parents, proper homes, food, access to a doctor's care. The foundation offers these poor souls a way to get on in the world. A path to a future that is less bleak."

The marchioness shocked Elisabeth by nodding knowingly. She waved her fork in the air. "A worthy cause, no doubt, and I salute it. Rainsleigh would do well to support it, if he's in the business of giving away money. Certainly any money redirected from that house of his would be a gift to us all."

Of all responses, Elisabeth had expected this one the least. She was momentarily speechless. She stole a look at

Aunt Lillian, who sat back in her chair and silently watched the exchange, a small smile on her face. *In no way*, Elisabeth thought, *does she appear to be suffering her due. In fact, she looks gratified.*

The Marchioness of Frinfrock appeared entirely unfazed by the conversation and was presently dickering with a footman about the cut of her fish.

Slowly, softly, chatter emerged up and down the table—couples whispering among themselves, debutantes giggling, oohs, and ahhs as the footmen set down the trout. Without thinking, Elisabeth stole a look at Rainsleigh. He looked up too, catching her gaze.

Their eyes locked, and Elisabeth's breath seized in her chest. Every part of her, in fact, seemed to tense and freeze. She felt immobilized by his very look. By great force of will, she was the first to look away.

Oh, God, his eyes were so blue, they shone. At this range, she could see the roughness of his emerging beard. She wondered absently what it would feel like to trace her fingertips across the stubble.

It was ridiculous—nay, it was *madness*—because her priority at the moment should be to stew over her own mortification and determine some way to make amends for her outburst. Instead, all she wanted to do was study him again, compare the man he had become to the boy of that night fifteen years ago. She wondered, and not for the first time, how he could not yet have married. How he enjoyed London. How he chose his home and the changes he made. Why he did not recognize her.

No, not that.

Thankfully, a footman appeared with the platter of fish, and they shifted to be served. Aunt Lillian took the conversation skillfully in hand, drawing in each guest, allowing everyone to bid some self-serving welcome to the viscount. Lady Frinfrock, she was surprised to see, did not insinuate herself again—in fact, she did not speak at all. She ate heartily, scolded the footmen consistently, and listened closely, but she did not interject.

When at last the meal ended, the ladies went through to the drawing room while the men lingered over port and cigars. Elisabeth was compelled by Lady Beecham to lead a game of Whist among the other young ladies. Ten minutes later, Quincy knelt beside her to whisper that Stoker had returned through the kitchen door and wished to speak to her. She could have wept with relief.

Elisabeth glanced at her aunt. Lillian discreetly shook of her head. *No, you would not.*

She stood up. *Yes, I would and I will.*

Beside her, Quincy cleared his throat discreetly. "Perhaps you would consider meeting the lad just there?" He inclined his head to the double doors of the balcony at the far end of the room. "The rain has prevented us from opening them tonight," he said, "but you may safely step outside. It's dry enough under the eave, and you will be away from the party but not too far."

"*Thank you,* Quincy. Please, tell Stoker."

"Very good, my lady."

Just as she made her way to the balcony, the men came through. Before she could stop herself, she sought out the viscount. He looked too, and their eyes locked again. Awareness tingled at the back of her neck and her arms above her gloves. She felt herself blush. For the first time in her life, she understood the need for a fan in an otherwise comfortable room. She hurried to the balcony.

The air was cool and damp, and she sucked in two gulps. The debutantes' heavy perfume had been suffocating. Now, perhaps, she could breathe again and reclaim some measure of calm, and *think*. Now, perhaps, she could answer how she'd managed to progress from shy and speechless in the stairwell to bold and verbose at the table. Or why she kept staring at this…this…man. No, not simply staring; she had been *blushing* at him.

Ultimately, she'd spoken to him very little—there had been no opportunity for private chatter at the lively table— but oh, how she'd wanted to do. And not about the weather. Or anyone's failing health. She'd gritted her teeth with each vapid new topic. Did no one want to learn about the viscount's life? His opinions on the current Parliament or prime minister? His impression of London? Where he'd been? What he read?

Elisabeth opened her eyes and blinked. She was being ridiculous. Of course no one else was interested in what he read. Why then, could she think of little else? Even while Stoker and his crew were darting around South London in the rain, risking their very lives.

And if they had spoken, where could it all lead? She had no wish to revisit their past. Almost certainly, he would eschew her charity work. She felt an interest—well, perhaps, if she was being honest, she could term it closer to an *attraction*, not that it mattered. Whatever it was, it had absolutely nowhere to go. Her interest (or attraction) was not greater than her desire to remain anonymous in their shared past.

She heard Stoker then, effortlessly scaling the garden wall, and she shook her head to clear it and straightened her shoulders. The youth deserved her full attention now. He rarely called on Denby House after sunset, and this was his second visit in one night. God knew what had happened with the scouting mission.

He leapt the railing and sank to the balcony floor, ever cautious.

She crossed her arms over her chest. "What is it? Is someone hurt?"

"Brothel's gone," he said, rising. "The whole lot, moved on. Again." He wiped his hands on his shirt. "Building's abandoned, neighbors won't talk. I could tell it as soon as we took position in the alley."

"Gone? But where? You were there not two nights ago!"

He nodded. "No accounting for it. They haven't left a trace, either. Some of the women had little dogs, street mongrels they fancied as pets, and they're gone too. Everything's gone."

Elisabeth turned away and clutched the railing. "We spent two months closing in."

Stoker grunted and shrugged. "I left the lads outside to watch for blokes who turn up without knowing. Sometimes there's a coded sign on the doorframe... something only regular customers would know. Gives them an idea where to find the new location."

"Don't approach these men, Stoker," she said. "Stay back, and for God's sake, *keep hidden*. It's almost like they knew we were watching. It frightens me."

"I'm not frightened, Lady E."

She smiled sadly. "Yes, of course you're not. You are never afraid. I sometimes think your courage is our most valued asset. I don't know what I will do without you."

He grunted and moved to the edge of the balcony, putting one leg over the railing.

She went on. "But I hope you are aware this does not change things about the school…"

He threw the other leg over the railing and began to pick his way down, disappearing into the rain.

Elisabeth leaned over and whispered fiercely, "I haven't forgotten, Stoker!"

He looked up. "Can I take a fresh horse?"

"Yes, yes, of course. Tell the grooms that I said so. Tell them, Quincy's horse—he's working tonight. But Stoker, did you hear? I haven't forgotten about the school!" His only response was the scrape of boot, rustling vines, splashing puddles. The fog and dark closed over him, and he was gone.

Elisabeth clutched the railing and stared into the mist. How would she ever replace him? Hiring anyone at all would take money away from the girls, and hiring someone remotely as effective and devoted as Stoker would require a fortune. But what choice did she have? Stoker had never accepted even a shilling of payment for his work, except the occasional coat or boots in winter, perhaps a hat at Christmas. The school would be his payment. He'd earned it and so much more. Anyone else? They would require a salary.

She turned and stared into the glow of the party, thinking of Rainsleigh in practical terms. His charity donation—one thousand pounds. If he did not know her after tonight, after she'd burst up from the table and spouted off his accomplishments like a devoted biographer, perhaps he never would. Perhaps she could safely apply to win the donation after all. Perhaps if she explained the specifics of her work in the vaguest terms. And limited their contact as much as she could. And never spoke to him again after the contest was over.

The chances of her foundation winning the money were very slim, indeed, but the need was surely as great as any other charity that might apply. Stoker would go away to school whether he liked it or not, and that would leave her without anyone to raid the brothels. She'd have to hire the work out. Not to mention, the building in Marylebone that she used as the foundation's headquarters was one of the oldest in the street, and its list of needed repairs seemed to grow longer every year.

She could not *not* apply, she decided, not in good conscience. If there was money to be had, she needed to have a go at it. Now more than ever. If she'd been a responsible, selfless person, she would have leapt at the chance to win the money as soon as Aunt Lillian mentioned it. Instead, she'd dickered around with her own delusions about the viscount and their history together, and their…their…

She shook her head. He did not remember her. He'd stared at her all evening, and he'd said nothing, alluded to nothing, and gave every indication that he had never seen her before, ever, in life.

It was a blessing, really. She could interact with him only enough to apply for his donation and then go her own way. After that, she would never see him again.

As for her own attraction to him? This could be tamped down. Bryson Courtland was a flash of girlish fancy, nothing more, and she'd buried it long ago. So now life had unearthed it (or rather, Aunt Lillian had)—but was the spark still there? Or was it a self-indulgent daydream, outdated and outgrown, too tarnished by the passage of time to shine?

"Lady Elisabeth?"

She jumped and spun around. Lord Rainsleigh stood in the doorway of the balcony.

"I hope I am not disturbing," he said. "Your aunt said I might find you here."

Oh, I'm sure she did, she thought, but she said, "By no means. I...I needed some air."

"You'll not get wet, I hope?"

She shook her head. "The rain has stopped."

The moment she said it, lightning cracked, a great wind swept from the east, and the skies opened. Cold, fat raindrops pelted the red oak beside the balcony and splatted against the bricks of the garden below. Elisabeth laughed and hopped beneath the narrow overhang of roof. He reached out to steady her, catching her around the waist.

"Here," he said, whipping off his evening jacket, "take my coat." Before she could refuse, he settled it on her shoulders. The soft wool, warmed by the heat of his body, closed in around her. It smelled like sandalwood and shaving soap and...*male*. She sank into the warmth, clasping the lapels together, holding it around her.

"Thank you," she said.

Rainsleigh studied her. "The charity prize..." he began.

The rain fell harder, faster, coming down in loud, rolling sheets. They were dry under the strip of roof, but the sound was deafening.

She raised her voice. "Yes! You are very generous! I...I intend to apply. On behalf of my foundation."

He leaned in, and she was struck by how tall he was. Had he been this tall at nineteen? He scrunched to remain under the eave.

She swallowed hard and spoke over the rain, "The newspaper was unclear about how to apply. Will you explain the process? I predict fierce competition for such a large amount."

"My secretary has the paperwork," he said over the rain. "But surely the staff of this charity you patronize will take care of the application."

She paused a beat. A gust of wind sprayed them with cold mist, but she barely felt it.

"'Tis my own charity," she said. "I am the founder, and I run it alone. There is no staff beyond a few servants, a teacher, and a nurse trained in medicine."

He was silent a moment, studying her. "I have not heard of a female at the helm of a charity..."

She bluffed, saying, "Well, you are new to town."

"Do you have advisors? Someone to guide you and oversee financial matters?"

No, she thought, but she said, "Will this be addressed on the application?"

"I don't know, to be honest. My secretary drew up the application."

The rain continued to pelt. She edged closer to the wall, taking hold of the tangle of wisteria on an iron trellis. She snuggled into his coat. "Well, I shall learn soon enough. I will call upon your secretary."

"When?" he asked.

Thunder boomed, and she jumped. He reached for her again. She felt his hand on her waist through the wool of his coat.

She answered, "This week?"

"Tomorrow?"

He was close enough to read her lips, so she answered quietly. "Very well. Tomorrow."

He nodded.

Nervously, she bit her bottom lip, and his gaze locked on her mouth. Thunder boomed again, closer this time, and lightning struck. Two pops split the darkness with bright white light, and she saw the intent expression on his face, clear as day. He was so close. Without thinking, she whispered, "I'm sorry about dinner."

He shook his head. His hand tightened on her waist.

She fought the urge to step closer. Half a step? A fraction of a step? "I am loath to hear what my aunt will say about my outburst. But I warned her. I had too much work to spare the time for a party, and my manners suffered."

"Work?"

She nodded. "For the charity. There is much work. Always. Especially tonight."

"This work keeps you too busy to eat?"

She laughed. "Was tonight's purpose really to eat dinner?"

Slowly, he gave a half smile, his first of the night. Her heart missed four beats. Thunder boomed again, and she allowed herself the half step.

He sucked in a breath.

She whispered. "Thank you for the loan of your coat."

He said, "Why are you not married?"

"Another question for the charity application?" She laughed.

He answered with a single raised eyebrow. Another look that she had remembered. Fondly. Foolishly. For fifteen years. *You were chattier when you were younger*, she thought.

She looked out at the rain and then back at him. Was he waiting for an answer? She forced herself to whisper, "We should return to the party."

To this, he said nothing, and for a thrilling moment, she thought he would suggest the opposite—that they stay huddled on the wet balcony—but then he nodded, dropped his hand, and stepped away.

She slipped from the coat and held it out. The cool night closed in around her, and she was immediately cold. She reached for the door. He held it open and, God help her, she brushed against him when she passed. His body felt hard and warm, solid and unmoving. She tucked the sensation away for later—for many, many laters. Their previous exchange had sustained her for fifteen years. This would have to last her for the rest of her life.

CHAPTER EIGHT

The morning after the Countess of Banning's dinner party, Rainsleigh held his pen over the notes from his last meeting with Dunhip.

~~Wife.~~

~~Solve.~~

Marry by year's end.

He hesitated only a second before crossing out the first two items, but honestly, few decisions felt more decisively right. By nature, Rainsleigh was a careful, measured man, but he was also decisive and swiftly capable of identifying value when he saw it. Elisabeth, he thought, was valuable. She also presented several other captivating qualities on which he would not allow himself to focus, but there was no mistaking it. She came from a good family. She was reserved and mature and clear-minded. She would be ideal for the viscountcy— and for him. Wavering and waffling and (God forbid) love sickness could be left to some other, less practical man. He'd set out to find a wife, and he'd done it. If only he'd known it would be this easy, he would not have burdened Dunhip.

Now, he'd have to deal with the secretary's thinly veiled disappointment.

He looked up at the loyal, eager man. "Dunhip, you may let go of the item I mentioned before." He cleared his throat. "About finding a wife."

"I beg your pardon, my lord."

Oh, not again. Rainsleigh added a note finality to his tone. "I believe I made myself perfectly clear."

"But, my lord, I wasn't given enough time." Dunhip began to turn oddly purple. "I wanted to ensure only the best—"

"It's not your fault, Cecil." Rainsleigh sighed. "I have identified a candidate for the position all on my own. Shocking, I know, but perhaps it's for the best. I will, after all, be the one to have to marry her."

"Found her on your own?"

Rainsleigh made a vague sound of agreement. He was disinclined to justify Lady Elisabeth to bloody Dunhip. "She's the daughter of an earl," he said. "Lovely girl—a woman really. 'On the shelf,' some might say, but her maturity suits me. Everything about her suits me. In any event, you may remove the task of wife-hunting from the heap."

The secretary nodded with faux pleasantness, staring at his knees.

"It was ambitious, I think, to pin the whole thing on you."

"As you say," said Dunhip carefully, "but would you have me look into the girl's family or her father's holdings? That is, before you—"

"Protecting me from mercenaries, are you? Bloody good of you, Cecil. I'm touched. But you needn't worry. She comes from an established family and is preoccupied with charity work. Doubtful she's stalked me for my money. If she intends to fleece me, it is for her charitable cause. To that, I will happily submit. Philanthropy is good for business."

"Very good, my lord." Dunhip sighed sorrowfully.

"Oh, but this reminds me, leave the paperwork for the charity prize on my desk. She intends to apply and may call today to collect it."

"She will marry you *and* apply for the prize?"

"That is the hope, Dunhip, and thank you for your confidence."

The secretary had the decency to look chastened. "As you say, my lord."

A heavy pause.

Dunhip cleared his throat. "What, might I inquire, is the nature of your betrothed's charitable cause?"

"We're not betrothed yet; I only met her last night."

This, Rainsleigh could admit, sounded a trifle reckless and precipitous when he said it out loud, but if Dunhip had been there, he would have seen. He would have *known*, as Rainsleigh did.

"I don't know about her charity," the viscount said. "Something to do with lost girls. The poor among us. Innocent children with no hope or some such."

Dunhip made a face. "My vision for the application was a very detailed description of the charity, along with specific initiatives for current and future work. We would not want to grant the money to a fly-by-night or an unproven group, my lord. If it pleases you, I can explain to her."

Rainsleigh picked up a file and flipped it open, studying the charcoal rendering of a dry dock. "I alone will be furnishing the paperwork to her, in particular, Cecil."

"Quite so. Of course. But, my lord, if I might be so bold, I've conceived the application such that we may sift the wheat from the ch—"

"I don't care how you conceived it, Cecil." He tossed the sketch aside and leaned back in his chair. "The application is immaterial. She's here for paperwork, but my motive is to see her again, learn more about her, ask her permission to call."

"Oh, but certainly, any woman in England would be honored to be called upon by you, my lord."

Rainsleigh laughed. " 'Certainty' is one of the few things that money won't buy. I cannot say what she might or might not be honored to do. All I know is that I want her." The words surprised him—out before he realized what he was going to say. He rubbed a hand over his neck and pictured Lady Elisabeth's face in his mind. It was a true statement. He *did* want her. Very much.

"If only everyone were as easy to impress as you, Dunhip," Rainsleigh said. "I don't intend to wheedle her for an audience, if that's what you think. It's merely…" He rubbed his finger across his lips. He wasn't entirely sure, he acknowledged, what he would ask her or why. He could hardly go in with his sudden designs on her future. All he knew was that he wanted to see her again.

"I'm sure you won't be surprised that I wish to do things properly," Rainsleigh finished. "If I intend to call on her, then I should ask permission first. It will sound more natural, I think, if she is already here on the charity errand. That said, leave the paperwork."

The secretary complied begrudgingly, and they worked on shipyard invoicing for an hour more, until the butler interrupted to announce a guest.

"The Marchioness of Frinfrock," Sewell intoned, handing the viscount her card. "I told her I would ascertain if you were 'in,' my lord, and she assured me that you are. Claims you promised her a tour of the house."

Rainsleigh thought about it, turning the card in his hand. *Lady Frinfrock.* His inquisitor from last night. His first inclination was to send her away, if for no other reason than he was exceedingly busy, and Dunhip was already in a petulant mood. Still, in hindsight, the old woman had done him a great service last night. The result of her interrogation was that, for once, everyone had the story straight. The guests left the Countess of Banning's dinner with answers to the questions no one dared ask. No one but this old bat. She'd pumped him for the unknown details of his life and allowed him to speak for himself—or rather, had allowed a certain ginger-haired lady to leap from her seat and rattle off an impassioned history that summed up everything in glowing terms.

The entire exchange was over and done in a quarter hour or less, and the only person who looked truly ridiculous was the marchioness. Clearly, she couldn't have cared less. The least he could do was give her a tour.

"I will see her," he told Sewell slowly, dismissing Dunhip with a nod.

Ten minutes later, the marchioness informed him of how the tour would go. "My companion is here to accompany me because the sheer distance we may travel within this mammoth structure might do me ill. Miss Breedlowe, *please*," she hissed to the tall woman beside her, "do not hover. I am not on the verge of collapse"—she shot Rainsleigh a warning look—"yet."

Rainsleigh nodded to the younger woman. "How do you do?"

The woman bobbed a respectful dip and inclined her head. With a gentle smile, she said, "It is a pleasure to meet you, my lord. I am Jocelyn Breedlowe."

"Miss Breedlowe, yes," he said, "I believe I've made your acquaintance once or twice before. Next door, is it?"

She nodded. "Indeed. When I am not serving as, er, companion to the marchioness, I assist the Countess of Falcondale with personal matters. Before they sailed for Far East, she spoke very highly of you."

"Let us not bore Lord Rainsleigh with your myriad occupations, Miss Breedlowe; we'll be here all week." Lady Frinfrock looked right and left. "Very well, Lord Rainsleigh. Let us commence. My God, is there a written guide? An atlas, perhaps?"

Their hour-long tour visited every room, including the closets and cupboards, with a triple turn around the garden. When they'd finally seen it all—indeed, when they'd heard a critical comment about nearly every detail—the marchioness pronounced the lone compliment of the day. "'Tis, at the very least, an improvement over the neglected heap that Lord Falcondale would have it be. You may call upon me about your garden drains before the next heavy rain."

"Thank you," he said, the only appropriate answer. He nodded to Sewell to open the front door and effectively send them on their way. He'd been patient and amenable for forty-five minutes longer than he was, on most days, capable. He'd only just turned to go when the marchioness could be heard gasping on the stoop.

"*But who is this?*" she breathed.

Gritting his teeth, Rainsleigh turned. A carriage had arrived. The marchioness now squinted disapprovingly into the glare on its polished door. "The Countess of Banning?"

Rainsleigh went still. Something like satisfaction seeped through his chest. In that moment, he became doubly motivated to be rid of the marchioness. Miss Breedlowe sensed his impatience and endeavored to spur the old woman along.

"It is likely," Miss Breedlowe said, "that the viscount will entertain numerous callers before luncheon. Let us find our own lunch and leave him free to attend other business."

"Other business?" the marchioness asked. "But he was at Denby House in the company of the countess for hours last night, as was I. The meal was interminable; I thought it would never end.

"*Oh!*" the marchioness went on, shaking her head. "But 'tis *not* the countess. 'Tis the *niece* of the countess." She shaded her eyes and watched a groom fuss with the carriage steps. "But surely she has not come alone. To call on you, Rainsleigh?" She peered back through the front door.

"I cannot say," he drawled, "but if it is Lady Elisabeth, she has likely come on the business of her charity. She expressed her interest in my charity donation last night, I believe."

The marchioness harrumphed and shook her head. She looked at Miss Breedlowe. "What is it about this house, Miss Breedlowe? Young women, turning up alone, with this business or that? If it's not one bachelor, it's another." She pointed her cane at Rainsleigh. "I urge you to apply to your erstwhile neighbor, Lord Falcondale, if you want to know how much carrying on I will tolerate in Henrietta Place. Very little, in fact. Better still, none at all."

Rainsleigh sighed. "I can assure you, my lady, there is no 'carrying on.'" The words were cordial, but he was rapidly becoming genuinely annoyed. Of all the transgressions of which he could be accused, he was most sensitive to imprudence.

He opened his mouth to offer his most civil version of *Get out*, but Lady Frinfrock spoke over him. "Take note, Lord Rainsleigh. Miss Breedlowe, God save her, has served as chaperone in instances such as this. Do you hear? I cannot speak for her, but I feel certain she would be predisposed if situations with young lady callers persist. I'm sure you are aware this is highly irregular." She looked back and forth between Rainsleigh and the young woman in the street. "Charity business or not."

Miss Breedlowe turned pink and sighed. "Oh, Lady Frinfrock."

Voices could be heard now—*her* voice—and Rainsleigh lost all interest in the conversation. "There is no cause for concern, I assure you," he lied, "but I appreciate your attentiveness and resourcefulness. Good day, my lady." He nodded to Sewell, and the butler assisted the duo down the steps and on their way.

In the next moment, Lady Elisabeth was inside, smiling, fussing with Sewell about her cloak, shooting Rainsleigh a glance and then away, looking around the marble entryway in wide-eyed wonder.

"Thank you," she said for a third time, declining the butler's help. She held a hand to the clasp on her wool cloak. "I won't stay long."

Oh, but you might, Rainsleigh thought, working not to stare.

Today, she wore pale green—the cloak, at least, was green. He was immensely curious about what she wore beneath it. Her gloves were ivory. Her hair was bound only at the crown of her head; the length of it spilled long and loose down her back. Last night, she'd worn it pinned. Now, he hoped to never see it pinned again.

She looked bright and energetic, standing in a beam of sunlight that spilled from the transom above the door. He had the unthinkable urge to touch her, as he had done, fleetingly, on the balcony last night. He was bombarded, he realized, with unthinkable urges. He cleared his throat and took a step back.

Elisabeth smiled at him again and craned to see the hall beyond. "Lady Frinfrock was not exaggerating, my lord. This is quite a house. It dwarfs the other houses in the street."

He stopped short of asking her if she liked it. "Fancy a tour?" he said.

She laughed again. "Oh, no, I wouldn't dream of detaining you. I've only come for the application. In fact, I assumed I would not see you at all. I thought perhaps your secretary could provide it."

"'Tis no disruption. But do allow Sewell to take your cloak. And please," he said, leading the way, "join me in the library."

The room into which Elisabeth was led reminded her of an aviary. An ornately carved, dark-stained-oak aviary with at least a thousand books. The ceiling was so high, birds could have flown freely, built nests, preened, sung, perhaps even migrated. She wondered if he considered this possible dual purpose. Likely not—although his desk, a massive slab of polished wood in the middle of the room—was littered with papers. To catch droppings? She almost laughed out loud. Nerves wreaked havoc on her composure.

Strictly business, she reminded herself.

Rainsleigh closed the door behind her and followed her in. "Please," he said, "let us sit." He gestured to a pair of plush leather chairs beneath the towering, floor-to-ceiling windows overlooking a lush garden.

"Oh," she said, studying the chairs that would position them knee to knee. "I will not tarry, my lord. If the application rules are at hand, I'll simply collect them and be on my way. I have my own work, as I know you do."

The viscount clasped his hands behind his back. "I was hoping to learn, firsthand, more about your work. Can you not spare five minutes?"

Could she? She bit her bottom lip and looked to the window. Well, yes. Of course, just…not in good conscience. Not without engaging in silly fantasies that had no place in a philanthropic transaction. Just as they also had no place in last night's perfectly mundane dinner party. Or afterward on the balcony. In the rain. With his coat.

Dear Lord. Why had she come here alone? Why had she relinquished her cloak?

Rainsleigh waited, staring at her in his intensely focused way. It would be rude, she thought, to deny him. Far be it for her to put him off, considering this unexpected degree of solicitousness. She was, after all, entering the charity contest to win.

She lowered herself into the soft leather chair. With a detached, professional tone, she asked, "What do you wish to know?"

"What do you feel I *should* know?" He leaned on the arm of the adjacent chair.

As little as possible, she thought. The fewer specifics he knew about the foundation, the better.

"Well," she said, hedging, "what is your goal for donating the money?"

He watched her. "'Tis no secret that the contest will draw attention to my shipyard and my name. Philanthropy has many advantages, as you know. But I'm not entirely motivated by my own ambition. I see the broader value in giving others a step up."

She nodded. "But this is the purpose of my foundation. To give others a step up."

"How many people do you serve?"

"At the moment? We have fifteen in residence."

He raised one eyebrow.

It sounded small, she knew. She huffed out a breath, searching for a better, vaguer answer. "Since the beginning, however, we have given refuge and aid to more than one hundred young women. We provide everything to the girls who come to us. Food, new clothes, lodging, education, a doctor's care. The foundation is everything from a safe haven, to a schoolroom, to a hospital, to a—well, to a home. Our numbers may be small, but we aim to serve every need of the girls who come."

"Your patrons are mostly children?"

"Young women, mostly. Sometimes they are younger. And we have never turned anyone away based on age. I have hosted girls as young as nine and as old as twenty-five."

"How do they find you, these girls? How do they come to you?"

Elisabeth chewed her bottom lip, thinking of the least colorful way to term it. "Actually, we seek out needy girls."

"Seek them out where?"

She took a deep breath. "We rescue them."

"Rescue them from what?"

"Deplorable situations."

"Such as?"

And just like that, she saw her bid for his donation drift away. To answer in any truthful way was to say entirely too much. She could lie, but what was the good in that? Worse, she found herself *wanting* tell him. His attentiveness drew her in. His probing questions validated her. His affecting ice-blue eyes…

She swallowed. "Lord Rainsleigh—"

He cut her off. "I beg your pardon, Lady Elisabeth, but do you know my given name?"

Bryson. Bryson Anders Courtland. Of course she knew it.

She shook her head.

"May I call you Elisabeth?" he asked. "My given name is Bryson—or Bryse, as my brother calls me. I would welcome a less formal address."

She raised an eyebrow. "Will all the applicants to the prize be invited to refer to you as…Bryse?"

"Only the ones on whom I intend to call."

Elisabeth opened her mouth. She shut it. She blinked at him. "I beg your pardon?"

He leaned forward. "Please don't think I'm dismissing of your work; I am not. I want to know everything about your foundation and the service you provide. But I also want to know everything about you. I am quite taken with you, Elisabeth. I should like to see you again. Very soon."

"Oh, God." Elisabeth forgot to breath. Their imagined rapport on the balcony had not, in fact, been imagined. He was *taken w* *h her?* He wished to know everything about her?

"Have I offended you?" he asked.

"No, you've simply…caught me unaware." It was the truth, not to mention the only excuse at hand. She could hardly say, *I've waited fifteen years for this moment.* Worse still would be her first impulse, which was to shove up from her chair and say, "Yes!"

There was, in fact, very little she could trust herself to say, considering the charity prize and her unwillingness to discuss their previous encounter. Considering the fact that she really did not know this man at all. She had only known him as a boy for one night.

"Would you consider a courtship?" he asked.

"Courtship…" she repeated. And now she did push from the chair and stood.

"Lord Rainsleigh," she began, "we've only just met. And what of my application for the charity donation?" *Sensible. On topic. Rooted in the real world, where sensible, topical, real-world things happen.*

He stood too. They were feet apart, face-to-face. "My personal interest in you will be entirely separate from my involvement in the donation. I can assure you it is only *you* I wish to refer to me as Bryse."

Bryse.

He had introduced himself as Bryson that night, so long ago, and despite her residual horror, she had clung to the sweet intimacy of that introduction. She'd devoted years of foolish fantasies to guessing whether those close to him referred to him as Bryson or Bryse or perhaps Court…

She looked up at him. *Bryse.* And now she knew. Now she was being invited to become one of those people close to him.

Cowardice compelled her to back away and retake her seat. "Forgive me, my lord." She spoke to her knees. "I don't know what to say, and that is a rare circumstance, indeed."

"I would also speak to your aunt," he assured her. "It felt appropriate to suggest the idea of a courtship to you first."

She laughed, in spite of herself. "I'd say so. Unless you wish to court my aunt."

"I wish for you," he said abruptly, and Elisabeth's head shot up. It was almost as if he knew she needed to hear it again, and again, and again.

I wish for you.

He crouched before her chair, spreading his arms, putting one hand on either side of her chair, caging her in. "How old are you, Elisabeth?" he asked.

"How old do you think I am?" A whisper.

"Twenty-six?" he guessed.

She shook her head. "No. I am the ripe old age of thirty. Far too old to be called upon by a bachelor viscount, rolling in money."

"Or"—he arched an eyebrow—"exactly the right age."

She laughed and finally looked away. And she thought he'd been handsome at nineteen. Her stomach dropped into a dip. She reminded herself to breathe.

"Why me?" she asked, looking out the window. "Why pay attention to *me?*"

His voice was so low she could barely discern the words. "Because I think you'd make an ideal viscountess."

An ideal what? Hope became a living, pulsing thing in her chest. It became her very heart. She fell back in her seat and closed her eyes, but the room still swam before her.

He went on, "You are mature, and intelligent, and poised. And devoted to your charity, whatever it is."

A thread of the old conversation. She sat up, determined to seize it before he could say another thing. "I've just told you what the charity is."

"You spoke in vague generalities that could mean a great many things. I let it go because I hope for more opportunities to learn."

Elisabeth breathed in and out, in and out. She bit her bottom lip again. She watched his gaze hone in on her mouth.

She closed her eyes. "My lord." She took a deep breath. "Rainsleigh…Bryson." She opened her eyes. "If your far-reaching goal is to earn an esteemed spot in London society, you're going about it entirely the wrong way. My charity is…unpopular, and no one has ever asked to court me before. It's really not done."

"Why is that?"

Because I have been waiting for you.

The thought floated, fully formed, in her brain, and she had to work to keep her hands from her cheeks, to keep from closing her eyes again, from squinting them shut against his beautiful face, just inches from her own, his low voice, his boldness.

"I'm very busy," she said instead.

"Then I will make haste."

"Is this because of last night? When I...challenged your dreadful neighbor?"

The corner of his mouth hitched up. "It did not hurt."

"It's very difficult for me to stand idly by when I hear a person misrepresented."

"And to think I was under the impression that you could barely abide my company. Your defense came as a great surprise."

"Oh...I am full of surprises."

"Is that so?" His words were a whisper. He leaned in.

She had the fleeting thought: *Dear God. He's going to kiss me...*

Bam! The door to the library crashed open.

"Bryse, I—" A man's voice froze them, nearly nose to nose. "Ah, I beg your pardon." The man laughed. "Bryse, I thought you were alone."

The man in the doorway was a blonder, younger, exceedingly more rumpled version of the viscount. His face was unshaven; his jacket, absent; his boots, filthy. He stared openly in amused shock.

All at once, Rainsleigh released her from the cage of his arms and stood. Elisabeth shot up, stepped back, and lost her balance. He caught her effortlessly and tucked her to his side.

"Beau," he said calmly, "a woodworker in Wales spent more than a year carving the relief panels of that door. Please don't whip it about like a stable gate. Where have you been?"

"The wrong place, obviously. Forget the door. I hope my tardiness will not preclude an introduction to your…friend?"

"Ring for Sewell, if you will," he said, nodding to the bell beside the door. "My *guest* is Lady Elisabeth Hamilton-Baythes, and now that you have scared her to death, she'll wish to flee, I'm sure."

"Flee? Not because of me, I hope."

"In spite of you, I'm sure."

Elisabeth rushed to assure him. "In fact, I was just leaving. I was here on a charity errand. Lord Rainsleigh may donate to my cause."

"I'd say the odds are pretty good," said the other man, walking slowly into the room.

Rainsleigh inclined his head to Elisabeth. "Do you mind if Sewell sees you to the door? This is my brother. He isn't fit for decent company, I'm afraid." He looked up at the other man and called, "Beau, say hello."

"How do you do?" said Elisabeth. She tried to tug away, but Rainsleigh did not release her.

"Very well, thank you," Beau said, winking at her. "Better now. You're a very pretty charity crusader, if you don't mind my saying. Puts me immediately in a charitable frame of mind. Will you stay for luncheon?"

Rainsleigh and Elisabeth said no in unison, and Rainsleigh added, "Now that you have graced me with your presence, Beauregard, you and I will take lunch at the shipyard, if you pl—"

"In that case," Beau cut in, "I won't be stay—"

"*Yes*," Rainsleigh said, "you will be. Do not think of leaving."

Gently, he set Elisabeth away and strode to his desk, gathering up a hodgepodge of parchment. Elisabeth drifted behind him, and he handed the papers to her in a heap. "I apologize for the disorder. Retribution from my secretary, I'm afraid. He wanted to distribute this himself and ply you for an early interview, but I sent him away."

Beau whistled lowly. "Oh, so this was one of *Cecil's* interviews...about the—"

"Will you change, Beau, before we tour the shipyard? You are part owner. The workers look up to you."

"Perhaps I will join Dunhip in retribution."

Rainsleigh ignored him. "Ah, very good, here is Sewell." He motioned to the butler who held the door. Leaning in to her, he said, "Good day to you, Elisabeth." His words were so low only she could hear. "You honor me with your call."

Elisabeth cleared her throat. "Yes, well. I believe I have what I need." It was the only thing she could think of to say. The butler waited, holding her cloak aloft. She took the garment and hastened to the door, down the hall, and out the front door, all but fleeing to her waiting carriage.

CHAPTER NINE

"Say it." Bryson sighed.

He collapsed into the chair behind his desk. "I cannot stop you, and I actually want to hear it. For once. Say it."

His brother laughed. "Say what? Which of the myriad remarks currently swirling in my brain would you find most useful?"

"All of them. What you think of her. The depth and breadth of your shock. Advice for next time, misinformed and wrong minded though it will be..."

"So there will be a next time?"

"I was in the process of asking permission to call. On *her*. A courtship. There will be a multitude of next times, I hope—not like this, of course. A *proper* call in her home, with her guardian, an esteemed aunt."

Beau laughed again. "*You're joking.* You'll do no better than your private library behind a closed door."

"Mind yourself, Beau. Lady Elisabeth is the daughter of an earl. Her aunt is one of the most highly regarded patronesses in London. You need only look at her to see that she is lady."

"Can I? Perhaps you're asking the wrong fellow. I don't care whose daughter *or* niece *or* second cousin she may be. I am judging by the look on your face when I walked in."

"What look?"

Beau shrugged, pretending to study the books on a near shelf. "Like you were two seconds away from pulling her out of that chair and down on top of you."

Bryson put his hands behind his head and stared at the domed ceiling. "Oh God, you're right." He looked at his brother. "Thank God you came, or I could not have accounted for my actions."

"Thank God? Bryse, I've robbed you of a bloody fantastic Friday morning! Do you know how many women I've plowed in a library? Of all the rooms in any given house, I believe the library might be my personal favorite, and I'll tell you why."

"Beau, please—"

"There's nothing like a sturdy, grommetted leather chaise," he went on wistfully. "No self-respecting study is without one. Ah, yes, here we are. What did I say?" He circled Bryson's eight-foot leather chaise and dropped onto it. "Although—sometimes the chaise is too much like a bed. Too conventional. Any library worth its salt will offer a wide variety of other expansive, horizontal surfaces upon which to lay someone back, if she is so inclined."

"I said, *careful.* You're talking about my future wife."

"Your what?" Beau shot up. "Wait. Stop. Forgive me. Perhaps I'm still drunk. I thought you said *courtship. Courtship* means tea and carriage rides and sonnets. Courtship does *not* mean marriage. Just last week you were going on about marrying someone pious, plain, and boring; someone Dunhip *and his mother* chose. And now you've squirreled away a perfectly lovely girl in your library, and you're talking about marrying *her*? Was she... Was this Dunhip's choice? If so, well done, Cecil."

"No, actually. I found her myself. Met her last night at a dinner hosted by Lady Banning, who also happens to be her aunt. I was taken by Lady Elisabeth nearly at first sight. She is everything for which I searched. Cecil will locate no better girl." Rainsleigh heard the protestation in his own voice, the urgency, but he was disinclined to pretend otherwise. The urgency was real. He *would* protest anyone who challenged him. Lady Elisabeth was the woman he wanted. Intensely. Immediately. *Now.*

Beau whistled lowly and turned away. "Well, she's very pretty. I'll give you that. What is she, a widow?"

"No. She lives as the ward of her aunt and runs a charity for lost girls or some such. To be honest, I'm only just learning her situation."

"Yet you're setting her up to be the next Lady Rainsleigh based on one dinner?"

Rainsleigh shrugged. "When I see what I want, I know it. There's no need to continue searching. I cannot be certain, but I think she is... amenable."

"Ha, I'll say. She looked very amenable to me."

Bryson ran a hand through his hair and pushed back from his desk. "Yes, and that may be a problem."

"Only you could see a problem in an 'amenable' girl locked in your library."

"She is an innocent. My... er, enthusiasm showed an astounding lack of judgment."

"Hmmm. How ironic. Astounding lack of judgment has given me years of untold delight. It *is* permissible, you know, to bend the rules, Bryse. Just a little. Or a lot, as is my view. But can't you see this is a good thing? How long has it been since you gave up your mistresses? Five years? Oh, God—*ten*? No wonder you're champing at the bit to get married."

"I gave up courtesans in order to earn this family some basic decency." He ruffled the papers on his desk, mindlessly sorting them into stacks.

"Well, you overdo," Beau said grimly. "You always have. Although, it couldn't hurt to play by the rules just this once. Now of all times. Have you heard that Cousin Kenneth has slithered his way back to town?"

"Kenneth Courtland? Dear God, no. I make it a point to hear as little about our Courtland relations as possible. If he's here, surely he cannot afford to stay long. Who told you? He dare not contact me."

"Navy mate of mine told me someone named Kenny was invoking the Courtland name for a seat at a card game in Pall Mall last week. Wound up pitched into the gutter, blind drunk. My mate said he'd racked up debts in excess of fifty quid."

"Splendid." Rainsleigh sighed, cringing at the thought of his idiot cousin claiming some connection to him. Kenneth was too weak and wretched to shame Bryson as he once had, but his lack of self-control was an embarrassment still.

"I would not worry too much," said Beau. "Kenneth's sins are not yours to atone."

Bryson chuckled. "As if that were possible. Even for me."

"Besides, you're obviously too busy becoming leg-shackled to a girl you've met once in your life."

"She defended me; did I tell you that?"

"Since when do you need defending?"

"I didn't need it, but she did it, just the same. An old-crone gossip called me out about Father at the party. I was ready with a set-down—the woman had been hectoring me all night—but before I could say a word, Lady Elisabeth leapt to my defense. Rattled off a list of my accomplishments and strengths. She knew all about me, Beau, and we had never met."

"Hmmm," his brother mused, "a Rainsleigh devotee. There was bound to be one of them out there somewhere, I suppose. You're in the bloody papers enough. So it was flattery, was it?"

Bryson made a dismissive sound. "No, it wasn't flattery. She understood the things that were important to me."

"Money and reverence?"

Bryson glared at him. "*Productivity and honor.*"

"Hmmm…so you say. And you're sure she's not a fortune hunter?"

"She is a ward of her aunt, as I've said, a wealthy widow who lives in Grosvenor Square. It's not the money. She knew me, Beau. She *knew* all about me."

"And yet she showed no hesitation," Beau teased.

"Well, I'd hardly say she's fallen into my arms. She is measured and reticent by nature. Another reason to admire her. I respect her caution."

"Caution toward what? Not the closed door of a library."

"Clever. No, I cannot say what, exactly, may make her hesitate. I asked permission to call on her just now, and she hedged. Perhaps I have acted too soon."

"The morning after making her acquaintance?" Beau scoffed. "Surely not. Twelve hours is only marginally obsessive."

Bryson ignored him. "I think she is afraid she will lose my donation to her charity if we are…involved."

"Ha—if I hadn't barged in on you, it's clear you would have promised the moon in exchange for…well, let me not be indelicate about my future sister-in-law."

"But this will be my struggle. Regardless of how alluring I find her, we cannot carry on, she and I. I've already had the poor judgment to secret her away in my library. My God, I have no idea what I was thinking."

"Well, I have some idea, and it's perfectly natural. You're an active man in the prime of his life. You should want to steal away with a pretty girl and have a kiss or what-have-you."

"What I *want* and what I shall have are two distinctly different things. Self-control is a virtue, widely known. I urge you to consider it. Rise above Kenneth, if you can—it's a very low bar." He sighed and returned to his desk. "You know, the old woman from the party has since suggested an available chaperone for hire. Perhaps I'll look into it. Elisabeth is thirty years old, and she seems wholly independent for all practical purposes. I cannot say what, exactly, is expected of any time we spend together, but I do know the limits of my lust. She is a very"—he took a deep breath and turned away—"beautiful woman. If her aunt will not arrange a chaperone, then I must."

"You know, Bryse, the more I hear, the more I am inclined to think you are *besotted* with the chit. Lust is one thing, but you've been going on about her as long as you've ever discussed your boats—if not longer. That's saying quite a lot."

"Well, she is attractive. I'll admit that much." He gave his brother a hard look. "But what use have I for…infatuation?"

Beau chuckled. "Use? Who bothers with usefulness when they are beset by so-called love at first sight?"

"Try *desire* at first sight," Bryson corrected. "Not that desire does me any good either. Physical intimacy is entirely out of the question before marriage, no matter how much I desire her. I will only enter into a courtship that is steeped in modesty and respect."

"Ah, yes, your bloody life creed." Beau tapped a *ba-dum-dum* beat on Bryson's desk and then backed away. "Modesty and respect. Sounds like a lark, Bryse. Good luck, mate—to you both. I wouldn't expect anything less."

CHAPTER TEN

"Elisabeth, darling, is that you?"

The Countess of Banning called to her niece from a stone bench beneath a trellis of drooping roses. It was well past tea-time, and Elisabeth had been working at the foundation since she'd left Rainsleigh's house that morning.

"Oh, hello." Elisabeth tugged at the ribbon of her bonnet and lifted it off, spilling her hair free. "I did not see you there. No ball tonight?"

"Perhaps not," Lilly said cryptically, beckoning her to the bench.

As a rule, Aunt Lillian attended a social engagement nearly every night of the week. It was rare to find her in the garden so late in the day. Elisabeth smiled at the unexpected surprise and tossed her bonnet on a stack of clay pots.

"Sorry to be away most of the day with no word," she said. "And hello to you too, Quincy." The large gardener winked from his spot behind the countess, pruning the climbing rose.

"We worked through luncheon," Elisabeth went on, "and tea. Were you—"

"Viscount Rainsleigh called today."

Elisabeth froze on the path.

"Already?" Her voice came out on a choke. She'd passed the day reliving their encounter in her mind again and again, searching for some misinterpretation or vagueness. She'd found none, but then again, she was hardly an objective observer. Her plan had been to wait and see. She'd never dreamed the wait would be less than a day. "Why did he…call?" Even now, she would not allow herself to assume.

"He asked for my permission to call on you."

"*Already?*" Elisabeth repeated.

The countess nodded. "He seemed wholly determined, in fact. Single-minded, one might say. You knew?"

"Yes…yes, I suppose I did." Elisabeth closed her eyes and raised a hand to her forehead. How, she wondered, had Bryson Courtland gone from a distant, pleasant memory that she conjured up only on occasion to a flesh-and-blood man who had called on her twice in one day? Who wanted to see her more?

"*I wish for you,*" he'd said.

His words had returned to her throughout the busy day. Her stomach had been a bittersweet swirl of hope and fear and disbelief.

"Darling," began Lillian, "I have told him yes. I hope this is the correct answer."

It's not, Elisabeth thought sadly, sliding her hand into her hair and looking at the sky.

"I was remiss?" the countess guessed.

Elisabeth settled onto the bench beside her. "Remiss? Well, this is a reversal. *Asking* my opinion instead of arranging it on my behalf."

"Do stop," said the countess. "We saw your glow after dinner last night."

"Oh yes. My *glow*."

Lillian snapped a rose from the trellis, considered it, and then tucked it delicately behind her niece's ear. "A courtship is a far cry from a dinner. He would not leave without an answer, so I guessed—I *hoped*. But I've worried for hours that I have said the wrong thing."

Elisabeth nodded. Her aunt was capable of some measure of restraint, but it took effort. Perhaps Elisabeth's protestations before the dinner had had some impact after all. If so, it was a huge concession, because Lillian wanted this so badly, and she'd been given no tangible reason why it could not be. But perhaps this was Elisabeth's fault. She had held the details of the abduction and rescue so very close.

Lillian went on, "The dinner was only meant to be an opportunity for you to meet him—or meet him *again*. Once and for all. If you've discovered that you have no attraction to the man, well, that is not my doing."

Elisabeth looked away. "Attraction is not the problem, unfortunately. How easy that would make things. Under different circumstances, I would be open to a courtship. But all things considered? I cannot."

"All things considered?" Lillian waited.

Elisabeth sighed, stretching her back and patting her hands on her knees. "Obviously, a courtship would jeopardize my bid for his charity donation. I need that money, Lillian. I've poured all but a fraction of the entitlement left by Father's death into the foundation. We are surviving, but his donation would do a world of good."

"*Pshaw*," said Lillian. "I'll pay for the charity prize myself. This obstacle is not significant. You only heard of the prize yesterday. Next."

"*And*," Elisabeth continued, rolling her eyes, "if he remembers who I am, then any future we may have will be doomed."

"Doomed, is it? And why is that?"

Elisabeth hesitated only a second. It was time. "Because," she said, looking over to her aunt, "if he remembers, he will be inclined to think I am, er—was, a whore."

Lillian barely managed to stifle a gasp. Behind them, Quincy's discreet footsteps padded away. She whispered, "You exaggerate the circumstances, Elisabeth. Why would he be inclined to think that?"

Elisabeth shook her head. "It's been so long since we've discussed the abduction, you and I." She turned and watched Quincy disappear into his potting shed. "Your respect for my privacy has been a necessary, cherished thing—essential to my healing. But I have not kept silent because I misremember. I know exactly what happened. He will, too, I'm sure—if he would but recall the circumstances."

"He discovered you in the dreadful brothel after the attack," recited Lillian—it was the only part of the harrowing night she really knew, "and he took you out and brought you across London. He brought you here to me. Well, not him, personally, as you showed up on my doorstep alone. But you said it was he, Elisabeth, who rescued you that night."

Elisabeth squeezed her eyes shut. "Yes, but I wasn't simply sitting on the hitching post waiting to be delivered. It was a brothel, Aunt Lillian. You've seen the scar on my shoulder.

For all practical purposes, I was being indoctrinated among the working girls there."

Lillian fell silent for a moment, studying Elisabeth's face. She shook her head as if she would not allow the story to go on. She reached out and placed her hand on top of Elisabeth's.

"I was in a bedroom when they brought him in," Elisabeth said. "Waiting for him—or dreading him, more like. What else was he to think?"

"A bedroom? But was he there as a customer, Elisabeth? I thought…I thought…"

Elisabeth shrugged. "He'd been dragged to the brothel by his father—he said as much. I said nothing at all, but he saw my shoulder, saw me dressed in rags. I was wretched, pathetic. The only thing propping me up was my will to survive." She looked away. "And *this* is why I did not want to sit with him at dinner last night. And *this* is why I cannot allow him to court me now. I am terrified that he will recognize me—or, more so, that he will *not* recognize me, and that I will be forced to remind him of the whole terrible ordeal."

Tears burned the corners of her eyes, and she squeezed them shut. "If he and I are…connected, the truth will eventually come out."

Lillian nodded slowly, reaching over and taking Elisabeth's hands in her own. "Forgive me as I muddle through." A tear slid down Elisabeth's cheek, and her aunt reached up to wipe it away. The tender gesture only brought on more tears. Elisabeth looked at the sky.

Lillian asked softly, "But would this be such a terrible thing? The truth? You were *not*, in fact, a…*that*. It would be difficult to tell him, but he seems like a fair and decent man.

You would survive it, if he knew. You both would survive this truth."

"Aunt Lilly," she whispered, her voice breaking, "you are like a mother to me, and I have not even survived telling *you*."

Lillian squeezed her hands. "Perhaps if you began with me then?"

"Perhaps you are right."

Lillian's head shot up. "What? Elisabeth, *wait*—"

"No," she insisted, "it is time." She wiped her eyes. She glanced at Lillian and chuckled through her tears. "Don't look so grave. I have owed you this."

When Elisabeth spoke, it was in the low, flat tones of forced detachment. She faced the open garden. She churned through the memories, angling to be specific but brief. "I'll start at the beginning. You know some of this. I was in the carriage with Mama and Papa when we were attacked. The highwaymen shot the servants first—driver, grooms, Mama's maid. Papa was next. Mama screamed and screamed. I honestly think they would have spared her (as they spared me) if she had not caused such a ruckus. But her husband was shot before her eyes. She was hysterical. They shot her to put a stop to her carrying on, and that left only me."

"Did they strike you, Elisabeth? Did they…"

Elisabeth took a deep breath. "Three of them wanted to…assault me there, on the side of the road, but the leader called them off. He told them he knew of a place that they could…'sell' me for a high price. But the money hinged on my being delivered untouched. This was the brothel."

Lillian nodded slowly. Her grip was so tight; Elisabeth wiggled to give them both some relief.

"They argued about this," Elisabeth said, "shouting back and forth as they searched our belongings. Ultimately, thank God, the leader won out, and they consented to let me be.

"They bound me instead, threw me over the back of a horse, and we rode through the night until we reached this certain brothel—the Bronze Root." Absently, she grabbed hold of the shoulder that bore the branded letters B and R. "At the time, I had no idea that such a place existed." Elisabeth took a deep breath before going on. "After the excruciating ride in an impossible position across the horse's rump, I was barely able to stand. I retched for five minutes. I wanted to die. I *prayed* they would kill me, as they had Mama and Papa. Meanwhile, they sold me, just like that, for ten pounds sterling. They held me down, and the owner branded my shoulder"—she reached for the scar again—"and I was thrown in among the owner's stable of very unhappy, very unfriendly prostitutes. I was told to make peace with my new life, because no one from the outside world would ever find me. I would be working 'on my back,' in a manner of speaking, as soon as they could lure a customer willing to pay the very high price they placed on me—a young, unspoiled, well-tended virgin." She ended this last on a whisper.

Tears rolled down Lillian's cheeks. She dropped the girl's hands and wrapped her arms around her. Elisabeth leaned into the hug, more to comfort her aunt than herself. Despite the years of silence and reckoning, this recounting of the tragedy affected Elisabeth less than she thought it would.

"After that," Elisabeth went on, "there were beatings, gropings, generalized…terror."

Lillian cut in. "But dearest, were you…" She let the sentence trail off, clearly unable to say the words. "The doctor I hired to treat you would not tell me, you know. He saw you for weeks, and he refused to ever say."

Elisabeth stared into her lap. She took three deep breaths. She had not thought about this detail in years. "I fought the doctor every time he endeavored to examine me. He didn't tell you because he did not know." She looked up. "Honestly, Aunt Lillian? Even I cannot say." She shook her head. Now the tears did come, closing her throat.

Lillian ventured a guess. "Because you were unconscious?"

"Because I was too young and naive to understand." She breathed in, trying to talk through her tears. "I was only fifteen years old and incredibly naive. The entire ordeal was a horrifying immersion in…depravity and violence. Mama had only explained to me in the vaguest terms what happens between a man and a woman. To me, one violation bled into the next—all of them were terrifying."

She went on, speaking briskly. "For all practical purposes, it is fair to say that I was…disgraced. The first night, I was left alone to recover from the branding and my general hysteria. But the next day, two prospective customers arrived. A 'sampling,' it was called. My clothes were taken from me, and I was presented to them naked. The owner and these men closed in and touched, and patted, and pinched."

Lillian, now crying too, muttered a desperate curse.

"So much value had been placed on my virginity—did they go so far as to finish the task?" Elisabeth drew her hand to her mouth and covered her trembling lips. Lillian pulled her so tightly to her side that she was nearly in her lap.

Finally, she lifted her head. Her voice was a whisper. "Was I raped by these three men? I cannot say. Their hands were everywhere. Perhaps? I...I *don't know.*" She shook her hair back. "What could this specific detail matter when I was subjected to all the rest? I can never claim innocence or purity after that night. Never. I can never entertain the advances of a respectable gentleman after that night."

"Elisabeth, *stop,*" said Lillian. "You were a victim, a child—"

"But don't you see?" she demanded tearfully, shoving up. "It doesn't really matter whether they did or they did not. You took me in, healed me, and gave me a safe and happy new home. Because of this, I have made my own way and built a rich, fulfilling life. On my own terms. In this life, neither innocence nor purity is a requirement. The same cannot be said for the life of the future wife of Viscount Rainsleigh, whoever she may be. For her, purity will be central. It will be essential."

She reached out and snapped a rose from the trellis. "And now you see why the viscount troubles me so. If anyone deserves an innocent girl, after the boyhood he suffered, it is he. And *this* is why I cannot entertain the idea of a courtship." She dropped back on the bench. "It's far too reckless, I worry, even to compete for the charity prize. If I was prudent, I would stay entirely away."

Lillian stared at her knees. "This is my fault. You said you were not ready, and I would not hear it. I thought you were simply being stubborn and needlessly independent. I thought you were being shy. I'd only heard that he'd rescued you, that he was dashing and—"

"He *did* rescue me. And he *was* dashing. But allow me to finish. I also had help on the inside. There was a prostitute there—a young woman called Marie."

She told her aunt about the plan to switch rooms and being given over to the young Bryson Courtland instead of his father.

"We know Marie's son," said Elisabeth, smiling. Finally, a happy detail. "*Stoker*. She sent him to me when he was old enough to make his way across London. I had told her where I would run if I managed to escape. She never forgot me and wanted a chance for a different life for her boy. When he came to me, I put him to work immediately. Marie has since passed away. The nature of that work leads to a very early grave. Her life was not easy, but she was a good mother to Stoker, and he loved her dearly. It is not only for me that he raids the brothels; he does it to honor her. How I'll ever get him to leave London to go to school, I have no idea."

"Oh, my darling, darling girl! I'm so incredibly sorry for what you endured. It is...it is far worse than I imagined, and I imagined quite a lot." Lillian gathered her up again and held her tightly. "And how grateful I am to Rainsleigh. That he did not take advantage but instead brought you to us. Oh my God, to think what would have happened if he had not been shown to your room..."

"Then I would have escaped some other way," Elisabeth said plainly. "I'm sorry I did not tell you sooner. For years, I could not bear to discuss it, and then I did not want to upset you. But you were correct; it was quite liberating to share it. I'm glad I've done it." She took a deep breath and stood up, straightening her skirt.

"Elisabeth? I'm...I'm sorry for pressing Lord Rainsleigh on you at dinner."

"I forgive you," she said with a laugh, "but you must now help me determine what to do with him. He has no idea."

"This, I cannot believe."

"Lillian—do not start. *He does not know me.* It's a miracle that he does not, but he doesn't."

"Well, this is simple. If he calls on you...if he courts you, Elisabeth, you must tell him."

"Oh, yes, how simple. If that is the solution, then I cannot see him outside the pursuit of his charity prize."

"But Elisabeth?" Lillian shoved off the bench. "I saw your rapport with him last night. And your defense of him against Lady Frinfrock. All those minutes out on the balcony? You should have seen the glow on your faces when the two of you stumbled inside. I believe you can find the words to tell him. He may come to understand."

Elisabeth shook her head and wandered away, toeing the primrose border with her shoe. Of course Lillian would hold this view. To her, everyone was one moonlit turn around the garden away from falling in love. "He may not." She looked up. "He works very hard to be...above reproach."

"But you are, in every way, above reproach."

Elisabeth shot her a skeptical look. "I run a charity devoted to rescuing child prostitutes. And our first meeting was in a brothel. To many—to *most*—I am highly reproachable."

"But he already knows about your charity. He said you called to his house for the application. Surely—"

"I have learned to discuss the foundation without going into detail about what, exactly, we do. I shall dance around the particulars."

"No more lies, Elisabeth?"

"No, not lies. I have never lied." She sighed. She reached the oak tree and leaned against it. "I will simply describe the foundation in vague terms."

"Fine, no more *secrets*."

Elisabeth turned her head and stared at Quincy, whistling as he emptied a watering can into a pot of ivy on other side of the garden. "Sometimes we keep secrets for a very good reason."

"Yes, and some secrets are happier than others," Lillian shot back. Elisabeth nodded and looked away.

Lilly marched on her. "You must tell him. All of it. Tell him everything, just as you've told me. If you do, and if he turns away, *then* we'll know what he's made of, and it will be proof that you would never suit. It will be a great disappointment, but you can cease thinking of him forevermore. *On the other hand*, if he is charitable, as I think he will be, then…"

"Yes," agreed Elisabeth, "*then*… What then?"

Lillian crossed her arms over her chest. "Elisabeth, is it possible that you were so traumatized by that night that you are, in a manner, put off from any sort of intimacy with a man? Perhaps, ever? Is there some barricade in your mind that will prevent affection or closeness? Is this it? Darling?"

Elisabeth considered this. She considered how she felt on the balcony with Rainsleigh last night, of how she felt in his library today. Heat rose to her cheeks. She shook her head. "No, I don't believe so. I have seen this with many girls in my work, but it is not the way I feel. It was mostly one incident, the second night. There is no barricade, as you say."

"If this is true, then you owe it to yourself to explore where a courtship may take you." She reached out and brushed an errant curl behind Elisabeth's ear.

Elisabeth leaned her head back against the tree. "So you say, but I cannot even think of how I would raise the topic. 'By the by, we've met before. Remember me from when you thought I was a whore, and we escaped a brothel together? Remember that night?'"

Lillian laughed sadly. "Well, that would do it, certainly. But you will think of the right words at the right time, of this I have no doubt. Any woman who can leap up from the table and rattle off a man's accomplishments in one breath can surely string together a few sentences to get the conversation going. I shall never forget the expression on Lord Rainsleigh's face when you defended him at the party. There is something special here, Elisabeth, something magical."

"Hmmm," she mused, shoving off the tree. It felt better, somehow, for having explained the haunted history to Lillian. Perhaps she should have done it long ago. Perhaps she could, indeed, tell Rainsleigh and survive that too. Not likely, but some bright, hopeful place inside had taken on a new glow. She tucked Lillian's arm in hers, and they began walking toward the house. "First things first. I will apply for his charity prize. If I manage to win that, it'll be magic, indeed. In the meantime, let us wait and see."

May 15, 1811

CHAPTER ELEVEN

May 15, 1811

> Dear Lord Rainsleigh,
>
> I am writing in response to your kind request to call. Your respectful manners do you credit, and on behalf of my aunt and myself, I thank you for your formality and your consideration of custom. I am honored. However, I hope you will not take offense when I insist that, at the moment, I must prioritize my desire to win your charity prize over any social or personal pursuits I may explore (with you).
>
> To that end, I respectfully decline your request. I cannot think it fair for me to spend companionable time with you beyond the bounds of the application process—not when other charities have only paperwork to promote their causes. I should like to earn your donation impartially, based on merit and need, as would any other group in town. Conversely, I would not wish to jeopardize my chances for the donation if you and I were to, in a manner of speaking, "not get on."

In short, my work is too important and our need too great to indulge the risk. I hope you understand.

Warm regards,

Lady Elisabeth Hamilton-Baythes

May 15, 1811

Lady Elisabeth,

I received your note. Enclosed is a bank note for £1,000 sterling, which I cede to your foundation as an independent donation, outside the bounds of the official charity prize. With this, I hope you feel less conflicted about competing interests, other charities, or what might happen if we "don't get on." I would see you.

Rainsleigh

May 16, 1811

Dear Lord Rainsleigh,

Your generosity is, indeed, impressive (if not entirely sincere), but of course I could never consider a relationship, romantic or otherwise, with someone who dashed off £1,000 simply to speed things along.

As much as I would love to earn any donation for my cause, I cannot, in good conscience, accept the money in exchange for my own time. For better or for worse, I am not for sale. If you would but allow me to furnish the completed application, sit for any interviews, and lead a tour of my facility—as required by the official contest rules—you would appreciate the irony of this statement.

Please find the bank note attached, with regret and thanks.

Elisabeth

May 16, 1811

Let the applications, interviews, and facility tours commence. Which best suits your immediate schedule?

Rainsleigh

May 17, 1811

Lord Rainsleigh,

I have not yet completed the application, which, as I'm sure you know, is exhaustive. Naturally, I want to get it right. I cannot imagine that you are ready to schedule interviews or tours when the written component is outstanding.

EHB

May 17, 1811

My lady,

Imagine that I am.

The paperwork interests me far less and may wait. Let us tour or interview presently—any step that allows us to pass time together. Name the hour, day, and location.

Rainsleigh

May 17, 1811

Rainsleigh,

As you wish. You may tour my foundation in Moxon Street near Regent's Park at ten o'clock tomorrow morning, if it suits your schedule. We are the sandstone building with the blue door.

For reasons you would know if I had been given the opportunity to complete the application, there are no signs or direction on the building; our blue door will be your guide. It is the only one in the street. I look forward to introducing you to our program.

EHB

CHAPTER TWELVE

"And where do you *procure* these girls, Elisabeth?"

Rainsleigh followed her down a sunny hallway of her foundation building in Moxon Street. So far, he'd seen the library, an art studio, a large parlor, a music room, Elisabeth's office, a tidy garden, and the laundry. He'd been introduced to several reticent but polite girls, all of whom regarded him with a mix of curiosity and distrust, and four pleasant members of staff.

It was thorough and impressive, whatever it was—but this was the thing. He could not say precisely *what* he was touring or *who*, exactly, were the benefactors.

The irony was, he'd approached the tour not really caring about the bloody charity. His purpose had been to see Elisabeth. How gratified he'd been that she had answered the door herself and led him on a private tour. But after an hour, his curiosity could no longer be tamped down.

"I beg your pardon?" she called, two steps ahead. Her voice was light, but she tensed and missed half a step.

He stopped walking. "These girls. Your patrons. Where did you come upon them? How are they chosen to receive your care? Where are their parents? Are they orphans?"

She nodded her head, but her voice was off. "They are orphans, in a manner of speaking."

"Which manner is that?"

"I believe I mentioned before that we remove them from deplorable situations in the slums of the city."

"Such as?"

She turned to face him and raised her chin. "Surely you are not so wealthy that you are unacquainted with poverty and cruelty, inhumanity—"

"On the contrary, I am intimately acquainted with poverty and cruelty. It's why I chose to award these donations from the start."

"I thought the donations gained publicity for your shipping company."

"That too. But you've just changed the subject. It was a legitimate question for a philanthropist who is motivated to effect change for the better, wouldn't you agree?"

"Oh. Yes, well. You'll forgive me if I am caught off guard. I was under the impression that your motivation was to see me."

He nodded, chuckled, and ambled closer. "Fair point. It *was* to see you. But now you have sidestepped my question a second time. Surely you know this only drives my curiosity."

"But I gave you an ans—"

"I am rich, Elisabeth," he said, stepping closer, "not stupid. On the contrary, my ability to discern evasiveness is one of the skills that has afforded me all of the lovely money that I now want to donate to your work. But first, I should like to know exactly *to what* and *for whom* I donate." He leaned closer with every word. His face was only inches from hers.

She sucked in a quiet breath. After half a beat, her chin went up. "The girls here were working as prostitutes when they came to me."

He stared.

"They were rescued," she went on, "from brothels. Or bordellos. Houses of ill-repute. They were brought here to start a new life."

Rainsleigh searched her face, his brain clambering to catch up. He prided himself on anticipating every given outcome to any situation. He had not anticipated this. "I'm sorry; did you say—"

"Yes," she said. "You heard correctly. After time with me—sometimes months, in other cases, years—we send these girls out into the world as fully healed, gainfully employed young women who can support themselves with honest work."

Rainsleigh struggled to digest this. "Does your aunt know?"

"Of course she knows. This work has been central to my life for as long as—well, for as long as I have lived in her care. She is one of my greatest benefactors, in fact. She pays the salary of our nurse—no small gift—and I am eternally grateful. You will meet her—the nurse—unless, that is, you find that you have lost your appetite for the tour."

"No," he said, stalling, *reeling.* "You'll forgive me if I take a moment to work my head around this...detail." He looked around the hall as if he was only just seeing it. "This certainly solves the mystery of your evasiveness. I had begun to think you were harboring a dragon in the cellar."

"No dragon. Though I have rescued the girls from the mouth of something far graver. But you need not agree. Ultimately, you don't need to support us with your donation. We have frightened away many a benefactor by putting too fine a point on the precise nature of our work."

"And this works?"

"Not really, but I do it reflexively now, I'm afraid. I am not ashamed of the work I do, nor of the girls I serve, but a vaguely worded summary yields more resources than the glaring truth. People are frightened of certain words."

Rainsleigh nodded. "I do not scare easily." He turned away. "But I am *surprised*." He turned back. "How did you become interested in this cause, in particular? Service to prostitutes?"

She nodded. "I should mention that once the young women enter into our care, we cease referring to them as prostitutes and simply call them girls. To answer your question, however, I...I met a young woman once." She faltered now, suddenly unable to look him in the eye. Her voice had gone off. He was confused by this. Surely he wasn't the first person to ask this question.

She took a deep breath. "This young woman...escaped a horrible place. She was terrified, running for her very life and entirely alone. Someone had—" She paused and looked at the floor, then out the window.

Rainsleigh waited while she composed herself. Doubtless, it was difficult for a woman of her station to manage the depravity that was inherent to prostitutes. But this returned him to his original question: why *this*? For a gently bred lady? Why *this* societal ill for *her*?

"Someone came to the aid of this girl," she finished. Her eyes darted away. "In the years that I've been helping these girls, we have learned that the escape from the brothel is only the beginning. What comes next is the real work. But the rewards are so very great. In essence, we are giving these young women their lives back. After coming to know this girl's plight, I could not turn a blind eye."

He narrowed his eyes, trying to reconcile what she said with what any other gently bred lady might say. Then again, no gently bred lady in his acquaintance would venture anywhere near the topic of rescuing prostitutes. It should have alarmed him. It should have put him off. Instead, he found his respect for her only grew.

He crossed his arms over his chest. "And so you, the daughter of an earl, niece to one of society's *grande dames*, prowl the streets of London, looking to rescue—and forgive me if I apply the wrong term to the wrong incarnation—prostitutes?"

"Yes." The blue-green of her eyes flashed with pride. "This is who my charity aims to save, and that is how the girls come to us. However, I personally do not participate in the work of locating or rescuing the girls—at least not as a front-line raider, out in the streets. I employ a handful of young men—you saw one of them at my aunt's party. He was with me in the stairwell. He has a team of lads with a similar... set of skills, and they discover new victims. Then they plan clandestine raids and rescue them."

He stared at her a moment, allowing each new detail to find a place in the rapidly reordered impression of her. "And what if they do not wish to stay here with you? These rescued girls?"

She sighed deeply, her expression turning indignant. "They all wish to stay here, my lord. Some may be temporarily lost to the lifestyle because it's all they've known but not for long. Not when we show them a different way. No girl is forced to remain in our care, but I am happy to report that very few leave after we explain an alternative and what we will do to care for them, what future they may come to know."

"And afterward? When you've served them? They go?"

"Yes. They go. They become chambermaids. Or kitchen help. Or find jobs in a mill. We do not release them until we've settled them in safe and sustainable employment. This is, you can imagine, one of the biggest challenges, and I do much of this work myself. While the boys discover and rescue the girls, I work with certain churches and other 'progressive' organizations to find positions for them in honest work. In between, they are taught by tutors, treated by the nurse, and enjoy the motherly or sisterly care of my carefully chosen staff. These generous women prepare them in every other way. It is an ambitious undertaking, I assure you." She smiled at him. "My life's work. I am very protective of it, I'm afraid. And quite proud. I did not originally intend to apply for your donation because the richest benefactors are typically put off by it, as I've said. But when we...er, met..." Her smile wavered and she looked at her hands. She appeared disinclined to go on.

Rainsleigh cleared his throat. "Lady Elisabeth?" he said carefully, "can I trouble you for a cup of tea?"

She looked up, puzzled. She gave a small, sad smile. He realized that she assumed she'd already lost. *You may have the bloody money*, he wanted to say.

It would be precipitous to tell her, but he knew this much. The charity was deserving, well-run, and deeply felt. The money was hers—the easiest thing to give. The greater challenge was accepting this new perception of Elisabeth herself. In his mind, he had already made her his wife.

Before he could catch himself, he mumbled aloud, "*Prostitutes. Why does it have to be prostitutes?*"

"For the exact reason that you've just asked. What interests me most," she went on, "are the very people from whom everyone else turns away."

"Please don't mistake me," he said. "I'm not judging you or your patrons, I'm cursing my own life. My father was a great purveyor of prostitutes, as you may have heard."

For this, she made no response. "You wanted tea," she said, leading him around a corner and down a dim stairwell. "Do you mind if we take tea in the kitchens?"

He nodded and followed her down. "My father sought to *employ* prostitutes," he said, filling the silence. "Not to rehabilitate them. It was a cornerstone of his reputation, actually. I believe he made it his goal to sleep with every whore in London. Such lady-loves were with him on the day he died. They allowed him to drown in three feet of water."

They reached the bottom of the stairwell, and she said, "I'm sorry, my lord."

"Don't be. Gladdest day of my life. But *he* is why I bemoan your work. Just selfish, I suppose. I've spent a lifetime trying to distance myself."

"I understand."

She didn't, he feared. "I cannot tell you how unsettling it was to see one—or two, or three—of them seated around the table at breakfast. How wrenching the ensuing fight between these women and my mother. Not that she was any more discerning. There were times when we barely had enough money for food, and she would return from London with new gowns and jewelry—luxuries that she could have only earned one way. 'Tis no different. I burned with shame over her exploits. It would be difficult to say, actually, which of my parents' proclivities humiliated me more."

She hovered on the bottom step. "Lives can be damaged in so many ways."

He smiled grimly, staring down at her, and she looked back with an expression so beautiful his heart lurched. Behind her, an empty kitchen glowed softly by the light of a dying fire. The bustle of girls and staff above stairs was a distant hum. They were alone.

"You'll forgive me if I find myself wondering why you could not deal in lepers, or prisoners, or lunatics? Some other exiled population."

"Too late for that, I'm afraid. The reality is, any money you give me will make a stir in the press. People will associate my work with you. We both know this is true. If you wish to avoid prostitutes because of some family history, well, then…"

"Elisabeth," he said, "I don't care about the charity prize. You may have the money, for all that."

"That's twice now you have offered me the money outright. I'm not sure how long I can politely refuse it."

"So don't."

"But you look so conflicted. I will not take what is unsettling to give."

"It's not the money. It's merely that this"—he gestured to the building above them—"endeavor of yours is unexpected, is all." He looked away and then back at her. "I hope you understand, Elisabeth. I would have you for myself."

"Ah, yes." A pause. "This again. Would it be ungracious to remind you that we've only just met?"

"Not ungracious, merely irrelevant." He dropped down a step. "I know what I want when I see it."

"Well, you cannot possibly want me," she whispered. "Not now. You've just said you want to distance yourself from…from…"

"Distancing myself from you is the very last thing I wish to do."

"Your reaction to my work is very clear—and understandable. I do not judge you."

He laughed. "You have only begun to know my reaction to you."

"But you cannot mean to *have me* in…er, one sense and deny this work in another. The two cannot not be separated." She licked her lips, and his gaze fell to her mouth.

"So I won't separate them."

"And besides"—her tongue touched her lip again—"I might not even fancy you."

"There is only one way to find out," he rasped, closing the distance between them. He dropped down the last step, leaned in, and kissed her.

She made a small gasp, a noise of surprise, and tension and, if he wasn't mistaken, anticipation. He smothered the sound, his lips slow and light at first, testing the fit. *Perfect.* No—better than perfect. What was better than perfect? So unbelievably better than he'd imagined, and he'd imagined quite a lot.

It was only meant to be a taste. Touch. Texture. Warmth. One kiss…two at most. He would not reach for her, and he balled his hands into fists.

Unhelpfully, she did not retreat. She tipped against the railing, reaching tentatively for his shoulder to steady herself.

He pulled back and stared into her sea-depth eyes, waiting for he knew not what.

The only sound was the rasp of her breath in and out, in and out.

She tipped her head, the smallest invitation, and he ducked to cover her mouth for another kiss—the last one—harder, deeper. Well, the *second*-to-last kiss.

But now the contact slowed, grew languid, one kiss melted into the next. He canted his head to deepen it. Her lips opened, ever so slightly, and she made another of the small gasps that he now viewed as an aphrodisiac and reward.

She pushed off the railing and went up on her toes, leaning against him, *falling* against him. He caught her, a reflex—a tightly wound, excruciatingly hopeful reflex for which he had been waiting for hours, for days, to perform.

He closed his arms around her, gathering her close. He'd wanted this since her aunt's balcony in the rain. She clung to him, and he felt every point of contact as surely as if she burned into him. When her tongue tentatively grazed his bottom lip, he groaned, lifting her against him. He pivoted, spinning them both, and backed her against the wall. *Leverage.* Something to push against. He raised his head to draw a ragged breath, and she reached for him, pulling him back to her mouth. He complied and pressed her back against the plaster.

The sweetness of the original kiss dissolved, replaced by something wilder. He took her face in his hands and angled her head, guiding the kiss. She gasped. He kissed her again, was rewarded again.

She was a dizzying mix of uncertainty and eagerness, her innocence as erotic as her enthusiasm. He lost count of the minutes, the kisses; he lost all conscious thought. Reality ebbed and flowed. His fingertips drifted to her hair, memorizing the texture, gently working free the wisps and curls. He left her mouth to trail kisses down her jaw to her ear and back again. She turned her head, offering herself up.

"This is madness," she said, turning her face to find his mouth again.

He descended on her lips. "Yes," he said between kisses, barely allowing time to breathe. "It was not my goal."

"I don't believe you."

He chuckled. "My fantasy, perhaps, but not my goal." He dipped to kiss her again, his hands falling from her face to her waist, wrenching himself closer, pressing her into the wall. She did not resist. God forgive them, she *surged*, pressing back.

She pulled away long enough to ask, "Why go to the trouble of asking for a proper courtship, only to come here and…?" She was breathless, the words coming out in a halting whisper.

"Because you *refused* my request to court you. This was the only way you would see me."

"So be it," she said, sighing.

"Oh, no." He chuckled, dipping down to her mouth again. "We must do it properly. Follow every rule."

"Too many rules," she mumbled.

More kisses. Her hands roved his biceps, his shoulders, his neck. She sank her fingers into his hair. It felt as if she would climb his body. He tried to laugh, but his mouth was occupied. Sound was swallowed by the next kiss.

Drawing a shaky breath, he pulled away and rested his forehead against hers. Their noses touched. When she blinked, her eyelashes batted his face.

"Lord Rainsleigh?" She tilted her head so that he was forced to pull back.

"I've asked you to call me Bryson." He slid his hands from her body and placed them on the wall, caging her in.

"My lord?" she began again and giggled. His heart lurched at the sound.

"I must know," she went on. "Are you truly not appalled by the nature of the work we do here?"

He narrowed his eyes. *Now* she would have him think? "I am appalled by *my* behavior here," he said. "With you."

"Now who changes the subject? It was only a kiss." She peered up at him.

He pushed off the wall and stepped away. "I hold myself to a higher standard, Elisabeth. I have to, if I intend to outrun the very low standard set by my parents."

"So very proper," she whispered. "Too proper?"

"There are kisses, and then there are *kisses*. This—as delectable as it was—is unacceptable. We are alone. I came here on an errand to support your charity; instead, I've had my way with you up against the kitchen wall. My God, it's like a bad novel." He tried again. "I have tried very hard to avoid reckless behavior. At the same time, I am intensely attracted to you, as you now see. That attraction is what concerns me. More than the nature of your work."

"Still not an answer, I'm afraid." She shoved off the wall.

He put his hands on his hips. "Does this charity give me pause? Yes. But not because of my delicate sensibilities. It is because I have spent my life endeavoring to distance myself from this particular *industry* and now, here it is, all tied up with you."

"It needn't be about me, my lord," she whispered.

"It is entirely about you." He stepped back to her.

"The courtship? But I have said no."

"And that is an answer I cannot accept."

"I am trying to win your money."

He leaned down to her ear and whispered, "I cannot imagine the others applicants being any more persuasive than you. You may have the money."

She rolled her eyes and shoved his shoulder. He grabbed her hand, holding it between them. The desire to kiss her again was so great it was painful not to lean in.

She stared at her hand in his. "This is wrong."

"Yes," he said, "but it can be made right. Let me call on you properly, Elisabeth. Let me take you to the opera. Let us ride in the park. Let us stay away from dark, empty kitchens." He paused, studying her. She did not deny him. "Let me consider the work you do here. Meanwhile, I'll show you that I am a gentleman. I was hoping it wouldn't come to this, but I'm afraid we will require a chaperone. I have learned of suitable candidate who might accompany us."

"Oh, God," she moaned, closing her eyes. She pulled her hand free. "I am too old for this. A chaperone? The opera?"

"Come now, Elisabeth. Are you ever too old for the opera?"

CHAPTER THIRTEEN

By all accounts, Miss Jocelyn Breedlowe was a poor candidate to serve as chaperone, and she knew it. At thirty-eight, she herself had never married. She had no particular training or experience in the comportment of young women. And although she denied it, even to her most suppliant, biddable self, she found frivolous, unearned entitlement to be a bore. And fewer souls were more frivolous and entitled than rich young ladies who aspired to land equally rich husbands with little more than pedigree and Papa's purse.

Despite all this, Jocelyn had chaperoned her first charge, Miss Piety Grey, in a brilliant love match—and with an earl, no less—and she remained close to that young woman, now the Countess of Falcondale, to this day.

But Jocelyn had not thought that Piety Grey was entitled. And Piety had never challenged Jocelyn's unmarried status. Their partnership had been a rare and fortunate thing.

Knowing this, she was reluctant to risk a second go. Employment was necessary to survive, of course, but she had her work as a paid companion to Lady Frinfrock. She had managed well enough, providing elder care, before her chaperoning of Miss Grey. As occupations went, it was steady and dependable, safe and familiar. She was proficient at it—beloved, in fact, by her former charges. Even Lady Frinfrock had grown to abide her.

So why take on chaperoning again? Why unpack her favorite hat and dress her hair? Why polish her shoes the day after a mud-strewing storm? Why knock on the door of a girl about whom she knew very little and invite every manner of the unknown?

One terrifying word.

More.

Jocelyn Breedlowe dared to want *more* than steady and dependable, safe and familiar. She'd tasted more in service to Piety Grey and, try as she might, she could not wash the taste from her lips. She wanted *more.*

"Hello," Jocelyn said, smiling pleasantly when the unmarked door in Moxon Street squeaked open just a crack. "Miss Jocelyn Breedlowe. Here to see Lady Elisabeth Hamilton-Baythes."

The woman in the doorway studied Jocelyn and then said, "I am Elisabeth Hamilton-Baythes."

But this was the same lady she had seen in Henrietta Place the week before, arriving at the viscount's house just as Jocelyn and Lady Frinfrock were taking their leave. She had been calling on Lord Rainsleigh—a young woman, alone—and the marchioness had not been impressed.

Well, if Jocelyn could say nothing else about the potential of this job, at least there was room to impress Lady Frinfrock (if anyone cared about that).

"How do you do?" Jocelyn went on. "I've come at the request of his lordship, Viscount Rainsleigh, to serve as possible chaperone." She raised her eyebrows expectantly.

"Oh, no," said Lady Elisabeth. "You're joking."

Jocelyn's smile went a little off. "*Ah...*forgive me, but—" She paused and tried again. "If I'm not mistaken, Lord Rainsleigh plans to call here at ten o'clock this morning. He suggested I should arrive a little early so that we might become acquainted. I'm sorry; did his lordship not discuss it?"

"Discuss it? Yes, I suppose he did," Lady Elisabeth said with a pained look, like a doctor had just imposed bed rest. "How silly of me to misconstrue his *discussion* as the way things would ultimately be. But please" —she peered right and left out the door, scanning the street—"do come in. Of course, you could not know."

Jocelyn smiled with a nod and slipped inside the cramped entry. There was no butler. In fact, there appeared to be no servants at all. Lady Elisabeth led the way, after giving Jocelyn a quick assessment, up and down.

Jocelyn applied the same quick once-over to the hallway, careful not to stare. The house was modest but tidy, certainly less opulent than she expected. It was no secret that the viscount was very rich, but she knew nothing about Lady Elisabeth.

"Mabel?" Lady Elisabeth called. "A *guest* has arrived. Come. Let us practice your greetings, if you please."

A plump adolescent girl with pretty brown eyes and a riot of curly blonde hair flounced from an adjacent room. Lady Elisabeth placed a hand on the girl's shoulder and said gently, "Mabel, this caller has just come in from the wet street. What would do we do to welcome her into the house?"

The girl nodded eagerly, swallowing hard. "My...but 'ow tall and thin you are, madam. You must be 'alf starved! Can we h'offer you refreshment?"

Jocelyn worked to keep her face neutral.

Lady Elisabeth cleared her throat. "Very generous, Mabel, but first let us offer to take her coat and umbrella, shall we?"

Mabel nodded her agreement and tried again. "Beggin' your pardon, madam. May I take your coat before we bring you something to eat?"

Jocelyn inclined her head graciously. "How kind. Thank you." She relinquished her coat. The girl took it, petting the soft wool.

Lady Elisabeth prompted. "And then should we bid her good morning and hang the coat? That's it. You've got it. Very good, thank you. You may return to your letters. I will call if we require tea."

"Oh, this one will surely be needin' tea, Lady E. Just look at 'er!"

"Fewer comments about the appearance of the guest, Mabel, may be in order. We would not want to say too much, would we?"

"Oh, but you could never say too much about bein' tall and thin, Lady E! Why, if I 'ad been that skinny, I could have gotten—"

"*That will be all*, Mabel," Lady Elisabeth cut in, winking at the girl and smoothing her hair over her shoulders. "Nicely done. Lovely."

The girl's eyes became huge and she nodded, turning to go. She'd only gone two steps before she reeled around, threw her arms around Lady Elisabeth's waist, and embraced her fiercely. Jocelyn blinked, unable to hide her surprise at the emotional display. Lady Elisabeth *oofed* at the force of the hold but seemed otherwise unalarmed. She patted the girl gently on the back and then whispered something in her ear. Jocelyn turned away to allow their exchange. Many admirable qualities presented themselves in that embrace. Lady Elisabeth was informal. She was gracious. Obviously, this young woman, whoever she was, regarded her very highly. Jocelyn stole a peek at them. As quickly as she had latched on, the girl drew away and hurried down the hall. Lady Elisabeth was a compassionate soul, then. Jocelyn had a weakness for compassion.

"This way if, if you please, Miss Breedlowe," Lady Elisabeth said, merging into a small cozy parlor. She did not invite her to sit.

"I hope you do not mind directness," Elisabeth began, turning to face her, "but I must lead with this: the very last thing I need is a chaperone."

Jocelyn nodded slowly, searching her repertoire of polite responses. There was naught but the truth. "I value your candor, my lady. But what—"

"Please call me Elisabeth."

Jocelyn laughed in spite of herself. "I beg your pardon," she said, bringing a hand to her mouth. "You've just reminded me of my last charge, now a dear friend. She had a penchant for given names."

"Well, titles won't be necessary, because the job is not necessary. I *am* sorry. I'm loath to put anyone out of work."

Jocelyn nodded. "I see. But you needn't worry—you have not impoverished me so much as surprised me. I...I had no idea you were not of the same mind as the viscount. He suggested that you were expecting his call—and, likewise, me."

"Oh, I know he is coming," Elisabeth said with a sigh, "just not on a personal call. We seem to be at odds over the designation of our…comings and goings."

"Quite so. I believe I saw—" She stopped, not wanting to accuse. She started again with a question. "Did I see you arrive at his house last week, as I was leaving with his neighbor, Lady Frinfrock?"

"Oh, right. That was you. But wait—" She made a horrified face. "Lady Frinfrock requires a chaperone?"

Jocelyn chuckled. "Er, no. I serve as a companion to the marchioness. I look after her health, keep her company—this sort of thing."

"Oh, God bless you. No wonder you seek work as a chaperone."

Jocelyn shook her head. "I don't seek employment so much as I was intrigued by the idea of change. I have only chaperoned one other young lady, and I quite enjoyed it. I have other pursuits. Please do not trouble yourself. I will not be made destitute if we don't suit. In fact, I was fully ready to decline my services, if you were too…too…" Jocelyn blinked, surprised that she'd revealed so much. She started again, "Let us say that you are none of the things that would drive me back to caring for those who are elderly. On the contrary, you are exactly the sort of young woman I should enjoy chaperoning, but I'll not stay if I am not required."

Elisabeth sighed. "Of course you would have to be lovely." She cocked her head. "Please"—she gestured, dropping into a chair—"Lord Rainsleigh has already called once, and now he's due back today. The problem with these visits is not that we have no chaperone; the problem is that these aren't *social calls*. He's not here to see me. If he is, he should not be. He was touring my foundation in consideration of a donation he may make. I called at his house in Henrietta Place for the same purpose. It's all very boring and official." She looked at Jocelyn, her expression imploring. She added, "This building is my charity foundation, a benevolence program for young women."

"I deduced there was some service to girls." Jocelyn settled on the near end of a couch.

"But there is *no* courtship." Elisabeth toyed with her hair. "We are not *courting*. He's wrong in this, but he will not be dissuaded. He is stubborn. Who knew he would be so stubborn?"

"I couldn't begin to—"

"The problem," Elisabeth continued, "is that he pretends to be in complete agreement with me—'tis not a social call—but then he goes and arranges for your service as chaperone. Either it is or it isn't. And it's *not*."

"Right," said Jocelyn cautiously. "I…I had no idea. I pride myself on discernment, but Lord Rainsleigh gave no clue of presumption or aggressiveness that would be, er, unwelcome. In fact, he approached me with the utmost regard for your reputation. Very adamant about it, he was. I assumed that you were the source of his concern—or your family."

Lady Elisabeth closed her eyes and shook her head.

Well, that settles it, Jocelyn thought. She took a deep breath and stood. "Clearly, if the viscount presumes too much, then indeed I am not required. But my lady? If I might be so bold as to suggest, it would be *your* responsibility, I'm afraid, to make this very clear to him. That is, if you do not wish to entertain him in this way—if you do not enjoy him…"

Lady Elisabeth looked up, and the expression on her face—the sudden blush, the bit lip, the wide eyes—told Jocelyn everything she needed to know about whether Elisabeth *enjoyed* the viscount or not.

Jocelyn sat back down. *Perhaps it's not settled.*

Elisabeth said quietly, "It doesn't matter if I enjoy him or not. He need not come here. What he needs is to *stay away*. This is the solution. He's come once already. He's seen the way I run the program. He's even promised the money. Why come again?"

"Oh, he's coming, I'm afraid. I heard him explain his devotion to his secretary when he took me on. If he does not have an earnest interest in your charity work, he may be using it as an excuse. He appeared very anxious to see you."

"Oh, God." Elisabeth stood up. "When did my charity become an excuse? Most people run from this charity, did you know?" She began to pace.

Jocelyn shook her head.

Lady Elisabeth continued. "You know who we serve? What we do here? I'm rehabilitating young women who were forced or fell into prostitution. You might as well know."

Jocelyn said calmly, "I suspected as much."

"Well, you're very astute."

"I am accustomed to observation."

"Right. Of course you are. Then, I suppose you've observed that I am thirty years old. That I run this foundation entirely on my own. That I am in the habit of near-complete independence. I live with my aunt, the Countess of Banning, and she and I are close, but she can't be bothered with playing governess to me—and thank God for that. We have our own rapport, and it suits us. My life would represent an exhausting challenge to any chaperone."

Jocelyn chuckled. "No one could be more exhausting than my last charge."

"Hmmm," Elisabeth said dismissively, still pacing. "How many girls have you spirited down the aisle, Miss Breedlowe? If you don't mind my asking? You seem rather young."

"Only one, in fact. My first charge was the neighbor of Lord Rainsleigh, Lady Falcondale—formerly Miss Piety Grey. They are abroad at the moment, away on a year-long trip, but they were friendly with the viscount before they left. Lord Rainsleigh is highly regarded by the earl, I believe. And my former charge, Lady Piety, seems to feel the same."

She paused, watching Elisabeth pace nervously around the small room. After a moment, Jocelyn continued. "It is accurate to say that I am not a *veteran* chaperone, Lady Elisabeth. And although Piety did *marry* Lord Falcondale, I had very little, if anything, to do with the union. It was their own complicated journey. I…I hope I do not offend you by revealing that I am not in the business of marrying off young women."

Lady Elisabeth made a scoffing noise. "Now you've endeared yourself to me even more."

Jocelyn smiled. "I am available to…support you, if you care for support. And to keep things properly done, which seems to be a priority for the viscount."

"It is the viscount's lofty priorities that I am trying to protect. By restricting his visits."

Jocelyn nodded. "The viscount does not strike me as a man easily restricted."

Elisabeth made a sound of frustration and dropped onto the couch next to her. "The viscount is a man *too* restricted. He is painfully aware of what other people assume. He suffered a difficult boyhood; his parents were far worse than neglectful. Now he tries to make up for their bad behavior by attaining perfection himself. Perfection is a very narrow path to travel."

"Undoubtedly."

"As much as I need his money, I am convinced that my charity is wrong for him. *I* am wrong for him."

"Forgive me if I suggest that he does not seem to think so."

"Yes," she said, and Jocelyn saw a sheen of tears in her eyes. "But he's got it wrong. He does…not…know."

"He does not know the nature of your charity?" Jocelyn prodded softly.

"No," she whispered. "He knows what we do here."

"Then what does he not know?"

She sniffled. "*Me.*" The word was barely audible. "Not genuinely. Honestly. I'm sorry; I've burdened you with far too much detail."

"Oh, I don't mind," said Jocelyn after a moment. "I've come all the way here. I might as well do some good before I go. Even if it is only to listen." She glanced at Elisabeth, who had closed her eyes. Elisabeth took a deep breath and laid her arm across her brow. She opened one eye and peeked at Jocelyn from beneath her sleeve.

This was another look Jocelyn knew. "If there is more to tell," Jocelyn said gently, "I should be happy to listen."

And then, while Jocelyn sat quietly beside her, Lady Elisabeth revealed to her a great personal secret. Speaking through some tears but more often in a flat, matter-of-fact tone, Lady Elisabeth informed Jocelyn of an unbelievable chapter of her own past—a past in which the viscount played an unwitting part.

When she was finished, they sat for many minutes in silence.

Finally, Elisabeth said, "He deserves an unsullied woman to make his wife. There are so few men about whom I could say this and mean it, but he is one of them."

"I wonder if it is fair to speak for him, my lady," Jocelyn ventured.

"Perhaps not. But I can speak for myself. I'm not sure I could put myself through the agony of saying the words to him. Of revealing it all to him. I'm not sure I could."

This admission hung in the air until it was dissolved by silence.

As with most things, there was a way it could be done. Elisabeth could find proper timing and courage and words. But Jocelyn would not invalidate her fear by trying to explain it away.

She put her hand on top of Elisabeth's and waited. When the younger woman spoke again, she implored Jocelyn to keep her confidence. "I cannot say what compelled me to burden you with it," Elisabeth said, leaning her head back. "We've only just met, and I tried to sack you before you'd even begun."

"I am honored that you trusted such a personal circumstance to me, and you may rest assured that I will tell no one."

Jocelyn paused. "I think, perhaps, it is the unknown, the anonymity of our first meeting that has allowed you to speak so freely."

"No," said Elisabeth, swallowing, "'tis you. I felt an immediate trust when you crossed my threshold. You took in the surroundings and showed absolutely no reaction. You were incredibly gracious with Mabel. I like you, Miss Breedlowe, and this is a rare thing indeed. There are very few people in London's established hierarchy that I actually like."

"But you like the viscount? The incredibly established viscount?"

Elisabeth dropped her head into her hands. "I'm behaving like a blathering, infantile ninny," she whispered. "Truly, I never cry. And I never enjoy anyone on first sight. *And I never cry*. And now look, all in the span of a morning. You should hear the atrocities endured by the girls who come into my care. *That* is the abuse that should bring tears to my eyes. These girls should be my only concern, but no. He has driven me to this. Oh, it was better before I met him, when I only just remembered him fondly." She closed her eyes and leaned her head against the heel of her hand, turning away.

Jocelyn put a gentle hand on her shoulder. "There is a particular strain of wretchedness that can come only from heartache."

"My aunt believes I should simply tell him. All of it. Immediately. That he will understand."

"And what do you think?"

"That I should remove myself from his life before he is ever the wiser."

Jocelyn raised one eyebrow.

Knock, knock, knock.

Both women jumped at sound from the door.

"He's here." Elisabeth stood, staring in the direction of the hallway.

Jocelyn rose beside her. "Likely. If you are not expecting anyone else."

Her eyes did not leave the door. She shook her head.

Jocelyn ventured, "My lady? Would you prefer I go?"

"No." A firm shake of the head. "Stay. Please." Elisabeth looked at her. "If you will. Unless it is more than you hoped to take on." She laughed without humor. "Well, of course it is that."

"On the contrary, my lady. 'Tis precisely what I had hoped to take on. 'Tis *more*."

Chapter Fourteen

With Jocelyn Breedlowe in place as chaperone, Rainsleigh wasted no time commencing the courtship. If Elisabeth did not agree to it in so many words…well, this did not keep the viscount from trying. Two days later, he asked her to dinner in his home, along with her aunt. Politely, she declined.

A day after that, he invited her to an evening at his box at the Adelphi Theatre for a performance of *The Magic Pipe*. Again, she sent her regrets.

Twice, he called on her at Denby House. Both times, he was uninvited, unexpected, and suspiciously close to tea. Thankfully, she was not home.

It pained her to decline him and not just because it was not her nature to be dismissive or introverted, but because she *wanted* to see him. They'd only just begun to learn each other, and there was so much more to know. He seemed to her a tightly wound clock—the minute hand was all tasteful propriety and the hour hand, stupendous wealth. The connected inner workings of the two fascinated and beguiled her. She found herself preoccupied by the thought of unwinding him.

And this thought brought her, always, back to the kiss. The feel of his large hands, fastening around her waist. The startling moment her tongue teased his bottom lip. The thrill of him deftly spinning her, backing her against the wall.

The memory haunted her at the most inopportune times, which was to say, all of the time. It swam in her consciousness as she tried to fall asleep. It broke the concentration in her quiet office while she endeavored to work. It lodged in her throat when Aunt Lillian asked her something, and she went sputtering, speechless, and blank. Like the village idiot. Like a woman possessed.

Never was it so apparent as on the journey from her office to Denby House at the end of each day, when she speculated on the contents of her aunt's silver calling-card tray. She wondered, with equal parts hope and trepidation, if his card would be there. She concocted a plausible excuse for any request that he might have made, all the while fighting off the fear that the tray would be empty.

Her aunt was little help, she of the round-the-clock cry of *Tell him*. Quincy agreed with her, as always. Stoker could not have cared less, as long as the discussion did not involve shipping him off to school.

It was Jocelyn, now woefully underused as a chaperone but, delightfully, a new friend who had taken to volunteering at the foundation, who offered the redeeming suggestion to which Elisabeth now clung: If she and Rainsleigh did not suit, then he never need know about their shared past. And the only way she would know if they suited was to spend time with the man.

They *must* interact, Jocelyn suggested, to know if Elisabeth's charity was too provocative or if he was too rigid to accept the terrible secret that she would, one day, be forced to tell him.

Guessing about it was neither fair nor accurate. They must know for sure.

To that end, she must give herself permission to accept some number of his courtship requests.

It seemed indulgent and cursory and too good to be true, but Elisabeth, God help her, embraced it and agreed to his very next call. He suggested a ride through Hyde Park, but Elisabeth countered with a request that they share a visit to the British Museum. Naturally, he would assume touring the exhibits and taking tea at the cafe, but Elisabeth had other plans.

If the purpose of spending time with the viscount was to determine their suitability, then she intended to deluge him with as many *unsuitable* aspects of her life as possible. Beginning with Stoker, who studied with his history tutor on Tuesdays at the museum.

Rainsleigh's regard for the boy and for Elisabeth's role in his life would be very telling, indeed.

"Do you have a mind for which exhibit you'd like to see?" Rainsleigh asked Elisabeth and Jocelyn, who accompanied them as chaperone. They mounted the great rise of stone steps to the museum entrance on the morning of this first official social call. "I haven't been to this museum in five years, at least."

Elisabeth kept her voice light. "Not *what* I wish to see, actually, but *whom*. I've brought you to the museum to meet a friend."

"A mummified pharaoh, perhaps?"

"No, although we might find my friend among the artifacts of Ancient Egypt. He is fascinated by that exhibit."

She felt him tense beside her. "Your friend is a gentleman?" The question, however nonchalant, sounded forced.

She shook her head. "No. A boy. Well, a young man, not yet eighteen. You've seen him before. I was lecturing him in the stairwell the night you attended Aunt Lillian's party. He's called Stoker."

Rainsleigh stopped walking. "A servant? We've come to the British Museum to call upon a servant?"

It was then that Miss Breedlowe asked to be excused to view the Mayan retrospective on beads and headdresses. Elisabeth encouraged her—they had tacitly agreed she might amble away if she could—and the chaperone hurried off.

Rainsleigh watched her scurry to an opposite hall, his expression unsure. Naturally, he was confused. Elisabeth couldn't blame him. Meeting a servant in the bowels of the dim, smoky British Museum was nothing like the ride in Hyde Park he had suggested. She suffered the first wave of doubt. Perhaps it would have been fairer to everyone to simply tell him that they didn't suit and refuse all offers.

There was little to do but put on a cheerful smile, gesture in the direction of Stoker's usual study spot, and lead the way. While they walked, she told him about Stoker and his life, beginning with his essential role in the foundation. She explained the number of girls he had rescued and his years of loyalty to her. Next she touched on his years of scholarship—his early interest in learning, her effort to teach him, and the eventual hiring of tutors. She and Aunt Lillian shared the cost of his education, she told him. Finally, she explained the university in Yorkshire that had accepted him as a student for the autumn term. The only omission was Elisabeth's initial meeting with the boy and why he'd sought out her, in particular. It was important to her to be honest and open in everything, except that very specific and painful intersection in their lives.

After she'd said this much, they wound their way through the dark, lantern-lit stairwell of the museum in silence. What more could she say? Hers was a narrative, she knew, that would send most noblemen sprinting to the door, likely laughing all the way. Rainsleigh was silent, but he remained.

"Ah yes, there they are," she finally said, closing in on a long polished table in a book-lined alcove adjacent to the hall on Ancient Rome, his tutor's preferred spot.

"Stoker enjoys Roman history most of all," she rattled on, more nervous now. "Until a few years ago, Mr. Bridges worked with him in Denby House. But the resources here are staggering." She called to the two bent figures at the table. "Hello, Mr. Bridges! Stoker? Look alive, if you please. I've brought someone to meet you. 'Tis a viscount, so you must employ your very best manners."

The duo pushed from their chairs and snatched hats from their heads. Mr. Bridges spouted his usual welcomes and how-do-you-dos. Stoker nodded and said nothing, staring at the floor.

"*Stoker*," intoned Elisabeth, "may I introduce his lordship, Viscount Rainsleigh. He is the gentleman who may donate the money we need to hire a whole cadre of men to work in your place when you go to school."

Stoker glanced up, studied the viscount, and then returned his stare to the floor.

Mr. Bridges scrubbed a chubby hand over his bald head and said, "Stoker still suffers from a few misgivings about the university, I'm afraid."

Elisabeth crossed her arms over her chest. "Stoker, I'd like you to look up, fix a pleasant expression on your face, and greet Viscount Rainsleigh. Then, I should like you to share with us your progress on the two things I've asked you to research since we last spoke."

Slowly, with the least amount of enthusiasm or free will, Stoker cocked his head and mumbled, "How do you do?"

"How do you do?" Rainsleigh repeated.

The youth nodded to his boots.

Elisabeth prompted, "And my two requests?"

Another shrug.

"There's a good lad, Jon, out with it," urged Mr. Bridges gently, nervously tapping a finger on the tabletop.

"It'll take *seven days* to reach Yorkshire," the boy finally recited. "And seven days to come back. But I haven't looked at the courses, so I can't say about the other." He looked up then, his face full of determined hurt.

"Stoker..." she began, but he moved away from the table and trudged to an adjacent glass box containing a crumbling artifact.

Elisabeth sighed deeply and followed, waving the tutor away. Stoker was not, by nature, a contrary boy—he *wanted* to please her—but he could not seem to accept this chance at a better life.

She rested her hand on the glass box beside him. "Are you anxious, Stoker, about being in school with the other boys? Is that it? Or is it the raids? Because you and I will devote the summer to selecting and training these new men."

"Not the same."

"True. It will not be the same. *You* will not be the same. You will be smarter and even more capable. Your world will grow. The raids will not be the same, but they will be sufficient."

There was more to say—about his fears, his commitment to saving more girls, about the life he might lead after a university education—but she took the very low road and implored him to accept the idea of school *for her.* As a *favor.* Out of loyalty to her.

It was a dirty trick but also the only argument she knew he would not dismiss. If she could begin with his compliance, even reluctantly, then she could slowly bring him around to viewing the school as gift instead of an obligation.

She took half a step back, resigned to leave him to sulk, when Rainsleigh appeared beside them, staring down into the glass cube at the filthy Roman whatever-it-was before them.

"A grave marker?" Rainsleigh asked, squinting in the lantern light.

Stoker looked at him. "It's a Curse Tablet from ancient Rome. And the stylus they used to write on it." He tapped the glass.

Rainsleigh nodded. "Curse Tablet?"

"A hank of soft lead. Shaped like a scroll. They wrote by bearing down with the stylus."

"The devil you say," whispered Rainsleigh, leaning in. "And we've got one here, from all these centuries ago?"

The interest engaged the boy. "Some of the script is still legible," Stoker told him. "See there? Carved into the surface."

"Hmmm. But why is it called Curse Tablet?"

"Used to record curses. That's what they believed."

"Rather rude of them, isn't it? Can the historians make out what this one said?"

Stoker shrugged. "Only a few figures are in Latin." He pointed to a squiggle. "The others are indistinguishable. An unknown script."

"You read Latin, do you?"

Stoker nodded without looking up.

Rainsleigh looked at Elisabeth. "Will you excuse us, my lady? Just a moment?"

Elisabeth blinked at him. She felt herself nod, and she drifted backward, standing beside Mr. Bridges, who tried in vain to make polite conversation. She only half replied, caught up instead with watching Rainsleigh's profile as he spoke to the boy. Stoker listened. What choice did he have? Although he did seem more relaxed. He stared at the viscount with wide eyes, watching him keenly. He nodded. Next, he asked a question. Rainsleigh answered and said something more. Listened again.

Five minutes passed. Stoker nodded and rubbed the back of his neck. Finally, Rainsleigh offered his hand. Stoker took it, and they shook. Rainsleigh nodded again and left him at the tablet. The viscount returned to her.

"Our intrusion keeps the boy from his studies, I fear," he said. "Carry on, if you will, Mr. Bridges." Then, holding out his arm to Elisabeth, he said, "My lady, should we locate Miss Breedlowe?"

Elisabeth eyed Stoker, now wandering beside the bookshelves. Mr. Bridges began thumbing through his book. She looked at Rainsleigh's proffered arm.

"Perhaps I should bid Stoker a proper farewell."

Stoker raised his hand across the room, an obvious dismissal. Elisabeth waved back. The boy didn't look.

"Very well," she said and took Rainsleigh's arm. "Thank you, Mr. Bridges. Do continue. My apologies for the interruption."

They left them, winding through the adjacent hall in silence. When they came to the first of several stairwells, she reached for the railing, and he allowed her arm to go free. It felt loose and wild by her side—ridiculous, as she'd spent thirty years without being led along by a man. When they reached the landing, she laced her fingers behind her back.

The silence continued. Another flight. A third. Finally, when she could not bear it, she said, "I would ask but one thing."

He laughed. "Only one? I will believe this when I hear it."

She allowed this, pressing on, "What do you think of our encouraging the boy? My aunt and I? Are we right to do it, in your view?"

He glanced at her. "I do not think you have done *wrong* by providing for him."

"What do you think of my bringing you here to meet him? Of course, your choice had been Hyde Park."

He glanced at her. "It introduces a...new perspective. There is one at every turn, with you."

They emerged on the second floor and entered the Greek wing, walking past eroded weapons, mounted fragments of aqueduct, and marble statues of armless nudes.

"It was foolish of me to suggest the park," he continued. "Ridiculous, really, looking back. My idea, if you can believe it, was to have my cook prepare a five-course meal and send it ahead with servants who would arrange a formal table in some soft, shady spot, with linens and china and crystal. There were to be footmen to serve us." He made a scoffing noise. "I sought to impress you as I would another woman, but I keep forgetting—you are not another woman."

"Indeed not, I'm afraid. But perhaps you would prefer a woman who would delight in uniformed servants in the park."

He said nothing.

"It's all right, really," she said. "If I'm being honest, few people have the patience or sensibility for…" She couldn't finish.

He shook his head. "I will not lie to you, Elisabeth. I have given my future a great deal of thought for many years. And when I envisioned my home and the woman who would be my partner in life, I saw a girl I would respect but not necessarily bother to know, not really. Not beyond her preference in furs and jewelry and our unified plan for presiding over the viscountcy. I could not envision…could not *fathom*…disappearing with her into the British Museum to encourage a young street boy about his university education."

Elisabeth nodded, her throat tight. "And you cannot bear it."

He looked down at her. "Would you like to know what I told your boy, Stoker?"

She stopped walking. She wanted this most of all.

"I told him that I had gone to university too."

"But of course you went to university." She laughed bitterly. Of all the obvious, unhelpful things to say.

"But also like Stoker, I did *not* board in secondary school before I went. I had no years at Eton, like my university classmates at Cambridge. I entered university after only having worked with the local vicar to guide me through my studies, learning on my own, much like Stoker. Actually with far less help than Stoker appears to have. There was no well-paid Mr. Bridges in my life, regrettably."

"He will appreciate this," said Elisabeth, relaxing. It was a useful thing to say, after all.

"He asked if I was prepared. For my studies at Cambridge, when I arrived."

"Please tell me you assured him," said Elisabeth. "He's a very clever boy. I have not seen his equal. But of course he will be prepared."

"I told him the reason I did not attend boarding school at Eton was because I was turned away. When I tried to enroll. A boy of thirteen."

Elisabeth took a step toward him. She had not expected this.

"Unlike Stoker," he went on, "I was eager—no, not eager, I was *desperate*—to escape the chaos in my parents' home and board in school. I longed for order and a routine and the possibility of a different future. The outside world was a mystery to me then, but I knew enough to know that, as the son of a viscount, even that wastrel like my father, I could begin Eton at age eleven or twelve.

"But my parents did not prepare me or enroll me, and they certainly did not deliver me. They didn't even mention the possibility, and they laughed when I asked them about it. So I discovered the schedule on my own, and I rode myself, on horseback, to the school. I arrived on the first day of the term with only a bedroll of meager possessions and my hat."

The museum behind Elisabeth dissolved as she listened to his revelation. She stepped closer still.

"Of course, I had not been officially registered and no tuition had been paid, but I tried to forge my way through the queue. It was far-fetched but not impossible, I suppose. But in the end, my absent application was not the problem. The problem was that even at age twelve, I could barely read or write. Arithmetic was entirely out of the question. All the other boys had had tutors from the earliest age. They spoke Latin and French. They were reading proper novels and solving geometry. If you knew my parents…" He shook his head. "They couldn't be bothered to provide my brother and me with meals in a timely manner, to put us to bed at night, to furnish winter coats. Tutors or even books were entirely out of the question. So I was turned away. Publicly. Scathingly. In front of the other boys and their parents. Sent home to 'study up.'"

He paused. Elisabeth waited, not daring to speak. She held her breath.

"Pitiful, isn't it?" He shot her an exasperated look. "But never fear. I've obviously learned to add two plus two."

"What happened?" A whisper.

"A young professor at the school overheard the incident and took pity on me. He discovered our address and sought me out, weeks later. I was mortified…belligerent and dismissive and rude. But I wanted it too much not to hear what he had to say. He explained to me what I would need to learn in order to apply again at the most remedial level. He could see by the disrepair of the house that paying for a tutor was out of the question, so he suggested that I find someone in the village willing to coach me…a vicar, perhaps.

"Looking back, I cannot believe I managed the shame and uncertainty of approaching the local vicar, but that tells you how desperate I was to succeed. He could have rejected me, too—certainly my parents were a bane to the villagers and tenant farmers of his flock—but he accepted my begrudging, terse cry for help, and we set to work."

Elisabeth whispered, "And you returned to Eton the next year."

He shook his head. "And I refused to go back to Eton, ever again. I resigned myself to forgo boarding school entirely, and I set my sights on university. This is what I told Stoker. He and I are the same in this. For me, it was Cambridge, but I have heard of this school in Yorkshire, and I assured him it is an excellent opportunity. One he would do well not to miss."

"And that he will be fully prepared? Did you assure him that you were ready by the time you went?"

Rainsleigh nodded grimly. "I was ready, and, if what you say is true, so will be Stoker. In my case, the vicar worked with me until I surpassed his knowledge. After that, I taught myself. And when the time came, and I finally arrived at Cambridge, I was ready. In some areas, I had already mastered the coursework."

"Thank you," she whispered. It was difficult to speak around the lump in her throat. "So you aren't regretful?" She ventured, finally. "About the park?"

He looked around again. "No, I do not regret the park, Elisabeth. It's simply…different. More."

"Too much?"

"No." He slowly shook his head. "Not too much."

His slow, quiet words seemed to shoot straight through her very soul, and she was propelled, quite literally propelled, to touch him. She leapt—no, not a leap, a lunge—straight for his chest.

He opened his arms at the last moment, and she fell against him with a short cry. She wrapped her arms around him and pressed her face against his chest. She wanted to feel the beat of his heart. She wanted to touch his heart.

"*Oof*," he said, and for a moment, he held his arms away. She thought he would decline the embrace, but slowly…tentatively…as if uncertain of his right, he settled his arms around her, securing her against him. She looked up, unable to hide the tears in her eyes.

"I will not have you pity me, Elisabeth," he said, his voice low. "It's…it's not a story I share easily."

Her answer was to rise up and kiss him. For this, he did not hesitate. His lips met hers more than halfway. He set the pace, reminding her of all things he'd taught her the week before. Within seconds, the kiss alone was insufficient, and he scraped his mouth across her cheek to her ear. He whispered her name, a plea, and she gasped in response. He moved lower, kissing her jaw, the expanse of her throat. She dropped her head back, inviting it all, tightening her hold on his shoulders as if she'd fall if she didn't cling to him.

"I tell you these things because the bloody picnic was…shortsighted," he rasped. "I am out of my depth."

"Good," she said on a breath, seeking his mouth, digging her fingers into his hair and then trailing her hands down his neck. She toyed with his collar, fingers working their way beneath. His cravat was in the way, but she continued to search, wanting warm skin, wanting *him*.

He growled and yanked the cravat free. He found her hand and flattened it over the exposed skin at the throat of his shirt. She thrilled at this, reveling in the hard muscle, the furl of hair, the hot skin.

"Elisabeth," he hissed, roving over her shoulders, arms, back, massaging his hands into the curve of her waist and then dipping lower still, gathering her bottom in his palms to press her against him.

A moan escaped her, and she felt herself push back. The pressure was both a relief and wildly insufficient. She pressed again.

Rainsleigh made a growling sound and tore his mouth from hers long enough to look around the empty exhibit hall.

"Wrap your arms around my neck," he rasped in her ear, and she complied. With the cravat gone, she could explore the skin of his shoulders beneath the collar of his shirt.

He lowered his head, kissing the expanse of breast above her neckline, and then bent down and scooped her up. She wrapped her legs around his waist without instruction.

While a new kiss blazed, he carried her between a giant stone urn and a naked statue to a small anteroom lined with glass display cases of ancient coins. There was a bench in the room, and he collapsed the two of them on it.

Oh, yes, that is better, she thought.

"You shatter my self-control," he panted.

She opened her mouth to defend herself, but she couldn't speak.

He scooped her close, tracing his hand down her leg to locate her ankle. "God, help me, Elisabeth," he moaned. "This is madness."

She hitched up her leg, and he found the hem of her skirt. His hand was beneath it in an instant, covering her slipper and inching upward…ankle, leg, knee. He rubbed, smoothing his hand up and down, going higher each time, nearly to the end of her stockings. Elisabeth stifled a cry, snuggling closer, cinching her legs more tightly around his waist.

Without warning, footsteps, distant but rapid, clattered through their pleasured oblivion. They froze. Two sets of feet by the sound of it, marching through the exhibit hall beyond.

Rainsleigh swore and scrambled to disentangle his hand from her leg, to set her off him, to stand up. It happened so fast, Elisabeth almost tipped over. He reached a hand out to steady her, leaning in the other direction to retrieve his cravat. She blinked and grabbed a display case for balance. "I have it," she whispered, breathing hard. It was only half untrue. She had hold of the case but not steady breath, or rational thought, or the desire to stop.

"Where the devil is Miss Breedlowe?" Rainsleigh said lowly, whipping his cravat until it unfurled and then stuffing it around his neck.

Still dazed, Elisabeth said, "Likely she would have preferred the picnic." She forced her hands to work, smoothing her skirt, straightening her bodice. She patted her hair; the pins were either barely hanging on or lost forever. Loose curls spilled down her back.

"We cannot let this happen," he said, jerking his cravat this way and that. "Not again."

The footsteps slowed, stopped, and then started again. He went still; and they listened. "We're in a public museum, for God's sake."

He looked up for her reaction, and she raised one eyebrow. *What's a girl to do?*

He growled, leaned in, kissed her again, hard and fast, and then grabbed her hand.

"This was my fault," she whispered, allowing him to tug her along. "I was overcome."

He stopped at the coin-room door and peered right and left, scanning the exhibit hall. "All the nude statues, no doubt," he said distractedly.

"It was *you*."

His head shot up, and he turned back to her, pulling the two of them out of the sight of the door. Grabbing her by the arms, he pushed her back against the wall. "We will find the bloody chaperone. *Now*. And you cease provocative declarations. I can only resist so much."

"I merely said, 'it was you,'" she whispered tartly.

His eyes, already hot-blue with passion, dropped, heavy lidded. He leaned in. She thought he would kiss her again, and she turned up her face. Instead, he put his mouth to her ear and growled, "And I merely put my hand up your skirt. I would have taken you right here, in a public building, with patrons and staff and bloody school children walking through. Do not push me, Elisabeth. My God—*please*. Have mercy."

She couldn't speak. The proximity of his lips, his voice in her ear, his body pressing against hers. She would have allowed it—she would have *hastened* it. Her body was on fire with need.

He stepped back, releasing her, pulling her from the wall and out the door. As they hurried along, he rolled his shoulders and stretched his neck. When they were in plain view, he yanked her forward, transferring her hand to his arm. He let out a long, slow breath. He slowed down, walking at an amble. Without looking at her, he led her to the stairwell in the far corner. Beside a crumbling pillar, two scholarly young men scribbled notes. They raised their heads and tipped their hats. Elisabeth smiled.

"You asked me, Elisabeth, if I could bear it—bear *you*," he said in the stairwell.

"Did I?" Her brain had shut down. She floated beside him.

"I assume you're referring to your charitable leanings and your progressiveness?"

"That's not at how I see myself. I simply meant…me. All of me."

He nodded, not looking at her. "I should like to be very clear. I have wanted you since the first moment I saw you. This, I think, has never been so clear. The answer is, *I can bear you.*"

She took in a shaky breath.

"Really, there are only *two* things I cannot bear," he went on, pulling her along. "You've just heard that rejection came very early and very harshly to me. Since boyhood, it has followed me, in some form or another, everywhere I go. When you will not see me, I assume more of the same. If we do not get on," he said, "so be it. But if you enjoy my company and have no other conflict, I…I do not like to *guess* at your affection."

She nodded. "I was rude with my excuses this week."

They walked a moment more, nearly to the main stair that descended into the lobby. "But what is the other? The second thing?"

Rainsleigh made a dismissive noise. "Oh, but the second thing is a trifle. A direct result of my own mother, I'm afraid—a woman I hope you never have the misfortune of meeting. She lives in my villa in Spain, thank God. Really, it's nothing that you have to worry about." He smiled grimly and led her down the lobby steps.

"Because…"

He chuckled. "Because 'tis chastity—my second priority. Although I feel silly mentioning it to you. Of course you are." He rolled his neck. "You remember the story I told you about my attempt to attend school? I omitted one thing. It's not important, really, and it's so utterly shameful, even now. But I suppose it applies. When the instructor from Eton called on our home after I had been turned away, he met with me, as I said. But when he was finished…" He paused on the bottom step. "*But when he was finished*—I'll never forget it—my mother stumbled upon us, and she seduced him. She lured him upstairs to her bedroom, just as I was bidding him good-bye. It was…" He shook his head, unable to finish. "So there you have it," he said. "After a lifetime of disgrace, debauchery, and lies, I want faithfulness and purity and honesty. Above all."

Elisabeth nodded, but the world around her went suddenly, starkly bright. Too bright. She could see every step, every crack in the stone, every sharp edge.

"To keep both of us safe from temptation," he said, "we shall have to insist upon Miss Breedlowe's vigilance. Ah, but look. There she is."

Elisabeth saw Jocelyn, felt herself take the steps across the lobby, but in her mind, she was suddenly still. In her mind, he strode off without her. A mile of cold marble stretched between them. She felt its hardness through the soles of her shoes. She was in a distant place—her very own museum. She saw the brothel, the highwaymen, Aunt Lillian's face when she opened the door to her so long ago. She heard Rainsleigh's words— *purity and honesty*—and she tried to square them with what she had, for so long, regarded as her own great shame.

Was she pure?

Oh, she was innocent of what had happened to her; this she knew. But did this diminish how she had emerged from the ordeal? Was she dishonest to withhold the circumstance from him? Even if it was all wrapped up in her deepest, most private shame?

She tried to blame him for making purity a condition of his devotion, but she could not. He had suffered his own trauma due to his parents' behavior. Who knew the depth of the abuse he had endured. He wanted someone fresh and clean. Perhaps it was wrong, but she wanted that for him.

She wanted it for him, almost as much as she wanted him for herself.

When they converged on Miss Breedlowe, she did not ask where they had been or why Elisabeth's hair had eroded into loose clumps of unfurled bun, trailing down her back. She begged fatigue, and they returned to the carriage.

"Are you...well?" he asked softly against her temple as he lifted her from the carriage in front of Denby House. "You are uncharacteristically quiet. I worry the...Greek exhibit unsettled you."

She avoided his eyes and scrambled for something to say.

He went on, his head bent beside hers, his voice barely audible. "I would die before I would dishonor you."

"I am well, Rainsleigh," she assured him, smiling up. "'Twas a lovely outing. Thank you. Do not worry about me. I quite liked the Greeks."

He studied her, and she forced herself to increase her smile. With some work, she added a knowing look.

"Very well, then," he finally said, stepping back. "If you're certain."

"Quite certain," she said, making up her mind. She would tell him. Not today. Not tomorrow. But soon.

Chapter Fifteen

Elisabeth had emerged from the museum on Tuesday with a vague, somber sort of quietness. She did not explain it, and Jocelyn did not press, but from that day forward, Elisabeth welcomed each of the viscount's calls. And, oh, how they came, swift and successive, some just days apart. Dinners, the theatre, rides through the park at the most fashionable time of day. Still, it was all very public and proper—so proper, in fact, Jocelyn made a point to detour frequently, tarry purposefully, and generally require a few moments more— *no, no, do go ahead without me*—at every footbridge or flower stall.

Unfortunately, the viscount allowed for little time alone. He was very clear. Impropriety must never be breeched. Any intimacy at all, it seemed, was entirely out of the question. Even at the close of a visit, when they returned to Denby House for tea, Jocelyn was always to be nearby.

She was a poor chaperone, indeed, to find fault in this, but could they not enjoy five sincere minutes alone? Even with Lady Banning in the next room? Even with servants in and out?

No time alone meant no time to be honest. Even so, Elisabeth declared—firmly, breathlessly after each outing—that she would tell him about their shared past, and very soon. But the declaration, somehow, never seemed to come.

On one call, Rainsleigh drove them across London to Blackwall, on the banks of the River Thames, for a tour of his expansive company, Courtland Ironworks and Shipping.

The weather was fine that day; even the filthy Thames seemed to sparkle, and Jocelyn and Elisabeth walked beside the viscount, taking in the massive construction yard in awed silence. Oxen-drawn wagons and carts rolled to and fro, pulling massive lumber masts, stacks of steel beams, and iron parts. Warehouses, as long as a city block, lined one side of the main thoroughfare. Coal, timber, iron, rope, and chain were cordoned off in pallets or coils in lots between each building. And before them, at the end of the wharf, was the swirling confluence of the Thames and what the viscount explained was Bow Creek, a direct route for Rainsleigh's ships to reach the sea.

Beside the water, a brittle web of scaffolding held the frameworks of three embryonic ships, their shape just distinguishable through a network of ladders and platforms. They rose to such heights—docked dry, high above the water—Elisabeth and Jocelyn had to squint and shade their eyes to see the tops. Jocelyn could not help but exclaim over the majestic sight of it. Elisabeth, too, was stunned, pointing and asking questions, amazed at the magnitude of Rainsleigh's work.

The viscount, Jocelyn observed, was much transformed inside his bustling empire: a quieter, more modest version of his usual self. He walked slowly behind the women, saying as little as possible, glossing over details about which another man would boast. Unless prompted by his portly secretary, he did not mention the staggering value of the ships or the amount of land and waterfront occupied by the operation, which was a little city unto itself.

"That will do, Dunhip," the viscount would say after his secretary had given an extended explanation of the scope and scale of any of Rainsleigh's endeavors.

Elisabeth took it all in with silent wonder, watching Rainsleigh as much as she watched whatever notable landmark his secretary pointed out. Jocelyn wondered how the obvious wealth, generally of so little interest to Elisabeth, would impress her. Two hours later, she had her answer.

"I should like to return to Rainsleigh's shipyard as soon as we can," Elisabeth told her after the viscount had returned them home. She lay back on the settee in the Denby House green salon, her arm thrown over her eyes. "Wasn't it the most remarkable place? I knew Rainsleigh was successful, but truly one must see it to believe. Ha! If only the old biddies who preside over the *haute ton* could see it. They would fall all over themselves to revere him, rather than forcing him to prove himself again and again."

"Yes and how modest the viscount was. He will not suggest a return trip, I dare say. You will have to ask this. But what will be your reason?"

"I'll return to arrange work for my girls. A new source of employment for them after they leave the foundation. They could sew sails. They could sweep warehouses. There is so much work that a diligent woman could do. Endless possibilities. I don't know why I had not thought of it before."

"You believe the viscount would welcome former prostitutes to work among all of those burly shipyard men?"

"They are not prostitutes when they leave me," Elisabeth reminded her.

"Yes, I know, but will Rainsleigh? Will his foremen and ship builder? That portly secretary seems very particular, indeed."

Elisabeth shrugged. "Yes. Perhaps you are right. This is uncertain. Maybe I am mistaken—blinded by my affections for the viscount, or stupid with hope—but everything I learn about him tells me that he is open. He is willing to help. He is generous, not simply with money but of spirit. He knows forgiveness. He can be made to see the mutual value of it."

Jocelyn cleared her throat. "Made to see the innocence of your shared past, Elisabeth? Perhaps that too?"

Elisabeth made a face and dropped her arm over her eyes.

Jocelyn continued gently. "If Rainsleigh is so open and forgiving, then perhaps the time has come. You know that my original suggestion was to see the viscount once or twice. Just enough to see if the two of you 'got on.' By now I believe that it has been established that you suit." Jocelyn stood up and crossed to her, looking down. Elisabeth closed her eyes, saying nothing.

Jocelyn continued softly. "Tell me some plan, Elisabeth. A vision. A schedule for the way you will manage it. To delay much longer will only make the revelation more complicated for you both. If he is all the things you believe, then *now* is that time."

Elisabeth spoke to the ceiling. "I have indulged myself. It's been like a dream." She looked at Jocelyn. "I... I don't want it to end."

Jocelyn nodded. "I cannot say for sure, Elisabeth, but I would be shocked—*shocked*—if your honesty brought about an 'end.' Of course you mustn't deceive yourself that it will be easy. *You* will be the one who has to say the words. Unless I am mistaken, his reaction will only soften the blow. It will be difficult, but it *can* be done. Isn't this what you tell the girls who come to you? That their past experiences do not dictate who they are or who they can become? If you believe this to be true, then you may tell the viscount without guilt or shame, because what happened to you fifteen years ago is *not* 'you.' The genuine 'you' is a woman he would be proud to call his wife—a woman that he shall want, regardless."

Elisabeth dropped the back of her hand to her cheek, swiping a tear. "You're right, of course," she declared. "I am going to tell him. Right away."

"Tomorrow?"

"No, no, not tomorrow." She sat up. "Tomorrow is Lady Whomever's dreadful ball."

"Oh, yes. Lady St. Clare. Indeed. Your first ball together."

Elisabeth nodded. According to Rainsleigh, a baroness, Lady St. Clare, held an annual 'do' the first weekend in June. He and his brother had been invited—their first formal invitation to a large society function. Rainsleigh had requested that she attend as his guest. Thankfully, Jocelyn was excused from this particular event, as Lady Banning would also attend and serve as chaperone.

"Aunt Lillian is delighted that we'll finally appear out together," said Elisabeth, "so of course, it will be more overblown than it would normally be. I can't possibly tell him then. Also, you won't even be there to support me. There's far too much going on tomorrow night to have the discussion *then*."

"Right," hedged Jocelyn.

Elisabeth continued, protesting far too much. "I would cry ill for the ball, I detest them so, but seeing Rainsleigh's shipyard today...seeing how he *deserves* to be among society, if that is what he wishes, of course I must go. If we carry on as we have, the future will bring more and more of these things, I'm afraid." She stared off into the distance. "Perhaps it will not be so bad—with Rainsleigh there." She smiled beseechingly at Jocelyn.

"No," she finished, "a trumped-up ball is hardly the proper setting for this discussion. I won't complicate a special night with my great, dark, momentous secret. I'll do it..." She faltered, looked at her hands, and then finished, "The day *after* tomorrow. On Sunday. I will ask him for tea with the express purpose of telling him. Then we'll know." She nodded. "Then it will all be over."

"Or then," countered Jocelyn with a wink, "it will truly all begin."

CHAPTER SIXTEEN

Elisabeth dressed for the St. Clare ball with a zeal and spirit that surprised even herself. She hummed as Bea laced her into a gown of green apple silk. She collaborated on the style of her hair—long, loose curls down her back. She was entirely ready, drifting around the parlor, enduring Quincy's good-natured teasing, long before Aunt Lillian swept down the stairs in her iridescent marvel of indigo-colored ruffle and flounce.

Elisabeth laughed off the suggestion of her eagerness, but of course it was true. She *was* eager. For all of her teasing about Aunt Lillian's social whirl, Elisabeth did not work so hard or sympathize with the downtrodden so stridently that she did not wish to have friends. She longed for diversion and a nice glass of wine just as much as anyone else. And, well, if Rainsleigh was amenable to a turn around the dance floor, all the better.

For so many years, she had been almost entirely alone—surrounded by girls, and staff, and street boys, yes—but except for Aunt Lillian and Quincy, otherwise *alone*. It had been a perfectly adequate way to live, really. And then, *he* entered her life. He was, she thought, the very best version of not being alone. Her feelings for him expanded every day— one part attraction and desire, another part engagement and respect.

She felt it when he strode into a room and she saw him for the first time on any given day. When he placed his large hand on the small of her back to usher her around two men quarreling on the pavement. When they poured over the newspaper together and debated the issues of the day. When she read to him, and he listened quietly, staring at her as if, on every page, she read his name. When he effortlessly lifted her down from her horse.

The thrill of it thrummed through her, and for some time after each contact, she floated.

Naturally, Lillian said she was falling in love, but Lillian felt that everyone was falling in love. She was ruled by her love of Quincy, and everyone else was pinned somewhere on the same romantic spectrum.

Love? Elisabeth could not yet say.

Every hour they spent together, she felt herself listing in what was surely this direction. But listing was one thing, falling was quite another. And only when Rainsleigh knew the truth and responded with compassion would she allow herself to fall. His response would prove the ultimate test. She needed only her own courage to tell him and to hear his response.

She speculated on this as her aunt's carriage wound its way through London to the St. Clare ball. What would it be like to love him in earnest?

"You are positively glowing tonight, Aunt," Elisabeth said, trying to distract herself. "How delighted you must be that we will finally embark on your favorite pastime together."

"But what favorite pastime?" said the countess. "Of course I am delighted that we are together. Don't think I haven't noticed that I've been thrown over by that chaperone of yours. Lovely woman. A touch on the thin side, God save her, but lovely. Still, she has usurped my role in this courtship."

"Count yourself lucky to be free from following me around." Elisabeth chuckled. "But I was speaking of the party. I know you adore nothing more than a lovely ball. This is why Rainsleigh hired Miss Breedlowe in the first place. You are too busy to play chaperone."

Lillian waved the notion away. "A ball? 'Twill be tolerable, I suppose. There are far worse ways to pass an evening, but it is all part of the fiction."

Elisabeth screwed up her face. "What fiction?"

"Oh, maintaining a distracting, predictable facade. Secluding this 'double life' that I lead." She laughed. "No spirited society matron, seen out every night, could possibly be carrying in on in secret with her gardener."

"Quite so." Elisabeth chuckled, a little less sure. "How ironic. All these years, I thought the 'double life' *allowed you* the freedom to indulge your love of parties. I thought you wanted to hide your relationship with Quincy so you could carry on being the spirited society matron."

Lillian held her head at an odd angle to protect her coiffeur from the stiff carriage seat. "Well, no, Elisabeth," she said, all laughter gone, "but if this is what you think, then I must be doing a very good job, indeed. Egad, how I must seem to you. Flitting around town as countess whilst Quincy stays at home alone, unable to make me his wife. Unable to be seen by my side without a trowel in his hand."

Elisabeth blinked, staring at her. An unaccustomed crescent of guilt began to puff up in her gut. "But of course I have nothing but respect and love for you, Aunt Lilly. And I know you love Quincy very much. I...I suppose I did not think about it all. A candlelit ballroom is such a natural setting for your great beauty and wit. I thought you both wanted this. If you marry Quincy, you will no longer be the Countess of Banning. To remain a countess is important, I know—for you. Above all else."

"No. What is important above all else, darling, is for *you* to have every advantage."

"*Me?*" Elisabeth tried to laugh. "But..."

Lillian stared at her a moment more, considering, and then she shrugged, smiling warmly and relaxing against the seat, sacrificing her hair. "If you thought I preferred being a countess to being with my Quincy, then you are very wrong indeed. We wanted you to have all the time in the world, and we worked very hard not to let on. Even now, I want you to do everything in your own time and way. But considering how well things have gone with Rainsleigh, a splendid match might be just around the corner, I think. You might as well know."

"*Lillian*," Elisabeth's voice shook. "I might as well know *what?*"

"Truly? You had no idea?"

"No idea about what? I haven't the slightest idea what you're talking about. I only meant to make conversation, acknowledging your love for parties."

"Oh, darling. My love for parties? But don't you see? If I am seen out, happy, active, popular—no one will guess. When you are settled, well, the charade may end. Quincy and I will quietly slip away. Simply, 'the Lady Banning has remarried. She relinquishes her title and has sailed from England with her new husband. Bound for the tropics.' Somewhere warm and sunny has always been our dream." She winked at Elisabeth. "In time, we will get there."

"Lillian"—Elisabeth struggled, suspecting the answer, dreading the answer—"are you meaning to say that the *only* reason you have remained in London, living life as a countess, is for me?"

Lillian cocked her head. "Come now, Elisabeth."

"But why? Surely I have not detained you *fifteen years?*"

Elisabeth thought back, her mind a whirl. She had learned of her aunt's secret relationship with the gardener slowly over time, in the weeks and months after she turned up at Lillian's door. She'd accepted it from the start and happily took on their deeply guarded secret. But never once had she considered the cost to them. In the beginning, she'd been too wrapped up in her own pain. After that, it simply *was.*

Oh, God, the sacrifice…

Lillian shook her head. "In no way did you detain us. We are very happy, as you can plainly see. Eventually, we will go. Soon, perhaps, if your affiliation with the viscount continues on course, and I suspect it will. For now, I would not dream of scandalizing and, let us be honest, *ruining* you. I cannot traipse off to a tropical island with the gardener. If we did this, your reputation would never recover."

"My reputation?" Elisabeth said, her voice far too loud in the closed carriage. "But what care have I for my reputation? Especially if it is keeping you and Quincy from your life together. Oh, but this is awful. I had no idea. Lillian! I'm so sorry. The sacrifice the two of you have made…"

"There has been no sacrifice, and you should never speak of it in that way. You are like a daughter to me, and I love you with all of my heart. Quincy too. Everything we have done has been out of love. It has been our own choice."

"My God," said Elisabeth, strangled. "You might have had *children* if you'd married and moved away."

"Stop. And what would I want with a baby to make me fat when I had a delightful, full-grown girl in you? Besides, Quincy and I do not suffer. We carry on behind the walls of Denby House exactly as we please. Eventually, we will realize our next dream. But for now, *you* are our dream."

Elisabeth fell back against the carriage seat. "I shall never be able to repay you," she whispered. "So many lives were forever changed that night. So many."

"Oh, my dear, you're viewing this in entirely the wrong light." Lillian tsked, fluffing her hair. "What I would not give to have my brother and your dear mama here with us, hale and hearty, but I could not have been more blessed to raise you in their stead. It has been an honor. And it is not over yet. Ah, but look, here we are. Let us not tarry. No frowning or sad eyes at a ball, if you please—that's no way to snare a viscount."

"How can you bid me to smile after all you've just revealed?"

"My revelation is entirely out of your control. Now, if you wish to bring Quincy's and my love into the light of day, then sew up this brilliant match with Rainsleigh, and we'll be half-way there. But it shall never happen with that tearful expression! There we go; there's a good girl. Lovely. You chose well, picking the green dress instead of the fawn. Not every girl could pull it off, but it looks stunning on you. Especially when you *smile*." She rapped on the window of the carriage door. "Do hurry," she called to the groom, "the static in this carriage seat is spoiling my hair."

Elisabeth descended the ballroom steps in a fog.

And *now* she was meant to be jovial? To smile and make conversation with new friends? To enjoy the food and wine and dance? What once seemed frivolous and leisurely now seemed urgent and pressing. The ball *must* be tolerable—the first of many tolerable balls she would endure as Rainsleigh's wife. Her strong feelings for him *must* remain strong—nay, they must soar.

And, above all, she must tell him. Now. Tonight. And he must take her great secret to heart and accept it, and he must be understanding and sympathetic. And then they must marry, sooner rather than later.

After that, he must take in stride the fact that his aunt-in-law is no longer the esteemed Countess of Banning but rather Lillian Greene, runaway newlywed, most recently of the British West Indies or Timbuktu.

Dear Lord.

As if meeting the man again, concealing their courtship, and then forcing herself to tell him her deepest, most hateful secret were not enough. Now was the pressure of Lillian's long-delayed happiness, and after that, the ramifications of what would be said when a countess married her gardener.

The venue for the ball, another sprawling Mayfair townhome, was like every other ball Elisabeth had been compelled to attend over the years. Admittedly, she had been to very few, but they always appeared to the same: Crowded, noisy, warm.

It made no difference. Tonight she would dance for her life—or Lilly's life. The sacrifice her aunt had made, not to mention Elisabeth's own, self-involved blindness to it, propelled her. She squinted in the uneven light of five hundred candles, searching the crush of color and silk for Rainsleigh. Aunt Lillian had been immediately swept away by friends and admirers. She'd suggested they circulate together, but Elisabeth sent her on. Lilly's social pantomime would be harder to watch, now that she knew the truth. She needed space and air; she needed—

Rainsleigh.

She saw him standing, tall and resplendent in evening finery, near the bright fire of a large hearth across the room. Her breath caught, and a swarm of butterflies launched in her stomach. She looked away. She forced herself to take a deep breath and to smile as she released it. Perhaps she *was* in love with him.

He spoke to his brother, a casually propped elbow on the mantel, his other hand in his pocket. He looked every inch lord of this incredibly over-bunted, flower-laden ballroom, of these finely dressed people, of this fine house—of the whole world.

But now his brother was pulled away, and Rainsleigh turned in her direction. Their eyes locked. The butterflies converged for a swooping flip.

He inclined his head. A slight, regal nod. She did not wish to be coy, but she would not grin. Or sprint to his side. With some effort, she slowly inclined her own head. A return nod.

"Lady Elisabeth?"

Grateful for a reason to look away, if only for a moment, she turned at the sound of her name. A young woman side-stepped a footman carrying a chair to hop beside her. She extended her hand, smiling brightly.

"Lady Elisabeth?" she repeated. "Forgive my impatience, but I must meet you. You don't know me—not yet—I am Piety, Lady Falcondale, Lord Rainsleigh's neighbor! Next door in Henrietta Place?"

"Lady Falcondale. How do you do?" Elisabeth smiled uncertainly. "Our mutual friend, Miss Breedlowe, has told me so much about you, including that you were newly back in town. Welcome home. But I had no idea to expect you at this ball. What a pleasant surprise."

Of course, Piety would be young, but Elisabeth had not expected her to be so beautiful. Or effusive. She wore a loose-fitting gown that did little to hide her obvious pregnancy.

"Oh, well, Jocelyn will confirm that I am full of surprises," Piety enthused, her honey-blonde curls bouncing as she pumped Elisabeth's hand. Her frank American accent grew more obvious with each proclamation. "I've bribed my husband to come because it may be the last such 'do' I am able to attend for quite some time." She patted her swollen belly. "He loathes this sort of thing, but I wanted to see for myself. We set sail so soon after I became a countess, I never had the opportunity to attend a proper ball before tonight."

"Oh," said Elisabeth weakly, looking around. "Well, if you've been to one of them, you've been to them all. But do not let me spoil it for you. Rainsleigh, too, looked forward to this night. I am trying to put on a brave face for him."

Piety chuckled and snatched up Elisabeth's other hand. "A brave face—ha! But you are stunning! Rainsleigh did not exaggerate."

"The viscount, er, described me?"

She nodded cheerfully. "Well, he told Trevor, who told me." She spun, gesturing to a tall, tanned, sandy-haired gentleman making his way toward them. "That's my husband. Trevor, Lord Falcondale. We sailed on one of Rainsleigh's ships, and the two of them have had much to discuss since we returned. But it's not all business, obviously. Trevor says Rainsleigh speaks often of you."

"Oh, well," said Elisabeth without commitment, glancing at Rainsleigh and then quickly away. She could feel her cheeks glow with color. She knew of Rainsleigh's enthusiasm for her, but it had not occurred to her that he would discuss their relationship with other people. The realization made her strangely uneasy. They were hardly carrying on in secret, but the more people he told about her, the more people would require excuses if her great secret drove them apart.

Carefully, she changed the subject. "Jocelyn has been looking so forward to your return. How long were you away from England?"

Lady Falcondale made a sound of exaggerated fatigue. "Oh, heavens, since well into last year. Long enough to, er, get our family under way." She touched her belly again. "We came home to have the baby. But how delighted we were to find Rainsleigh had moved in for good. When we left, the house was a worksite, and he only dropped by now and again. It was a lovely homecoming to have him in residence—and to be getting on so well with you."

"Yes," said Elisabeth, barely able to keep up.

Piety went on. "But perhaps my happiest discovery was to learn that dear Jocelyn is working again as a chaperone. All the better. I do worry for her sanity when she is in the unrelenting company of Lady Frinfrock."

"Please do not joke about the unrelenting company of Lady Frinfrock," said a male voice behind them. "Far too grave a threat."

Elisabeth turned. It was Piety's husband, Lord Falcondale. He placed a possessive hand on the small of his wife's back.

"How do you do?" he said, "Lady Elisabeth, I presume?" He made a small bow over her hand. "Thank God. I thought my wife would burst with anticipation."

"How do you do?" said Elisabeth, smiling more easily now. "Rainsleigh and Miss Breedlowe speak so highly of you—both of you."

"High praise from Rainsleigh?" said the earl. "Now I know he's besotted."

"I knew Rainsleigh was over the moon," gushed Piety, "when I heard about his donation to your charity. He does like to throw his money around, but then I learned of the nature of your foundation. And I *knew*."

"The viscount has been most generous," Elisabeth managed, surprised to discuss her work. And Rainsleigh's money. And especially his alleged state, *over the moon*. It occurred to her that she, alone, viewed their courtship as a small, private, experimental thing.

"Ah, but here's the devil himself," Falcondale said, watching Rainsleigh make his way to them. "Thank God. He's finally screwed up the courage to say hello."

Elisabeth inclined her head, watching dancers part and the room open to him. Her heart began to pound. He cut a slow, determined stride across the parquet floor. She allowed a small smile, watching him watch her as he came.

"Lady Elisabeth is a peach, Rainsleigh," Piety enthused when he reached them.

Elisabeth laughed, barely managing to screw on a straight face while Rainsleigh affected a formal bow over her gloved hand.

"My lady," he said. "It's a pleasure."

Elisabeth resisted squeezing her fingers around his hand. "The pleasure is mine."

"Finally," said Falcondale. "My God, Rainsleigh, I was beginning to think you'd forgotten which one she was. Sporting of you to say hello. Lovely girl, by the way." He shot Elisabeth a smile. "But my wife and unborn child require sustenance. Who fancies a turn at the buffet? The sooner we eat, the sooner we may leave for home."

Elisabeth did laugh then; Piety too. Rainsleigh offered his arm, and Elisabeth took it, grateful to feel the solidness of him at last. She tightened her hand around his bicep and saw his jaw clench, as it always did. It thrilled her to see him respond to her.

"How are you enjoying the evening, my lord?" she asked.

"Well enough," he said. "I had a moment's…unease that you had changed your mind and wouldn't come."

"Oh, yes, how anxious you looked when I arrived, rushing to greet me."

His eyes narrowed, but she saw him fight a smile. "You look…verdant," he said.

"As I am not a forest, may I assume that means nice?"

"You may assume that means beautiful. You've left your hair to hang down your back. My preference."

"Is it? What luck; it's mine too. But of course you know that long, loose hair is hardly current. People will talk, and not in a good way. Individualism is not to be encouraged in settings such as these."

"Hmmm. Another stroke of luck, as you seem impervious to 'talk.' "

"I've made the effort to turn up here, just to be with you. So that people will talk about that too."

"You *came here*," he whispered into her ear, "to enjoy the evening with me; everyone else and their *chatter* be damned."

Elisabeth pressed on, enjoying herself. "The gossip in the ballroom is positively echoing in my ears." She affected a meddlesome tone. " 'But who is the gentleman we've never before bothered to invite? Oh, it's Lord Rainsleigh. And how well-heeled he is. I cannot imagine what took us so long to include him. But who is that *verdant* spinster beside him with the unkempt hair?' "

"Ha!" Rainsleigh barked a laugh. "I assure you that is not what's being said. In fact, I could stand for a little less talk in this ballroom, as 'spinster' is hardly the word the men here are ascribing to you. I was unprepared for the amount of male attention you would receive. I don't like it."

"Pity to wait your whole life to go to a fancy party, only to discover it's no fun at all."

"Let me be very clear. I can take or leave the bloody ball. I don't enjoy the other men staring at you. Is your dress, perhaps, missing some part of the neckline?"

Now she laughed. "Perhaps you should do something possessive and demonstrative—and quick."

Rainsleigh made a growling noise. "It's reckless to be without Miss Breedlowe. I don't care what your aunt says. She will be a hapless chaperone, I fear."

"You have no idea."

"Beg your pardon?"

She shook her head. "Come now, what possible impropriety could happen in a crowded ballroom?"

"If only you knew my parents."

"I'm glad I did not know them."

He stopped, looking down at her. "Yes. So am I."

"But we will be nothing like them," she assured him, hugging his arm more closely. "I am only here to meet your friends—who are lovely, by the way—and because it is important to you. You are only here because you *can be*. Where's the risk in that?"

"Careful, my lady, you might just enjoy yourself."

"I already am."

In that moment, she longed, deeply, to rise up on her toes and kiss him. If they had not been in a crowded ballroom, swirling with watchful strangers, she would have done it. "I want to kiss you," she whispered.

Rainsleigh growled again and swept her along.

CHAPTER SEVENTEEN

"Let me guess," Beau Courtland drawled, sidling up beside his brother. "It doesn't live up to your expectations?"

A footman passed with beef pies on a tray, and his brother scooped up two, eating the first in a single bite. "Too much idle diversion? No ledgers to tally? Certainly no boats in sight."

"Clever…" mumbled Bryson, not really listening. Across the room, he watched the Countess of Banning introduce Elisabeth and Piety to yet another circle of guests.

"Have you seen Kenneth?" Another footman passed, this time with drinks. Beau juggled the pies and took up a glass. "He has no guile, the sod. Standing vigil beside the drinks table as if he's just come off Lent."

Bryson tore his gaze from Elisabeth and stared at his brother. "Kenneth Courtland is *here*? *Why*?"

Beau shrugged, making a face. "I don't monitor the comings and goings of our cousins, but it was hard to miss him. Strolled in on your coattails. I thought you saw him. I told you last month that he was back in town, trying to use the family as currency."

"It's one thing to lie to bookmakers and card dealers but quite another to show up at a proper ball. My God, why did they let him in?"

"God only knows. The butler is better dressed. Do you send him money?"

"I've never sent him a shilling. I keep Aunt Fay in small house in Wales, but nothing more. She has no other means." He turned back to the ballroom, seeking out the degenerate relative. "He should not be here."

"Fancy I should speak to him?" Beau sighed. "He knows better than to come close to you."

Bryson shook his head. "Stay away from him. If there's any justice, he'll be ignored and scuttle out before there's any harm. Best not to associate." They watched Kenneth, standing alone with a tankard, his dated, threadbare suit near to bursting at the seams.

After a moment, Bryson added, "I intend to make an announcement before the night ends. Hopefully, he will have loped away before then."

Beau chuckled. "What announcement? Playing the shipbuilder extraordinaire so soon? Just because you've been invited, doesn't mean you have an audience. No one discusses business at these things, Bryse." "Not an announcement to the room," he grumbled, "to you. To Falcondale and his wife. Lady Banning and Elisabeth."

"Announcement? About what?"

"It's a...proposal." He cleared his throat.

Beau choked on a mouthful of champagne. "Proposal for what?"

"Clever. Very clever. Not *for what*. To whom. Marriage. To Elisabeth. It's why I wanted you here."

"Well, it's not why I came!" Beau wiped his mouth with his sleeve.

"And I thought it was because I'd asked nicely."

"I came"—Beau was shaking his head—"because a certain lonely diplomat's wife suggested she'd save a dance or two—or *more*—for me. My God, Bryse. All this bloody marriage talk again? You've only known this girl for a month."

"I have wanted to offer for her since the first night we met."

"Oh, right. How could I forget: 'When you know, you know.' There's a term for this phenomenon, you know."

Bryson sighed. "Hmmm, and what is that?"

"*Love*." Beau laughed. "I never thought it would apply to you, but why not? Even the mightiest sometimes fall."

"Stop, before you injure yourself. God save me from your dramatics."

"You're besotted. Smitten. Shot by cupid's arrow. Naturally, a wedding would be next."

"*The wedding* will unite two esteemed families, so you may cease your romantic drivel."

"Oh, it's drivel now, is it?" asked Beau. "Well, I'm not the one racing to the altar with a girl I've only just met."

"Yes, but not because you lack romance. You're not headed to the altar at any speed because you detest the idea of monogamy. So be it. I do not have the same luxury. As viscount, it is expected that I should marry. It's the proper thing to do."

"I'm not suggesting that you avoid marriage, Bryse— in fact, I like Elisabeth very much. Congratulations on your…how do they say it? *Love match.*" Beau took a long sip. "It's sweet, really. And to think, not six months ago, all you loved was money and title and your great bloody house."

"I cannot expect you to understand," Bryson said on a sigh. He waited a beat and then added, "Elisabeth and I are fond of each other. And I desire her. But it would be reckless and silly to base a marriage on anything quite so fanciful or fleeting as *love.*" Bryson thought for a moment longer. "It would be irresponsible."

"God save us from that," Beau mumbled.

Bryson narrowed is eyes. "Elisabeth's manners and breeding, her chastity and modesty make her exactly the bride for whom I searched—or would have searched, if I hadn't met her on that first night."

"Ah yes, here we go with the manners and breeding and chastity and modesty," Beau recited. "Is she to be your wife, Bryse, or your nun?"

Bryson looked away. "Make no mistake. If I did not marry her, I would not be able to resist her."

"Aha! And so the truth comes out." Beau lifted his glass in a mock toast. "Pity you cannot find some manner of discreet interlude that might preclude immediate shackling. Something to hold you over for six months…the summer, perhaps. I suppose you'd never considered some time alone with her in the carriage on a moonlit night? Or another 'interview' in your library? An idle tryst to smooth out the edges, rather than bolt to the altar on your way to the bed."

"I will not dishonor Elisabeth," Bryson said harshly. "She is chaste and unsullied and wholly pure. It would be an insult to…have my way with her in a bloody carriage seat. She is a lady. She deserves the sanctity of marriage and a proper bed—at the very least." His expression blazed. His brother had taken the joke too far, as usual.

Beau whistled again, shaking his head. "So you say. But I urge you not to disparage a nicely sprung carriage seat until you've tried it."

"*Beau,*" Bryson growled warningly.

"After you're married, of course! When that sanctified marriage bed of yours grows tiresome."

"I'm beginning to wonder why I asked you to come."

"That's another thing! Marry her if you must, Bryse, but why offer for her tonight? Why *here?*"

Bryson nodded. This was fair. "I had planned to approach her at home. Next week, perhaps. But I've already spoken to her aunt. I have the jewelry in my pocket. I thought perhaps tonight would add a little bit of romantic flourish. Borrow a page from your book."

"Don't pin this on me! I'll never propose marriage—not here or on the bloody moon. This is your choice, Bryson, and I, for one, am shocked. What does your society rule book say about this sort of song and dance? You've just said that love was 'reckless' and 'fleeting.' What about spectacle? Surely there's at least a chapter on discretion, subtlety, good bloody taste."

"I do as I please." Bryson sighed. "And now it pleases me to do this. I wish to be very clear. To Elisabeth and to her aunt." He turned, studying his brother. "Don't you see? With this ball, we've come full circle. We've not been included before tonight. Did you see where we were seated at dinner?"

"Yes," grumbled Beau, "nowhere near the diplomat's wife." He shook his head. "Count the accolades if you must, Bryson;

that was always your dream. I've done nothing but hold you back. Congratulations. You're soundly revered. Now you may attend a society party every bloody night of the week. But why cause a stir at your very first one? If you propose tonight, what will be your next trick?"

"It's not a trick, and the proposal isn't meant to put on a show. It's a gesture. I will demonstrate"—he lowered his voice and looked away—"that I am worthy of her." A pause. "This ball proves it. I am accepted everywhere she may wish to go."

"You were always worthy of her, and from what I know of Elisabeth, she doesn't even enjoy balls for all that."

"It's a symbol," he said through gritted teeth. "I cannot expect you to understand."

"No, you cannot. Exclusion doesn't trouble me. In fact, I prefer it. Far less bother. You cannot find this evening jacket comfortable, Bryson, you cannot." He tugged at his stiff collar.

"There are more important things in life than comfort."

"Obviously, as you're racing to the altar at breakneck speed."

"You think my life with Elisabeth will lack comfort?"

"No, no, I think your life with Elisabeth will far exceed comfort. I think it will be an exercise in constant compromise—and good for you both for finding each other. Pity you don't *love* her, but far be it for me to assume. The less I know about love, the better."

Bryson took a long drink, watching Elisabeth and her aunt return from the dining room with drinks and saucers of cake. "Before this conversation devolves any further, I would like to gather up everyone and get on with it. She and her aunt will not stay much longer. The dancing has preoccupied most other guests. I should like to do it without an audience."

"Have you considered what a small, dare I say *nonexistent* audience you would have had in the privacy of her parlor?"

Bryson shook his head. "Her aunt is here. You are here. My friends are here. I won't make a spectacle. Just a small announcement before we all go. A bit of flourish. Something special for all of us to remember."

"Afraid she'll turn you down if you go it alone?"

Bryson finished his port. "Perhaps a touch," he said, smiling grimly. His brother shook his head, wisely making no further comment, and Bryson tapped the lapel pocket that held the ring.

CHAPTER EIGHTEEN

It took considerable effort to convene Falcondale and his
wife, Elisabeth, and Lady Banning in the arched alcove at the
back of the ballroom. Bryson had scouted this dim, secluded
corner because it was far enough from the musicians to be
heard over the instruments, and far enough from the food
and drink to hold little interest to other guests. A few couples, inappropriately secluded in the shadows, hurried away
when he led the group to the chosen spot.

"Forgive me for tearing you from the party," Rainsleigh
began when they gathered around him. "I beg just a moment
of your time to…celebrate."

"You've sold another boat?" guessed Falcondale.

"No. Something more important than the boats." He
stole a look at Elisabeth. She was watching him cautiously,
an uncertain smile on her face. He was more nervous than
he expected, and he bore on. "I asked you here to celebrate a
betrothal."

Lady Banning let out a muffled shout but then quickly
clamped a hand over her mouth.

"A what?" Elisabeth laughed. She looked between Bryson and her aunt and back again.

He swallowed and forced himself to follow through. "Lady Elisabeth Hamilton-Baythes," he said, dropping to one knee. "Will you do me the honor of becoming my wife?" With shaking hand, he held out a ring. Topaz and diamonds glinted on a thin band of gold. He looked up.

She stared back with an expression that fell somewhere between surprise and stone-cold shock. Her eyes were wild and large, her mouth halfway open. She raised her hands but then froze in mid-air, as if she was about to burst into applause.

Rainsleigh watched her, feeling the timpani boom of his pulse in his neck. Beneath his cravat, sweat beaded and rolled down his back. He willed her to say something while everyone watched, while he held his very breath.

She bore on in frozen silence, her eyes fixed on the ring. She seemed incapable of looking him in the eye.

But then her aunt finished the shout she had begun, and Piety joined her with a near-yelp. Lady Banning launched herself at Elisabeth, and her enthusiasm propelled her. Elisabeth blinked—once, twice—and her hands fell to her sides. He could see her taking very quick, shallow breaths. Lady Banning rained down tearful kisses, shaking her back to life. She hustled Elisabeth against him, and he was forced to his feet to catch her. She allowed it, falling against him, and she hid her face against his chest.

He had the fleeting thought, *Oh God, what have I done? She is abashed. Or overwhelmed. Or opposed.*

The Countess of Banning and Lady Falcondale embraced and cried and exclaimed, while Beau and Falcondale did their best to awkwardly contain them. Other guests drew closer, curious of the commotion. Women leaned to each other, whispering. Necks craned, eyes squinted into their corner of the ballroom. A handful of the couples on the dance floor stopped waltzing altogether to stare in their direction. He caught sight of his cousin Kenneth staggering from the drinks table, as if to join them.

God, no—that's all this situation bloody needs.

He sought out his brother's gaze and jerked his head toward Kenneth. Beau nodded back and left the group, striding to intercept.

Meanwhile, Falcondale's wife shared the happy news with one nearby woman and then another. Details of the betrothal spread from group to group in two directions. Curious onlookers drifted closer, staring, remarking. Judging? Perhaps. He couldn't be sure. Mostly, he saw open curiosity, fascination. They bore witness to colorful gossip in the making.

At least the baroness's venue provided an esteemed backdrop. And the countess's undeniable enthusiasm lent aplomb. She veritably bounced up and down as she discussed the happy news with a growing circle of her matronly friends. Elisabeth was already a subject of interest because it was so rare to see her out. And now this.

Rainsleigh pivoted reflexively, blocking her from the scrutiny. She went along, still uncharacteristically quiet, her pliant body warm against him. He was painfully aware that she had yet to utter one crucial—and crucially absent—word.

"Elisabeth?" he said in a low voice, speaking to the top of her head.

She looked up. She smiled. Not a beaming smile, not the smile he expected, but not a dismissive or regretful smile either. Slowly now, deliberately, she unfolded her arm and reached out.

The ring. She wanted it.

He slid it on her finger in a rush. His hand shook. It had felt more substantial and easier to hold in the jeweler's shop.

"A topaz," he whispered. "Unpretentiousness. For you."

"And the diamonds?" she whispered back.

"The highest quality. For me."

She nodded, staring with a dazed expression at the twinkling ring on her finger.

Before he could stop himself, Bryson said, "May I take this to mean you have…accepted the offer?"

Her head shot up. She looked surprised. She bit her bottom lip and smiled again, blinking back tears. She nodded, and he could finally breathe again.

"But Bryson?" she asked. "I would speak to you alone, please? Tonight. Right away. Is there some place we may go to have a conversation in private?" Her voice quavered.

This unexpected request dimmed the glow just a little, but he ignored it. "Of course," he said. "Let me just inquire—"

"My aunt will know," she said and reached for the countess.

Moments later, Lady Banning led them to a wide corridor at the opposite corner of the ballroom. Elisabeth burrowed into him as he escorted her on his arm, but she said nothing, staring resolutely at her aunt's back.

"There is a map room along this hall," Lady Banning explained, leading them down the corridor. "Ah, yes, here it is. The baroness's sons are hobbyists, and she has relegated their cartography to a former parlor."

They were just about to disappear into the room when Rainsleigh heard his brother call his name. He looked back to see Beau trotting down the hall in their direction. Rainsleigh signaled him: *Not now.*

Beau shook his head—two slow, heavy shakes—and kept coming. Rainsleigh stopped, alarmed by his dark look.

Elisabeth slipped from his arm. "Bryson?"

"I'll be right in," he assured her, keeping one eye on his brother. "Please go along. I must have a word with my brother."

Elisabeth looked uncertain, eyeing Beau as he jogged to them.

"It won't take a second," Bryson assured her carefully. "Look. Your aunt is already inside. Wait with her for me?"

Elisabeth consented, disappearing after her aunt, and Bryson strode to meet his brother halfway. "What is it?" he snapped.

"It's Kenneth."

Rainsleigh shrugged. His brother would only interrupt him if something had gone horribly wrong with their cousin. "A drunken scene?"

Beau shook his head. "No. Not that. I hustled him outside and down the street easily enough. It's merely...it's what he was saying as we went. He was blathering on. No one of consequence heard, but it worried me. I had to tell you."

"Blathering about what? What did he say?"

Beau glanced at the map room behind Bryson and then back. "He was going on about Elisabeth, of all people."

"What about Elisabeth?"

"He happened to be beside her at the buffet, and in his inebriated state, he apparently tripped and fell very nearly at her feet."

Rainsleigh gritted his teeth. "Did he touch her?"

"No, no, it was nothing like that. He was on the floor, and she stepped out of his way. But apparently there was some floundering moment where he looked up at her—stared at her, I assume—and he…" Beau faltered.

"Say it, Beau. Kenneth fell and what happened? Did he speak to her?"

"No, not that I'm aware. As far as I know, she went on her way, but Kenneth claims to have passed the remainder of the night *watching* the two of you."

"Watching us?" Rainsleigh repeated, incredulous. It made his skin crawl, but he failed to see the impact. "And?"

Beau nodded and exhaled uncomfortably. "And—look, I know it's madness, but Kenneth has become convinced that Elisabeth looks like someone he's…encountered before."

"Elisabeth encountered *Kenneth*?" Rainsleigh wanted to laugh at the ridiculousness of this, but something about the look on Beau's face stopped him. Instead he said, "Elisabeth and Kenneth hardly travel in the same circles. In fact, Elisabeth is rarely seen out. Encountered where?"

Beau gave a bitter laugh. "That's the ridiculous bit, and I why I came for you." He paused again, eyeing Bryson as if he did not trust his reaction. He took a deep breath. "It was something about a night of whoring—years ago. You and he and Father…"

Rainsleigh seized at the mention of their father, and he struggled to hear the rest of what Beau had to say.

"It was nonsense, obviously," Beau went on. "Why would Elisabeth be in a *brothel*? He said it was fifteen years ago; she would have been little more than a girl. I've issued a very strident warning to him—cease all conversation of his misguided 'recollection,' whatever it may be, and I think he understood."

Rainsleigh himself was scrambling to understand. "*What* about Elisabeth and a night of whoring?" He worked to keep his voice calm while anxiety knifed his gut and twisted. "Tell me again. Everything. Everything he said. He claimed someone who looked like Elisabeth was seen in a brothel *with* Father?"

Beau sighed, shaking his head. "It was something about a night when you were at Cambridge. On a lark, Father, along with Kenneth and Uncle Bernard, took a carriage from Rossmore Court to London so that Father might sample the pleasures of some luminary whore, a great nubile beauty. Apparently Father fancied young women—one of the many predilections to which I would rather not be privy, but Kenneth thought it was a laugh."

"Yes, yes, but what about Elisabeth?"

"Among the whores who may or may not have been this acclaimed ladybird, Kenneth claims he saw Elisabeth—or the young Elisabeth of years ago. As I've said, she would have been little more than a girl at the time. So—"

"Rather swift memory," Bryson said, "to recall a look-alike from years ago."

Beau shrugged. "Apparently, Kenneth and Bernard had been sent ahead the night before to scout out the proclaimed courtesan, and this is the girl they were shown—the one Elisabeth favors. One can only guess she was also ginger-haired. Kenneth hardly seems like a chronicler of subtle detail. Oh," Beau added, "the fiction is complete with this bit. I can't believe I forgot. Kenneth claimed *you were there too.*"

"What?"

Beau nodded, chuckling. "According to Ken, they'd abducted you from your bed and hauled you along purely to torment you. To parcel you off with some experienced ladybird…to 'make a man of you,' that sort of nonsense." He looked philosophical. "Actually, it's the only part of the story that rings true, sadistic bastards."

The story went on, Beau filling in more details, but Bryson had stopped listening. A distant buzzing rose in his ears, drowning out all other sound.

Parcel you off to bed with some experienced ladybird…

To 'make a man' of you…

Bryson's head shot up.

He looked at the door through which Elisabeth had entered, then back at his brother, and back at the door. In his mind's eye, a memory unfurled. Long buried—long forgotten, *purposely* forgotten. It came slamming back now with a vividness and clarity that mocked real life.

He remembered.

Oh, God.

It was her.

"Beau?" he managed to rasp. His voice sounded strangled. "Who else heard Kenneth? Who?"

Beau studied him cautiously. "I told you; no one, really. It was a long rambling story, his speech was slurred, and I was hustling him out with due haste. Someone would have had to follow us to piece together the whole thing, and no one did. Why? My God, but you've gone white. What's wrong? Bryson—stop. Wait!"

He was already walking away. Slow, steady strides. Hands clenched into fists. It was all he could do not to break into a run. While he walked, he conjured up an image of the girl in his room that night. Red hair. Turquoise eyes. A brand on her shoulder. She had been beautiful, but oh, so young. A girl.

He stopped in front of the door to the map room. Beau rushed up behind him, reaching for him, but he jerked away. "Leave us," he hissed. "I wished to be alone with my betrothed."

Working to steady his breathing, he swallowed hard and stepped inside, slamming the door behind him.

CHAPTER NINETEEN

Elisabeth hadn't expected the door to slam, and her head shot up.

Bryson strode into the room, not looking at her, not speaking—he did not even acknowledge her aunt.

Inexplicably, she stood.

She watched him prowl the room, the sound of his boots on the marble tile barely audible over the pounding of her heart. His expression was granite.

"Lady Banning," he said suddenly, partially turning. "Please, remain." Elisabeth jumped at the bite in his voice.

"Not tonight, Rainsleigh," Aunt Lillian declared lightly, pushing up from a chair. She gave Elisabeth's arm a squeeze and bustled toward the door.

He began, "It wouldn't do to be secreted away alone—"

"You are engaged to be married now," she called over her shoulder. "This affords you ten minutes alone, I should think. Especially if I acknowledge it. I will not go far. The nearest corner of the ballroom. And I shall leave the door standing open, just a little. Elisabeth is not seventeen, and you are hardly a dandy." Without a backward glance, she slipped into the hall. They were alone in the silence.

Elisabeth looked down at her twinkling engagement ring. It seemed odd now that a hard, twinkling stone would be her only reminder of his affection, but he would not meet her eyes. And his demeanor was off. Closed and dark. The unexpected distance was like an intrusive third person in the room.

She had planned to go to him, to take him by the hand and lead him to the settee so that they might have their talk. Now she forced herself to venture one step in his direction. She cleared her throat. The secret could not wait. Not even five minutes more.

"Bryson," she began, "there is something I must—"

"Let me see your shoulder, Elisabeth," he suddenly said, looking up. His eyes were ice-blue and hot with anger at the same time.

"I beg your pardon?" She shuffled one step back.

"Your shoulder. On the right. Let me see it."

"Wha—" she began, but then his awful request sank in. She felt the blood drain from her face.

He knows.

Oh my God.

He. Knows.

She looked again. His face was tight with agony, hard and closed off. She took a cannonball to the belly with that look. She reached for a chair to support her, struggling to stay upright.

He knew.

Not *her* way, not by *her* words or memories—but still, he knew. Tears shot to her eyes, and she felt her cheeks go warm, despite the clammy sweat of shock. Her mind leapt to the defensive, a wheel spinning for the most appropriate, diffusing thing to say. Her first impulse was to explain herself. Her defense was weak, perhaps, but legitimate. And he was a decent man—thoughtful and fair—and she had rehearsed this much with Jocelyn and Aunt Lilly. If they could but remain calm, if she could find the words. She lifted her head to implore him and—

The hardness of his gaze struck her mute. Anger, hurt, disbelief—she saw it all, plainly on his face. All of her solutions and excuses felt suddenly flat and one-note. She resorted, lamely, to shaking her head.

He started to her. "Perhaps you did not hear me," he said, rounding a desk. "I want to see your shoulder." His voice belonged to a stranger.

"You would have me disrobe?" she managed to say. "Right here?"

"Do it. Do it, or I will peel the gown back myself."

She scuttled behind an adjacent chair. "You most certainly will *not*." Now her own outrage flared, eclipsing her shock and shame. "You will not touch me."

He kept coming, and she darted behind the next chair and the next. "What is wrong with you, Bryson? You are behaving like a madman."

"Mad, am I?" he bit out. "Perhaps that's the result of learning I've been lied to. *For weeks.* Do not ask me what is wrong."

"I will ask you. I don't care what you think I have done. I haven't *lied,* and I do not deserve undefined aggression from you."

"Undefined?" He laughed bitterly. "What an accurate term. How very *undefined* the nature of our relationship has been."

"What's happened?" she asked again. "What did your brother say to you?" She darted behind an easel of maps. She was nearly to the wall. She looked at the fireplace behind her and then back at him. Would he really dare touch her?

She gambled and stepped out from behind the chair and stood tall. "Watch your tone, Rainsleigh," she said. "I will not be dominated by you simply because you are incensed. Rest assured, I will scream if you touch me."

"My *tone?*" He stopped in front of her, and she held her breath. She found the courage to raise her chin.

"What do you discern *in my tone?*" he asked quietly. "Pray, define it for me, because what I *feel* is adrift."

"You are not *adrift,*" she said as levelly as her voice would allow. "You are angry. But how can I address your anger if you do not say what is wrong?"

He studied her a moment, and she had the thought that she must suddenly look like a stranger to him too. Her chin went higher still. Let him look. She *willed him* to see that she was the same woman from the happy weeks before. "What did your brother tell you?" she whispered, staring into the narrow blue slits of his eyes.

"Oh, he explained the most unthinkable circumstance."

"Unthinkable?" She took a step toward him. "Also *unspeakable,* I presume. Can you not even say it? I cannot defend myself if we do not say the words. But perhaps that is what you want."

He threw out his arms. "What defense can there be for lying to me for weeks—for weeks, Elisabeth?"

"I did not *lie*," she corrected firmly, loudly—possibly too loudly. "I have never lied. I simply have not…I didn't…"

He shook his head and turned away. He began to pace. "Now who cannot say the words? How could you keep this from me? My God…" He stopped pacing and leaned over a desk, planting his hands wide. "Did you remember me? When you saw me at your aunt's party last month? Did you remember me from"—he cleared his throat—"my father's trip to the brothel?"

She opened her mouth to speak and then closed it. She met his eyes and nodded.

"*When?*" he demanded lowly. "*When* did you remember me?"

"I…I have always known you."

"Your long, glowing monologue to the marchioness at your aunt's dinner that night?" he said, realization dawning. "You leapt to my defense because you knew my life. You *knew me then.*"

"Yes," she whispered. But then, louder and stronger, she said, "*Yes*, I knew you then. But I deserve to know what your brother said about my past. We may not even be talking about the same thing."

"Oh, judging from your reaction, I think we are."

"You *think*, but you don't know—listen to yourself! There is too much at stake not to have an honest conversation. This is the reason I wanted to speak to you after the betrothal."

He let out a sad, angry laugh.

"Laugh if you must, but it was. Why else would I immediately insist that you come away from your friends and this party to a private room?"

"I don't know," he said coldly, looking her up and down. "Why else might a woman of your previous vocation ask to come away to a private room—"

"How *dare* you," Elisabeth gasped. Adrenaline shot through her veins like a lightning strike, and she charged on him, striding across the room with fists clenched.

He watched her come and went on. "According to your aunt, there is leniency now that we're promised to each other. I'm sure that door can be locked."

She made a shrill sound of frustration and rage and stopped dead. His words opened up a chasm between them that could not be crossed. With shaking fingers, she reached for the betrothal ring that now pinched the skin of her left hand. Pulling to the point of pain, she worked it off.

"You are mad if you believe you will ever touch me again. I have seen a lot of unfeeling cruelty in my life, Bryson Courtland, but your behavior here tonight is cruelty unmatched. You are merciless."

"Mercy?" he growled, rounding her, staring at her naked hand. "You wish for mercy? Here is mercy: Replace the ring on your finger, miss, because the betrothal still stands. I will not be jilted by you and become the subject of endless, speculating gossip. Not after I have toiled my entire life to avoid such talk."

"Oh, and you're so certain that being jilted is worse than being married to a liar."

"Would that you had merely lied," he ground out.

"Meaning what?"

He squeezed his eyes shut and sucked in a calming breath. When he spoke again, his voice was low and emphatic. "When we go through with the marriage, no one need know that you were a—"

"*Do not* say it," Elisabeth rasped. "You have no idea about that which you speak."

"I saw you, Elisabeth—that night. I saw the brothel. I know what my father likes. I think I have some idea."

"You are sorely mistaken, my lord," she said, her voice barely under her command, "if you think I would ever bind myself to a man who would treat me so cruelly."

"Cruelty? Where is the cruelty in offering marriage to a thirty-year-old spinster with no other prospects?"

"Oh, now flattery on top of all else!"

"And who runs a scandalous charity that I now know was founded from *personal experience*. My God," he said, sounding inspired. "You had the opportunity to tell me the day of the tour. When you explained the history of the foundation. We spoke about it at length. *Why didn't you tell me?*"

"Because it is excruciating to discuss it, and I never speak of it! Not with anyone. It is my own private pain, and I would not casually bring it up to a man who just happened along. I had every reason to believe that you would *happen away* very soon."

"I wasn't simply *a man*, Elisabeth. I was…" He let the pronouncement fade away and tried again. "You would conceal it even from me?"

"By all means, I could conceal it from you. Until recently, I had not even revealed it to my aunt. It is a devastating, mortifying thing to put to words, Bryson. I wanted to be certain of your affections—certain enough that you would not respond as you have tonight. And besides, we were busy becoming acquainted. The time was never right. And I was *afraid*." Her voice broke, but she spoke through the unshed tears. "Do not think I have kept this from you lightly. I have agonized over it since my aunt forced us together at her dinner. For what it's worth, I was going to tell you tonight."

"Fine—good," he said, putting his hands on his hips. "Tell me now."

"No."

"Yes."

"No, Bryson, it's over—it's too late."

"Why, Elisabeth? *Why* is it too late?"

"Because you've been wretched to me, and accusatory, and unfeeling, and hateful. And after tonight, I will refuse to see you ever again."

"On the contrary. After tonight, we will marry."

"Stop saying that; we will not marry."

"Some women in your position might consider it a great generosity to take you as my wife."

Elisabeth took in a sharp breath. His words were like a knife, cutting each time a little bit closer to her heart.

Rainsleigh spun away and strode to the mantel over a low fire. He shook his head, staring into the flames, and ran a frustrated hand through his hair.

They were achingly familiar mannerisms; she had seen him do it fifty times before. Like a fool, she had the reflex to comfort him, to run to him and seek comfort from him in return. She would not—not now, not ever again—but to go against the impulse put a crack in her heart. She wrapped her arms around herself.

"Why, I wonder, did I believe I deserved more than this?" he suddenly said, speaking to the fire. "Considering *my* parents? Considering the squalor from which I came? There are things one may never overcome."

Elisabeth let out a small sob. "You feel sorry for yourself? Because you've been saddled with *me*?"

He looked at her. The pain on his face was clear and deep. "You've won no prize in me, either, Elisabeth," he said gravely. "I have a fortune but little respect."

"I don't care about your respect. Find your own happiness, Rainsleigh, independent of how the lords and ladies of bloody Mayfair regard you."

"There is no happiness without respect. This I know."

"Oh, God," she rasped, feeling the crack in her heart split completely. "I can't believe I held you in any measure of affection all this time."

"Affection is not necessary to our union."

"This offer improves every time you open your mouth. If you think I should fall at your feet in gratefulness simply because you'll have me…because you are rich, and powerful, and it will save me from eternal spinsterhood…you do not know me at all."

"Oh, I think we've well established that tonight."

Elisabeth blinked, determined to keep the tears from rolling down her cheeks. "Bravo," she said brokenly, "and perhaps we have. But pray, do not fret. I can describe myself in one breath: I live a very full life. My work is important. I have enough money, all on my own. I can be perfectly satisfied devoting my life to saving innocent girls from attitudes likes yours."

He made no response, and it occurred to her that she was finished here. He would hurt her more, the longer she remained. She had only one more thing to say.

"Your proclamations are not law, my lord," she told him. "Not to me. I will *not* marry you; you cannot force me. I couldn't care less about the gossips." She reached out and took up his hand. Without looking away from his sad, blue eyes, she dropped the engagement ring in his palm.

His fingers had not even closed around it when she turned and strode to the door.

"Oh, no you don't," he said through gritted teeth, and she heard him lunge.

She broke left, skirting a table. He went the long way around but was faster. She pivoted right and sprinted a diagonal line. He anticipated this and caught her around the waist, pulling her to him.

"Elisabeth," he whispered against her hair, "please." There was a new note of desperation in his voice.

She shook her head against his mouth. "Let me go."

"You are upset," he continued, not budging. "I am upset. I feel blindsided and betrayed. I have handled this wrongly, possibly unforgivably. But please, do not do this. It was ambitious, perhaps, to indulge in the fantasy of a marriage with cheerful affection. Life is not so fanciful. We can still marry and succeed."

She wriggled, trying to break free. "I am already a success. Even better, I am *free*. It was the only saving grace that came of my parents' deaths. I have the money to do as I please. You are mad if you think I will marry you."

"Freedom," he said on a breath, "is one of the few things that money cannot always buy." He loosened his hold but did not let her go.

"Oh, yes, how restricted you are." She gave her arm a yank and pulled free.

"If I intend to build a new reputation for the viscountcy, which I do, then I am very restricted indeed."

"If you're so concerned about your reputation, then tell everyone *you* jilted *me*. I don't care. There is your freedom. You invest too much in what these people think about you, Bryson. You are a slave to a way of life that is almost impossible for a flesh-and-blood human to maintain."

"You're wrong," he shot back. "It is entirely possible. You don't know the value of it, because you were not brought up in the stench and shame of the opposite. Whatever…happened that landed you in the brothel that night must have been a mere dot on the chronology of your life. I cling to high standards now because I mucked around in the gutter for too long—for years. Half my life."

He watched her watching him, and her expression must have been pained, because he suddenly reached out. "Are you hurt?"

She hopped out of his reach. "High standards, you say? Yes, how high they seemed when you strode into this room, demanding that I pull off my dress. You assumed the very worst about me."

"You misled me for weeks, Elisabeth."

For this, she had no new answer. Her greatest wish now was to go. She backed away.

He reached a hand out to her—a gentle hand, supplicating—but she shook her head. She turned and walked to the door.

He called after her. "Why did you go along with the courtship? If you knew our past was such a barricade? I must know. I pursued you, yes, but you could have denied me, put a stop to it, refused to see me."

She stopped, considered this, and gave the answer to the door. "I went along with it because I enjoyed you."

"Isn't that enough on which to base a marriage?"

"Not anymore." She reached for the knob.

"Elisabeth," he called. "Wait—"

"Good-bye, Bryson." She sighed. It took no effort to walk away. She heard him rush up behind her, but she didn't break stride. She opened the door.

"Elisabeth, I said wait," he repeated, a harsh whisper, but she had already slipped into the hallway and gathered herself up to flee.

She turned...and faced Aunt Lillian and a dozen of her collected friends. They strode down the hallway to her, their smiles champagne bright.

Bryson burst through the door behind her and came up short.

"Ah, here they are!" Aunt Lillian sang, her smile the brightest of all. "The match of the century! We've waited more than ten years for this. The ladies have come to congratulate the bride- and groom-to-be!"

"Do not think of disgracing me," he whispered.

Elisabeth's anger spiked again, and she glared. And now he would *threaten her*? After everything else?

But his face was devoid of threat. He looked…panicked. Desperate. It was the only thing that stayed her.

She gritted her teeth, angry at herself now too. She owed him nothing, least of all sympathy. Even so, she swallowed hard, fixed her face with a blank expression, and turned back to the women. They descended, and she allowed them to cluck around her while she said nothing at all.

Five minutes later, her aunt mercifully bore her away.

Chapter Twenty

Elisabeth refused to see him for ten days.

He called in person, every day, beginning the day after the ball, including Sundays. He did not insult her with flowers. He did not write.

The first five days he was turned away by a member of staff. On the sixth day, Lady Banning herself loomed behind the servant and broke in, just as Rainsleigh handed over his card.

"I hope to make more clear what my man has failed to convey," the countess said tiredly. "Elisabeth will not see you, my lord."

"I understand, your ladyship, but if she would but permit me—"

"The reason she will not see you," Lady Banning cut in, "is that she is devastated and heartbroken. In my experience, the only remedy for these conditions is time. To see you only winds back the clock."

He had been prepared for the countess's anger and scorn, but he was not prepared for sadness.

"I would apologize to her, Lady Banning," he said, pressing on. "I behaved abominably; if I could only admit that to her."

"I will tell her," she said, sighing, backing away, and shutting the door.

On the tenth day, Elisabeth herself came to the door. It shocked him to see her, and his gut responded a half moment before his brain remembered that he was no longer permitted to be cheered by the sight of her face, that her beauty did not unnerve him, that his chest should not expand with what felt like light when he saw her.

"Lady Elisabeth," he said, blinking at her, fighting to control his expression.

"If I receive you, will you cease calling?" she asked.

He had not expected to bargain. "If that is what you wish."

"That's no answer, but please be aware: You will cease coming here. Furthermore, in the few moments you will be permitted to say whatever it is you wish to say, you will not raise your voice."

"Yes...I—"

"Or insult me."

"Correct."

"Or inform me of my great luck in accepting any offer you may toss at my feet."

"Yes."

"You will not demand to peel back any corner of my garment to examine any hidden area of my body."

"God, no—Elisabeth..."

"You may come in for ten minutes if you promise to abide by these stipulations. And it cannot be said enough: after you've gone, you may never come again."

He gritted his teeth. "Thank you."

She narrowed her eyes at him, quite aware, he thought, that he had not, in fact, promised. She retreated into the house, leaving the door open. He breathed deeply and followed.

Trailing her silently would be just one of several humilities, he knew. She would not be cordial or pleasant. She would not feign pleasantness. This was the price for his rashness and lack of control.

The price for her dishonesty was the reason he'd come.

They walked silently, him behind her, in a single line. He stared at her back, marveling that he had ever known the liberty of touching her there. Now she seemed as remote as the moon.

She led him down the long hall where he'd first seen her. *No*, he corrected—where he'd first seen her *again*.

She wore the same blue dress, then as now. Her hair was down. He was unaffected, he reminded himself, by the sight of her hair, or how the bodice of her dress gave way to the fall of her skirts, or her singularly regal walk. He reminded himself that he'd come here to subjugate himself in order to gain her cooperation and not because he…wanted her.

The last ten days had been an exercise in restraint. He restrained himself from pounding on the Denby House door after he had been turned away, and he restrained himself from putting a fist through the wall when he returned home.

The restraint, perhaps, was second nature, but the extreme need for it (especially to rein in door-pounding and wall-punching) was new, and he hated himself for it. Never had he felt so out of control. From the moment he remembered her, his control had vanished, and rashness took its place. He'd behaved abominably in the map room at the ball. And when he returned home, he agonized over it, helpless to put her out of his mind. He could not stop thinking about her. She'd willfully mislead him for weeks—a gross manipulation—*and yet he wanted her still.*

His days were consumed with thoughts of her. Why she'd lied? Why he had not seen the lie? How had she found herself in a brothel that night? Would she ever consent to see him again so he could learn the answers? Worst of all, would they still marry?

He had to know. Never in his life had he respectfully appealed to someone again and again, only to be turned away. Yet every day he awoke anew with the fresh compulsion to see her again.

And so now, ten days later, here he was. *Seeing* her. He could not fully acknowledge the rush of great relief.

She led him to a small receiving room, a dim and airless anteroom, tightly crowded with spindly furniture, devoid of cushions. The message was clear: *You will not linger.*

The room was so small there was no escaping closeness. The chairs were huddled together around a cold grate. She took a chair but he stood.

"May I impose on you to shut the door?" she asked.

He looked behind him at the heavy door. By habit, he was cautious of being alone with her, but what could it possibly matter now? He pulled it shut. The tiny room now appeared even smaller. Elisabeth said nothing and stared up. She waited.

"May I sit?" he asked.

"If you prefer."

His wooden chair scraped loudly on the stone floor as it took his weight. He cleared his throat. "I am sorry to be a nuisance these many days," he said. "I was trying to convey my urgency and determination."

"In this, you succeed. What do you want?"

He blinked. "An opportunity to apologize. To explain myself."

"There's nothing to explain, Lord Rainsleigh. Our mutual offenses against each other—and I count myself as complicit, I have wronged you too—are too astounding to make amends. That is my thinking on the matter. In fact, I am shocked that you have persisted. You were very angry."

"Yes, well, anger was only half of what I felt. I think what caused my truly uncivil behavior was that I felt deceived." Even now, he had trouble saying the words without his heart pounding, without a bitter edge sharpening the ends of his words. He went on. "Regardless of what I felt, it was no excuse for what I said. I…I am sorry. I handled the situation very wrongly. Please accept my heartfelt contrition."

"Very well," she said, standing up. "Now will you go?"

He stared at her, hustling to his feet.

He had prepared for coolness and hurt but not…indifference. Her voice was low and flat. She stood perfectly erect but was in no way anxious. Her arms were folded gently across her chest. He looked at her face, at her smooth, unfurrowed brow and relaxed mouth. She arched one eyebrow.

Did she care not at all? He cocked his head, looking deep into her eyes. That was when he saw the rims, faintly red. The bright, unshed tears. The unique aquamarine had deepened to a lonely shade of blue. His heart lurched.

This is what you want, he reminded himself. *Regret. Vulnerability. Give.*

He forced himself to continue. "If you will indulge me, I had hoped to hear…your story."

"What story?"

He bit back a fatigue-laden sigh. Of course she would not make it easy.

"The story of how the daughter of an earl and the niece of a countess was working in a brothel when she was barely fifteen."

"Oh, that story. Not much to tell, really. I did it for pin money, of course."

"I know this is not a joke to you," he said lowly. "You have not been to your office in Moxon Street for days. Miss Breedlowe is very loyal to you, but when pressed, she revealed that you are…troubled."

"Let me be very clear, your lordship, or you may leave straightaway. You are not privy to my comings and goings, so do not monitor me. And do not harass Miss Breedlowe. Do not." She sat back down.

"As you say. But I will hear this story." He retook his seat and leaned forward, his chair groaning. "Not as a path to forgiveness, Elisabeth. I will hear it because I deserve to know. Considering the time we spent together."

"Yes, well, *considering the time we spent together,* I deserved respect and compassion when you—" She looked away. "When I received quite the opposite."

"I can do no more than apologize, Elisabeth. I was out of my head, and I will regret it forever."

He saw her blink. She was crying.

He continued in a low voice, "You are being stubborn to your own disadvantage. I think you *want* to tell me."

"No." She shook her head, speaking to the wall. "What I want is for you to leave and never come back." When she looked at him again, her eyes were dry. "But as we both know, we cannot always get what we want."

"Life is about choices, Elisabeth." He leaned back in the unaccommodating chair. "You can choose to tell me or choose not to tell me. But *you* decide. There is no overlying rule of thumb for this. And I am imploring—begging—you to tell me. You can make up your mind and do it."

"Fine, Rainsleigh," she said tiredly. She dropped her head into her hand and scratched her brow. "But please know that I am not being fickle, if that's what you think. I am not withholding the events of that night in order to punish you. I abhor talking about it—which is the reason I had not yet been able to discuss it with you earlier. And especially after the way you behaved."

"If it makes any difference, I should say that my reaction had mostly to do with me, and my own frailty, my own history, my own relationship with my father."

"But *I* was there. *I* bore it."

"Yes," he said, "you were there." He felt a regret so deep he couldn't breathe. Elisabeth, of all people, had been the recipient of what he now regarded as an emotional caving in. He would regret this, perhaps forever.

Suddenly, she said, "All right, I will tell you. But first let us acknowledge that life is *not*, in fact, 'about choices,' as you say—not always. Life may also be about managing whatever one is dealt, learning to cope, and not giving up."

He nodded to this. He'd told himself that to hear the full account, if she would give it, would be something he did for her—something he gave her. A chance to explain herself. But now his own heart pounded as if it were hammering its way out of his body. He had to fight the urge to grip the arms of his chair. He couldn't say why, really, but *he* wanted to know. He was desperate to know.

She sighed and began. "When I was fifteen, after a visit to my aunt in this very house, my parents' carriage was set upon by thieves on Windsor Road. My mother and father were murdered in cold blood while I watched and waited in terror for my turn at the hands of the highwaymen. However, the attackers did not murder me. Instead, they strapped me to the back of a horse and hauled me to a brothel at the edge of London. There, they sold me to the proprietor, whose scheme was to offer me to whichever deranged man fancied himself rich and selective enough to rape a young innocent."

"Elisabeth…" He gritted his teeth, bile nearly closing his throat.

"Oh, yes," she said flatly. "After the brothel owner bought me, he branded me—not unlike a head of cattle—which is the mark you demanded to see on my shoulder in the map room. Clearly you remember it from…that night."

"Elisabeth," he rasped, running a rough hand over his face. Images from that night flashed in his mind. The shock at seeing a girl so young and lovely in his room. Her obvious state of distress. The sight of a hot-iron brand on human flesh...

He made an anguished sound, half wail, half growl, and shoved away from his seat. He paced the three steps to the wall and back. He felt her watch him, considering his reaction.

"I appreciate that you are horrified, Rainsleigh," she said, "but spare me the shock, if you please. What did you think? That I took up residence in a vermin-infested brothel because I admired the chef?"

"I'm sorry," he said, and he wondered if there would be a limit on the number of times he could effectively say this. "I suppose I did not think."

"A fair supposition," she said, shaking her head. "Next, the brothel owner put me on display for prospective clients."

"What do you mean, 'on display'?"

"Perhaps you should ask whoever revealed to you that it was me at the brothel that night."

"I beg your pardon?"

"Whoever informed you that you were betrothed to a whore." She paused.

His mind raced to make sense of this.

"Someone must have told you. You didn't remember for weeks, and then you did," she said. "Who spoke to you?"

Bryson clamped his eyes shut. "My detestable cousin Kenneth. He followed my father around like an enchanted monkey in those days. I haven't seen him in years, but he came to the baroness's ball, uninvited. Apparently, he tripped at the buffet table and floundered around at your feet. He got a long look at you and managed to dredge up some gin-soaked memory in his tiny brain. He relayed it to Beau, who…informed me."

"A cousin…" Elisabeth repeated absently, sitting up in her chair. "Did anyone else hear?" Her voice took on the first notes of distress.

He shook his head. "No one heard, and my brother has since paid Kenneth an unforgettable—and unforgettably *painful*—visit. He will not be a problem. In fact, he is, even as we speak, *relocating*. To New South Wales."

"You had him shipped to Australia?" She was openly surprised.

"It was a journey long overdue." With this, he smiled. After a moment, she smiled too. It was a slow, sad sort of smile. Something began to unspool in his chest at the sight of that smile. He took his first full, clean breath in ten days and then looked away.

Chapter Twenty-One

Do not smile, do not smile, do not smile at me.

Elisabeth blinked at the back of Bryson's head, grateful he had turned away. He smiled so rarely—she'd only seen it four or five times in their acquaintance, including their original meeting so long ago—and she had considered each one a gift.

But there was no room for gifted smiles in this exchange; they'd already spoken too long, and she had said too much.

What difference could it make if his smile was rare or authentic or that it nudged her very heart? She had not agreed to see him so that they could grin at each other.

But this begged the question: why had she agreed to see him? To answer this, she tried to decipher why he'd really and truly come. For ten days in a row, he'd come. At the ball, his disgust—nay, his revulsion—could not have been more clear. Yet here he was. Contrite. Humble. Compliant.

It was possible, she thought, that he really did wish to apologize. It was possible he wanted to understand. He was charitable in that way, even about things to which he was opposed.

It was also possible he wished to extract a silent vow from her to ensure the safety of his sterling reputation forevermore. Ha! As if she might gossip about the details of a night she could not even explain to him. As if she would boast about her broken engagement.

Whatever the reason, the smile was gone now. It had not been unpleasant, but ultimately it told her nothing, while his intense expressions and conciliatory tone told her less. Silence expanded in the small room, filling up the sunny corners where they looked when they could not look at each other. Sweaty awkwardness, she thought, would be next. After that, there was a chance she would well up and sob. She might as well finish it and hustle him out before it devolved into that.

"Shall I go on?" she asked.

"If you can bear it."

He stared at her, waiting, and she thought, *Now he's only being polite.*

"Elisabeth?"

"Yes?"

"It is an understatement to say that I did not comprehend the pain that you endured, nor the difficulty you would, naturally, suffer when forced to revisit it, especially to a suitor— especially to *me*. I...I know that I expressed my regret before, but please, allow me to say it again—to *mean it* again. I...I have been thoughtless and cruel. I had no idea. I am so very sorry."

"Thank you," she said. Now he sounded as authentic as his smile. "Have you heard enough, then?"

"If you will tell the rest, I should like to hear it."

She took a deep breath and rushed to finish it, striving for the flat, emotionless tone that allowed her some measure of detachment and made the horrible words seem less raw. She told him about Marie, the switched rooms, her own plan to escape. She told him how terrified and ashamed and grief-stricken she had been.

She wanted to tell him how his kindness and humor and outrage at the situation had, quite possibly, saved the last remaining embers of her spirit as much as his strength and cunning had saved her life...but she did not. Those were the admissions she'd planned for her own telling of this tale, the one that was never allowed to be. This version was for his information, and he was now duly informed. She need not elaborate.

"And you won't have to threaten me with deportation to New South Wales," she joked sadly. "I never speak of those dreadful four days. The girls at my office do not know, even though it would do them no end of good. 'Tis not a story I willingly share, for obvious reasons."

"Elisabeth," he said, looking down at her, "I do not wish to deport you. I wish to marry you."

She stopped breathing. "You what?"

"The marriage, Elisabeth, it...it..."

"Bryson, *no*." She leaned back in her chair and closed her eyes, laying a hand across her brow. The room, suddenly, seemed too bright. "No, no, *no*. I can't believe you've come here, asking this."

"It's not a question, Elisabeth. You've already accepted me."

"Well, I un-accept!" She tossed her arm out and stared. "That goes without saying."

"Elisabeth, hear what I have to say on the matter. Please."

"Whatever you say is…is deranged!" she said, marveling at his nerve. "Not only did you make me painfully aware of your opinion of my lack of suitability as your future bride, but I am no longer the least bit…amorous toward you."

He closed his eyes and rubbed the back of his neck. He turned away. "The marriage I propose would not require either of us to be…amorous," he said quietly.

"Well," she scoffed, "if you term it like *that*…"

"You have not heard my offer."

"Perhaps, but I'm not thick. I know that you are wealthy and powerful and that marriage to you would make me a viscountess. I know that any woman in England would be thrilled to accept you."

"Not *that* offer," he said, turning back to her. "The offer I came with today."

"You came today to apologize. You said so yourself. In fact, you promised you would not wheedle me with offers of any kind."

"And I have apologized, but I implore you, at the very least, *to listen* to a new offer."

"The old offer…the new offer—do you realize that you sound like you're buying a second-hand carriage?"

"If you marry me, Elisabeth," he said, pressing on, "if you *save me* the embarrassment of a broken engagement, I promise that as my wife, your foundation will know unlimited resources. Forever. A new building, if you wish, a larger staff, a new team for your raids—professionals, the very best—to replace Stoker. I will also fund his education and underwrite your continued support of him."

Elisabeth stared at him, amazed. He would not. "Bryson." She faltered. "Escaping gossip and the loss of a betrothed could not be worth all of that to you; it could not."

"You have no idea how difficult respect is to earn," he said bitterly. "In contrast, money is the easiest thing for me to give."

"Not love." The challenge was out before she could stop it.

He took a deep breath. "Look, Elisabeth, I know I did irreparable damage to our…rapport at the St. Clare ball. Likewise, you misled me for weeks. We need not pretend that this can be patched over with one conversation. I won't insult you by suggesting your cooperation can be bought, even with money that goes to your beloved foundation. What I suggest is more like…a business agreement."

"I beg your pardon?"

"A contract of sorts. I will marry you and make you a wealthy viscountess with far-reaching influence toward social change and pots of money to give to rescued prostitutes or whomever your compassionate heart desires. You will marry me, and I will suffer no damage to the reputation I have worked so hard to cultivate."

"This is not an equal trade." She was too stunned to do more than state the obvious.

"Well, I also gain a wife who happens to be exactly what I was looking for when I set out to find one. Mature. Steadfast. Modest."

"Oh, God, you *do* think of me as a used carriage."

He smiled again. Elisabeth smiled too, although only for a second. This was madness.

"*Bryson...*" she said sadly, shaking her head.

He went on, explaining in calm, even tones. "The image we will show to the world will be that of a devoted couple, mutually respectful, loyal, and faithful. In private, at home, we needn't, er, pretend that we share anything more than an amicable business agreement that benefits us both."

"Meaning?"

"Meaning separate lives, separate interests—I have my work; you have yours—separate schedules..."

"Separate bedrooms."

He looked up. "Well, naturally. Even if we had—" He stopped himself and looked away.

He cleared his throat before he went on. "It is customary, I believe, even in traditional unions, for a lord and lady to reside in separate chambers. My house is expansive by design. The viscountess's suite is luxurious, to say the least."

"When I dreamed of our marriage before, Bryson, I had no intention of sleeping anywhere but in your bed." Another admission, out before she could stop it. His reaction—a clenched jaw, a flush, a balled fist—was satisfying, even now. One last opportunity to provoke him.

He gritted his teeth. "Well, then perhaps you will not balk at my last stipulation."

"I'm balking at all of it—the entire scheme. What is your last stipulation? That I sing in the church choir?"

She watched him turn in an agitated circle, collecting himself. "I will require children."

Oh.

"Of course," she said. "An heir."

"If I am blessed with a son," he said amicably, "yes. But if you bear only daughters, so be it. I would not keep you as a…brood mare."

"I do believe this is the most romantic proposal I have ever known."

"I tried for a romantic proposal, Elisabeth. At the ball. It was not to be."

"Yes. Well. You may have a difficult time procreating with your wife if she is alone in her luxurious viscountess's suite."

"If you agree," he said, pressing on, "some…*rotation* can be agreed upon, put down in writing for us both. Strategically timed appointments, possibly slotted in for a full year at a time."

It was now Elisabeth's time to close her eyes.

How in God's name had she arrived at this moment?

Why not simply be left alone, never to know love or children, but to live peacefully and helpfully without enduring this cruel irony?

Tears formed behind her eyelids, and she bit them back.

It was too late. He'd already read her expression. "It all sounds very rigid and impersonal, perhaps, but it is more in line with the relationship I first conceived of for a marriage, before we—before. Nearly every other facet of my life is put down on a schedule, and it makes for far less complication. My own parents were slaves to their passions. And they abused so many people—each other, most of all—because these impulses fuel equal parts recklessness and selfishness. It is no way to live."

"No," she heard herself say.

She would not feel sorry for him. His damaged boyhood would break anyone's heart, but his heart was not hers to mend. She had suffered damage too, a different kind, and it was because of that damage that she had tried valiantly to stay away. It was why she would stay away now, despite his smiles and his regret—and his offer. Her damage only upset him more, he'd made that plainly clear.

Surely he would easily find someone else to marry. She wondered idly if she might impress upon him (as a concerned bystander) never to propose *strategically timed appointments* to whoever this future wife might eventually be.

"Elisabeth?" he said, prompting her. "Will you say something? Do you understand what I propose?"

"Yes, I understand. It has shocked me, but I can comprehend it." She looked at him. "Of all the reasons I thought you persisted in ten days of relentless calling to our front door, I never dreamed that you wished to carry on with a wedding."

"I rarely break my promises. And I was promised to you."

"But only for thirty minutes. And a disastrous thirty minutes they were."

"The incident changed the nature of our union, but it need not change the fact that we will, in the end, unite."

"Bryson, I…I cannot. Don't you see? Any arrangement between the two of us is ambitious at best. I know that we will both eventually forget the discomfort of the…'incident,' as you call it. But marriage is a far more complicated thing from which to recover. Marriage is forever. I will always be that girl from the brothel; I will always have tried to hide it from you for far too long. You will always be the man who blamed *me* when you discovered my secret. I shall never forget your reaction."

He stood again, running a frustrated hand through his hair. "I will forget," he insisted. "I have not asked about what happened there—at the brothel. Before I arrived and bore you away. It does not matter to me."

"This only proves my point. Naturally it would come back to this. You *cannot* forget."

"It is not your fault, obviously. You were a victim. I can abide this."

"That's very decent of you," she said, squinting her eyes. She stood up. "And what if I wish to talk about it? What if I wish to tell you? Would you hear it then?"

"Of course," he said, but she saw the unease in his eyes.

"Don't worry. I've said I detest talking about it, and that's true." She dropped back into her chair. "Ironic, that. This is precisely the type of damaging silence we discourage from the girls at the foundation."

"Look, Elisabeth," he said. "I haven't the capacity for openness or gentleness, for the unconditional compassion that you do. I know I feel wretched for you and what you endured, that I feel fury toward the men who did this to you. But I don't know what you need from me to make it palatable for us to proceed."

She opened her mouth to remind him, but he spoke over her. "I know what you do *not* need, and I will not treat you so callously ever again. Whatever else you want, I stand ready to serve. I'm sorry I cannot guess it, but you need only tell me."

She marveled at him. "You have said everything right. I needn't tell you anything except marrying me to avoid *gossip* is wrong. There are worse things."

He turned away, sighing heavily and looking at the ceiling. "I see. You cannot forgive me. I am not repentant enough."

"On the contrary, you seem duly repentant. But whether you are truly sorry does not matter so much as your reaction the *next* time I do something to stun you or hurt you or disappoint you. The *next time* you misunderstand. Yes, I can forgive you. But how can I know when you will next launch into a maddened rage? I am mindful of others' feelings, and I am not rash or secretive, but eventually, I will displease you. And I cannot survive in a marriage—traditional *or* businesslike—wherein I live in fear of your unsubstantiated anger."

He studied her for a moment, considering this. He nodded to the floor. "For this, I have no defense. I had not...not thought of it. I can vow to you that I am not some dormant madman who might explode every time he's provoked." He looked up. "Of course, I have no proof. But you must remember that I strive to be temperate in all things. Another talisman of a childhood spent in dizzying chaos. My parents' ceaseless shouting nearly defeated me. I hold my temper in check because I hated it so very much. I will not run mad if you mislay the key to the cellar."

"So you say," she said softly.

He stood up and walked three steps to the wall and back, chuckling. "Right. Now I feel compelled to ask: *What other* life-altering secrets that strike at the heart of my deepest insecurities could you withhold from me, Elisabeth? Is there something *else* I should expect to discover from a smug, hated cousin after a public gesture? Perhaps if we cleared up that now, we can cut off 'unsubstantiated anger' at the bend."

It was a joke, and Elisabeth smiled along sadly, working to suppress the tendrils of hope that had begun to twine around the fractured trellis of her heart. He should not be so honest. He should not lay himself so bare. He should not be more open and authentic than he had ever been, just as she was

ready to say good-bye to him forever. She blinked, sighed—
and then she remembered.

Aunt Lillian.

Quincy.

In her miserable, self-involved sadness, she'd forgotten
that she *did* have another life-altering secret—one that she
had mourned as much in these last ten days as her own broken heart.

She stood up. "As a matter of fact, I do have such a secret."
She watched him closely, crossing her arms over her chest. He
wished to press this marriage? He insisted that she was his
model wife? Let this be the ultimate test. He would fail it, of
this she was sure. But then they would both know.

He stopped pacing and turned around. "You're joking."

"*No.*" She shook her head. "I will tell it to you, here and
now. When you hear it, if you still wish to marry me, I will
consider your…arrangement."

"Truly?" He took a step closer.

"*Wait* until you hear it. And remember your promises
upon entering this house. No shouting."

"Oh, God, Elisabeth, what is it?"

She took a deep breath, drawing her hands up in front of
her chest and clasping them together. "My aunt, the esteemed
Countess of Banning, has been carrying on a twenty-year love
affair with her gardener. A man called Benjamin Quincy. They
are fully committed and intend to marry. They have been in
love since shortly after her aged husband's death, years ago—
the old earl. Quincy is like an uncle to me, and he's adored
by everyone in this house. My aunt is madly in love. I'm sure
you've seen him. He is never far from her at his duties."

Rainsleigh stood stock-still, staring at her.

"It is why Aunt Lillian never remarried," Elisabeth went on. "She was waiting until I was settled. She would not damage my reputation by running off with a member of staff. Of course she will lose the title, the house. If I were not married when they did this, I would have nowhere to go. It's to be a whole new life for them. On a tropical island, apparently, which is their dream."

"A tropical island…" he repeated faintly.

"In the Caribbean Sea."

"And you've…known all along?"

"Well, I've known since I came to live with her after I…well, after you rescued me. In the beginning, I was preoccupied with recovering. I knew only my own pain and grief. By the time I emerged from the fog, I had grown accustomed to Quincy. Their relationship is very natural. He is a wonderful man. They are very happy."

"And they are determined to run away? To leave London and marry?"

"Determined is the wrong word. It is their most fervent wish—well, after seeing me happy. I am trying to convince them to go, even while I remain here alone, but they are very committed to me."

"Indeed." His expression was unreadable.

"I was going to tell you," she said.

"I can see now that you've had a growing list of things to tell me." He raised an eyebrow, and she laughed. It was a small laugh at first, a chuckle. She tried to stifle it, but then she was laughing in earnest. Two weeks of agony let loose in a torrent of laughter and tears combined. She put a hand on the back of her chair to support herself, bent over laughing. She stole a look at him. He stared back, shaking his head. *Disgusted*, she assumed, but then she saw his achingly familiar wrinkled-cheeked smile, and she felt something dislodge in her heart. A talon or a thorn—some sharp, heavy thing that had pinned it down. Now it simply let go. She swallowed her laughter and wiped away her tears.

"Would they consider waiting until after the wedding?" he asked, looking mildly pained.

She blinked at him, certain she'd misheard. "I believe that was the plan. They would not miss my, er, wedding."

"What has become of the Banning earldom? Who became earl when the old earl died? Your aunt is not a dowager, so there was no one with a wife, gunning to be countess."

"There was a distant cousin who is said to be lost at sea. Solicitors of the estate pursued him, but the young man was never particularly interested in the title before he set sail. Lord Banning married my very young aunt in a desperate attempt to produce a suitable heir. But he died before…"

"And so she has chosen instead *the gardener*." He sounded as if he were trying to convince himself.

"Quincy fought valiantly in the war," Elisabeth said.

Bryson dropped into his chair. She moved to sit opposite, watching him.

"You see?" he finally asked, looking at her. "You see how calmly and rationally I am responding to this news?"

"Oh, so now you're telling me that you can weather the gossip of my aunt's great escape?"

"If they will consider a few suggestions I might offer on the timing and the strategy of their departure—yes."

"But they must actually go, and they must actually wed."

"Oh, yes they must."

She thought about this. He was a man of his word. If he promised it, it would be done. Aunt Lillian and Quincy—finally married and openly living as man and wife. The reward for their long-awaited happiness was nearly enough to make her immediately consent. Their sacrifice all these years had been for her. She could now make one for them, could she not?

A moment later, she asked, "And you would not promise the money for my foundation if you did not mean to give it?"

"The money is yours. Your good work will flourish."

"And…and…" Her voice grew stronger now, more demanding, "May I find employment in your shipyard for the girls I rehabilitate? Sewing sails or sweeping up? Whatever honest work you may have for them?"

His eyes grew large, and he scratched his jaw. He made a faint growling noise.

She shrugged. "It is the right thing to do."

He growled again, shifting in his chair. He'd tossed his coat over a quilt stand, and he leaned back and reached inside it now. She watched him pull out the ring she'd dropped in his hands ten days before.

"The agreement comes with jewelry," he said. "Part of our public appearance." He handed it to her.

She reached out and took it, their fingers brushing in the exchange. "Shall I remove it when we are behind closed doors?"

He blinked. "If you prefer."

"Perhaps we can add the rotation of the ring to the strategically timed appointments…" She turned away to slide it on.

The weight of it was a conscious thing. She had only worn it for a moment in time, but she had felt its absence since she'd pulled it off that night. Like ripping off a layer of skin. She opened and closed her finger, trying not to stare at it.

When she looked up, he was watching her carefully, intimately.

"Does that mean you agree to the marriage? The business arrangement?"

"Either that, or I am stealing this ring."

"And you are…content?"

"Oh," she mused, unable to resist gazing at the ring, "let us not classify the vivid spectrum of our current contentedness." She tore her eyes away. "Yours or mine."

He nodded, allowing the topic to dissolve. What more was there to say? She could identify only two truly happy things: Her aunt was now free to marry and go, and she would never have to worry about resources for the foundation again.

As for the rest of it?

Well, marriage to him could not be worse than the last ten days without him had been.

CHAPTER TWENTY-TWO

The irony of the wedding, Rainsleigh thought, was its utter perfection. He and Lady Banning had thrown the whole affair together in just three weeks' time, not that anyone could guess. The church dripped with flowers. The musicians and robed boys choir transported the audience to an angelic realm. The esteemed guests—a mix of the countess's society friends and Rainsleigh's well-heeled shipping clients— were a colorful bouquet of hats and fans and sugary-colored spring finery.

The ceremony was at St. Paul's, an obvious choice, but he and Lady Banning had clashed over the site of the breakfast. As Elisabeth's guardian, the countess had expected to host the guests at Denby House in Grosvenor Square. But Rain-sleigh had pressed for a grand feast in his new townhome in Henrietta Place. He'd gone to the expense of building and furnishing the bloody thing; what more legitimate reason to trail all of influential London through its doors than his own wedding?

If circumstances had been different…if his and Elisa-beth's relationship had been as it was before…then perhaps he would be less inclined to exploit the exposure. But now? Now the purpose of their union *was* exposure. He married her so that no one would talk about a showy engagement that fizzled out. And even before that, he'd chosen her because she appeared to be an ideal wife.

As to the wedding, he would have curtailed any detail if she would but have asked. But she was never at home when he called to discuss the wedding with her aunt, and Lady Banning assured him that she had no preference whatsoever. When he insisted that he should hear it from her, he was given no choice but to write her to ask what she wished. A note came back by her boy, Stoker. One line:

I have no preferences for the wedding. Do as you wish.

Well, he had wished to host the bloody wedding feast. In the end, Lady Banning conceded, as her home could not easily be made ready to host three hundred guests in such a short period of time. Rainsleigh would have his way, and the party was set for Henrietta Place.

After the venue and the food, there was the matter of the dress. Rainsleigh and the countess agreed it must be exquisite and unique and unforgettable—and complete in three-weeks' time. Rainsleigh had wanted to buy it—he'd wanted to buy everything—but her aunt would not be swayed, and she paid triple to London's most esteemed modiste to have a singular frock rushed into production.

In the end, it was worth whatever the price. When Elisabeth emerged from the vestibule at the far end of St. Paul's, Rainsleigh worked to curtail the jaw-drop and intake of breath. He had not seen her in twenty-one days. He had thought of her many times in those weeks (if he was being honest, he thought *only* of her during that time), but the memory of her beauty did not compare to the living, breathing golden glow of life. Or perhaps she had, in fact, never looked quite so lovely as on her wedding day. Whatever the reason, he could not look away.

Ironic, because he had meant to glance at her once and then to look anywhere else—one of many moments about which he'd lain awake at night, planning in advance. His brother had teased him for plotting simple reactions, but it was a way of assuming control of an event that, despite the design of every detail, had felt wildly out of control. And anyway, why should he stare? It would be too personal. Staring revealed too much.

But oh, when the moment was upon them, detachment was lost to him. No reaction this strong could possibly be concealed. The full scope of his desire surely burned in his eyes.

The dress was perfection. No garment had better suited her, he thought. The design was simple—light, gauzy fabric of the finest silk, falling in yards and yards from tiny gathers at an empire waist. It was the color of forest in the shade. The contrast against Elisabeth's lightly bronzed skin, freckles, and red-gold hair was nothing short of ethereal in the sunlit church.

And her hair? He'd never known her to wear even the simplest jewelry, but today she wore a sparkling coronet, diamonds mounted on a slight silver setting, as beautiful as it was regal. From the crown fell her veil, with her hair pulled back from her face and then long down her back.

When Rainsleigh recovered from the sheer shock of her breathtaking beauty, he began searching her face. Was she unhappy? Resigned? Was she afraid? Bitter? Regretful? Did she approve of the flowers and the music and the great many guests?

Did she approve of him?

He could not say. She returned his gaze. Her blue-green eyes grew large. She smiled a little. And then she was the one who coolly looked away. Her eyes darted away, and she remained transfixed on the stained-glass window above his head until the bishop invited them to kneel.

When the ceremony began, she glanced at him only when the vows called for it. She repeated the familiar words in low, even tones. Her hand was warm and steady when he slid the ring on.

At Rainsleigh's request, the ceremony was classical and formal, and there was no place for a kiss. When it was finally over, the bishop bade the bride and groom to face the guests, and he intoned, "Lord Bryson Anders and Lady Elisabeth Rose Courtland, the Viscount and Viscountess Rainsleigh."

And then it was done.

Rainsleigh could not resist and stole another long, searching look at her face. If she gave some reaction, any at all, he would not miss it.

She stared back, cordial but vague, her beauty heartbreaking at such close range. And then she stared out at the great crowd with her chin high. He felt an unaccustomed clench in his chest, a physical reaction to her profile, or that raised little chin, or simply to the fact that she was standing so closely beside him again. He forced himself to look away.

Adhere to the plan, he ordered and proffered his arm to lead her down the aisle. Her hand settled over the top of his hand, light and stiff, barely touching. A formality. The message was clear. She could march independently down the aisle in the same way she'd marched up, but she would follow convention. She would play along. Resigned. Formal. Entirely for show.

It's what you wanted, he reminded himself.

Before you met her, when any future wife was but an ideal. And after you knew her, after you really knew her. You wanted this. Resigned and formal and just for show.

It it's all you wanted.

In that instant, while hundreds of guests beamed up at them, Rainsleigh felt deeply, crushingly sad. Sadder than he had been in a very long time.

Underlying the sadness was anger. Only a spoiled child would demand something, receive it, and then declare it not enough.

But it's not enough, he thought, forcing a grim smile.

It's not bloody enough.

They were silent in the carriage to the breakfast feast, each on opposite seats for the short ride to Henrietta Place.

Elisabeth could have made some idle chatter, but she refused to be trite. She would not prattle on about the beauty of the church or the flowers and the songs—not when there were so many more pressing and important things to discuss. When Rainsleigh had proposed (well, when he had proposed the second time), the conversation had been painful, but it had also been frank and honest. She could not bear for them to become disingenuous and petty now. If there was any hope for civility between them, they must have honesty or nothing at all.

The quietness felt strange in the closed carriage, not to mention rude, but she allowed herself to lean her head back on the soft leather seat and embrace it. He had pressed for this arrangement; surely the burden was on him. She closed her eyes, willing the gentle sway of the vehicle to while away her regret for what might have been.

When the carriage turned onto Henrietta Place, Rainsleigh cleared his throat, and she opened one eye. He watched her.

She sat up.

"Elisabeth," he began, "I thought we should discuss the domestic...er, positioning."

"All right." She had no idea what this meant.

"My housekeeper, Mrs. Linn, is very proficient at running the house and managing staff, working in tandem with Sewell, the butler. I have told her that you will direct her in your preferred level of involvement. Please consider your own work at the foundation and choose what best suits you. It makes no difference to me either way."

Elisabeth nodded. If he meant what he said, this was a generosity indeed. She had no time for (or interest in) running his overgrown house, but naturally, it would be expected of a wife. "Thank you," she said.

"Your trunks from Denby House arrived yesterday, and I instructed Mrs. Linn to see your things put away in the viscountess's suite. I hope that is acceptable."

"It is," she said carefully, searching the statement for deeper meaning.

"You may arrange the suite as you see fit," he went on, "and send out for anything more you require. I hired a man to furnish the suite in the style of a lady of means with a considerable wardrobe. God knows if he got it right."

"I will look forward to settling in," she said, but she thought, *I don't care about the room. I don't care about the trunks or Mrs. Linn.*

They'd said so very little to each other since he'd learned her terrible secret. Was there nothing he wanted to discover, now that he could look on her real, true self? Nothing at all?

But perhaps he could not bear to look upon her real, true self.

She had no idea how to ask this, of course. And honestly, was it her right to ask? This was a business arrangement, after all.

"I am aware of your…fatigue," he continued. "I thought I'd show you to your chambers tonight, and perhaps Mrs. Linn can take you around to every nook and newel in the morning. Since we are not bothering with a wedding trip, I assumed we would each resume our normal lives and schedules tomorrow."

In response to this, she could but nod. She tried not to think of the grand tour of his house he had planned before their courtship had so abruptly come to an end. It was his idea of an outing, and he suggested it more than once. He'd said Miss Breedlowe would chaperone, as in the visit to his shipyard. He had not yet asked her to marry him, but he had alluded to "learning her preference" for changes to decor or the function of rooms. He'd hinted at a suitable guest room for Stoker on school holidays and a "second office" for her beside his own.

What a difference three weeks made. Now someone named Mrs. Linn would provide the tour. Now Elisabeth would discover her new home by walking in the front door as a resident. It was only her second time.

"After the crush of the reception, I assume you'll want to take supper in your rooms," he finished. He pushed the carriage curtain aside with one gloved finger and looked out the window.

"Perhaps. Yes," she said quietly, mortified to hear a quaver in her voice. "It might be best."

Now? she thought, swallowing hard. Now *I will cry?*

She'd endured the lavish ceremony, the dazzled guests, and the misguided vows with dry eyes, and *now she would cry?*

The carriage bounced to a stop in front of his house, thank God, ending the conversation. The door flipped open, and a line of liveried servants could be seen standing sentry outside. She blinked, swallowed hard, and braced herself for more of the same.

Chapter Twenty-Three

Quincy was not a guest at the wedding breakfast. Elisabeth had seen him at the church, seated in the back beside Stoker, but he was nowhere to be found in Rainsleigh's elaborately bunted garden or ballroom.

When she consulted Aunt Lilly, she was told that Lilly and Quincy had decided not to raise the topic with Rainsleigh when the guest list was set. They were grateful for the viscount's understanding about their...circumstance, and they did not wish to embarrass him or shock guests at the wedding. They would not elope for another month.

"Please do not fret over it, darling," Lillian told Elisabeth when she pulled her into a far corner of the garden. "You made the decision not to take part in the planning, and so we made such choices without you. Quincy is here in spirit."

"But he should be here in *body*," Elisabeth said, her voice breaking.

Elisabeth had needed the intervening weeks between the proposal and the wedding to make peace in her mind with the agreement and her new life. *Perhaps it was indulgent to leave the plans to others,* she now thought. Yet another bungled thing. She squeezed back tears.

"Quincy is like a father to me," she said.

"And you are the daughter of his heart. That is why he made the sacrifice." Lillian handed her a plate of wedding cake. "But come, please do not be sullen. It is the last thing Quincy would wish. Let me get a look at you in the sunlight. Just stunning. I couldn't be more pleased with the color of this dress. But, oh…" She frowned. "Do take more care with the hem on these outdoor paths." She stooped to cluck over Elisabeth's skirts.

"I'm never sullen," Elisabeth said, sniffing the cake. "And what could sullenness possibly matter now? We're married; isn't that enough? Your dastardly plan has been realized. Although I feel compelled to point out that you nearly missed the mark—"

"Nearly but not entirely," Lillian mumbled, shaking dust from Elisabeth's hem.

"And anyway, the marriage is not an authentic one. Do you know what we discussed in the carriage from St. Paul's? My baggage. The trunks. The housekeeper, Mrs. Someone-or-Other. It's a *business agreement,* Lilly, there is no love or romance—your personal life's quest." She took a tentative bite of the cake. Sugar and butter melted in her mouth, and she sunk her fork in again.

"But what *business agreement?*" scoffed Lilly, studying Elisabeth's coiffeur. "The marriage will *overflow* with love, once you settle in. It seems ambiguous now, but it is only a matter of time."

Elisabeth shook her head. "Our relationship will be nothing like what you enjoy with Quincy; it will not be like Mama and Papa." She was swamped with sadness, saying the words out loud. "We are to be associates, he and I. What use has he for a dishonest wife? Or for a wife who cannot be the virginal vessel of innocence for whom he waited so long?"

"So be someone better—be *yourself*. Waited for a vessel, has he? Make him burn *for you*." She snatched a pin from Elisabeth's coiffure and then reapplied it to her coronet.

"*Ouch*." Elisabeth rubbed her head. "It's all an operetta to you, naturally. 'Burn'? Honestly, Lillian."

"You think I am being whimsical?"

"I think you're being ridiculous." Elisabeth didn't want to talk about it. Talking about it only inclined her to believe. And she *should not, would not* believe.

"But you are so much more—so much *better*—than the boring wife for whom he thought he waited. You are a gift to any man but especially to him. He needs only to unwrap you. And you need only to assist him."

"He will not touch me," Elisabeth said. The cake was suddenly far too sweet in her mouth, and she balanced the fork on the plate. "He said so himself. You'll remember the conception of children is to be set out, a year in advance, on a scheduled rotation. I can only assume this allows him to become very drunk before he embarks, so he can suffer through it."

"Now who is being dramatic? You know nothing about men, darling, especially a man who stares at you as long and as hungrily as Rainsleigh does. If he wants innocence, he certainly has that in you. You can't see his considerable desire for you, even now. But he is stubborn and ashamed of his behavior—as well he should be. It may be up to you show him how to seize that desire."

"I will not manipulate him, if that's what's you mean." She had misled him enough already. He could not bear any more, and neither could she.

"I mean, allow yourself to be the woman he cannot resist. Believe me, it will not take much."

"I hardly see myself becoming irresistible to a man who has vowed only to touch me for the purpose of getting an heir, and only if it's already on his agenda."

"Oh," cooed Lillian, "but these are the best sorts of men to persuade."

"You can say that because every man wants you."

"I can say that"—Lillian dusted off her hands and smoothed her own skirts—"because *Rainsleigh* wants *you*. All joking aside, Elisabeth, you know I would not give you to him if I did not believe the two of you were very well suited, or that nature will eventually take its course. I have every confidence that you will emerge happy and in love. Think me dramatic or addled by blind hope if you must, but you will see. You will see."

"The only one addled here, dear Lillian, is me," Elisabeth mumbled, turning to stare out at the crowded garden. She spotted Rainsleigh immediately, half a head taller than everyone else. He looked up in the same moment, and her traitorous stomach did a flip. Their gazes locked. He stared but did not smile.

Elisabeth nodded grimly and looked away. "I simply want us to get on with our lives," she said softly. "The arrangement suits me in the same way it suits him. I merely have a new address."

CHAPTER TWENTY-FOUR

"I should like to know, Rainsleigh, how you prevent this goldfish pool from flooding the garden when it rains?" Lady Frinfrock cornered the viscount beside the rear garden wall in the third hour of the wedding feast. He'd been shocked to turn around and discover her still going strong.

"You've paid no mind to flooding," she went on, waving her cane at the perfectly dry beds, "none at all. You've been lucky with the dry spring we have enjoyed, but when the rains return—and they always return—you will lose half of these beds; mark my words."

"How astute of you to notice," Rainsleigh said, looking over the plumage of her hat for some reason to step away. "Perhaps you would be so kind as to have a word with my gardener."

"Perhaps you would take an interest in your own property," the marchioness harrumphed. "Servants can only do so much. 'Tis the lord of the manor who steers the vessel. Servants merely swab the decks."

Rainsleigh had no idea how to respond to this statement; moreover, he didn't care. In fact, he couldn't remember when he had cared less about the house or the garden or the bloody drainage. He struggled to keep a pleasant expression on his face and scanned the crowd again for Elisabeth.

She was near the pergola, her back to him, surrounded by a circle of Lady Banning's friends. He frowned. Were her shoulders drooping? Was she massaging the back of her neck? He worried she had become over-tired. The countess's friends were a trial for her on any day, and today had not been any day. The preparation, the ceremony, and now going on three hours at the reception. He had not once seen her sit. He cleared his throat, glanced at the marchioness mid-scold, and prepared to make some conciliatory statement and walk away.

"Ah, there you are, the happy groom." His brother strode into view, bearing drinks in both hands, thank God.

"And *hello*, my lady," Beau said to Lady Frinfrock. "Don't you look lovely in that orange hat?"

The old woman turned, squinting at his brother's voice. "Ah, Mr. Courtland." She shaded her eyes. "'Tis you. Tell me, how does it feel to wear a proper cravat for perhaps the first time ever in life?"

"Splendid, actually. Just like a noose. But Lady Falcondale and Miss Breedlowe are looking for you, I believe. Something about your opinion on the food being left out too long in the sun?"

Bryson opened his mouth to assure them that the food was of the finest quality, tended by the most professional staff, but Beau winked at him and gave a subtle shake of his head.

"Oh, it's been ruined, I dare say." The marchioness sighed, already stumping away. "Only a foolish man would set out such a feast in the heat of the day."

"Enjoying the party as much as the marchioness?" Beau asked when she was gone. He handed Rainsleigh a drink.

"How long do you think it will go?" It was three o'clock in the afternoon.

"The marchioness? Come now, Bryse, she is unpleasant, but we mustn't refer to her as '*it*.'"

Rainsleigh sighed. "The *party*. How long will the party go?"

"Oh, right." He looked around. "Well, it's your event, Bryse. Bring it to an end whenever you wish. In my experience, parties desist when the spirits run dry."

"I worry Elisabeth is tired." He stared at her across the terrace. She looked ethereal, as if she existed only to inhabit this garden.

Now she moved, raising her hand to wave to Miss Breed-lowe, and the outline of her body could be seen in gauzy relief through the layers of her dress. Long, slim legs; the tight tuck of her waist above the flare of her hips; her flat stomach and pert breasts. A pang of lust shot through him so acute that he tossed back his drink one gulp.

"Hmmm. What about you, Bryse?" His brother followed his gaze. "Are you...*tired*?" He chuckled and shook his head.

Rainsleigh smirked and turned back to Elisabeth. How, he wondered, would she receive the suggestion that they take their leave? A departure now would not be unacceptable for the bride and groom. But depart and go where? They were already at home. He would risk her rejection, and happily so, if he could think of some alternative destination. He'd already suggested dinner in their separate rooms, and she'd agreed. Was this what she wanted?

She was turning now, walking with the group as her aunt led them into the ballroom.

"Do what *you* wish, Bryse," Beau said, more serious now. "You cater to the standards of strangers and what they think is right, or appropriate, or proper, et cetera, et cetera. Can you not make time for your own desires tonight?" He turned to look at him. "For once in your life, Bryson, what do *you* wish?"

"I wish…" Rainsleigh paused, considering this. "For her to be happy." This was the truth.

Beau nodded. "Unselfish to the very core. Right. Of course you do. Very well, I'd start by asking her what the bloody hell that might be."

"Yes," he said, handing his empty glass to Beau. "Ask her. For once, you may be right."

Rainsleigh wove his way through the party, following Elisabeth and the laughing, trilling group inside. Business associates and other guests rushed up to wish him well, but he waved them away. When Elisabeth reached the great hall, she slowed down and fell behind Lady Banning and her friends. They didn't seem to notice, and she stopped altogether. When they moved on, she carefully began to back away.

Only steps behind, Rainsleigh fell in line behind her. Intentionally, he allowed the two of them to collide.

"*Oh!*" she gasped, bouncing off his chest. He steadied her, catching her around the waist. She was an irresistible bundle of silk and veils.

She tried to spin. "I beg your pard—"

"Only me," he said gently. His hands lingered.

"So it is," she said, hopping two steps back. "I didn't see you there."

"Are you enjoying yourself?" he asked.

She hesitated a moment. "It has been a grand party, Rainsleigh."

He glanced around them. "So grand, I worry it may never end. I am concerned about you. Take care that you don't become over-tired."

She chuckled. "Yes. I believe even my aunt is tired, and that is saying quite a lot."

"You know I can bring the party to an official close," he said. "One round of thanks and then send everyone on their way. If you are tired, I shall have no qualms about empting the house."

"And have this be the gossip of the party?" she teased. "How lovely it was until the viscount booted everyone out. No, let them enjoy your hospitality. You should enjoy it too. I may"— she cast a glance around, looking at the stairs and then back to him— "may slip away to my bedchamber, if I can find it."

An image of Elisabeth alone in her bedchamber settled in his brain, and his pulse jumped.

He hesitated, wanting to get the next bit exactly right. "I should be happy to show you around upstairs," he said.

She turned back to him. There was a light in her eyes he had not seen in some time. "I thought you had relegated this task to your housekeeper," she reminded him. "Mrs. Linn, was it?" She cocked a delicate eyebrow.

Was she flirting with him?

"Mrs. Linn is terribly busy at the moment," he said, and he extended his arm.

She took it, looping one hand beneath and placing her other hand on top. She nudged close. Her skirts swished against his boot as they began to walk. She looked behind her to check the location of her aunt, and her hair tickled his hand. He felt the outline of her breast against his arm. It was all he wanted—no, that was a lie. He wanted considerably more, but he would accept this.

"There is a balcony," he said, climbing the marble stairwell, "that overlooks the garden. We can sit there, unobserved, and watch the guests filter out from above. I'll ring for a dinner tray if it pleases you."

"That sounds divine, actually," she said, allowing him to lead her up. "A balcony, you say?"

"Hmmm. I had it built for star-gazing, actually, and I can show you—"

Just as they reached the top step and turned onto the landing, the distinctive sound of Lady Frinfrock's froglike voice rose from the hall below.

"I've waited long enough," she was saying, "I will see this illustrious music room wall."

Rainsleigh and Elisabeth froze for two beats and then slowly turned in unison. There was the marchioness, stumping toward the stairwell with her cane, flanked by her friend, Miss Baker, and Lord and Lady Falcondale, Rainsleigh's friends from next door.

Elisabeth went tense beside him. "*Oh*," she murmured, fatigue clear in her voice. "Sign of a good host, I suppose, if your guests feel free to roam every level of your house."

"It's your house too," he said, swearing in his head. "And I cannot imagine their business up here."

Moving deftly, he steered Elisabeth to the corner of the landing and then stepped back, so they were out of sight. He looked at her. "Ignore them; they will pass. You are tired. It's not worth the effort."

"Even if I was wide awake," she said, "I'm not sure I would have the fortitude to deal with your neighbor. We've already discussed the color of my dress, the style of my hair, and the flavor of the cake." She let out a weary sigh. "If an idea did not originate with her, she considers it open for debate."

He chuckled and looked right and left. Elisabeth's bedroom door was adjacent to the corner, but they could not make it there without colliding with Lady Frinfrock and her entourage. His own door was beyond that, an even greater risk. The landing ended behind them with a small cupboard door.

He swore again and looked back at his neighbors. They continued to come, ascending the stairs with alarming speed, considering the marchioness's cane. He looked down at Elisabeth. She shrank behind the corner and leaned her head back against the wall. She closed her eyes. "I'm all right," she said, sighing. "I just need a moment."

Rainsleigh nodded, searching her face. The perfect constellation of her freckles was irresistible, he thought. He would never grow tired of looking at her.

But now they would deal with the neighbors. He sighed, backing away. He checked their progress on the stairs. He swore. He scanned the landing again.

"Elisabeth," he said, suddenly inspired, "take heart." He grabbed up her hand. "I don't think we've yet been spotted." He tugged her off the wall.

"What do you mean?" She laughed, staring at their clasped hands.

"Follow me." Staying close to the wall, he whipped open the small door to the adjacent cupboard. With a quick glance over his shoulder, he gestured for her to step inside.

She laughed again but hesitated only for a minute. Lady Frinfrock could be heard bearing down on the upper steps now, just feet away from the landing. Elisabeth hopped in.

Rainsleigh shot a glance over his shoulder. Falcondale rounded the corner, and he caught his gaze. His friend cocked one suggestive eyebrow. Rainsleigh raised one finger to his lips and silently shook his head. *Not a word,* he mouthed, and then he nimbly stepped inside behind his wife.

Elisabeth laughed, and he shushed her gently, nudging her further in. She ignored him and laughed more still, struggling to untangle her veil and skirts from various mop and broom handles propped against the wall. When she was free, he reached around her and pulled the door shut with a click.

"*Shhh,*" he said again, but this only seemed to elicit more laughter. Now she was entirely out of control, and he settled his hand over her mouth to cup the sound. He shushed her again, but it was no use. Her composure dissolved in a fit of giggles, and she lost her balance. Rainsleigh swore, laughing now too, and broadened his stance to support her. He caught her up with his free hand.

The moment his palm closed over her waist, the laughter stopped. Silence settled around them like the curtain on a stage, and their other senses came alive. He smelled the perfume of her hair. He looked down and saw her profile in the darkness. He felt…*oh, God*. He breathed deeply, savoring what he felt. Her lips under one hand, her body beneath the other.

"Please tell me this is not my bedchamber," she whispered against his fingers.

With considerable effort, he drew his hand away from her mouth. "A cupboard," he managed to say.

"I think they saw us," she said. "I *know* they saw us."

"Lady Frinfrock only sees what stares her in the face," he whispered, and she laughed again.

"*Shhh*," he reminded her, and something about the darkness and the proximity propelled him to rest his face against her veil and hair. He breathed in. She leaned against him, her back to his front, and his heartbeat ricocheted against her. Meanwhile, her bottom…*oh, God*…the delicious curve of her bottom was tucked against him, a perfect, *perfect* fit.

But now they heard footsteps outside the door, laughter, voices.

She tensed, and Rainsleigh tucked her closer. Elisabeth nestled back, and he made a low, strangled noise. His body had, perhaps, never been so acutely, strainingly aware of another human form.

The footsteps and voices grew louder, louder. They were right outside. Rainsleigh held his breath, oblivious to the irony of hiding from his own wedding guests—oblivious to everything but the feel of his wife in his arms.

And then, just as quickly as they had come, the footsteps began to fade. They were left with nothing more than the overwhelming sensation of each other's proximity and the sound of their own shallow breath.

"Elisabeth?" he finally said, his voice barely audible. His mouth was just inches from her ear. He need only dip his head a fraction of an inch to touch it to his lips to its softness.

"Yes?"

"Are you…" He forgot what he intended to say.

She wiggled, setting off a surge of pleasure that tested the limits of his self-control.

He released her waist, desperate to get a handle on his desire, and his body *raged* at the separation. He clenched his fists at his sides to prevent himself from snatching her back.

Free of his grasp, Elisabeth now began to fidget. She adjusted her veil, her skirts, her coronet. Despite the gap between them, each tug and pat brought her pressing up against him. He swallowed a groan.

"Sorry," she whispered, but she kept moving, puffing the sleeves of her dress, smoothing her hair.

Now she shuffled, staggered a step, and began to turn. Slowly, silently, she revolved to face him in the tight space. When her back was to the door, she leaned against it and tipped her head up. In the darkness, he could barely make out her face.

He swallowed. A moment passed. Two. Three. A hundred. Time ceased to make sense. He knew only the beats of his own rapidly pounding heart.

The door behind her creaked, and she jumped. He reached out to steady her, and his fingertips brushed her knuckles, the lightest of contact. It felt so incredibly right. As right as anything he'd known since he'd last held her, weeks ago. He reached out again. A glancing brush, a graze on her arm. The third time, she opened her fingers and captured his hand. Their linked fingers sank into the layers of her gown.

She tugged slightly—or did he?—and their faces were closer now. A whisper apart. He felt her breath on his neck. His own breathing seemed out of his control.

A thin line of light glowed beneath the door, and when he'd stared long enough, he could make out the curve of her eyelashes against her cheek. These became a defining feature, a landmark. He watched them shut, and open, shut again. He heard her lick her lips. It was his undoing.

He lowered his lips to hers and kissed her. Slowly, gently. He was deliberate, and cautious, and careful. Just in case.

She did not turn away. She tipped her head higher, receiving him, welcoming him. He closed his eyes and tasted. She was, at the same time, familiar and new. Forbidden and his very own. A moan escaped him, and he squeezed the hand he held. She opened her hands and spread her fingers, closing them again around his, entwined.

His only purpose in the world became the feel of her lips, the scent of her, the feel of her hair brushing the backs of his hands.

He drew away—not far, just enough—and balanced his forehead on hers. He willed himself to go slowly, to catch his breath. For a time, they did not move, they merely…*felt*. The dark closet locked them away from past and future, from the whole bloody balance of the earth.

It was their first real embrace since the museum, as imminent as it was unexpected. What had been a slow-burning, day-long desire now roared through his body like a maelstrom. Now he dipped down to kiss her again, ravaging her mouth like a starving man. She dropped her head against the door and received the kiss, returned it, fed it.

"Elisabeth," he heard himself say, "I cannot."

She turned her head to draw a ragged breath. He descended on her neck.

"Cannot what?" she asked.

"*Stop*," he said, scooping her up, reaching for the doorknob, and pushing it open. "I cannot stop."

He glanced right and left, not really caring who might see, and kicked the cupboard door shut behind them.

He looked down at her. She did not fight him; she felt close and snug in his arms. She buried her face in his chest.

It was enough. He strode down the hall, all the while his mind spun, justifying, reasoning. It was the night of their wedding, after all. The dynamic between them was not amorous, not anymore, but the marriage was real. Was it not his right—his *duty*—to consummate the union? In the lifetime that followed, he would have only intermittent claim to her body, but did the arrangement not afford him *this* night?

He came upon his bedchamber door and jerked it open, maneuvered them inside, and slammed it shut. He fell against the door and put his lips to her neck.

"Elisabeth?" he said, speaking against her skin, "I've no right to ask this, but I would consummate the marriage tonight."

"Oh," she said, winded, against his ear. He felt her hand reach up inside his jacket and clasp the fabric of his shirt.

"If you are amendable," he said, soldiering on. The roar of blood in his ears made it difficult to think. "We need not make it romantic or overblown. There is a way to do it without descending into, er, pleasured oblivion."

That was a lie, but his brain was barely functioning. Later, he would marvel at the utter ridiculousness of this statement. Even in the moment, he wondered how many wholly false promises he would pass off as truth.

He went on, rambling now, dropping intermittent kisses on her neck between words, "Consider it a duty of marriage, if you must. Detach. You'll remember how to do this, I'm sure, from your time—"

She made a strangled noise and the words froze in his throat.

He jerked his head back and stared at her.

She looked up, blinking. Her mouth fell open. Her face had gone white.

Oh, no.

He hadn't thought. His brain was shot. The words—they simply...

And he—

"*Elisabeth...I didn't...*" he began.

Her arms fell, and she struggled, trying to pull away. He set her down. She staggered and reached for the closed door to steady herself. His hands shot out to catch her, but she shrank away.

She shut her eyes, working to control her breathing, and pressed a hand to her mouth.

After a long, horrible moment, she said, "Of course." Her blue-green eyes swam with tears, and his own heart stopped. "I'll *remember how to do this from the brothel,*" she went on, "That is what you would think."

CHAPTER TWENTY-FIVE

Elisabeth felt as if he'd doused her with icy water. "The brothel is ever present in your mind," she said. "I understand. I would expect nothing less."

He rasped, "Elisabeth—no."

"Your preoccupation with it is no different than any other bridegroom's would be." A pause. "If anything, you are far more charitable. So charitable, in fact, I allowed myself to forget." She tried a sad smile. His face was taut with misery; she could actually see his regret.

She looked away. "The great irony, of course, is that you are not a proper bridegroom. Not really. And I am not a real bride. We are *colleagues*."

"It is *not* ever present in my mind, Elisabeth," he said. He turned to the door and leaned against it, bracing his hands wide. "I don't dwell on the past—mine, yours, anyone's. My own past is wretched. What matters to me is the future." He paused, staring at the door beneath his hands. "And now, what matters is the present." He looked at her over his shoulder. "*Now* matters to me very much."

Elisabeth considered this. He stared back, his blue eyes studying her, *imploring* her. She had seen many versions of that same look over the course of the day. Each time, some subtle, nuanced quality caused her own heart to bob up a little, as if it were trying to hop out of her chest to capture whatever feeling shone there. If she had to name it, she would call this look…desperation. She'd seen it when she'd walked to him down the aisle. When he'd said his vows. When he'd taken her from the party. And she saw it now. It seemed to say what words could not.

She looked away, wondering if this could possibly be enough. A look. A desperate look that had grown increasingly more desperate as the day wore on. She shook her head. Perhaps…perhaps it could make up for words that he could not seem to say, but it could not take words away.

"Elisabeth," he said, studying her, "I cannot believe that I am asking you to forgive me again—but I am. I have behaved abominably. There is no excuse."

She waited.

"And I do not say that because I would like to make love to you. It is not an appeasement to have my own way. I…I am lost. I…it is an entirely new sensation, and I cannot say I enjoy it. But I can say that the solution seems to be…you."

Something about the admission caused her heart to bob again, rising up, seeking him. She took a deep breath and felt herself begin to nod.

"I am not angry, Bryson," she said. "And I should like to consummate the marriage, as you said." This was the truth. Isn't this what she had demanded—that they all simply tell the truth? He had done so and laid his apology at her feet.

"We are here, in your room," she went on. "We've just been married. We might as well consummate the union, as you've said. I will rely on you to…make it as you wish. If there is a less 'overblown' way to go about it, and that is what you prefer, then let us do it."

As if to prove herself, she looked purposefully at the massive bed that dominated the far wall. It was a raised, canopied affair, with a sheer curtain cordoning it all the way around, shrouding the coverlet and a heap of pillows at the headboard.

He pushed off the door, watching her study the bed.

"I should warn you," she said, suddenly overcome with nerves, "I don't…won't know what to do."

Lead me, she wanted to add, *sweep me away again.*

He took another step toward her. The look on his face was still desperate, but something new also lurked there. Purpose? *No,* she thought, forcing herself to stand her ground. *Possession.*

Her heartbeat ticked up, and she babbled on. "It is a rare situation indeed that finds me at age thirty in my familiar little world, not knowing how to proceed. I know you regard me as a veteran seductress because of—"

"Elisabeth, no." Another step.

She held up her hand and rushed to finish. "But whatever you think of me, you are, almost certainly, mistaken. So…" He was coming for her, but suddenly it wasn't fast enough. She was running out of things to say. "I will rely entirely on you to direct the, er—well, to direct me." She blushed, warmth spreading from her hairline downward, like a veil of shyness had been drawn across her face.

His expression was less careful. His eyes melted into a deeper, hotter shade of blue.

She felt compelled to add, "You do know what to do? Don't you?"

"Yes, Elisabeth," he said gruffly. "I know what to do."

You do know what to do? Elisabeth's question resounded in his head. The understatement of the century. His knowledge of "what to do" seized him with such excruciating clarity that, at the moment, he felt as if he knew little else.

And yet. Not like this. Not—how had he described it?— *unromantic* or *overblown*. Without descending into *pleasured oblivion*. Ever poetic. Ever impossible, especially since pleasured oblivion was the only state he now wished to pursue.

Meanwhile, despite her prompting, it was clear Elisabeth was nervous. Likely, she longed to get it over with. She was exhausted and wished to lose herself to sleep. He'd insulted her grievously. The least he could do was to make it quick. And painless. And, as he'd so impossibly termed it, *not overblown*.

He crossed to the gentleman's chest beside the bed and yanked open a drawer. First things first. He would free himself from the constricting cravat, the jacket, the heavy boots.

"I appreciate your accommodation," he told her, reaching for the top button of his waistcoat. His voice was gruff, abrupt, harsher than he intended.

She answered, "Should I lie down on the bed?"

Oh, God. He groaned inwardly.

"Or snuff the candles?" she continued helpfully.

"Elisabeth—"

"I...I think I shall," she said, but she didn't move. Instead, she watched him unbutton his waistcoat.

He glanced at her. Her open curiosity made his pulse jump. Some unknown stripe of male vanity bade him turn, just a little, allowing her to see. He made quick work of the buttons, flicking them open with short, impatient movements. First the waistcoat, then the shirt. He raised his chin, fumbling with the pin in his cravat. He yanked it free, nearly rending the linen, whipping it from his neck.

"The candles are as good a start as any," he said. "At least one of us has some notion of how to get on." He shrugged free of the waistcoat and flung it on the back of a chair. The shirt, he left hanging on his shoulders, baring his chest.

"You said you knew what to do." She sounded breathless.

"Under normal circumstances, yes, I suppose I do." He jabbed at his cufflinks, plunking them into a glass tray with a clatter. "You're doing a lot of talking. In future, there will be less talking." He fell into a chair to pull off his boots.

"Oh, right," she said. "In future. The 'strategically timed appointments.' "

He looked at her. "You agreed to the pursuit of children."

"Yes, but I never agreed to conceiving them in silence."

"No. You would never agree to that, would you?" He laughed briefly, ending on a frustrated sigh. "You see, Elisabeth, I find myself deciding upon the lesser of two evils. Should you 'lie on the bed,' as you suggested, while I drop my trousers and lumber on top of you? Or should we go to bed, so that I may accost you in the middle of the night and hope that you're half asleep?"

She bit her lip. "Neither of these sound half as pleasant as...the cupboard."

His head shot up, and he stared at her, unsure of what he'd just heard.

She held his gaze for a moment, her aquamarine eyes wide and courageous and...*hot*? She looked away, suddenly abashed—and he knew. She *did* want him.

His body's response roared to life, and he shoved away from the chair.

"I couldn't agree more," he said, coming upon her. "But first, will you disrobe? Take off the dress. If nothing else, we can begin there."

Elisabeth blinked at him, trying to comprehend this new mood. Had it been a mistake to mention the cupboard?

She was operating without a script, mincing through so many layers of hurt and distrust. She could not remember ever feeling so uncertain. But she'd already mentioned the closet. If nothing else, that had propelled him from his chair across the room.

And now he appeared aggressively, urgently...attentive. His movements were distracted and impatient, but his eyes remained levelly locked on her. He watched her as if she might, at any moment, turn tail and run.

For better or worse—silly girl—it was a look that *intrigued* her. She wanted to revel in it.

Collecting the heavy mass of her hair and veil in one hand, she dropped it over her shoulder. "I cannot remove this crown or dress without aid. It took two maids and my aunt to bind me into it," she said.

His gaze dropped to the bodice of her dress and back up to her face. "Of course it did. Naturally. Inevitably. And what should we do about that? I have been charged with the impossible task of bedding you without…inciting you. Few things are more inciting than undressing a woman."

Yes, please, incite me.

She said, "You will have to do it. Or ring for a maid."

"No maid. Turn around."

"I am not afraid of you," she asserted. She reached up and began to pull the pins that held the coronet in place from her hair. "Please be aware."

"That makes one of us. *Turn.*" He made a spinning motion with one finger.

She narrowed her eyes, considering him. When she finally complied, she spun slowly, watching him over her shoulder as she went.

He stepped to her proffered back, grabbed what must have been the first available lace, and yanked. The dress was a thatch-work of hooks and eyes, buttons and holes. One pull would have little effect. Still, she was overcome with the closeness of him and the deft, efficient pressure of his hands. She quickly pulled at the network of pins in her hair and tugged the veil free. The coronet listed sideways. She grabbed it and tossed them both on a nearby chair.

"Are you finished?" he asked.

"Are you?" she answered.

His only response was to clear his throat and return his hand to the lacings. He pulled. Elisabeth listed this way and that as he worked his way down her back.

The only sound was the rustling of his loose sleeves and the slipping and snapping of silk. She became increasingly aware of the warmth on her neck. Occasionally, he would draw a lock of hair out of the way and graze her skin. Awareness crackled up and down her spine.

"Hold still," he said gruffly. "This dress lacks only lock and key."

She tilted, and he palmed her waist to steady her.

When the sweet relief of looseness finally freed her ribcage, she drew her the first deep breath in hours. Hook by hook, her posture relaxed, the blood returned to her middle. The gown went slack, and he attacked the laces of her corset. She drew a deep, shaky breath. Cool air touched her spine. The gown gaped at the neck, the bodice and corset sagging.

"Right," he said, his voice clipped. "Out."

She clasped the fabric to her chest and held up a finger. "One question…"

"No more questions."

"I feel very strongly that there should be unlimited questions."

"Fine. What is it?"

"Surely you don't expect me to decipher that bed. Not without assistance."

"It's *a bed*. It does not require deciphering. You are stalling."

"Yes, but you are sprinting. And if I'm meant to step out of this dress, I will be naked—well, nearly naked. And as such,

I'd like to know my destination. It's the bed, I assume. But to be honest, I'm confused by the curtain and the pillows and—are there steps? It's so high off the floor?"

"Confused?" His voice broke. "My God, Elisabeth, there is only so much I can—"

His hands froze on the neck of the gown at her shoulder. The room fell quiet.

She shivered. "Bryson?" She half turned, trying to see behind her. "Bryson?"

Oh. And then she realized.

The scar.

After fifteen years, she rarely gave it a second thought. How could she have forgotten?

In this, it would be…glaringly, fundamentally, obviously…*un*forgotten. A grotesque reminder of what had brought them together and, likewise, what drove them apart.

The sight stunned him, obviously. It repulsed him.

It was ironic, really, for all her worry about not knowing what to do, about saying the wrong thing or behaving the wrong way. She had mortified him without doing anything at all.

"Elisabeth," he said, his voice barely a whisper.

She sucked in breath to say something—to implore him to cover it up, to make some small joke or apology—when slowly, carefully, he leaned down and placed the lightest, softest kiss to her shoulder.

"Elisabeth," he repeated. "*Sweetheart.* I'm so sorry."

The endearment nearly toppled her, but he reached to catch her around the waist. He held her up. While they stood together, stock-still, he bent and kissed the scar again.

"I…I wanted so badly to do this that night, all those years ago. I wanted to care for you, to make it better."

She shook her head. "I was damaged in so many ways. I could not have borne it if you had touched me."

"And now? Tonight? Can you bear it, Elisabeth? If I touch you?"

"I cannot bear it if you do not."

He groaned when she said this, and dipped to collect her, sweeping her off her feet. The wedding dress hung loosely from her body, and she buried her face in his neck. He carried her across the room to the bed, slowly lowering her, scattering pillows.

"I may have misrepresented what will happen here," he whispered, hovering above her.

She waited.

"Detachment, I'm afraid, will never be the guiding force when I make love to you. Ever." He lowered his face to hers and nuzzled her lips, once…twice. Not a kiss, just a brush. She chased his mouth with her own, and he growled, kissing her harder, and dropped on top of her.

She sighed and wrapped her arms around him, drawing him in. She'd fantasized about this—what it would feel like to have the weight of his body on top of her. It was a perfect kind of heaviness, a pressure so essential, she wondered how she would ever feel truly satisfied without it again.

He went up on his elbows to gather her beneath him, staring down at her, taking in her limp, half-stripped gown. His eyes filled with appreciation and need.

The kiss that followed was languid, thorough, and, for a moment, she was lost to it, but now she explored, her hands drifting from his neck to his hair and down again. She moved lower, grazing the edge of his collar until it gaped, revealing his broad back. She massaged his neck, fingers reaching deeper with each pass. She felt the hard, muscled plates of his shoulder blades, larger than her hand. All the while, he kissed her, and her own body melted into a dark, hot pool of need.

Consciousness left her, and a fog of sensation descended. They had never felt so much. Time stopped or spun; she didn't know, and she didn't care. He devoured her mouth like a man starved, pulling up only to gasp for breath.

She laughed, reaching for him, and he rasped, "You find this amusing?"

"No—yes. I am delighted that you—" She couldn't finish. He settled in on her neck, stringing kisses from her collarbone to her ear. "I'm delighted," she said simply.

"Oh, but we haven't even gotten to the good bit yet," he said against her throat. "I waited so bloody long, Elisabeth. I'm taking my time."

"Take whatever you wish," she heard herself say, and she arched upward, pressing against him, an instinctual move that was rewarded with a newer, brighter sensation. She heard herself sigh. *"Oh, Bryson..."*

He hadn't expected her to implore him.

Hell, he hadn't expected her to do much more than lie there. Now, she reached for him, pulling on his shirt in something akin to desperation.

The kiss in the cupboard was nothing compared to this.

Take whatever you wish…

Please…

Acknowledging this was, perhaps, his last thought before all sanity fled, before his very existence was taken over by an ever-escalating ladder of need—lips, breath, the skin behind her ear, handfuls of her hair, lips again.

And to hear her respond with the same desire? To feel her surge beneath him? As if her beauty and spirit and intellect were not enough, now she would heap on sensuality as well?

He was not a deserving man, but his ability to resist her snapped.

"Will you take this off?" he heard himself ask, tugging at the slipping bodice of her unfastened dress.

She rose up and turned away from him, drawing down the straps of her shift. She shimmied then, pushing the shift, sagging corset and bodice to her hips. When she lay back down, she was bared before him. His mouth went dry. He devoured the perfection of her body.

She wiggled more, letting out a frustrated giggle, trying to work the dress and shift over her hips. He was helpless to assist; he could but stare. She fell back, watching him watch her. A hank of apricot hair fell forward, and she shrugged beneath it, flipping it shyly over her breasts.

"No, don't," he said, reaching out, dusting the hair away.

She sucked in breath at the contact of his knuckles to her breast, and her eyes went wide.

His breath hitched, and he touched her again. His hands now moved of their own accord, driven by instinct and need. She met him there; her desire mingling with his own. He touched her because he could not *not* reach out. She arched up to meet his hands.

He leaned in to taste first one breast, then the other, and she turned her head to the side, straining against the pillow, eyes now shut. Nothing prepared him for this response.

Now she surged upward, her body seeking his. Her gown was in a wad between them, and he tore it away.

He sat up, motivated to be rid of the dress, and she whimpered when he moved away from her. She propped herself on her elbows.

The sight of her, bared to the thighs, hair spilling around her, flushed, lying in his bed, was an image seared forever in his brain. He forgot the dress and kissed her again.

"I want too much," he growled, pulling away, tugging on the tangle of silk and petticoats with new fervor.

"Making up for lost time."

"Oh, God, how I have wanted you," he said. "*Want* was never the problem."

Finally, the dress gave, rolling down her hips. He hooked his thumbs in the sides of her drawers and rolled them down, too, swallowing hard, watching as the descending silk exposed her thighs, long legs, trim ankles. Then it was gone altogether, and he tossed it to the foot of the bed. She was naked except for her stockings and garters.

"Bryson?" she sighed, kicking a little, swishing her legs on the coverlet like a mermaid on dry land. "Now you?" She reached for him.

He yanked his shirt over his head. She gasped at the sight of him, naked to the waist. This reaction surprised him, and he looked up.

She laughed. "You are beautiful." And she began roving her hands over his shoulders, down his arms, kneading the muscle. "So strong. How are you so strong?"

He watched her hands on his body, mesmerized. "Punting boats on the river. Years of it. Since I was a boy." He pushed her back down. Another kiss. "*You* are beautiful," he moaned, leaving her mouth for her neck. "More beautiful than I deserve."

"That's what you said"—he caught her mouth again and kissed her—"on my aunt's balcony." Another kiss. "In the rain."

Against her ear, he whispered, "I have never spoken such truth."

She laughed again. "I couldn't believe you were really there…saying it…about me."

"I couldn't believe you were *allowing it*. I thought you were too proud."

"No. Not too proud." She grew still. "Too afraid."

He looked up, staring into her turquoise eyes. "Afraid of what? Not me?"

She turned her head sideways on the pillow. "Afraid I would never find myself where I am right now. If you recognized me. If you knew."

Her neck was exposed, and he ran his mouth along the smooth olive skin until he reached her shoulder. He kissed the delicate point of it. "I wish you had simply told me that night."

"I couldn't." Her voice cracked.

"I know."

She took his face gently in her hands. "Do you?"

He kissed her palm, nodding.

She sighed, wrapping her arms around him, drawing him close. She wrapped her legs around him in the same manner, twining around him in a full-body embrace. She buried her face in his neck.

It was meant to be a tender moment, he knew. Intimate. A milestone on the journey from where they had been to where they...might go. God help him, he wanted to savor it, to hold her tightly, but the proximity of her breasts to his bare chest, the feel of her legs wrapped around him, the canted position of her hips cradling his desire...

His body pulsed with the most fundamental need. He was helpless against her. He could sustain the embrace for only a handful of seconds.

His trousers still separated them, but he rocked downward, seeking relief.

She gasped.

He rocked again, and again she sucked in breath. He caught her mouth in a kiss and thrust a third time. For this, he was rewarded; she surged up, arching off the bed.

He growled, reaching for her thigh. He felt a silk stocking and traced it to the garter, fumbling with the fastener. When the hook released, he yanked the stocking off and massaged his way back up her leg. She shuddered and moaned beneath him.

He reached for the other leg while her hands whirled through the hair on his chest, tracing the muscle, radiating circles higher and lower. She drifted to his belly and then lower still, her fingers nudging the button on his trousers.

He laughed. It was either that or cry tears of joy.

He made quick work of her remaining garter and stocking. He allowed her sweet torture with the buttons of his trousers, trailing kisses down her neck and shoulder. When she cried out in frustration, he shushed her gently and took up her hands, kissing them, and unbuttoned the trousers himself. While she watched, he stripped them off and flung them over with her dress. His desire was impossible to hide, straining against his drawers. He glanced at her, watching her eyes go huge at the sight of him. He chuckled, kissing her again, pressing her back into the pillows, settling on top of her, reveling in the dual sensation of relief and greater need.

"Elisabeth." His voice rumbled between kisses. "Have we avoided descending into oblivion?"

"I...cannot say," she said, arching her body beneath him.

He groaned.

"Well, then"—another kiss—"I'm not doing my part. When we descend, you will know it. There's still time."

She laughed until he covered her mouth with his.

CHAPTER TWENTY-SIX

Elisabeth's last solvent thought was, *Why would we ever try to circumvent this? On purpose?*

Never had she known such a beautifully unified, concerted, pleasurable effort toward…toward…

Well, she could not say toward what, precisely, but whatever it was, they were going there together, both of the same fevered mind, with bodies that strummed with mutual pleasure.

She knew little else than a growing urgency—a stoking—a quickening toward an ultimate…*something*. She could not identify it, but her body informed her that she wanted very much to achieve it—that she *must* achieve it.

He captured her mouth in a deep kiss and gently used his knee to tap her legs apart. He made a growling noise, called her name on a hiss. She understood. She took a deep breath, and her legs fell open. He growled again; his body coiled. Pain knifed through her, and she gasped at the startling contrast to the building pleasure she had felt only moments ago.

She forced her muscles to release. Relax. To trust.

The pain subsided with each heartbeat. She felt her body expand.

"Breathe, Elisabeth," he rasped.

She drew a shaky breath. And another, and another. Slowly, the pleasure returned, and then built, and then very nearly consumed her.

Bryson moved slowly at first, but as her breathing increased, so did his pace. With every sigh, he kissed her harder, more desperately. Suddenly, his movements weren't fast enough. She pushed back—a little at first, and then more, more; she couldn't breathe. She cried out. Her brain went solid white.

After that, a shattering.

A million iridescent pinpoints of pleasure spun to the tips of her fingers and toes. Her breath came back in a rush. Her eyes flew open. She saw his face. Strained. Intense. Eyes tightly shut. Beautiful. Beautiful. He'd done this. Beautiful.

She leaned up and kissed him. One small peck on the tip of his nose. He caught her mouth and devoured it, kissing her more fiercely now than ever he had before.

She rocked her hips gently, marveling at the new sensation. Fullness. Tightness. Friction. Heat.

Bryson made an indistinguishable sound and dropped his face beside hers, burrowing in her hair. She rocked again.

"Elisabeth." He breathed into her neck. "I cannot resist…"

She rocked again.

Bryson growled into her ear. She turned her head and found his earlobe. Tentatively, she nibbled.

A guttural moan.

She latched on and sucked, rocking her hips again, steadily this time.

The urgency inside her spooled anew.

Bryson reared up, calling her name—an oath, a vow—and moved inside her, faster, more urgently. The friction was a new kind of pleasure. Conscious thought began to slip away.

She looked up at him. He stared down, blue eyes boring into hers. He dropped to her mouth for a kiss. She found it difficult, suddenly, to keep up. She opened her lips to receive him, clasping his shoulders to hold on.

She heard herself cry out, and the shattering seized her again. Blankness and iridescence, all in the same breath. A surge of sensation unfurled in her body.

As she drifted back to earth, color and shape fuzzed back to view. He shouted now too, echoing her need. She felt him tense and opened one eye. He was stricken. He shuddered and then collapsed on top of her, panting. By some miracle, she found the strength and coordination to wrap her arms around him and hold him tight.

When explosive sensation finally…gradually…dissolved into a heavy fatigue, Bryson looked down at his wife and thought, *More.*

It was his only thought.

More.

Soon—now. Forever.

More.

If it had not been so immediate, so essential, perhaps it would not have triggered the inveterate, *No.*

No, this may not consume you.

No, she will not consume you.

An entirely different voice, his reliable wariness, the ingrained ruthless restraint of more than thirty years of self-possession. *No, no, no.*

Because this was the very definition of "consumed."

The compulsion he felt now. The fullness inside and the lightness out. The emotional tether from his chest to her heart. The *more*.

Beneath him, Elisabeth shifted. It occurred to him to roll off her. He lifted his head from the pillow and risked a sidewise glance.

Her eyes were demurely downcast, thick eyelashes dusting the freckles of her cheeks. Her pink mouth was swollen.

She blinked, and he felt his heart lurch.

No.

She looked up and smiled a small, shy smile, snuggling closer. There was no hesitation in the way she touched him, no battle with her own will. She was without guile or self-conceit or doubt. Meanwhile, he felt like he was falling, falling, falling—and it scared him to death.

To moor himself, he did exactly the wrong thing—which felt exactly like the right thing—he tightened his arms around her. She responded by sliding one, delicate foot along his leg and looping it over, locking the two of them at the ankle. She looked at him and sighed a satisfied sigh. They were nose to nose.

"What is it?" she asked softly, and his heart lurched a little more. She reached out to trace his stubbled jaw with her index finger, scraping his cheek with the back of her hand. He closed his eyes. She could touch him for a thousand years, he thought, and he would still want more.

"Are you... well, Elisabeth?" he finally managed. When all else failed, there were always manners.

She considered this a moment. She said, "Yes. Quite well. Are you well?"

" 'Well' does not begin to describe what I am."

"If this bout of lovemaking did not descend into 'pleasured oblivion,' Bryson, then I must confess, I am curious to embark on a one that does."

He laughed in spite of himself. Her closeness made him amorous, but her eagerness made him hard. "I misrepresented my ability to detach, I'm afraid," he said.

"I'm glad," she whispered, leaning to him. While he watched, she kissed him. One, quick peck. A demure, goodnight kiss. But, oh, God, save him, she lingered, and he found himself incapable of pulling away. He took over at once, kissing her deeper, feasting on her mouth. He broke away only to mark her, scraping his beard against her cheek, her ear, and back to her mouth.

He ran his hand down the landscape of her body, steadying it on the delicious dip of her waist. He dragged her more tightly against him. Her curves fit exactly to his swells. She opened her arms, wrapping one around his neck and sinking her fingers into his hair.

Their mouths met, and thoughts drifted. He could barely hear the words *no* or *careful* or *lost*. In truth, he barely heard the thunder of his own heart. What began as lazy, amorphous desire took immediate crystalline shape. She arched against him, shooting a jolt of pleasure from his brain to his groin.

"Sleep, Elisabeth?" His words rumbled against her lips. A final, fleeting effort at restraint.

She made a wordless sound of protest and flicked her tongue against his lip.

He answered with a kiss, and she sealed it, looping her arms beneath his shoulders and digging her fingers into the muscles of his back. She tangled both of their legs; they were a knot of thrumming sensation that pulsed as one.

Tomorrow, he thought—or endeavored to think—he would explain to her that taking her to bed must not lead to an…emotional precipice. He would tell her that they must be careful not to fall over the edge for his own sake. He had the viscountcy to think of—it was all he'd ever thought of—and it was important that he not become distracted.

Tomorrow, they would revisit the contract.

Tomorrow, he would gently remind her that…that…

She arched again, and all reminders fled.

He lodged his knee into the mattress and pushed, rolling them, pulling her on top. She let out a little shriek.

It became a benchmark, that shriek. How many ways, how many times could he make her do it again?

CHAPTER TWENTY-SEVEN

Bryson was gone from the bed by the time Elisabeth awakened. Slowly, eyes still closed, lying very still, she slid her hand across the empty spot where he had lain.

Coolness.

He had been gone some time.

Whispers rose from the corner of the room, and she listened, pretending to sleep.

Bryson's voice—he said something to do with Dunhip. Also something about his brother. "No valet," she heard him say. "Yes, a breakfast tray—just the one."

A whispered answer from a servant and, *click*, the door closed.

Now she heard footsteps. The iron poker against the grate. The thud of a log dropping into the fire and the hiss of flames on new wood.

She opened one eye. The sun was up but not bright. Shadows from the grate animated the ceiling. Her stomach growled, and she wondered at the time. She glanced through the thin bed curtain in the direction of his footsteps.

He was near the basin, splashing water on his face. He wore breeches and boots but no shirt.

Careful, she told herself. *Very, very careful.*

She'd known all along that Bryson was too complicated and their labyrinthine history too deep for the marriage to attain rosy perfection after one heated night.

It made no difference that she felt suddenly, radiantly happy. It made no difference that he, most likely, felt happy too. All that mattered was that he had left the bed and dressed in silence. All that had mattered was that she was alone. She tried to recall her aunt's words. *You are a gift*, she'd said. *He need only unwrap you. Show him how.*

"Good morning," she ventured. She edged up, holding the bed sheet loosely against her still naked breasts.

He turned. "Good morning." His formal voice. He cleared his throat and turned away.

Taking care to avoid the bed, he walked to a towering, double-door wardrobe.

She kneed to the edge of the bed and nudged the curtain aside, staring at his back.

I know the feel of that back.

He was ticklish along the ribs.

His strength was in his shoulders.

His hair curled, just a little, along the back of his head.

She would tell him this, she thought. When they'd made love, he had told her she was beautiful again and again, and it thrilled her to know that he found her desirable. He should know the same thrill.

Telling him this, telling him so many things, would be the only way to move beyond a future of formal, wordless mornings and waking up alone in bed.

She would tell him that the idea of a marriage in public but a separation in private was *not*, in fact, what she wanted. What she wanted was to be married to him all the time, including right now, in the cool, cloudy light of morning after a night of transcendent passion.

Including always.

And I will tell him that I love him.

This final revelation formed in her mind all at once, but she knew it was already embedded into her heart. Like the mesh of an iron gate can be swallowed by the trunk of a growing tree. The iron remains, and a tree grows through it. Two very different entities become one.

The love, she would tell him, did not destroy her, or hobble her, or even sweep her away. It was simply a new version of herself, a stronger version. A version so unique, only the two of them could create it.

He should know this, she thought, and he should admit as much himself.

But not yet, perhaps.

Not when he would rather stare into his wardrobe than look at her, sitting naked on the edge of his bed.

"What time is it?" she asked. "Not too late, I hope."

She slipped through the curtain and padded to the center of the rug. She pulled the sheet with her and wrapped it loosely around her body.

"Not yet eight o'clock," he said to his shirts. "But I must seek out my brother. And Sewell and Dunhip. Mrs. Linn.

We left the party last night without a backward glance. Fitting, at the time, but now I must ensure that the guests made their way home without further incident. That no one made off with the silver or drowned in the goldfish pond." He put his hands on his hips. He ventured a look over his shoulder. He had not expected her to be away from the bed because his face went from agitated and distracted to attentive and hot.

He turned away, his knuckles white on the doors to the wardrobe.

It encouraged her, that look, and she opened her mouth to say some intimate, personal thing, something playful and light, but he cut her off. "We have much to discuss, Elisabeth," he said. He cleared his throat again. "You and I."

She took a step back. "Yes, all right. Let us…discuss."

"Not now." He fished inside the wardrobe for a shirt.

"Very well. When?"

"At dinner, perhaps? In the meantime…" He shrugged into a shirt. "You may—"

"You needn't feel responsible for my time, Bryson."

She said it lightly, cheerfully, although it was an important statement, and she meant it. He wasn't responsible for how she spent her days. His nights? This, they would discuss, just as he said.

"I will make my way to my own suite after you've gone," she told him. "And then I believe I have an appointment with Mrs. Linn. After that, I have work, actually. Miss Breedlowe and I will call at the shipyard today. We're discussing the assimilation of five of my girls who are ready to begin employment outside of my foundation. I've already been in touch with Mr. Dunhip about it. He will meet us, if you can spare him."

"Yes, yes," he said, taking care not to look at her. "I appreciate your…diligence."

"Diligence." She chuckled. "I suppose. But I'm not a squirrel, Bryson. The foundation is like a vocation to me, and I work very hard at it—but you know this. Nothing about me has changed. The foundation is a priority, and I am not one to laze about the house."

He nodded, glancing at her. She raised her chin and allowed the corner of the sheet to slip, just an inch. Heat flared in his eyes, and he looked away.

"I've work as well," he said on a cough, "although it will be put aside until I've squared business with the various vendors and tradesmen I employed for the wedding. May I…" He stopped and then started again. "I will rely on you to find your own way to your suite since you are not yet dressed. It's just next door, actually, and I'll be happy to send a lady's maid to attend you."

I prefer your suite, she thought, but she said nothing. She would wait. If he was determined to run, let him run. He said they would speak in time; he preferred formal meetings. She would wait until dinner. It would be a provoking conversation, frank and personal, but certainly it could happen at dinner. And hopefully conclude in his bed.

"Very good, my lord," she said. "Until dinner. I will return to bed and allow you to dress."

CHAPTER TWENTY-EIGHT

"You took her to bed." Beau rested his hip on the breakfast table later that morning and crossed his arms over his chest. "I can't believe it. After all the talk about a contractual union. Cold and separate and platonic at home. You couldn't last—not one bloody night. Well done. I, for one, am gratified. My money was on the week, but I'm happy to be proved wrong."

"Gratified to know that you'll keep chatter light and decorous, even at breakfast," Bryson said, glancing up from his paper to glare at his brother. When Beau raised his eyebrows, Rainsleigh said, "Why would you say that?"

"The look on your face. The moment you walked in."

"What look?"

"Terror. Mixed with want. *Terrified want*, I'd call it. You thought she might be in here, taking breakfast. You *hoped* she'd be here."

"Colorful." Rainsleigh turned the page. "If you cannot be a sailor, perhaps a novelist?"

"Meanwhile, I happened to see Elisabeth in the kitchen, and you know how she looked?"

"Why were you in the kitchens?"

"You couldn't know this, but some guests prefer to take their leave by the kitchen door. I was just seeing the last guest out. Lovely woman. A widow of a certain age. She wishes you all the best, by the way."

"Beau, please." Rainsleigh drained his cup of coffee, pretending he wasn't waiting anxiously to hear the relevant part of this story. Beau had seen her.

"The point *is*," Beau continued, "Elisabeth was in the kitchen, meeting her boy Stoker. Heaped him with orders about her charity and then offered him a tart and a piece of fruit. All this before nine o'clock. And you know how she looked?"

Beautiful, Rainsleigh thought. *Exhausted. Sated. Confused. Abandoned.* He looked at his brother, forcing himself to wait out his dramatic effect.

"She looked pleasant, and useful, and lovely, really. As I said, another clear sign."

"Clear sign of what? That gainful enterprising residents in this house now outnumber you two to one?"

"Well, that too, perhaps. But I was going to say it was a clear sign that her new husband took her to bed."

"Careful, Beau."

"Let me prove my point. There are precious few events in life that elicit such cheerful altruism from a woman. Making love to her is one of them."

Rainsleigh wiped his mouth and pushed back from the table. "You know what I think? I think it's a wonder any woman will consent to go to bed with you at all."

"And yet..." Beau rolled off the edge of the table and stretched his neck.

"Elisabeth is inherently *pleasant*," Rainsleigh went on. "And extremely capable. Generous to a fault. It was nothing motivated by me."

Beau nodded sagely. "Say what you like about the sex, but I know she slept in your room last night. Heard it from a footman."

Rainsleigh stilled. "*Which* footman?"

Beau ignored him. "You are aware that taking your new wife to bed is *allowed*, Bryse? Please tell me you know this."

No, not like that—not for me, he thought, but he said, "I have no idea what you're talking about."

Beau went on jovially, "You knew this would happen. She promised heirs in that bloody contract of yours. You told me yourself that you've wanted her in your bed since you met her. Why are you so unhappy? You cannot tell me it was unpleasant."

Rainsleigh almost laughed out loud. Easily, it had been one of the best nights of his life. He strode to the open doors of the breakfast room and pulled them shut. He walked back. He grabbed hold of the back of his chair. "Like a fool, I thought that once or twice would be enough," he said. "For a time. I thought my, er, *need* would be assuaged." He looked up at his brother.

"Once or twice?" Beau raised his eyebrows.

Rainsleigh shot him an exasperated look and pushed up. "I am overcome. She is all I think about. From the moment I left her, hours ago, I've been in a bloody daze. To be honest, it's a miracle I left the bed at all. I only went because I feared that I had somehow made her uncomfortable or ashamed. We were so…" He let the sentence trail off. Wisely, his brother said nothing.

After a moment, Rainsleigh said, "I left her alone for privacy's sake and to clear my own head. And yet? She consumes me still."

Beau held out his hands. "So what? You're *consumed*. Can you not embrace it, embrace *her*, and return to the bed and remain there until you feel more like yourself? Take a wedding trip and lose yourself, if that's what you want."

"What I want is control."

Beau shook his head and turned away. "Well, you've done this to yourself. Ten years with no mistress? The most chaste courtship the world has ever known? Of course you feel preoccupied."

"Not preoccupied—obsessed, more like." Rainsleigh wandered to the window and nudged the curtain aside.

"Lovely. Be obsessed. There are far worse things that might take up your time. What are you afraid of? That we'll starve because you're too busy plowing your wife to sustain the fortune?"

"It's not the money. The money was a means to an end."

"*Ah*," Beau said darkly. "Your lifelong quest to be revered. Bloody noble, Viscount Golden, Lord Immaculate, to-the-manor-born rubbish. A lot of rubbish, if you ask me."

"Only you would consider an ancient title to be *rubbish*. It is an honor and a privilege to be born to the House of Rainsleigh, one I take very seriously."

Beau laughed. "Only because you made it so! It was a bankrupted laughingstock before you inherited."

"That is precisely why I have worked so hard and resisted so much. Can you not see why it is important to me—nay, crucial—to hold tight to my standards of excellence for this family? Why I may not allow myself to become distracted?"

"Have you considered that no one bloody cares as much as you?" He drifted in front of a hanging mirror and studied his reflection. "I won't tell a soul that you'd rather make love to your pretty wife than preside over the *haute ton*, but allow me to let you in on a little secret. I'd wager that most of the heads of these so-called 'great families' feel the same way."

"No." Rainsleigh turned from the window. "They do not. Not the men I admire. The men I respect aren't *obsessed* with their wives. It's not the way proper married couples get on."

"Because *proper couples* are married to their cousins," Beau shot back, moving beside him and yanking the curtains wide. "Or are neighbors with thirty years difference in age—a union arranged for money or land or horses. You married Elisabeth because you fancied her. And now you want to—"

"I *married her*," interrupted Rainsleigh, "for her grace and modesty. Her compassion. And maturity. Her heritage. Her loveliness—yes, but not..."

"Her body?"

"I was going to say her irresistibility. But nothing and no one may be irresistible to me." Rainsleigh breathed heavily. "*This* is how I have restored the viscountcy. I strictly regulate my access."

Beau groaned, falling against the wall beside him. "Let go of the notion of bloody *restrictions*. Please. In this one, small, indulgent corner of your self-denied life. You overreach. It will hurt Elisabeth to reject her, not to mention you deny yourself for no good reason." He slapped his palm against the wall. "As a favor to me. Stop with the incessant talk of propriety for the sake of the bloody family!"

"I will not be like our parents," Rainsleigh countered firmly. "I shielded you from all but a fraction of their rapacious carryings-on. You did not see the full extent, and thank God."

"No, you won't be like them," his brother said slowly, reasonably. "*In no way* are you alike. So why would your marriage be? You will be faithful and true to Elisabeth. This is the crucial difference. This, you will do."

"The difference is, I will be detached," Rainsleigh vowed, turning to him. "As I always have been. Especially in this. I cannot allow her—" He stopped himself and cleared his throat. "I cannot allow my *desire for her* to consume me."

Beau made an indistinguishable sound of frustration and slapped his hand against the wall. "Now there's an unworthy goal if ever I've heard one. She's a lovely girl. She likes you. Your only foolishness is to deny yourself what she offers. Marriage is not for everyone, I'll allow. I would be a particular failure at it. But I assure you, the institution was *invented* for men like you." He waited for some response to this, but Bryson said nothing.

Beau went on, "I cannot tell you what to do, Bryson, but heed this very rare bit of entirely accurate advice. Do not be so adherent to what you deem 'proper' that you lose sight of what is precious. You've nearly done it once already. Don't do it again. For the first time in your life, leave your quest for propriety and control at the door. And then walk inside, and shut the bloody thing behind you."

Chapter Twenty-Nine

"We shall come bearing gifts when we meet Mr. Dunhip, Rainsleigh's secretary," Elisabeth told Jocelyn Breedlowe later that morning as the Rainsleigh carriage rolled away from Henrietta Place. "It will be the first of many ploys to win him to our side. Cake, fresh from the baker's, certainly. We will stop en route, but what else? He seems to be the sort of man who would appreciate fresh-cut flowers, does he not? He is fastidious, in a way. Fussy."

"I...I cannot say," Jocelyn managed, studying her friend. She had only agreed to accompany Elisabeth so that the new viscountess would not be alone. Elisabeth had just endured an overwrought wedding to a man who did not love her. Jocelyn thought it was the least she could do.

But what an unexpected attitude from the new bride. Elisabeth was cheerful and fresh-faced, smiling, excited to the point of gushing at the prospect of new jobs for foundation girls. Jocelyn could not remember when last she had seen her friend quite so happy—certainly not before the St. Clare ball.

"Well, if he does not care for flowers in the office," Elisabeth continued, "he may take them to his mother. Rainsleigh claims they are very close. This, I could have guessed, honestly."

On and on it went from there, even after they stopped for cakes and flowers. Elisabeth gave animated discourse about conscripting Mr. Dunhip, about training the girls and putting them to work as soon as possible. She was so quick to laugh, so good-spirited, Jocelyn could not find a moment to ask what exactly had transpired after Elisabeth and Rainsleigh mysteriously disappeared from the reception.

"Elisabeth?" she finally ventured when they neared the shipyard. "I am gratified to see you in such good spirits. I was worried about your…fatigue. You disappeared from the wedding without a good-bye."

"Oh, the wedding was dreadful, was it not?" Elisabeth said, feeling around for the pins in her hat. "Such a crush— and strangers, all of them. They came under the auspices of wishing us well. I'd never seen most of them before in my life."

"Was the viscount happy?" Jocelyn fished.

Elisabeth considered this. "I'd say, the viscount is struggling to designate his current state of mind. There were moments of happiness, yes. We hid in a cupboard. After that, he took me to his room."

"Hid in a *cupboard?*" Jocelyn repeated. But then she saw the look on her friend's face and thought perhaps she had begun to understand.

"Oh, yes," said Elisabeth, biting down on a smile. "I'm sorry we did not say good-bye."

"Please do not apologize," Jocelyn said carefully as they pulled into the shipyard. She glanced at Elisabeth's broad smile and busied herself tucking the paper around the bouquet of flowers they'd procured for Mr. Dunhip. A stable boy darted out to care for the horses and help them down.

"There's nothing more to say, really," Elisabeth volunteered while they waited at the office door. She looked at Jocelyn. "Since the moment Rainsleigh came back into my life, I have teetered between the fear that he would remember me and the longing that he would want me. Now he knows everything, and he is the one who teeters. I can only be true to myself and wait for him to sort it out. In the meantime, I feel better than I have in weeks. He will come around, I believe. Ah, but here is Mr. Dunhip. Your sweetest smile, please, Jocelyn. It is imperative that we earn his cooperation."

They worked with Cecil Dunhip until luncheon, learning the various trades in the shipyard, talking over possible positions for the girls, discussing payment and a schedule. At noon, Elisabeth sent the secretary home for the midday meal, and Jocelyn went in search of the stable boy to procure their own food. She had scarcely pulled the door open when she collided, or nearly so, with a middle-aged gentleman, nicely appointed, with tall hat and cane, standing on the stoop. His carriage, or what she assumed was his carriage, was parked behind him. Jocelyn saw the figure of a young woman inside.

"I beg your pardon," Jocelyn said, stepping back. "I did not see you, sir." The man made no reply. Silence stretched on and on. "I hope you have not waited long," she said, but he said nothing. She tried again, "We did not hear your knock."

"Oh, I did not knock," the man said enigmatically, studying her carefully.

Elisabeth swept behind Jocelyn with a stack of papers and a heap of torn sail. "Lord Rainsleigh is not in the office today," she called over Jocelyn's shoulder. "Offer to take the gentleman's card, please, Miss Breedlowe."

Jocelyn opened her mouth to make the request when Elisabeth reversed and popped her head back into the doorway. She peered out at the man, cocking her head. Under the women's collected scrutiny, the man's expression fell. Cleary, he was disappointed at missing the viscount. He took off his hat and turned it in his hands, looking out at the unfinished ships in the distance. He sighed. He looked back at the women uncertainly.

When he said nothing more, Elisabeth pushed out on the stoop. "Forgive me, sir," she began softly, "but are you…acquainted with Lord Rainsleigh? You appear…" She laughed, a nervous, worried little laugh that Jocelyn had never heard before.

The man blinked at her and did not answer.

Elisabeth continued, "Forgive me, but you look as if you could be *related* to the viscount. How similar the two of you appear in stature and even face. I've never seen anything like it." She glanced back at Jocelyn, seeking concurrence. Jocelyn looked again. Now that Elisabeth pointed it out, Jocelyn could, indeed, see the resemblance.

The man who looked like Rainsleigh remained silent. He simply stared, considering Elisabeth with a cautious sort of squint.

"Perhaps I can be of assistance, sir?" asked Elisabeth. "I am Lady Rainsleigh, the viscount's wife."

"I...I read that Lord Rainsleigh was set to marry," the man answered in almost a whisper. He studied Elisabeth as if it would discern the position of her heart.

Elisabeth laughed nervously again. "Ah. Were we remiss with an invitation? I hope not."

He shook his head. "Do I resemble his lordship? Truly, Lady Rainsleigh?" His voice was full of wonder. He appeared to hold his breath.

Elisabeth nodded. "Does my husband know you, Mr...."

"Mr. Raymond Eads," the man provided slowly, as if he waited for her to recognize the name. He made a small bow.

Elisabeth smiled gently but shook her head.

He clarified, saying, "Mr. Raymond Eads...of Berkshire. My daughter, Miss Lucy Eads, has accompanied me." He gestured to the young lady in the well-appointed carriage behind him. "We are in London on other business, and I thought we'd...call."

Another pause. Elisabeth did not press, but her small smile looked forced. "Would you care to join me in my husband's office, Mr. Eads?" Elisabeth finally asked. "Other business has detained the viscount today, and his secretary is out. My friend and I were managing some of our own charity work here in the shipyard. But we need not hover on the doorstep like deliverymen. Please, if you would feel more comfortable leaving a card or message for the viscount in his office, I am happy to show you inside."

Jocelyn stepped across the threshold to stand beside her and placed a hand on her elbow. "My lady?" Jocelyn whispered, worried about the safety of inviting a strange man to an empty office.

"Do not fret, Jocelyn," Elisabeth assured her, already taking a dazed Mr. Eads by the arm and leading the way. "Mr. Eads, shall my friend entertain your daughter?"

"She will prefer to await me in the carriage, Lady Rainsleigh," Mr. Eads said following her slowly.

"If you are sure," said Elisabeth briskly, holding the door. She looked at Jocelyn. "I won't be ten minutes." And then she swung the door to the viscount's private office.

Twenty minutes later, the door swung open again, and Jocelyn bolted to her feet. Elisabeth, thank God, appeared very much as she had when she'd disappeared inside Rainsleigh's office, although now her arm was tucked snugly against Mr. Eads's chest. Their heads were bent, and she was telling him something softly, patting his hand, while he nodded and dabbed his eyes with a handkerchief.

Elisabeth looked up as if to assure Jocelyn, sparing her a quick wink, and then she walked the man out the door. There was naught for Jocelyn to do but wait beside their untouched lunch on the desk. Through the window, Jocelyn saw Elisabeth and the man exchange a few more words, a half embrace, and then Elisabeth waved good-bye to him as he climbed the steps of his carriage, and his coachman drove them away.

"Well, that explains quite a lot," Elisabeth said. She closed the door and leaned against it.

"I'm afraid to ask," said Jocelyn. "What is it? You alarm me, Elisabeth, when you disappear behind closed doors with a strange man. I sent for Stoker, just to be safe. Most of all, I was terrified that Rainsleigh would turn up, and I'd be forced to explain it."

"Yes, that would have been ill-timed. Dunhip would have been all wrong too. I was sorry to leave you out here alone."

"Please do not worry for me," Jocelyn said. She waited, watching Elisabeth chew her bottom lip, lost in thought.

After a moment, Jocelyn said, "I sent the stable boys for lunch, as you asked."

Elisabeth looked up and pushed off the door. "Oh, lovely. Thank you." She wandered to the basket of food. "I'm sorry to have worried you. I could see that Mr. Eads sought an audience with the viscount or someone close to him. That he had some burden he wanted to share. I know the signs from working with my girls."

She looked up from the basket. "And I was right. Turns out, he knew Rainsleigh's mother as a young man." A pause. "You might as well know."

"Oh," began Jocelyn uncertainly, realization slowly dawning.

"*He*—Mr. Raymond Eads," she continued, returning her attention to the basket of bread and cheese, "claims to be Lord Rainsleigh's father." She looked up. "His *true* father, Jocelyn. Long lost. Back to say…well, I'm not sure what he intends to say."

"Oh," Jocelyn repeated, a strangled, airless sound this time. She felt her eyes go huge. "Which would mean…"

Elisabeth nodded, left the basket, and breezed past her to the desk. She began to gather her paperwork. "Which would mean, my husband is in store for the surprise of his life."

CHAPTER THIRTY

Rainsleigh stared at the marriage contract strewn across his desk and scowled. It was coward's way out. Trotting out *paperwork* to discuss their marriage. Impersonal, and stilted, and silly, but his brain was gruel. He could conceive of no other way to begin—assuming, that was, he managed to embark on any conversation at all.

Sewell knocked in the same moment that Rainsleigh checked the clock on the mantel. He shoved to his feet like a man on trial. It was ridiculous; he had counted the bloody minutes until he would see her again, but now he felt unprepared. Yet another stupefying result of his fevered regard for his new wife. He thought of little else. How could he bloody work if all he did was think about taking her to bed?

"Enter," he said. He left the contract on the desk and strode to the windows. She would speak first, he thought. Let him hear what she had to say, and he would carry on from there.

"You've had me summoned to the library?" she asked.

He turned. She was irritated; he could see it on her face. She ignored Sewell, which wasn't like her, and Bryson dismissed him with a nod.

Perhaps he would not wait for her to speak. "I was not certain that Mrs. Linn provided a sufficient tour."

She narrowed her eyes, drifting to him. "Well, I've seen the library, as you well know." She crossed her arms over her chest.

"Fine. You've seen the library. Regardless, I should like to walk you 'round the house myself. This should feel like your home, Elisabeth." He swore in his head. "This *is* your home."

"Bryson," she said, holding up her hand. "Stop."

He stared at her hand. Unease climbed from his gut and grabbed him by the throat. He looked to her face and back at her hand. It occurred to him that the topic of restraint was but a trifle compared to some complaint from her. God forbid she have some request that might take her away from him.

"None of that matters now," she said.

He leaned against the wall beside the window, hoping to appear casual rather than weak-kneed. In what way, he wondered, would a tour of the house *not matter now*?

"May I sit?" she asked purposefully, already heading for a chair.

He nodded, watching her. She wore the simple blue dress today. Her hair was down her back. Her cheeks were flushed as if she had rushed to reach him.

She settled in a chair adjacent to the window, stealing sideways glances in his direction. She closed her eyes for a moment and put a hand to her mouth. She looked, he thought, as if she prepared to taste something for which she had great dislike. It scared him in a way nothing had scared him in a very long time.

She took a deep breath, opened her eyes, and smiled the dreadful smile of someone with complicated, unhappy news. "Today," she began, "when I was in your office at the shipyard, a man called, looking for you."

She paused, looked out the window, and then back at him.

"A man?" He crossed his arms over his chest. The topic of "a man" was the very last he'd anticipated.

She nodded. "He is called Raymond Eads." She watched him with a wary sort of anticipation. "Of Berkshire—although, originally, from Wiltshire."

The name of Bryson's home county thudded into his consciousness like a dull kick.

"Ah," he said harshly, turning his face away, "an old *neighbor*, was it? You've had an earful, then, I'll wager. Even after fifteen years in the grave, I still receive notices of my father's debts. Or perhaps it was stolen property?"

She stared at him sorrowfully.

"And now you're to hear them, too? And on your very first day as my wife? My apologies."

She remained silent.

Shame welled within him. "What did he want, then?" He forced his voice to remain calm. "And where was Dunhip? He knows what to do when these phantasms of the past float to the surface." He shoved off the window and paced a distance, only to spin back. "I knew it was careless to send you to the shipyard alone. But you could not wait, oh no—"

"Bryson," she said levelly, "it was not that. It was nothing to do with your father. Not directly."

"Then what?" The question was a whip. The unease had grown into a mild thudding panic.

"Would you sit?" she offered gently.

"No, I will not sit."

She nodded and looked away. She took a deep breath.

"My God, Elisabeth, what is it? Who is *Raymond Eads?*"

She leaned back, settling into the chair. "Raymond Eads is a man of some property and means—the owner of several maltings—in Berkshire. He is a widower. Just this year he lost his wife. And he has a seventeen-year-old daughter. He read the announcement of our marriage in the newspapers and was, apparently, compelled to seek you out. It is an errand he has put off for some great many years, but he made a vow to his dying wife that he would finally put the matter to rest."

"Naturally. And what matter is this?" He'd begun again to pace, but he stopped now and turned to study her, shoving his hands in his pockets to contain them. She stared back serenely.

"It was a confession," she finally said. "Meant to be made in person, face-to-face, with you."

"Well, he's failed at that, clearly, considering he's burdened *my wife*. What I don't understand is, where was Dunhip? You should not be parsing through confessions of villagers, whoever they are, when you are alone in my office."

"We had sent him home for luncheon."

Rainsleigh growled in frustration. "Typical. He is powerless to the demands of his bloody stomach."

"He would have been little help. The confession was of a highly personal nature. I cajoled Mr. Eads to tell me—very nearly drew the words out of him—because he was so clearly in distress. It was providence, I think, that placed me there, alone, when he came." She watched him. "But you may disagree. I cannot predict."

"Cannot predict *what?*" He crossed his arms over his chest. "Say it, please, Elisabeth. Now I'm speculating on your safety, alone in the office with a strange man."

"Oh, Mr. Eads is a gentleman, some fifty-three years old, and he was accompanied by his daughter."

"*Say it*, Elisabeth."

She nodded. "He claimed, Bryson, that your mother— Lady Este Rainsleigh, who you have mentioned many times now lives in Spain—visited his father's blacksmith shop some thirty-five years ago. The viscountess's mare threw a shoe as she galloped to the village, and she called at the shop for repair. Mr. Eads was a boy of eighteen, still living in his parents' home. It was there," Elisabeth went on, "that your mother caught sight of young Mr. Eads and, apparently, liked very much what she saw. According to him, Lady Rainsleigh contrived a way to chance upon him in a more private, fortuitous moment, and, as Mr. Eads terms it, he was 'overcome.'"

She paused, watching him closely.

Overcome? The word echoed in his brain, but he had no breath to speak.

"As an innocent yet healthy boy of eighteen," she said, "yes, he was simply overcome. Este was beautiful and provocative and aggressive. Persuasive to a point of irresistibility, despite

Mr. Eads upbringing by well-intentioned parents in a devout home. He could not, he said, resist your mother."

"Elisabeth," Rainsleigh cut in, barely able to keep bald-faced fear from his voice, "please tell me that you do not intend to recount this vividly familiar tale—my mother's paramours are *innumerable*—to illustrate that she is a whore."

"He claims to be your father, Bryson."

Rainsleigh blinked. He ceased drawing breath. He felt his throat close in the same moment his heartbeat leapt into a sprint.

Silence sucked the air from the room.

She spoke over it. "Mr. Eads claims he was altogether caught up. For nearly a month. They were…frequently together. Whenever they could steal away. There were countless interludes, he said."

To his mortification, Rainsleigh felt his knees begin to buckle. Tremors followed—his hands, his throat, his very chest seemed to vibrate. He still could not draw breath.

He grabbed the back of a chair. "You should not subjected to such base talk," he managed to say. "I don't care who he claims to be. Why assail you, my lady-wife, with his sordid tale of licentiousness? Blacksmiths and interludes and being overcome."

She chuckled sadly. "Eventually, you will come to terms with how I spend my days, and with whom. I am accustomed to 'base talk.' Who better to hear it than me? To be honest, I encouraged him. He was very distressed. He wanted to tell someone—you, obviously. But when you were not there, I was more than willing to allow him to unburden himself."

"You were *deceived*," he gritted out, his body strumming with terrified anger.

"Pray," she said softly, "let me finish."

He glared at her, unable to speak. His grip on the back of the chair was almost painful. He wanted to tear the leather. He wanted to hurl the chair through the window and shout through the shattered glass. He wanted to run through the gash left behind. Anything to compel her to *cease* explaining the unthinkable.

She did not. "The sixth Viscount Rainsleigh—the man you knew as your father—and Este had quarreled, Mr. Eads said, and the viscount had gone away in an angry huff. Este told Mr. Eads she had been abandoned in Wiltshire with no means to follow her husband to London. She was very resentful, and when she met the young Mr. Eads, she allowed their passion to sweep her away."

Rainsleigh searched the words for some incongruity, a telltale behavior or choice that did not align with what he knew of his parents.

He found none.

Everything she described was exactly as immoral and selfish and reckless as he would expect.

Still, he shook his head. Slowly at first and then faster. The more she spoke, the more he shook his head. It became harder and harder to breathe.

"Mr. Eads, in contrast, was plagued with guilt and shame," she went on, "even while desire for your mother entranced him. Within a month, he managed the wherewithal to refuse her. Their affair ceased, and Este was livid. Six weeks later, your mother sought him out and informed him that she had become pregnant, and that he was the father of the child. Mr. Eads was, he says, terrified and thrilled at the same time. He begged her—although in vain, he knew—to leave the viscount and run away with him—to Ireland…or America—so he might provide some meager existence for her and the child."

She glanced at him, and he looked away. He could not bear to look at her; he could not bear to hear what she had to say, but she *would not stop*.

"According to Mr. Eads, Lady Rainsleigh only laughed," Elisabeth said. "She told him about the baby only to spite him; she had no intention of leaving the viscount. In fact, she had written to her husband in London, made amends, and begged him to come home to her. He was set to arrive any day. Their union would carry on, and she would have the baby— have *you*—under the auspices of the viscount's paternity. You would be raised as the viscount's child. She would deny the affair, she said, until the day she died.

"And so Mr. Eads was powerless. He allowed her to go on her merry way, along with the baby she carried, although it nearly killed him. He could not argue the logic of the unborn child being raised as an aristocrat instead of the illegitimate offspring of a villager who, at that time, amounted to nothing. He wanted you to have all the benefits of a nobleman, and even more, he wanted you to have a father who was married to your mother."

"Stop saying *you*." Rainsleigh's voice cut through her narrative like a blade. "Do not say it again when you refer to *me* as this…bastard child." He dropped his hand from the chair. He trudged three heavy steps. He tried to pace, but his legs would not move.

It was unthinkable, the history she described. Another horrible ruse borne from bitterness toward his parents. Mr.

Eads, whoever he was, had been wronged in some way, and this lie was his revenge.

Bryson managed one step. The settee was there, and he went down on the stiff leather with one knee.

"Bryson?" Elisabeth said gently. He heard her rise. "I cannot imagine the shock and anger that you feel in this moment, but I believe it is something with which we must reckon." She paused. "You should see this man. He *looks like you*. The resemblance is so great; in fact, I thought you had stepped inside the office this morning, suddenly aged twenty years. And you cannot deny that his story rings very…possible. Knowing what you've said of your mother. If he—"

"*How much?*" he asked tersely.

"What?"

"How much will it cost me in shillings and pounds to bring about a reckoning? This tale of unrequited, adulterous lust?" He heard the blood rushing in his ears, and he spoke louder and louder to hear over the sound. "There are times when you fight extortion, you see, but other times, you simply say pay the liar to go away."

"I understand that you are no stranger to ghosts, as you call them, from a lifetime ago. You have a protocol, a way to cope—but this is different. This man wants nothing, except possibly to know you…to say how incredibly regretful he is…to tell you that his abandonment has haunted him all of his life. He made a promise to his dying wife that he would finally unburden himself of this lifelong secret. He wants to grow old in peace with his daughter. You have a sister, Bryson. You and your brother could come to know her."

He whirled on her. "You speak of *my* brother? Did this man mention his name? Did he have some elaborate explanation for the questionable paternity of Beau as well? I should like to see him try to weave the strapping, stable-boy narrative seven years into the future, when he was born."

Elisabeth shook her head and drifted to the settee, settling on the end. "Mr. Eads said he fled Wiltshire after you were born. He could not bear to stay. He assumes Lady Rainsleigh conceived Beau within the bounds of her marriage to the viscount. Mr. Eads said he was living in Berkshire by then. When he fled Wiltshire, he found work as an apprentice to the owner of a malting in Berkshire. The owner had no sons; when the man died, he willed the operation to Mr. Eads. It was a stroke of good fortune, but only a hardworking man of intellect and steadfastness could make a go of it. Which he, in every way, appears to have done." She paused, watching him. "Whether you like it or not, Mr. Raymond Eads seems to be diligent and honest and everything one would expect from someone who started with nothing and worked hard to earn success." She reached out and touched Bryson's face. He squeezed his eyes shut, resenting the contact—resenting the whole bloody story and especially her obvious favor of it—but he could not pull away. He leaned into the coolness of her palm.

"*Just like you*, Bryson," she finished in a whisper. "In manner, in integrity, certainly in appearance, he is, in many ways, *like you*." She nudged closer to him. "I would not bring it to you here, now—not like this—if I did not suspect that there is truth in what he claims."

"*He. Lies*," Bryson rasped. "He lies, and I resent that you would be so easily fooled." He turned to glare at her, but the expression on her face brought him up short. He blinked. She was lit with compassion—beautiful, damnable compassion. He looked away.

"Insulting me may feel satisfying in this moment," she said gently, "but this is something you cannot buy or bully or marry to make it go away. It's also something that could change the course of the rest of our lives. Possibly for the better. Just think, Bryson—the man you despise so much, the man you thought of as your flesh and blood, might be no part of you after all."

He laughed bitterly, jerking away. "Careful what you say, *my lady*. Do you hear yourself? I cannot imagine the reality has been lost, even on you. If what your *Mr. Eads* says is true, if I am not the son of Franklin Courtland, sixth Viscount Rainsleigh, then I am not, in fact, *seventh* Viscount Rainsleigh. I am not a viscount at all; I am a bastard. And you are not a viscountess. You are married to a man with no name."

Elisabeth dropped her hand and sat back on her haunches. "How can you think I care about that? Bryson? Please tell me that you do not."

"Well, you should care!" He shoved off the settee. "It's no small thing to accuse a man of being a bastard. To threaten to strip him of his title, to single-handedly make him the son of an…an…unmarried blacksmith!"

"You're not listening." She sighed. "Mr. Eads is not a blacksmith; his father was. He is a man of industry. And he wishes to accuse you of nothing. He proposes to tell no one but you. It was only because I drew the story out of him that he told me."

"Drew the story out, did you?" He strode to her. "Are you deliberately trying to ruin me?"

"What I'm trying to do," she said, standing, "is set you free."

"From what? Respectability? The pride of a rich heritage, an ancient title? The simple decency of being a man of known parentage?"

"From *lies*, Bryson."

"Well, this is a novel goal, coming from you."

She gasped and stumbled back.

His arm shot out, and he grabbed her. "*No*, that's not what I meant. Elisabeth, *please…*" He shut his eyes, straining to control the rioting emotions that threatened to overwhelm him. "Forgive me. You have been taken in by this man. It is not your fault. He is the liar—you cannot know the lengths to which these people will go to extort me. I lashed out, and that was a mistake. I'm sorry." He gave her a gentle shake. "I have vowed to be unaffected by these sorts of ghosts, but this one has caught me unaware. I've never had anyone's claims strike so directly."

He was afraid to open his eyes, to look down and see misunderstanding, fresh hurt, or, God forbid, disgust on her face. He drew breath to go on, but she shuffled under his grip and turned. He felt her move in. She placed her hand on his chest.

He opened his eyes.

"Your reaction," she said softly, "is exactly what I would expect. You will have more anger and denial and resentment as we go. We must sink to the bottom of what this man says before we rise up. But we shall do it together. I am here to weather it with you, Bryson. I would not have presented it to you in this manner if I meant for you to go it alone."

He opened his mouth to speak, closed it, and then opened it again. He said, "I think perhaps what I find the most astounding is how convinced you already are that he is telling the truth." He stared at her. "You *believe* this stranger is my illegitimate father." His voice had gone harsh again—even as he leached comfort and strength from the touch of her hands on his chest, even while he studied her upturned face, searching it as if it held every answer. He glared down, daring her to deny it—*demanding* that she deny it.

I am Rainsleigh. My entire life has been about little else.

"It doesn't matter what I believe," she said softly. "Because I know *you*. And I know that *you* will not dismiss it until you have discovered the absolute truth. Your honesty will see it through, whatever the answer may be. I simply want you to know that I am here. For you." And then she leaned in, resting her head on his chest, sliding her hands around his waist, drawing him tightly against her.

"Elisabeth," he managed to say, "please. Leave me. I will…" He took a ragged breath. "We will start again in the morning. I will not take supper."

She did not move, except to squeeze him harder, burrowing against his chest. He smelled her hair—sweet, full of sunshine—just below his chin, and he fought the urge to drop his face against it. He stood taut and still beneath her hold.

"I understand," she finally said. "I expected this. And I will go. But please be aware that I will not sleep in the viscountess's suite." She slid her hands from his back and stepped away, turning toward the door. "Ever again."

CHAPTER THIRTY-ONE

He came to her in the middle of the night. She awakened to the sound of the door crashing against the wall. A heavy candelabra clonked unevenly on the tabletop. His boots hit the floor with a heavy, one-two-*thud*.

She was fully awake by the time he loomed over her. She lay still, eyes wide, heart hammering.

He slid the bed curtain to the end of the canopy and fumbled for the covers, flinging them back to reveal her curled beneath.

Her night rail was voluminous—a gift from her aunt—yards and yards of thin, white fabric, bunched up now, around her thighs. She blinked in the dim candlelight, watching him ravish her with his eyes.

He wore only his trousers and shirt, opened at the neck. His hair was wild, his eyes were heavy, half-lidded. She could smell the brandy from where she lay.

"I sent a messenger," he said lowly, finally looking at her face. "To Spain. He'll take a boat from Portsmouth to Bilbao. I'll have some answer by next week from my mother."

Elisabeth nodded. In her mind, she had no doubt. Her only uncertainty was Bryson's own journey to the truth. It could take years, she thought, regardless of what his mother said. There was always the chance that he would never accept it.

She rose to her elbows. "Right. Next week."

"I felt compelled to include your description of this… *Raymond Eads*"—he could barely say the name—"in the very real possibility that she cannot remember one former lover from the next."

"He was easy to describe," she said, sitting up higher. "Because he looks very much like you." Her hair fell around her shoulders, a nuisance; she had not bothered to braid it. Except, oh—

His gaze was fixed on it. The heat in his eyes flared, and he swayed. He widened his stance. He steadied himself on the headboard.

"And how is that?" he rasped.

"Well, he is tall, with broad shoulders, and although his hair has turned to white, a few strands of black remain. His jaw is rough with stubble, even though I'm sure his valet was fastidious about his shave."

Bryson rubbed his own emerging beard, swaying again. "Careful. I shall think you prefer to be taken to bed by *Mr. Eads*."

"Don't be stupid," Elisabeth said softly, reaching out to him. The top of her gown fell from her shoulder, and his gaze locked on the exposed skin.

"Not stupid, my lady," he said, swaying again. "Merely a bastard."

She sighed and let her outstretched arm fall.

"My fathe—" He stopped again, squeezed his eyes shut. "*The viscount* looked nothing like me at all."

"I'm not surprised." After a pause, she said, "Bryson? Will you come to bed?"

"Elisabeth," he began, addressing the bare skin of her shoulder, "you should go. I…I *want you* to go."

"Go? Go where? My God, Bryson, it's the middle of the night."

"Go," he repeated. "Out of here. Back to your own bedchamber. Back to your aunt's house. You…you cannot stay." He put one knee on the bed.

"I very well *can* stay, I am your wife, and I will stay. Come to bed."

"Elisabeth," he repeated, "our *rapport* in and out of bedrooms is…*was* something I intended to discuss. With you. In the library tonight."

She narrowed her eyes. "This, now? Truly? 'Our rapport?' "

"Typically, a gentleman and his wife reside in different chambers. I designed this house with this arrangement in mind." He looked around. "*Now*, of course…"

"Oh, yes, *now, of course*, we will relocate to a one-room hovel in Wales, and if you wish to avoid me, you will have to stand in the garden." She sat up and crossed her legs like a child. "Look, if sleeping in separate beds was to be part of my life as a viscountess, then I'm glad I may be one no more. I will embrace the hovel in Wales."

"Our contract clearly stipulated that—"

"Our contract is null and void, as it should have been from the start."

"Because I am no longer viscount?" he guessed bitterly.

"Because it was ridiculous."

"Elisabeth," he repeated, "I plan to pursue an annulment."

She considered this, working to control her reaction. It was a test. Each statement was a test. He tossed it out and then waited, tense and watchful, for her to agree.

"On what grounds?" she asked casually, allowing the gown to fall down her arm.

He leaned more heavily on the mattress, thinking this over. "Fraud. When you married me, you believed me to be a viscount. You were to become Lady Rainsleigh, as far as you knew. Instead, you married the bastard son of a heartless woman and a blacksmith." He lost his balance and tipped forward on the bed, scattering two pillows.

"When you meet Mr. Eads, Bryson, you will not think of him as a blacksmith—"

His head shot up. "He is not a viscount."

"No, he is not. Although he is painfully aware that you are. His plan for meeting you, by the by, was that the reality of your birth remain a secret. The world at large need not know that you are not the son, strictly speaking, of the previous Lord Rainsleigh."

"Beau is the rightful viscount now." He growled, fumbling with the buttons on his shirt. "I will not take that from him."

"You're so certain Beau wishes to be the viscount?"

"It doesn't matter what Beau wishes! I worked too hard, for too long, and made too much progress to *pretend* to be the viscount when I am not. It's why you must be sent away."

She sighed in frustration and reached up to help him pull the shirt from his shoulders. He caught her wrists in his hands, holding her still. "Elisabeth," he rasped, "I will not drag you through the scandal that this revelation will create. The ensuing humiliation will be diabolical. No lady of quality would remain bound to a man who was stripped of his title and his paternity." He dropped her wrists.

"Perhaps I am not a lady of quality," she mused, shifting to move behind him. She pulled his shirt away and rose up against his back. She rested her chin on his shoulder.

He turned his head, his mouth inches from her own. "But it was never a real marriage, was it?"

Another test.

"Wasn't it?" she breathed, pressing against him. She slid her palms up and down the muscled ropes of his arms, and she tucked her nose to his neck. He smelled like sweat, and brandy, and *him*. He growled and turned his head, seeking her mouth.

"We made inane agreements after we'd said horrible things," she whispered against his skin. "Our pride would not allow any other way. But it was you…" She lifted her head and gently bussed his cheek with her lips. His skin was warm. His whiskers prickled her mouth. She felt the muscles of his shoulders and neck go taut.

"*You* contrived the agreement that saw us married," she went on, "that brought us *here*."

She touched her lips to his beard again, relishing the prickle. "Here is precisely where I want to be. I don't care if you are Bryson Rainsleigh…" Another pass of her lips—now more like a kiss.

He craned to her, stretching, reaching to catch her mouth.

"Or Thomas Coachman. I…I love you, Bryson."

She paused and allowed that statement to settle in. He went very, very still. His breath seemed to stop. She kissed his mouth, and he returned it, light and cautious at first, a nibble.

She swiped his lip with her tongue.

He growled, descended, and overtook the kiss, devouring her mouth. She leaned in for another soft kiss, but he pivoted, wrapping his arms around her and pulling her into his lap. "I am drunk," he said, falling back, taking her with him.

She stretched out her legs and settled on top of him, seeking the correct fit, his contours to her curves, his hardness to her soft. They were lost to the kiss. She came up to breathe, and he allowed it, although only just barely. He captured her mouth again, gathering up fistfuls of her gown, pulling it over her head. When she was naked, his hands roved her body retracing the curves he'd learned the night before with possessive ferocity.

She melted against him, loving the freedom she had to be above him, the solid hardness of him beneath her—loving, most of all, his hands massaging her body to life. He cupped her bottom, scooting her to just the right place, and her legs fell on either side of him.

He groaned, releasing her long enough to fumble with his trousers. When he'd kicked them free, he grabbed her by the hips, lifted her, and settled her with a precision that took her breath away. She sank onto him with a sigh. He groaned again, wrapping his arms around her, fusing them, and she lost herself to his taste, and his scent, and his body.

Bryson could not remember the last time he'd awakened to the desolate after-effects of excessive drink. He opened his eyes and then shut them. The punishing light of morning pierced his skull. Slowly, he shoved up in bed, and the room swam. He reached out, and his hand collided with a soft, warm body.

"Move slowly, I think," she mumbled, her lips brushing his bare arm, "in your condition."

"Elisabeth…" he began gruffly, harshly—a warning.

"At the very least, please tell me you can recall last night," she whispered, stretching beneath the covers.

No amount of drunkenness could make me forget last night. "Yes. I remember."

He glanced at her, a snug, bean-shaped form under the sheet, a jumble of red curls lay on the pillow. "It was the last time."

She made a punishing sound of frustration and flopped onto her back, staring at the ceiling. "Oh *no*," she threatened. "You wouldn't."

"I am struggling, Elisabeth," he rasped. "Please do not make it more difficult than it is."

"I will be difficult, because you've gone stark, raving mad. I knew you were cagey," she said with irritation, "but I did not know you were destructive. We have married. You *forced us* to marry, and now you would…you would—what, exactly, would you have us do?"

"I am releasing you from the 'forced marriage.' "

"Well, I reject your release."

"Oh, God. My head aches too violently to quarrel about it."

"Pity, because it's no small thing to reject your wife, especially if said wife is me. And we will quarrel about it. Quarreling, in fact, is a very generous term for what we will do. Did you think I would simply say, *Yes, my lord,* and toddle off as if we'd never met?"

"Ha!" he said bitterly. "I thought you would utter a prayer of thanks and sprint."

"But why?"

"Why? *Why?*" he growled, fishing in the covers for his shirt and shoving his arms inside, "Because I am in no condition to be a decent husband to you! I am…adrift." He laughed bitterly. "Adrift does not begin to describe what I am." He glanced down at her, and she glared back.

He shook his head at the ceiling. "Everything I ever knew; everything I believed and worked for, everything on which I staked my very identity is now gone. And not simply gone, but stripped from me and strewn in the gutter for everyone to see. The precise spectacle for which they've waited all along. Worthless Rainsleigh. Like father, like son. It was only a matter of time."

"But that's just it. He was—"

"It makes no difference that Franklin Courtland was not my actual father! I am a bastard now, which is more of the same. Scandal and shame follows this family around like a stench that can never be washed away, no matter how relentlessly I have tried. There's no surprise that it's now attached to me. I could only stay ahead of it for so long." Another bitter laugh.

"You would refuse, entirely, the plan of keeping Mr. Eads's introduction a private matter, known only to you? If you approach it this way, you may carry on as viscount, and no one else will be the wiser. You are fair, and temperate, and compassionate. You are successful and generous. You are more *noble* than most gentlemen will ever be. Only a few trusted people need to know what happened, all those years ago."

"*I* know," he said, "and I can barely live with myself for the knowledge. This…*this* is what I now reckon with. How can I reckon with you too?"

"I require no reckoning, Bryson," she said softly, calmly, "I simply *am*."

He rolled away, reaching for his trousers.

"Now who sprints?" she said softly.

"Bloody well better believe I'm sprinting. Look, Elisabeth, after the first night, it became clear that I…I wanted you too much. The intensity of my desire for you concerned me enough, but now…" He broke off, moving to the edge of the bed to drag his trousers on. When he spoke again, he forced himself to mimic her calmness. "You needn't martyr yourself to me after three days as my wife. My identity is vague, at best. I cannot say what I will do, who I will tell, or how it will resonate. I feel broken. It is not your job to put me back together. This is not to be the life for which you signed on when we married."

"So *ironic*," she said, dazed. She sounded as if she was talking to herself. She went on. "Because the life for which I signed—and I mean that quite literally; I *signed a document*— was really not my preference at all. Together in public, separate in private? No. I would be together with you always. *Even* when you are adrift. Even when you are broken—especially when you are broken." She turned to stare at him. "Tell me, what kind of a woman would I be if I deserted you now? When you are reeling from the biggest shock of your life?"

He said nothing, and she went on. "You cleave to everything honorable and noble and pure. Well, what of basic loyalty? Of selflessness? Please tell me that you do not think I would be so invested in my own standing or comfort as to abandon you now."

"I do not expect you to abandon me. *I* will go."

"Go where?" She scrambled up, sitting gloriously naked on her knees in the center of the bed.

He jerked his gaze away. "I've told you; I *don't know.*"

"Will you come back when you reach some decision?"

"You should not pursue me!" he gritted out, leaving the bed. It killed him to move away from her, like the tide refusing the moon, but distance was the only way.

"You do not dictate what I do," she declared to his back. "Perhaps I should not want the young women who come to my foundation, but I do. Perhaps I should not want Stoker to go to university, but I do. Perhaps I should not want happiness for my aunt and Quincy, but I do—no, wait!" She stopped suddenly. He heard rustling; the bed curtain slid open. She moved from the bed and stomped in front of him, holding her night rail clutched tightly to her chest.

"Actually, I *should* want these things," she said, fumbling with the voluminous gown, shrugging it on. "I will not apologize for being compassionate, and I will not apologize for wanting you." Now her voice broke. He felt his own throat coil into a knot.

"I am not doing it to punish you," he said quietly. "I do it to protect you. It is because of my regard for you that I send you away."

She whispered, "Then you must hate me very much, indeed."

"Elisabeth," he growled. He turned away and trudged to the basin, setting his hands wide and leaning over the bowl.

"Where do you intend for me to go?" she said to his back. "I have told you how I feel. But I will not *beg you* to accept me. If your own pride, or fear, or lack of regard for me is too great to accept my support and…" She faltered, and he gripped the cool marble to keep from going to her. "And my *love*, then, you win. You have proven that I will always be second to your own embattled pride. And as painful as it may be, I am not capable of being second, not with you. I will fare better alone than to be rejected again and again by my own husband."

"If only it was that simple."

"Another vague indifference meant to push me away," she marveled. "Fine, I am *away*. And I ask you again: where do you wish me to go? Back to my aunt's? Shall I remain here and live a separate life, as described in the idiotic contract? Will you set me up somewhere to live as a jilted wife? What do you intend?"

"I do not know!" he said, slapping his hands on the marble and rattling the bowl. It was the truth. He did not know where he wanted her to go, or for how long, or if he would allow himself to indulge in her ever again. He only knew that he could not have her now.

She was silent for a moment, and he had the panicked thought that she had already gone. He craned his neck around. She was walking to the door.

"If you won't *reckon* with me, as you put it, at least please talk to your brother."

"I will not tell my brother until after I've spoken to Eads."

She stopped. "Mr. Eads? You will meet him? When? Today?"

"*Meet* is too civil of a term for what he and I will do." He turned back to the basin.

"I would accompany you," she said, "when you meet Mr. Eads." She advanced on him, holding the hem of her gown off the floor. "I insist upon it. The man is fragile, and hopeful, and terribly afraid. You are angry at him, which I understand, but please. We must strive for civility and grace. He trusted me."

Her continued defense of this man made him want to howl. Did she not see that Raymond Eads had stolen away *her* identity too? She had been Lady Rainsleigh for all of one day!

"Bryson?" she prompted.

He turned to look at her. "How would you designate me?" he asked. "If Mr. Eads is 'fragile' and 'hopeful' and 'afraid?'"

She narrowed her eyes, crossing her hands over her chest. "I would designate you precisely as I have always known you to be. *You*, yourself, have not changed, only some small part of your past, entirely out of your control. And I would describe you as capable, and honorable, and, like Mr. Eads, very much afraid."

CHAPTER THIRTY-TWO

"You shouldn't have come, Elisabeth," Bryson said. He wouldn't look at her. Instead, he stared at the paneled door to the hotel suite that housed Mr. Raymond Eads.

"It makes no difference that I've come," Elisabeth said. "What matters is that *you* have come. I'll go as soon as I've seen this through. Someone has to be pleasant to this man. It's the least I can do. I feel responsible."

"To *him.*"

"Do not," she warned. "You have rejected any responsibility I feel toward you." She took a deep breath. "I'll need ten minutes to make introductions, and then I will go. You could not have been more clear."

"I said that I would go."

"And leave me alone to look after that massive house of yours? Please, do not bother."

It was their first exchange since she had left his chamber in the early morning. She'd asked a maid to inform her when he ordered the carriage brought around. When he climbed in, she was already seated on the opposite bench. He had not ejected her, as she feared, but the short ride to Mr. Eads's hotel had been silent.

Now he stared down at her with sad blue eyes, distant and distantly angry. There was a new hardness there. It had not wavered, not even when he was drunk, not even when they had made love.

It was why she had finally consented to leave him. The revelation about his parentage would devastate him—this she knew. What she had not known was how he would ascribe her into that devastation. Cleave to her or push her away? The answer was resounding. He pushed, and she was tired of fighting.

She raised her hand to knock a second time, but the heavy door creaked opened just a crack. A uniformed maid peered out. Her eyes flitted over Elisabeth and then fixated on Bryson, growing wide. His resemblance to Mr. Eads would shock anyone, and this girl was no exception.

"Hello," Elisabeth said, trying to draw her stare from Bryson's face. "Lord and Lady Rainsleigh, here to see Mr. Eads. I sent a message ahead, but perhaps he has not—"

"Let them in, Nell, let them in!" called a familiar voice from beyond the door. "Do not just, stand there, girl. Let them in!"

As introductions go, this one unfolded slowly, somewhat like a dream. First they heard the voice, then they saw the man. He filled the doorway—as tall as Bryson, his thick hair gone white but otherwise the same. Blue eyes, gentle and soft, met Bryson's hard stare.

"You've come," Mr. Eads said quietly, his voice cracking with emotion.

She looked at Bryson. No amount of stoicism could disguise the open shock of confronting an aged version of his own face.

She smiled at Mr. Eads, but he saw only his son. He made no effort to hide his appreciation of Bryson's broad shoulders, his great height, his large hands. Bryson was always impeccably turned out, and today was no different. She could see her reflection in the sheen of his boots. Mr. Eads marveled at it all.

"I hope you'll forgive our rudeness," she said. "Please tell me that my boy, Stoker, reached you with our note."

"No rudeness at all, Lady Rainsleigh, I assure you." He did not break his gaze from Bryson. "We had been waiting for any word since yesterday. We rejoiced at the message."

"Lord Rainsleigh," said Elisabeth, "may I introduce Mr. Raymond Eads? Mr. Eads, Bryson Courtland, Viscount Rainslei—"

"*Stop*," gritted out Bryson. "Let us cease with the repeated use of what is now a wildly inaccurate name."

Mr. Eads reared back as if Bryson had slapped him, and Elisabeth shot Bryson a warning look.

"If you'll but show us the way, Mr. Eads," she said, "we should be delighted to join you inside. It might be best, I think." She looked right and left. "My husband has experienced quite a shock upon learning of your…news." She grabbed hold of Bryson's arm and tugged.

He stared at her hand.

"Bryson, *darling*, come inside."

Mr. Eads finally realized his duty and stepped back, gesturing them in. "My apologies. Of course you should not languish in the hall." He looked back, watching Bryson remove his gloves and hat. "I have never met a viscount before."

Bryson's eyes narrowed into slits, and Elisabeth squeezed his arm.

"Your rooms are very nice, Mr. Eads," she called.

"We generally take rooms in Knightsbridge," he said, "but for this…just in case…I thought, Mayfair. I've read all about your new house in Henrietta Place, Lord Rainsleigh."

Bryson wouldn't answer, and Elisabeth gritted her teeth.

They followed him down a black-and-white-tiled hallway into a small, well-appointed sitting room with large windows that overlooked the street.

"The maids have the windows up for the morning breeze," he explained, hurrying to shut them, "but the carriage traffic sends up a cloud of dust and stench. I warned them. They are accustomed to the clean air of the country, I'm afraid—we all are. London is a jolt to the senses every time." He muscled a window shut.

"You've visited London before?" asked Bryson. He stopped in the doorway. Elisabeth tried and failed to pull him into the room.

"Very rarely," Mr. Eads answered, ducking out from behind a curtain. "I am the owner of four maltings in Berkshire, and my business is mostly with the local barley farmers and the brewers. Only rarely am I required in Town, usually to consider new equipment or settle some banking matter. Once every five years, perhaps? My late wife and I had planned to host our daughter, Lucy, in a London season, but she claims she has no wish for a debut, God love her. She is a country lass, like her mother." He slammed the last window and dusted his hands together, turning to face them.

"Had you sought me out previously, Mr. Eads," Bryson asked, "on your infrequent visits to London?"

"Oh, after you began your ship making, I allowed myself to get as close as the road in front of the shipyard gate. Once, perhaps twice, a visit. It's difficult for an old man to be inconspicuous when he's hanging out the carriage window for the best view, but I have tried to be so careful, my lord." He moved to a chair near the fire. "Oh, how I marveled at the size of your operation, the obvious efficiency and success of your company, the grandeur of your ships."

He paused and looked dreamily into the distance, locking his fingers together beneath his chin. "I did not wish to be selfish with my interest, you see. I knew that you resembled my people—resembled *me*. Your rise has been well-documented in the papers, and I have read every word. The sketch artists—they bring portraiture to life, do they not? Although, I must say," he shook his head, pointing at Bryson up and down, "nothing could prepare me for how striking a man you have become."

Again, Bryson said nothing. Elisabeth rolled her eyes and left him, taking a seat adjacent to Mr. Eads.

"Your parents must have been so proud," Mr. Eads mused, and Elisabeth cringed.

"What do you *want*, Mr. Eads?" Bryson asked.

"What do I want?" the older man repeated hollowly, as if he could not understand the words. He shook his head vaguely. "Do you mean today? For our introduction? I want to make your acquaintance, I suppose. I want come to know you, if you are amenable to such a thing—but this would be entirely up to you. Certainly, I will settle on whatever makes you—" He chose his words carefully. "On whatever you require. It will be enough for me," he declared, "It is everything, just to clap eyes on you. And to meet your lovely wife."

Mr. Eads went quiet, clearly wanting to say the correct thing. "I should like to tell you that I am proud of all that you have achieved. To tell you that you were loved, even though you did not know me—"

"What *tangible thing* do you want?" Bryson interrupted. "What are your monetary demands?"

"Bryson," warned Elisabeth, shutting her eyes.

Mr. Eads said, "Monetarily? Oh, no, you misunderstand. I have all the money I require." He looked confused. "I hope you did not come here expecting to be extorted. Not by me."

"That is exactly what I expected. It is what I expect it still."

"I ask nothing of you, my lord, except that you hear my deep regret for not knowing you until now. In fact, my failures to you are legion." He laughed sadly. "It is *I* who should be asking *you*: what, if anything—anything at all—may I do for you?"

Bryson stared at him, cocking his head to study him from a different angle. He almost appeared to consider the request. Elisabeth had never seen him look so desolate, even at the St. Clare ball.

"What would I like?" Bryson asked facetiously. "For myself? Oh, well, I should like my *title* back. My legitimacy. My name. My honor. And while you're at it, I should like these things for my wife as well. I should like to never have to reveal to my younger brother—who abhors establishment, and rules, and society life—that he is suddenly a wealthy viscount, with responsibilities and expectations and boundaries that will hem him in. Oh, but wait. Now the title will come with a sordid scandal that he can never overcome, and all of the respect, and acceptance, and position for which I have worked my entire life will be worthless. It will have…no value whatsoever. What, I ask you, has *no* value? Ashes? Do ashes have value? I am left with the ashes of a great house, burned to the ground. Make that all go away, will you, Mr. Eads?" finished Bryson. "*That* is what I want."

Mr. Eads looked back and forth between Elisabeth and Bryson. "This is your allegiance speaking," the old man said. "The loyalty you feel to the father who raised you."

"*No*," gritted out Bryson, "I abhor the man who raised me. The day he drowned was the happiest day of my life."

"Because you became viscount."

Bryson opened his mouth to speak, but then he closed it. The hardness in his face fractured into a scowl. "No. Because my tormentor was dead."

"So now you abhor *me?*" It was the tiniest hint of a challenge.

"I do not abhor you, Mr. Eads; I do not know you. I abhor what has been *done* to me. I conduct my life with an incredible amount of self-control, you see. And the irony of your secret paternity is that it was entirely out of my control." He closed his eyes, composing himself. "But that is neither here nor there. If you cannot name something that you *want*, Mr. Eads, then I should like to know what you *intend*.

"You seem to think I have turned up in your hotel on a social call, but in my mind, I am here to determine how to carry on with my life. In this, I am entirely at your mercy. It is not a position that I enjoy. My wife claims that you are a man of some responsibility and means. If this is true, then surely you understand how difficult this is for me. The sooner I understand what you would do next, the sooner I may begin to pick up what is left of my life and find a way to go on. And the sooner I may release my wife."

"Release your wife?" Mr. Eads said, gasping. He gestured to Elisabeth. "But surely my presence will not disrupt your relationship with this dear woman?"

"And why the bloody hell not?"

"Bryson—*no*," Elisabeth snapped. He would not use her as an excuse. He was grasping at straws, desperate to heap blame. What harm could come from making the smallest effort? Bryson ignored her, finally leaving the doorway for the windows, likely because Mr. Eads was walking to him. "Elisabeth is a gentle lady from an esteemed family. She married under the auspices of our shared nobility. She was promised to become a viscountess. And what is she now? The wife of a bastard with no name at all."

"But you were raised to be Viscount Rainsleigh," objected Mr. Eads. "My intention was for you to remain as such. I only wished to know you *in private*."

The old man paused, thinking about what he'd said. He dug in his pocket and pulled out what appeared to be a miniature portrait. He gazed it a moment and then cupped it protectively in his fist. "Oh, but we knew the risk," he said. "We knew it was a selfish thing to do, but my heart has ached for so long. My late wife urged me to, at the very least, endeavor to meet you. To be honest, I did not know yesterday if I would say the words. And then I met your beautiful Lady Elisabeth. She compelled me to share the secret—not that I blame her, oh no. She made the telling easy. And telling her felt *so*…" He paused and smiled tearfully at Elisabeth.

She squeezed her eyes shut, spilling her own tears.

"Telling her absolved me in a way I cannot describe. But I never intended my own peace to come at any cost to you, my lord. I never wanted to alter your life."

Elisabeth opened her blurry eyes to smile at him. How gratifying, she realized, to have a champion when she had been battening up against Bryson's iron will for days. She'd nearly forgotten the reason for which she fought while Bryson indulged his own rage. He would not listen to reason, but this did not mean she could not speak it. She would not repay Mr. Eads's gratitude by keeping silent now.

She held out her hand to the older man. "Please do not be misled, Mr. Eads," she said levelly. "Bryson does not push me away because I object to his new identity, he pushes me away because I interrupt the deeply controlled manner in which he leads his life. The control may be less necessary now, and that frightens him."

"*Elisabeth*," Bryson warned from behind her.

"What?" She whirled around.

"*Do. Not.*"

"Do not, what? I'll not have you suggest to Mr. Eads that I am devastated—nay, that I am affected at all, except to sympathize with the pain of you both. I could not care less who your true father is."

"But why *couldn't* he remain the viscount?" begged Mr. Eads. "And you, his lady-wife? No one need know! Stripping you of the title was never my goal!" His voice sagged to a new low; he held his hands out in desperation.

"Because it is *a lie*," snapped Bryson. "I am *not* the viscount. I have not worked years to restore honor to the viscountcy to now *masquerade* as a member of the nobility that I am not."

"So you are not specifically related to the Rainsleigh viscountcy—so what?" countered Elisabeth, gripping the back of her chair. "What could it possibly matter, unless blood trumps the sacrifices that you have made?"

"Blood trumps everything!" he said.

"Bollocks!" she shouted back. "It has been *your* talent, Bryson, your hard work, and your own, inherent honor—not some genetic elixir from the odious man you thought was your father—that restored the title. *You* did this. If you wish to remain Rainsleigh, I think you should do it. No one need know. Mr. Eads could not be more clear about his discretion. The House of Rainsleigh is entirely your design. Carry on, and do not look back."

"But the previous viscount was…was *odious?*" stammered Mr. Eads. "I left you to him to give you every advantage. To be raised by a titled gentleman, in a sprawling estate, with servants and schools and the leaders of the country as your friends! Please, my lord, tell me the viscount was not…cruel to you? When you were a boy?" His sawing whisper barely made it to the end of the question.

She thought Bryson would refuse this answer too, but he shook his head, and said to the window, "The viscount beat me. Regularly. When he did not beat me, he mocked me. When he did not beat me or mock me, he taunted me with liquor and women and things I would not mention in front of a lady."

"*No!*" Mr. Eads cried in hushed agony, his hands outstretched.

"The title he gave me was worthless, soiled by his selfish, bacchanal existence. There was *no* advantage; in fact his greatest joy was to hobble me. He wanted me in the gutter with him. Perhaps…perhaps he always knew." He glanced quickly at Mr. Eads and then away. "The estate was decrepit and host to unspeakable degenerates. I financed my own education. I had no friends."

Mr. Eads's body shook. Thin, desperate tears jumped down his cheek. Elisabeth looked away, but she heard him move, staggering around furniture. Bryson stared rigidly down at the street.

Now he will reject him face-to-face, she thought. It had been a mistake to come. She wiped away more tears. It had been a mistake to entertain Mr. Eads at the shipyard. *I am too ambitious*, she thought. *I am selfish. I want too much.*

No one knew more than Elisabeth that not every story had a happy ending. Not every father and son discovered each other. Not every wife managed to show her husband the power of forgiveness and love. What made her believe that she would be the person to bring these things to light? Her love for him? Her admiration for the courage of Mr. Eads?

It wasn't enough.

"Please, Bryson," whispered Mr. Eads, his voice breaking when he called his son by his given name. "I will not go so far as to ask you to forgive. I will not even ask you to understand the trap I found myself in with your mother. But please, my boy, *please* allow me to simply tell you how deeply, regretfully sorry I am. So sorry, from the depths of my soul."

He reached the first window and kept coming. "Every day, I thought of you," he said. "Every day my late wife and I said a prayer for you. Please accept that my torment over losing you, at not knowing you, is real. Acknowledge it, just once, if you can. And know that you will not have to bear the horrible memory of it—whatever it was—alone anymore, even if we never speak beyond today. Because I will agonize with you, nay—on *behalf of you*. Oh, if I could, I would bear the memories for you—bear them away."

Bryson's jaw was clamped so tightly, Elisabeth thought it would snap. He refused to look at the older man. If he could, she thought, he would clap his hands over his ears to block out all sound. He kept his eyes locked on the street.

When Mr. Eads reached him, the older man choked out, "May I...may I touch you? Bryson? May I shake your hand? You asked what I wanted—well, that is it. To put my hand in the hand of my son. To touch you in the way I never could, in the way that I always hoped Lord Rainsleigh did. My heart is broken, learning that he did not, the stupid, stupid fool."

Without waiting for an answer, Mr. Eads extended a shaking hand. It hovered there, unmet, for three seconds...four...

Elisabeth wanted to crawl over the chair and shove Bryson in his direction. She wanted to take up Mr. Eads's hand in her own. She *willed* Bryson to meet Mr. Eads halfway, just this once.

Finally, after an eternity of stillness, Bryson moved his eyes from the window and stared at the quavering, outstretched hand. His breath came harder, so hard his shoulders rose and fell. Elisabeth worried that he might slap his father's hand away, and she opened her mouth to call out his name—a plea, a demand, a threat—but he squeezed his eyes shut and thrust his left hand out. He stopped just short of touching him.

Mr. Eads closed the space and grabbed hold, joining their palms.

For a long moment they simply stood, connected, hands gripped, together but apart.

Bryson refused to open his eyes, but Mr. Eads drank in the sight of him. His face was a canvas; Elisabeth saw affection, hope, joy—he veritably radiated love.

"Oh, my boy," he whispered, closing his other hand on top of their joined hands. He bent his face over them and pressed his cheek to the back of Bryson's hand. He turned his head and kissed his son's knuckles. He breathed in, weeping tears of relief.

Throughout it all, Bryson stood, eyes closed, body rigid. He allowed it.

It occurred to Elisabeth that her presence in the room had become superfluous. The moment was private, intensely so, and here she sat, taking it in from four feet away.

She staggered to stand.

She wiped her eyes with the back of her hand. Perhaps she'd been too greedy. Not two happy endings but one. One…was enough.

Mr. Eads finally loosened his hold, allowing Bryson to pull away, but he did not. Bryson grabbed him back, catching Mr. Eads by the forearm. He gripped the older man's arm. He clung, like a man falling off the side of a boat. Mr. Eads reacted immediately, hauling Bryson against him, wrapping him in a tight embrace.

Through fresh tears, Elisabeth saw Bryson hesitate only half a second, gape in disbelief, and then fall against him, squeezing his eyes shut again. His father slapped him on the back four times and then locked his arm there and seized him.

Elisabeth put a hand over her mouth to stifle the sound of a sob.

Now I will go. She somehow managed to turn away, to walk uneven steps to the door. *I've done what I came to do.* She looked back and saw Mr. Eads move his hand to his son's head, digging his fingers into Bryson's hair, holding his head to his shoulder. *I told him I would go, and now I will honor what I said.*

She forced her legs to carry on, down the hall, around a corner. She leaned against the front door and cried, allowing the tears, finally, to really come. *He needs time. They will both require so much time.*

When she opened her eyes, the wide-eyed maid was there, hovering, accompanied by a girl of about sixteen with black hair and blue eyes. Bryson's sister. It could be no other.

Elisabeth turned her face away.

"Careful," said the girl gently. "There you are." She pressed a handkerchief into Elisabeth's hand. "Now, then. Lady Rainsleigh? How can we help?"

Elisabeth felt a cool hand against her shoulder. She shook her head.

"Should I call for your husband?" the girl asked.

Another shake, more violently this time.

"Leave them, please," whispered Elisabeth. "They are getting on so...well. But I have stayed far too long. I apologize. If you'll excuse me." She fumbled for the doorknob.

"Yes, all right," said the girl, stepping back, "if you're sure. Can we not bring you a cup of tea? Another handkerchief? Our footman, Charlie, can accompany you outside if you require fresh air. Or I can—"

"No, no—you are kind, but no. Thank you. I must—I have promised I would go. And now I shall." This was the plainest, most painful truth. She'd traded his cooperation for her promise to go. She would keep her word.

The girl looked unconvinced. "But the men know you are leaving? Your husband? My father? I am Miss Lucy Eads, by the way."

Elisabeth shook her head. "They are…occupied. If you please, allow them ten minutes more, perhaps? Your father will likely summon you when the time is right." She glanced over her shoulder. "I'm sorry to steal away, but I must."

"Yes, yes," said Lucy carefully, hopping out of the way. "I won't detain you."

Elisabeth nodded, pulling at the door.

Go now, go now, go now—or you will never go.

"But Lady Rainsleigh, what should I tell Lord Rainsleigh?" the girl called. "About where you have gone?"

"*Home*," said Elisabeth—her first clear, loud statement since the crying began. She pulled the door open and walked through. "If he asks, you may tell him that I have gone to my home."

Chapter Thirty-Three

Bryson couldn't say how long he clung to the old man. Five minutes? An hour? When he finally emerged from the morass of emotion and memory and a host of feelings he could not name, a full day might have passed. He felt wholly…transported.

Although not so transported that awkwardness had not set in. Not so much that everything was immediately resolved. But he was transported…*enough*. Enough to stop fighting.

He cleared his throat. He gave a nod against the old man's shoulder. He stepped away. He looked out the window and stared at the street.

I always knew. He marveled at the thought.

He glanced at the old man and then away.

He remembered, distinctly, shivering in his bed, alone at night, listening to whoops and hollers, to stray gunshot, to wicked laughter from his parents' endless parties a floor below. He had been so frightened by the chaos, the shrill women and dodgy men, the debris he and his brother would pick through the next morning. But most of all, the man he

knew as his father had frightened him. How could he belong
there, in that house, he had wondered, time and again, if he
was always so bloody afraid?

He wanted to tell him—Mr. Eads. In the same way he had
suddenly, urgently, wanted to embrace him, he wanted to say
to him: *Somehow, I always knew.* He would not, however. Not
yet. Possibly not ever.

Ah, but somehow Eads read his mind. "You suspected
it all along, didn't you?" His voice was full of wonder. "You
knew you were not his flesh and blood? And I? I was not there
to claim you." The joy on his face dissolved into misery. His
eyes watered again.

Bryson tore his gaze from the window to watch him,
considering this—considering what the bloody hell to do
next. They had known each other for all of an hour. Too
much was at stake. He couldn't suddenly make room in his
life for this man because he *resembled* him, or because he
seemed to embody selflessness and regret. A lifetime of distrust did not simply *disappear*. What if he was an incredibly proficient liar, bent on blackmail after all? What if he
promised discretion today but could not resist telling a few,
trusted friends or relatives tomorrow? Oh, God, what if he
ever told anyone at all?

Of all the times in his life when he employed caution,
when he reveled in it, *now* would be the most essential time.

He could not go along just because something about
Mr. Eads felt…right.

Or could he? Because all of a sudden, it did not seem to
matter so much that he was no longer viscount. It was brand
new, this feeling. When he'd first allowed himself to consider

that he had no hereditary right to the title, it had felt as if his arm had been cut off. But now? Now it simply…*was*.

Not ideal, of course—not for him or for Beau—but it did not feel…impossible.

In fact, what a relief to suddenly, simply, *be*.

Mr. Eads blew his nose noisily, and Bryson was compelled to explain his silence. "Forgive me, Mr. Eads. I am struggling to know how to proceed. You have been more than generous, and my behavior when I arrived was hostile, I know. I never allow myself to assume, and I don't make allowances quickly. I have survived in my life due, in part, to shrewdness and caution. Bear with me, if you will."

Mr. Eads agreed so heartily his entire body seemed to nod. "Oh, but I can only imagine, my boy." He waved his handkerchief like a flag. "You may navigate my enthusiasm as you see fit. I do get ahead of myself, especially when it comes to, well, family. We have all the years ahead of us to make peace, if you desire it. Rome was not built in a day."

Bryson gave him a small smile. He had never met a man so willing to concede. It added to his legitimacy, certainly. Very few swindlers knew patience, and he was willing to wait.

Before he could stop himself, Bryson explained, "I suppose my most urgent reckoning is: *why*? Why bother, now, so long after the fact? If you, indeed, seek no recompense from my fortune or from knowing a"—it was still difficult to say— "a *viscount*, then why not leave well enough alone? You have lost your wife, but you claim to be happy in the company of your daughter. You also claim to be solvent—even rich, one might say. You've seen my business in the newspapers, my marriage too; so you have proof that I am well. Why dredge up what never could have been?"

"Because *I*, too, always knew," Mr. Eads said. "In the back of my heart, *I always knew*. Deep down. You were not well in the care of the previous viscount. I *knew* your mother could not look after you properly." He stared at him with eyes glistening. His voice broke. "I knew you would search for someone—search for *me*—and I would not be there." He dabbed his eyes. "Perhaps I have not admitted it out loud—not even to my dear wife, although likely she assumed—but I think I always knew." His voice closed off, and he tapped his fist against his heart, two times—*thump, thump.*

Bryson looked away. He heard Mr. Eads take two steps closer to him.

"The guilt from that worry, that pain?" the older man went on. "*That* is why. The urge to seek you became too powerful to resist. I wanted to discover that I was wrong, that you had been happy and indulged."

The two most absent conditions from Bryson's boyhood: happiness and indulgence.

"If nothing else, I hoped to find you happy *now*," finished Mr. Eads. "It was to be enough. But then I happened upon your beautiful wife instead of you, and she spoke so lovingly about your life, your new marriage. I thought, perhaps a man with a wife such as this could come to know me without bitterness. If I made it clear I did not wish to expose the paternity to anyone else. Lady Rainsleigh made no such promise to me, but I knew that any man who chose *her* would be a man I could, at the very least, *try* to come to know."

"Elisabeth," Bryson said hoarsely, suddenly remembering, looking around. "Elisabeth?"

But where had she gone? She should hear this. She would know what to do with the emotional tsunami that threatened, now, to pull him down. This meeting had been her design.

He looked to her chair, to the four corners of the room, to the doorway. She was gone.

"Did she go?" he asked, feeling the first flare of alarm.

"Oh, but perhaps she did," Mr. Eads said, smiling and looking around. "She might have slipped from the room to grant us privacy. I've become so emotional in my old age." He made for the door and hallway beyond. "I have asked my daughter, Lucy, to remain upstairs until I discovered how our meeting would go, but knowing her, she has drifted as close as possible. She will have intercepted Lady Rainsleigh—likely the two of them are taking tea. Come—no, no, you needn't look so concerned. We shall find them presently."

"Yes," Bryson agreed absently, but he thought, *She's gone. She's gone. I've driven her away, and she's gone.*

His heart began to pound. He hurried after Mr. Eads, barely restraining himself from setting the old man out of his way, running ahead, and shouting out her name.

"Lucy?" sang Mr. Eads. "Lucy? Lamb?"

"Elisabeth?" Bryson called.

Mr. Eads craned around, puzzled. "But was she unwell, my boy?"

Bryson called again, more urgently this time, "Elisabeth!" *Please don't be already gone.*

"Papa?" answered a voice in the distance. "Papa, we are here. May I…"

The voice belonged to a girl of about sixteen—to Lucy, he presumed. He nearly collided with her, darting around the corner. She came up short, clasping her chest.

Bryson croaked, "My wife—have you seen her? Lady Rainsleigh?"

"Oh," said the girl, "I worried this would happen. She was so upset when she left."

"*Left?*" His voice was too loud, too imperious, but Lucy did not blanch. The eagerness in her expression fell to concern. She was a pretty girl, black hair and blue eyes. Just like Mr. Eads, she had that familiar look of…well, of him.

The girl said, "Not thirty minutes, she's been gone. She forbade me from calling for you, my lord. She was very insistent. And she said she was meant to go alone."

"But why would she go?" wondered Mr. Eads. "Would the reality of my confession upset her?"

"No, no," Bryson said dismissively, "your confession is the only thing that has kept her with me for so long. Oh, God, what have I done?"

"What *have* you done?" asked Lucy. "She was quite upset when she left."

He shot her a surprised look. He was not accustomed to being challenged by young ladies. She raised one eyebrow, clearly not intimidated.

Bryson nodded. "The story of…what I've done is so terrible and one-sided and unbelievable to have gone on this long. My entire purpose these last six weeks was to have Elisabeth for my own, but I have I failed to…to…"

He dropped his head in his hands and rubbed his eyes. Dear Lord, he'd failed in so many ways. Most grievous of all, perhaps, he'd failed to acknowledge the love that she had so freely given him.

And oh, how he loved her. His heart soared with it. He just learned that he was a bastard. He had no name, no title, and he didn't even care. Because of love. For her.

He *ached* with it. He almost laughed at the irony. If it had not been for Elisabeth, he would never have known that this ache—this urgent, breathtaking ache—*was* love unacknowledged. It only hurt if he turned away. As he had been trying to do *for days*.

But what had she also taught him?

He lifted his head.

It didn't have to be this way.

He could choose to acknowledge the love—hers, Raymond Eads's—he could choose to acknowledge it all. He could choose to stay.

When he looked at Lucy Eads, all trace of pride was gone. "What I've done is refuse to give myself to Elisabeth," he said. "I reserved the most vulnerable part. I was afraid of the depth of my love for her, and I tried to keep her at arm's length. She would not stand for it, and we quarreled. We quarreled just this morning. I threatened to send her away."

He blinked, realizing the magnitude of what he had just said.

He turned to the door. "My hat? My gloves?"

"Nell! His lordship's things," bellowed Mr. Eads, scuttling after him to the door.

To Bryson, he said, "But surely she will listen to you when you go to her. She is a forgiving woman; this I know. You will make it right. If you can say it so plainly to us, you can make it right."

"There are so many wrongs to be made right," Bryson said, "possibly too many. Repeatedly, I have pushed her away. I have blamed her for things that were not her fault. I have—"

"Oh, but you must tell her!" said Mr. Eads reaching for the door.

The maid tripped up with Bryson's things, and he swiped them from her, shoving into his gloves. Speaking to himself, he said, "I was so afraid of being overcome. I never wanted to fall victim to any pleasure that would make a fool of me, like every pleasure made a fool of my fath—"

He stopped himself. He froze with his glove halfway on his hand. He looked at Mr. Eads.

The older man smiled at his son. "Marriage is the place to indulge your pleasure, my boy. Here is where you revel in it. This love you share with your wife is what bolsters you and sends you out in the world to take on every other fear and temptation."

Bryson nodded, shoving his hat on his head. "Yes, well, I did not know. I did not know if what I felt was right. I was never shown."

"We start today," said Mr. Eads quietly, his voice breaking again. His daughter stepped to his side and grabbed his arm.

Remarkably, Bryson felt his own eyes fill with tears. He could but nod.

"Go!" urged Mr. Eads, ushering him out the open door. "Hurry to her! We will not depart London until we have had some word."

Bryson was almost in the hall before he paused, turned, and asked, "Miss Lucy, I beg your pardon, but did she happen to say where she was going?"

"She said, 'home.'"

"Home?"

"No," Lucy corrected herself. "She said, 'I'm going to *my* home.'"

Chapter Thirty-Four

There was a warm but spacious room in the rear of Elisabeth's foundation building that she had designated long ago as the reception room for new girls on the night of a rescue raid. Originally conceived as living space for a married butler and his housekeeper wife, the room connected to the kitchens and led to the garden.

It was anchored by a long table, thick and sturdy, that was lined on both sides by low benches with cheerful pink cushions. On the night of a raid, the table would be laid with warm bread and salty cheese, sweets, milk, ham, and fruit.

Along the wall was a small cot, also made up in the sweetest pink, with soft linens and fluffy pillows, and warm blankets folded at the end. Two bookshelves offered picture books and simple novels on the higher shelves; an array of bonnets, ribbons, and fans on the lower. A large crib in the corner was filled with dolls in frilly dresses and explosively curly hair. Near the fire, which illuminated the room with warm, orange light, lay three friendly dogs and a cat.

By design, the room was meant to appear irresistible to frightened, deprived, lonely girls. The dogs, the fripperies, and the dolls were the result of years of consideration. Elisabeth wanted each girl, no matter how frightened or displaced, to feel welcome and curious and open to the program that the foundation would offer her if she elected to stay.

Despite the food and the toys, the blankets and the pets, a final, crucial element was the large, arched door that led to the garden and the outside gate beyond. Both door and gate remained open—wide and gaping—while the girls were welcomed in, situated, introduced, and fed.

Open doors posed all kinds of security risks, and it meant that Stoker and his lads remained outside, patrolling, on alert and in danger for more than an hour while the girls settled in. Still, to Elisabeth, the open doors were essential. A lock on any room, she knew—even a comfortable and safe and inviting room—could be just as terrifying as any of the places from which they had come.

To that end, they kept the doors open, even on cold nights, even in the rain. There was to be no question about anyone's will in the matter of a rescue. If a girl did not wish to stay in Elisabeth's care, she need only walk through the open door.

It was, she thought, looking around this very room, exactly the manner of choice Bryson had given her. An open door. A way out. He did not mean to reject her so much as to say, *This is all my heart can allow. Manage with this much—this little—or go.*

Or perhaps she was being too generous.

Perhaps he did simply reject her.

She sighed, reminding herself that the marriage he had offered was hardly the husbandly equivalent of a warm, inviting room. But for some women, it might have been enough. It simply was not enough for her.

She looked around the spacious room at chores that needed to be completed before the next group of girls came. She smiled hopefully at Jocelyn Breedlowe.

Jocelyn was shaking her head. "I cannot possibly handle this—not alone, Elisabeth."

"You can, and you must," Elisabeth countered softly. "The sooner I leave, the better."

Jocelyn's head still shook. "But all the way to Yorkshire?"

"Stoker may never go if I do not personally escort him to the school. And Rainsleigh has bade me go, so...two birds, one stone. That said, the raids and acquisition of newly rescued girls must not stop simply because I am away. Not when you may be here to do the important work."

"But I've never even been present on the night of a raid."

"Oh, it's really rather exciting," Elisabeth said, sliding a crate of food from the market down the table. "You will enjoy it, I think. The other staff will help you. You bring a calming presence that will be a boon to the rattled girls. They will need you more than ever, with Stoker gone."

"You have too much confidence in me. I don't understand why you and Stoker cannot wait. The raid is just three days away."

Elisabeth hefted a sack of flour aloft and looked at her. "And where else am I to go? My aunt is relocating to the other side of the moon. She mustn't even know. And I cannot go back to Henrietta Place."

"You could live here for a time." Jocelyn began to unpack the provisions.

Elisabeth shook her head and plunked the flour on the table. "Rainsleigh would seek me out; maybe not soon, but eventually. You saw him hound me—for weeks, he has hounded me, even when he was furious with me. He tracks me down so he may hold me at arm's length. I cannot take it anymore. I cannot."

"Perhaps he will track you to Yorkshire?"

Another head shake. "This circumstance with Mr. Eads will keep him quite busy, I'm afraid." She thought about this, thought about the two men embracing when she'd left. "I could have helped him sort it out. It would have been the perfect opportunity for us to function as a little team, working toward a common goal. To turn to each other for support and counsel. But Rainsleigh does not want a wife in this way. He doesn't want a wife at all. He wants a figurehead."

The crate was empty and she carried it to the door. "No, I will not stay, I cannot. He has offered me the opportunity to bow out, and I will take it."

"But he would not wish you injury nor harm. It is dangerous for a lady to travel alone in a public coach for so many days."

"I won't be alone. I shall have Stoker with me. It's not the Orient, Jocelyn, I'm only going to Yorkshire."

"You are *not*," said a male voice from behind her, "going to Yorkshire."

Elisabeth froze.

Slowly, she turned around.

Rainsleigh filled the doorway, hovering on the garden stoop.

The bottom fell from Elisabeth's stomach, and she stared, taking in his handsome face, red with exertion. Had he run here? His chest rose and fell as he took in great gulps of air.

"Please tell me you have not chased me here," she managed to say. He looked resigned and ruffled and sad, and she reminded herself of her own determination and sadness. She was determined not to be affected. With great force of will, she turned her back on him and walked to the basin. There were potatoes, fresh from the market, and a pail of water. She took up the scrub brush, wet it, and selected a potato.

"Chased you is exactly what I have done," he said, ducking through the door. "And I will chase you all the way to Yorkshire if I must."

"You mustn't."

"No," countered Rainsleigh, crossing his arms over his chest, "*you* must not. You won't. Not now."

"I'm going," said Elisabeth, stressing the words, "and you cannot tell me what to do."

"I am your husband, and I very well may tell you what to do, if it pleases me."

Her head shot up.

"But it does not please me," he finished, raising an eyebrow. "However, I will *ask* you not to go."

"And why?" It was out before she could stop herself. She scrubbed the potato as if her life depended on it and then dropped it into a bowl before taking up the next, angry at herself for engaging him.

"If you'll excuse me," mumbled Jocelyn, "I'll just check on the girls' sewing..." Before Elisabeth could stop her, she slipped discreetly through the kitchen door.

"You cannot go to Yorkshire because I need you. Here. With me. Because I am lost without you."

"Lost?" She dropped the potato. "*Lost?*" She reeled around, pointing at him with the dripping scrub brush. "Spare me the hyperbole, please. I know of no other man more capable than you. Only you could lose your entire birthright and have a self-made, independent fortune waiting to sustain you in exactly the same style."

"I don't require you to *navigate my life*, Elisabeth. I need you because my life is worthless without you in it. The money? The boats? Even the birthright—it means nothing to me if you are not at my side."

"Bryson..." she began, shaking her head. She turned back to the sink and picked up another potato. "This week has been the sort that would drive any man to edge of sanity. First the wedding and now Mr. Eads? Even you can be expected to flounder a bit. It is precipitous, I think, to judge your needs based on all that has happened since Wednesday."

"I needed you before Wednesday," he countered, taking a step toward her. "I needed you on Tuesday"—another step— "and Monday, and every day before that. I have needed you since I first saw you disappear into your aunt's stairwell."

She dropped the brush again and threw the potato into the pail with a *plunk*. "Two nights ago, I told you that I loved you, and you...you said nothing. A day later you began to talk about sending me away. I am stubborn, but I am not stupid. It's too late." She lifted a section of her skirt and dried her hands.

"It is never too late," he said. He was close enough to touch her now. She turned again to the sink.

"I know this, only because of you. I have the figure of a real father now, because of you. I have an entirely new future with no title and certain scandal—"

"Because of me," she said to the potatoes.

He leaned in, speaking in a low voice, "I was going to say, *but I am at peace with it—because of you.*"

She shook her head, refusing this logic, refusing, even, to look at him. "You are *at peace* with all of this *at the moment,* Bryson. *At the moment,* all things seem possible, because you are swimming in bad luck and poor timing, and I am a proficient source of support who does not judge. But what if all was well with your world, and it was *my* life falling apart? What if I was wretched? What if *I* needed to rely on *you*? Because this, too, will happen. It's only a matter of time. Life, as you must know, is not exactly as you direct it."

"Yes, and thank God," he said on a breath. "Because I never would have directed my life to know you."

"That's a lie; you have hounded me. You hound me still. But not for what I want or what I need. Not for forever."

"Hear what I have to say, please," he said softly, reaching out. He caught her wrist and held it gently. "I have more than hounded you, Elisabeth, I have pursued you with a single-minded vigor. Not only is out of character for me, but it has been exhausting. In my right mind, I should never have endured. In my right mind, I should never have set my sights for a woman who runs a charity for prostitutes, who was in possession of a deep, dark secret that she revealed in her own time, rather than mine. Who—and I am speculating here— blackmailed me for her charity and the extradition of her aunt—before she would agree to marry me."

"Don't forget, who was not even a pure, virginal bride," Elisabeth interjected flatly.

"Oh, you were a virgin, but that is beside the point. What I was going to say, was—"

"Wait." She pulled her wrist from his hand and reared back. "Stop. What did you say?"

"You were a virgin; I thought you knew—"

"How was I to know? Why, why...didn't you tell me?"

"Oh, well," he hedged, "I was distracted, I suppose. It didn't seem important at the time. It's not important."

"But my almost-certain 'impurity' was the primary reason I didn't tell you about the brothel," she whispered. "You wanted a virgin." She came to the bench beside the table and dropped onto it.

"No, I wanted you, Elisabeth," he began carefully. "I didn't care that you were a virgin; I only cared that you were mine. That is all I have ever cared about."

"But how can I be yours if you will not allow yourself...to belong to me in return?"

"Oh, my darling," he said, crouching before her, taking up her hands, "I want nothing more than to belong to you. Forever. Please, can you overlook my stupidity, and reticence, and fear, and every other bloody barrier I have erected between us? Can you help me show you that I"—he looked away, squeezing his eyes shut, and then looked back at her—"that I *love you*, Elisabeth. And that my greatest wish is to remain in our marriage—our *real* marriage—starting now, until death, like the bishop said?"

She blinked down at him, fighting for control. Her mind was a tangle of desire, and fear, and fledgling hope.

"Whatever life brings," he continued, his voice breaking, "if you will have me. I want only you, and I want all of you, just as you are. I give the whole of my heart into your safekeeping."

"And I'm expected to believe that your fear of…of…intimacies has just disappeared?"

"Oh, Elisabeth," he said, burying his face in her lap, "that was the first thing to go. Please." He looked up. His eyes glistened, but there was a slight smile on his face. "We shall sleep in the same bed, always—beginning tonight. My bed, your bed, on the rug before the fire—whatever strikes us. I said that you could not go to Yorkshire, but I only meant that you could not go without me. If you wish to make the journey with Stoker, then I shall go too. Wherever you go, I shall go."

"But Bryson—why? Why the change of heart? Is it merely because you turned around and I was not there? How can I trust this?"

He nodded. His blue eyes darted right, as if searching for…for…It occurred to her that she had no idea what he would say. She had expected some of his speech when she saw him walk in the door—well, she had *hoped*. But the answer to this? This was essential.

She could not threaten to flee to Yorkshire every time he detached from her. She had to trust that he would not force distance between them ever again.

"The strangest thing occurred to me when I grabbed hold of Mr. Eads and embraced him," he finally said, looking at her. "Did you see it before you went? When he shook my hand? We actually stood in the center of the room and embraced. I wept on his neck like a child."

"Yes, Bryson, I saw."

"It occurred to me then that some things exist naturally in a man's heart and in his head...but some things must be modeled; they must be taught. I am naturally moderate and temperate, and making money is second nature to me. However, I had no idea how to properly love. No one showed me how."

"Oh, Bryson..."

"It sounds pathetic, and I suppose it is, although I never felt remorseful about it. I was simply confused. But Mr. Eads, even with my deep, angry suspicion of him, demonstrated an elemental truth in that admittedly awkward embrace. An epiphany. I thought, '*Oh, this is how it feels to allow someone to love you.*' After that," Bryson said, bringing her hands up to his mouth, brushing her knuckles with his lips, "finding you, telling you—*showing* you—became my only purpose. Mr. Eads, if he turns out to be what he claims, will show me more, no doubt; but the primary instructor will be you, Elisabeth. If you can bear it. If you are willing to give your husband a second ch—"

"Fourth," she corrected. "If I am willing to give my husband a *fourth* chance."

"I've bungled this shamelessly, haven't I?" He flipped her hands and pressed a slow kiss into one palm, and then the next. He did not break her gaze.

She sighed, feeling herself relent, feeling as if she would perish if she did not touch him. His hair, typically so styled and brushed back, flopped over one eye. He looked dashing, reckless. She pulled one hand free and reached out, running her fingers through that tuft of hair.

"Please, Elisabeth," he rasped, leaning his head into her hand.

Before she even knew she'd moved, her head began to nod. Tears flooded her eyes and spilled down her cheeks. She pressed her hand into his scalp and leaned in. She pulled him tightly against her.

"Yes," she whispered, "yes, Bryson, yes." How could he possibly think she could deny him?

He dove for her then, gathering her in his arms and surging up in the same push. She clung, returning the embrace, holding on. Her feet dangled above the ground. Slowly, he spun with her, pressing his face against her chest.

"I can't believe I was a virgin," she said absently, speaking into his hair.

He raised his head and released her, sliding her down his body. "Please tell me that *this* is not the chief impression you take from this conversation. Elisabeth, please. It makes no difference that you were a virgin."

"No, no, I understand, and of course your confessions were…gratifying, but, well, I have wondered. For years, I have wondered." She stared at his throat, considering this.

"If it makes you feel better," he said, his voice suddenly gravelly and lower, "I can assure you, madam, that you are a virgin no more."

Her head shot up. The heat in his eyes caused her to gasp. She laughed and shuffled two steps back.

"Oh, no, you don't," he teased, lowering his lips to her neck. He nuzzled her. The rasp of his beard left a trail of desire. "I have not survived the wholesale scramble of my entire world to be denied sex from my wife."

She laughed again, her skin suddenly ablaze, thrumming with desire for him. She dropped her head back, inviting him to kiss her, surrendering to him.

"But Bryson," she whispered between kisses, "we've no bed here."

He broke the kiss long enough to look around. "I see a bed," he said, capturing her mouth again, "against the wall."

"The cot? That is a soft place for the girls to huddle when they arrive after a raid."

"Perfect," he growled, pulling away long enough to sweep her feet out from under her and carry her there. "You were a girl who was once rescued, by me, I should add, and I have wanted you since that night." He nuzzled her ear. "Shhh, please don't tell anyone. I was deeply ashamed of it for years." A kiss. "And I want you still. God, so, so much." Another kiss.

"Elisabeth, my love." He collided with the cot and collapsed the two of them on the creaky mattress. Before she could right herself, he hauled her onto his lap. She laughed again, straddling him. He said, "If only I had known back then that you would end up rescuing me too."

"Bryson," she said, sighing and rocking against him, "love me."

"Forever, Elisabeth," he promised, and he gathered her to him.

EPILOGUE

By some peculiar irony, the two announcements appeared in the *London Times* on the very same day.

The first was a quarter-page article—an interview, more like—of the former Lord Rainsleigh, now Mr. Bryson Courtland.

"After years of balancing the responsibilities of a land-owning nobleman with the demands of shipbuilding, Mr. Courtland had announced his intention to abdicate the title of viscount to his younger brother," the article said.

The "new Viscount Rainsleigh, Mr. Beauregard Courtland, a sometime sea captain of no fixed address," the article went on to say, would assume the responsibilities and stewardship of the Rainsleigh viscountcy, while the elder Courtland focused on the expansion of his shipping empire, supported the charities favored by his new wife, and indulged in leisure travel.

For all the worry about timing and wording and a rather lengthy quarrel with the editors about his brother's distinction of "no fixed address," the article ultimately raised very few eyebrows. Around London, in fact, it elicited negligible gossip, scandalized no one, and was mostly forgotten by page three.

What could be said, really? The former viscount had been an unremarkable fixture in society's nighttime whirl—his wife too. Beyond their lavish wedding, the two of them were rarely seen out and received few callers. For years, it seemed, both of them had been regarded as charitably minded and quiet and no fun at all.

More fun, perhaps, was the *second* article, even though it was not really an article—more like an announcement buried on the last page, it was set in small text between the land auctions and the pork futures.

Despite its obscurity, the contents of the piece left its mark. All over town, coffee cups clinked into saucers, eggs slid from forks, and servants were summoned to fetch hats, coats, and gloves.

"Countess to Relocate; Grosvenor Square Townhome Offered to Let," the headline read.

Bryson and Elisabeth had written the piece themselves, lying in bed, tinkering with the wording, scribbling and scratching out, trying to pare the thing down to only the essentials. For a fee, the editors had been kind enough to run the piece verbatim.

The former Mrs. Lillian Price, Lady Banning, widow of the late Godfrey Price, eleventh Earl of Banning, has announced her marriage to Mr. Benjamin Quincy.

Mr. and Mrs. Quincy plan to relocate to the tropical island of Bermuda in the Caribbean Sea by year's end.

Fresh inquiries to the whereabouts of the late Lord Banning's heir, a distant cousin, presumed lost at sea some ten years ago, have been dispatched. In the meantime, Denby House, Mrs. Quincy's former townhome in Grosvenor Square, has been made available to let. Inquiries about the property may be made in person to the estate agents at Blinklowe, Dinkle, and Tuft in Barnes High Street, London.

The ensuing shock, supposition, and gossip in the wake of the article was immediate—and immediately divisive. Perhaps Elisabeth described it best when she wrote to her aunt: "The scandal was significant. I'd peg it somewhere between moderate and acute."

If Bryson and she had been in London when the scandal churned, welled, and then crested, Elisabeth said, they might have given it half a thought. Maybe.

But then again, perhaps not.

They were very busy, Bryson and Elisabeth. Busy with each other; with their respective businesses and charity work; with relocating Stoker to Yorkshire and setting him up in school.

Most of all, perhaps, they were very busy cajoling Beau to emerge from his shock and denial and (to be honest) extended drunken ramble so that he might learn what would be expected of him, now that he was Viscount Rainsleigh.

He was resistant, to say the least. And, for a time, absent. He moved out of the house on Henrietta Place, although he did not go missing for long.

But that, perhaps, is a story for another time.

This is the story of the virgin and the viscount. One who found her virginity but realized she did not require it—not in the way she thought. And the other who lost his viscountcy and discovered…precisely the same thing.

ACKNOWLEDGMENTS

The author would like to thank early readers of this book whose thoughtful critiques and encouragement were invaluable to her journey as a writer: Janet Marlow, JoLynn McEachern, Teresa Montgomery, and Julia Quinn. Thank you Dave Goldstein for coming up with Kenneth. Thank you Chelsey Emmelhainz for taking a chance on my work and teaching me to cut it for public consumption. And thank you to my critique partner Cheri Allan for making my first draft palatable for editorial consumption. Finally, thanks to Mr. Michaels and my children for being my real-life happily-ever-after.

Don't miss the first sparkling romance in Charis Michaels's Bachelor Lords of London series,

THE EARL NEXT DOOR

American heiress Piety Grey is on the run. Suddenly in London and facing the renovation of a crumbling townhouse, she's determined to make a new life for herself—anything is better than returning to New York City where a cruel mother and horrid betrothal await her. The last thing she needs is a dark, tempting earl inciting her at every turn...

Trevor Rheese, the Earl of Falcondale, isn't interested in being a good neighbor. After fifteen years of familial obligation, he's finally free. But when the disarmingly beautiful Piety bursts through his wall—and into his life—his newfound freedom is threatened...even as his curiosity is piqued.

Once Piety's family arrives in London, Falcondale suddenly finds himself in the midst of a mock courtship to protect the seductive woman who's turned his world upside down. It's all for show—or at least it should be. But if Falcondale isn't careful, he may find a very real happily-ever-after with the woman of his dreams...

Available now!

CHARIS MICHAELS believes a romance novel is a very long, exciting answer to the question: "So, how did you two meet?" She loves to answer this question with different characters, each time she writes a book. Prior to writing romance, she studied journalism at Texas A&M and managed PR for a trade association. She has also worked as a tour guide at Disney World, harvested peaches on her family's farm, and entertained children as the "Story Godmother" at birthday parties. She has lived in Texas, Florida, and London, England. She now makes her home in the Washington, DC, metro area.

Discover great authors, exclusive offers, and more at hc.com.

Give in to your Impulses . . .
Continue reading for excerpts from
our newest Avon Impulse books.
Available now wherever ebooks are sold.

ONE LUCKY HERO
The Men in Uniform Series
by Codi Gary

STIRRING ATTRACTION
A Second Shot Novel
by Sara Jane Stone

SIGNS OF ATTRACTION
by Laura Brown

SMOLDER
The Wildwood Series
by Karen Erickson

An Excerpt from

ONE LUCKY HERO
The Men in Uniform Series
By Codi Gary

Violet Douglas wants one night where she can be normal. Where she can do something for herself and not be just her siblings' guardian. So when she spies a tall, dark, and sexy stranger, she's ready to let her wild side roar. The last thing she expects is to see her one night stand one week later, when she drags her delinquent kid brother to the Alpha Dog Training Program.

"You done throwing a tantrum?" he asked.

As his hard body moved into hers, tension hummed around them. "I was not—"

"Yeah, you're revved up into a full-on hissy fit, but I'm going to overlook that while I . . . clarify a few things."

The way his voice softened on those last four words made her body tighten, especially when she realized one of his legs was pressed between hers. His wide shoulders blocked her view of who might be watching them, and his hands were braced flat just above her shoulders. If she moved a fraction higher, he could graze her bare skin with his thumb, and just the thought of it made her nipples perk up against the sheer lace of her bra.

"First of all, yes, I was rude to you, but not because I wasn't attracted to you."

Violet held her breath at this, her eyes riveted to his lips.

"I was trying to save you."

Huh? Save her? She could hardly concentrate on what he was talking about, his proximity casting a spell of confusion over her. Maybe she'd been binge watching too much

Charmed, but she was too caught up in the obsidian flecks in his brown eyes to fully process.

"From what?" Was that her voice? It was soft, dreamy, and not at all normal.

And good God, but were his lips inching closer? "From me."

"Are you dangerous?" Silly question. *If he was really dangerous, you wouldn't be putty in his hands.*

His right hand moved, and he began trailing one of his fingers along her temple and cheek, until the very tip smoothed over her bottom lip. "I would never mean to hurt you, but I'm not looking for anything serious."

That woke her up a little, and she frowned. "Neither am I."

His finger dropped, and he stared down at her grimly. "You say that now, but—"

"Okay, you know what, that's enough." The balls on him, getting her all revved up and then acting like she was just a soft piece of feminine fluff who didn't know her own mind. Putting her hands up against the wall of his chest, she pushed hard, but he wouldn't budge, so she settled for pointing her finger up between them, wagging it in his face. "Don't act like you know me or what I want. Don't just assume that I'm looking for a relationship because I have ovaries. I have too much going on in my life to handle anyone else's wants and needs, so the last thing I'm looking for is a boyfriend. And you might have learned that if you had bothered to spend more than ten minutes at a time talking to me tonight, instead of running away like a big wimpy asshat."

He leaned back but still didn't let her escape. "Big wimpy asshat, huh?"

Lifting her chin up, she didn't back down. "Yeah, that's right."

For several moments, he did nothing but stare at her, and the intensity in his eyes made her twitch. Finally, he nodded, as if coming to terms with his new title. "Fine, I made an assumption. I'm an asshat."

"Happy we agree on something," she said.

"But I didn't come here today looking to hook up. I planned to drink some beer, chill with my friend, and eventually head home to bed—alone."

Violet flushed. "Well, it's not like I was trolling for just anybody. If that were the case, I would be dragging Robert off to have my way with him in the parking lot."

"Are you saying I'm special?" he asked.

It was a loaded question, and her answer could be taken a hundred wrong ways. Why was it that the first guy she'd actually actively pursued had to be so complicated?

"Nope, you're absolutely right. Nothing special about you. There are still a few hours left for me to meet someone who doesn't make snap judgments and would love to make out with an attractive single woman who hasn't been kissed in six months, so if you'll—"

Dean's mouth closed over hers, stopping her tirade with the sheer heat of his soft, deep kiss. Violet melted on impact, her eyes rolling back as her lids closed. She opened her lips to the thrust of his tongue and felt a pool of joy bubbling up in her lower abdomen.

Holy shit. And you thought the sunshine was hot.

An Excerpt from

STIRRING ATTRACTION
A Second Shot Novel
By Sara Jane Stone

When Dominic Fairmore left Oregon to be all
he could be as an Army Ranger, he always knew
he'd come back to claim Lily Greene. But after
six years away and three career-ending bullets,
Dominic is battered, broken, and nobody's
hero—so he stays away. Until he learns Lily has
been the victim of a seemingly random attack.

Lily is starting to find a life without Dominic
when suddenly her wounded warrior is home
and playing bodyguard—though all she really
wants is for him to take her. But she refuses to
play the part of a damsel in distress, no matter
how much she misses his tempting touch.

The door swung open and a large figure filled the doorway. The light from the parking lot made it difficult to identify his features. But she knew him. She'd know him anywhere.

"Now?" she cried as fury rose up partly driven by the pinot noir. But after all this time, how could Dominic Fairmore walk in holding a freaking key in the middle of the night?

Beside her, the dishwasher moved as if Lily's one-word cry had been a directive. Out of the corner of her eye, she saw Caroline reach for the pie dish. And then it was hurling through the empty bar. The pie collided with the target, covering Lily's ex with a mixture of berries, sugar, and homemade crust. The tin dish dropped to the floor.

"What the hell?" the man roared, whipping the pie from his face.

A year ago, Lily would have laughed at the sight of Dominic covered in dessert. She would have smiled and offered to help clean him up. She would have been happy he'd returned home. And she would have set aside all of the lingering heartache from their last and supposedly final breakup.

But too much time had slipped past. Too much had changed. And for him to show up now? In the middle of the night when her fear rose to fever pitch? For him to waltz in here without even knocking?

She felt Caroline's hand close around her arm and pull as if trying to drag her away. Lily grabbed her wine glass and hurled it at the door. She missed and the glass fell to the ground three feet in front of her and shattered.

"Turn around and leave, Dominic," she snapped as she allowed Caroline to pull her behind the bar, into relative safety. Only she'd never be safe from the man she'd loved for so long, because he didn't aim for her face or her arms.

He went for the heart.

"You had your chance to come back," she added as Caroline released her.

"Lily, please calm down," Dominic called.

From their position behind the bar, she heard the door close. Caroline glanced at her. "You know him."

She nodded. Caroline pushed off the ground without a word. And Lily followed her, turning to face the former love of her life, who had stepped just inside the door.

"Ryan dragged me back," he said. "At Noah and Josie's request. How do you think I got the key? Or does your friend here throw food at everyone who walks into the bar?"

"It was the only thing I had," Caroline said simply. "Noah locked up my gun."

"Remind me to thank Noah in the morning," Dominic said dryly.

His hands dropped to his side, abandoning the attempts to wipe away the pie that had hit its target with near-perfect aim. Lily glanced at Caroline. She wasn't sure she wanted to see the dishwasher with a firearm.

Then she glanced back at Dominic. Marionberries clung to his beard. He'd always been clean-shaven. But now, his dark hair was long and it looked like he'd lost his razor around the same time he'd kissed the rangers goodbye. She'd loved the hard lines of his jaw and the feel of his skin against her when they kissed. But this look . . .

She ached to touch and explore. He looked wild and unrestrained, as if he didn't give a damn, as if he didn't hold anything back. Her gaze headed south to the muscles she'd wanted to memorize before he left. He appeared bigger, more powerful.

Impossible.

He'd always been strong, able to lift her up and press her against the wall. He'd held her with ease while she fell apart . . .

And with that memory, her fury and her fear opened the door to another entirely unwelcome emotion—desire. It was as if they were forming a club determined to barricade her heart, mind, and soul against the feelings that might help her return to her calm, steady life. But no, her unruly emotions took one look at the bearded, buff man in the bar and thought: *touch him!*

An Excerpt from

SIGNS OF ATTRACTION

By Laura Brown

From debut author Laura Brown comes a heart-poundingly sexy and wildly emotional New Adult novel about a Hard of Hearing woman, struggling to accept her "imperfections," and the gorgeous Deaf man who helps her see that she is perfect for him.

An Excerpt from

SIGNS OF ATTRACTION

By Laura Brown

You know those corny movies where the love interest walks in and a halo of light flashes behind them? Yeah, that happened. Not because this guy was hot, which he was, but because the faulty hall light had been flickering since before I walked into the room. His chestnut hair—the kind that flopped over his forehead and covered his strong jaw in two to three weeks' worth of growth—complimented his rich brown eyes and dark olive skin, which was either a tan or damn good genetics.

Not that I paid much attention. I was just bored.

And warm. Was it warm in here? I repositioned my hair; thankful it not only covered my aids but also the sudden burning in my ears.

Dr. Ashen stopped talking as Hot New Guy walked over to the two women, shifted his backpack, and began moving his hands in a flurry of activity I assumed was American Sign Language. Chic Glasses Lady moved her hands in response while Perfect Ringlets addressed our teacher.

"Sorry. My car broke down and I had to jump on the Green line," Ringlets said, speaking for Hot New Guy.

Car? In the middle of Boston, was this guy crazy?

Dr. Ashen spit out an intense reply. Chic Glasses signed to Hot New Guy, who nodded and took a seat in the back of the room.

For the next two hours—the joy of a once-a-week part-grad class—I watched the two interpreters. Every half-hour or so they switched, with one standing next to Dr. Ashen. They held eye contact with one spot near the back of the room, where Hot New Deaf Guy sat. I'd never seen ASL up close and personal before. My ears, faulty as they were, had never failed me, at least not to this degree.

From the notes the students around me took, pages of it according to the girl on my left, this class was a bust. I needed this to graduate. Maybe my advisor could work something out? Maybe—

Beep. Beep. Beep.

Dammit. To add insult to injury, my hearing aid, the right one, traitorous bitch, announced she needed her battery changed. Right. This. Second. And if—

Beep. Beep. Beep.

I reached into my purse, rummaged past lip-gloss, tampons, tissues, and searched for the slim package of batteries. I had no choice. If I ignored the beeping it'd just—

Beep. Beep. Beep.

Silence.

Fuck. My left ear still worked, but now the world was half-silent. And Dr. Ashen was a mere mumble of incomprehension.

I pulled out my battery packet only to find the eight little tabs empty.

Double fuck. No time to be discrete. I tossed the packet onto my desk and stuck my head in my bag, shifted my wallet, and moved my calendar. I always had extra batteries on hand. Where were they?

A hand tapped my shoulder. I nearly shrieked and jumped out of my skin. Hot New Deaf Guy stood over me. It was then I noticed student chatter and my peers moving about. Dr. Ashen sat at his desk, reviewing his notes. All signs I had missed the beginning of a break.

Hot New Deaf Guy moved his fingers in front of his face and pointed to the empty battery packet I had forgotten on my desk.

"What color battery?" asked Perfect Ringlets who stood next to him.

"I... Uh..." The burning in my ears migrated to my cheeks. I glanced around. No one paid us any attention. Meanwhile I felt like a spotlight landed on my malfunctioning ears. Hot New Deaf Guy waited for my response. I could tell him to get lost, but that would be rude. Why did my invisibility cloak have to fail me today? And why did he have to be so damn sexy standing there, all broad shoulders and a face that said, "Let me help you"?

He oozed confidence in his own skin. Mine itched. Heck, his ears didn't have anything in them, unless he had those fancy shmancy hearing aids that were next to invisible. The kind of hearing aids I assumed old dudes wore when their days of rock concerts gave them late onset loss. Not the kind of aids someone who had an interpreter at his side would wear.

At a loss for words on how I was supposed to communicate, or where my jumbled thoughts headed, I waved the white flag and showed him the empty packet like a moron.

He nodded, twisted his bag around, and found the batteries I needed.

I glanced around the room again. No one looked at us. No one cared that a hot guy holding out a packet of hearing aid batteries threw my world off kilter.

This class was going on The List of Horrible Classes. Current standing? Worst class ever.

He tapped the packet and signed. A few movements later, much like a speech delay on a bad broadcast, the interpreter beside him spoke.

"Go ahead. Sharon says this guy has a thick accent, must be hard to hear."

This could not get any more humiliating. I glanced at Perfect Ringlets, who I hoped was Sharon, and she nodded.

"Thank you." I took out one battery, pulled off the orange tab, and popped it into the small door on my hearing aid before shoving it back in my ear. Hot New Deaf Guy still hovered over me, wearing an infectious smile, a smile that made my knees weak. I handed the packet back. "You don't wear hearing aids, why do you have batteries?"

He watched Sharon as she signed my words while putting the batteries away. "I work at a deaf school. Most of my students have hearing aids and someone always needs a battery. I keep a stash on hand," he said via the interpreter.

"That's nice of you."

He smiled again. I wished he would stop. The smiling thing, I mean. Every time he did, I lost a brain cell. "My name's Reed." He stuck out a hand when he finished signing.

I looked at his hand, a bit amazed at how well he could communicate with it.

Not an excuse to be rude. I reached for his outstretched hand. "Carli."

Sharon asked me how I spelled my name. Reed looked at her instead of me. When I touched him, a spark of some kind ignited and dashed straight up my arm. A tingling that had nothing to do with my ears, or his ears. His eyes shot to mine and I froze. Unable to move or do anything human, like pull my hand back. All I could think of was the fact I'd never kissed a guy with a beard before.

An Excerpt from

SMOLDER
The Wildwood Series
By Karen Erickson

In the second book in *USA Today* bestselling
author Karen Erickson's Wildwood series
stoic sheriff's deputy Lane Gallagher has
lusted after his brother's ex for years . . .
but will he ever let himself have her?

The man was a complete idiot.

Like straight-up ignorant, ridiculous, gorgeous, stubborn, infuriating, sexy, elusive, and arrogant . . . yet sweet at the oddest times.

Delilah Moore frowned, tapping her fingers against her desk. She was at the dance studio trying to get some work done and failing miserably. And she definitely didn't like that bit about him being sweet intruding on her mental hissy fit. She wanted to hate Lane Gallagher right now. Hate him with the built-up anger of a million frustrated women because that's exactly what she was. A frustrated woman who was sick to death of being rejected by the only man who had ever given her true, real butterflies fluttering in her stomach.

Well, not *real* butterflies. Just that fluttery sensation one had when one saw the person she had feelings for. Not lust, not infatuation, not any of that shallow crap she'd experienced time and again as a way to try to rid her system of Lane once and for all. That stuff never lasted.

Nope, irritatingly sexy, aloof Lane Gallagher was the only one who ever made her feel something *real*.

No one else had ever done it. Not Weston—Lane's younger brother—when they were briefly together. They'd been in high school and in lust; that was it. None of the other guys she'd gone out with had ever made her feel much either—and she'd gone out with more than a few. She wasn't a celibate nun. She was a woman with needs, damn it. Had even had a couple of steady boyfriends over the years. Though for the past two years, she'd been so consumed with running her own business she'd sort of forgotten all about her own needs.

And she was too damn young for that sort of thing. She should be living it up! Having the time of her life! Look at West and Harper. Those two were up to no good in the best possible way. Harper glowed. That's what regular bouts of sex with the man you're madly, passionately in love with did for a girl.

Delilah, on the other hand, had thrown herself at Lane time and again. She'd barely escaped a horrific fire three weeks ago. Lane had seemed so relieved to find her, had held her so close and whispered comforting words in her ear while she'd practically trembled with nerves and adrenaline and fear. She'd savored the sensation of his thick, muscled arms around her. The way his lips had moved against her temple when he spoke and how he'd stroked her back with his big, capable hands. She'd melted into him, closing her eyes on a sigh, imagining all the delicious ways he might kiss her. Lips she'd never touched before but that she knew would taste like heaven . . .

And then he'd set her away from him, offered up a gruff,

"Glad you're all right," and practically ran away from her, never once looking back.

Jerk.

That had been the final straw. She hadn't really seen him since. And she was glad for it. So incredibly glad. Maybe she could finally purge him from her thoughts for good. She'd been kicked to the curb for the last time. The very last time . . .

The bell above the front door chimed, letting her know someone had entered the studio, and she sat up straighter at her desk, pretending she was actually getting work done versus daydreaming—more like day *scheming*—about Lane. She figured it was Wren, her best friend and business partner, coming in to work.

"Did you bring coffee with you?" Delilah yelled when Wren still hadn't made an appearance in the back office that they shared.

There was no reply.

Weird.

She rose to her feet, tucking a stray hair behind her ear as she made her way out of the office, down a tiny hall to emerge into the waiting area. All the breath expelled from her lungs when she saw who stood there with his back to her, eating up all the space with his mere six-foot-two presence.

Stupid Lane Gallagher, Wildwood County deputy sheriff, at her service. Ha, like he'd ever *service* her.